Parkhurst Boys, and Other Stories of School Life

by

Talbot Baines Reed

Parkhurst Boys, and Other Stories of School Life
by Talbot Baines Reed

ISBN: 978-93-63056-00-8

Published by

DOUBLE 9 BOOKS

2/13-B, Ansari Road
Daryaganj, New Delhi – 110002
info@double9books.com
www.double9books.com
Tel. 011-40042856

This book is under public domain

ABOUT THE AUTHOR

Talbot Baines Reed was an English author of boys' fiction who lived from April 3, 1852, to November 28, 1893. He created a type of school stories that lasted until the middle of the 20th century. The Fifth Form at St. Dominic's is one of his most well-known works. He often and regularly wrote for The Boy's Own Paper (B.O.P.). Most of his writing was first published there. Reed became a well-known typefounder through his family's business. He also wrote the standard work on the subject, History of the Old English Letter Foundries. John Reed was a colonel in Oliver Cromwell's army during the English Civil War. The Reed family came from him. Their home was in Maiden Newton, which is in the county of Dorset. They moved to London at the end of the 18th century. Andrew Reed (1787–1862), Talbot Reed's grandpa, was a minister in the Congregational Church and the founder of many charitable organizations, such as the London Orphan Asylum and a hospital for people who could not get better. He was also a well-known hymn writer. His "Spirit Divine, attend our prayers" can still be found in many hymnals today. Talbot Baines Reed grew up in a happy family where Charles Reed was very religious and thought that tough outdoor games were the best way to raise boys.

CONTENTS

Chapter One
My First Football Match

It was a proud moment in my existence when Wright, captain of our football club, came up to me in school one Friday and said, "Adams, your name is down to play in the match against Craven to-morrow."

I could have knighted him on the spot. To be one of the picked "fifteen," whose glory it was to fight the battles of their school in the Great Close, had been the leading ambition of my life—I suppose I ought to be ashamed to confess it—ever since, as a little chap of ten, I entered Parkhurst six years ago. Not a winter Saturday but had seen me either looking on at some big match, or oftener still scrimmaging about with a score or so of other juniors in a scratch game. But for a long time, do what I would, I always seemed as far as ever from the coveted goal, and was half despairing of ever rising to win my "first fifteen cap." Latterly, however, I had noticed Wright and a few others of our best players more than once lounging about in the Little Close, where we juniors used to play, evidently taking observations with an eye to business. Under the awful gaze of these heroes, need I say I exerted myself as I had never done before? What cared I for hacks or bruises, so only that I could distinguish myself in their eyes? And never was music sweeter than the occasional "Bravo, young 'un!" with which some of them would applaud any special feat of skill or daring.

So I knew my time was coming at last, and only hoped it would arrive before the day of the Craven match, the great match of our season—always looked forward to as *the* event of the Christmas term, when victory was regarded by us boys as the summit of all human glory, and defeat as an overwhelming disgrace.

It will therefore be understood why I was almost beside myself with delight when, the very day before the match, Wright made the announcement I have referred to.

I scarcely slept a wink that night for dreaming of the wonderful exploits which were to signalise my first appearance in the Great Close—how I was to run the ball from one end of the field to the other, overturning, dodging, and distancing every one of the enemy, finishing up with a brilliant and mighty kick over the goal. After which I was to have my broken limbs set by a doctor on the spot, to receive a perfect ovation from friend and foe, to be chaired round the field, to be the "lion" at the supper afterwards, and finally to have a whole column of the *Times* devoted to my exploits! What glorious creatures we are in our dreams!

Well, the eventful day dawned at last. It was a holiday at Parkhurst, and as fine a day as any one could wish.

As I made my appearance, wearing the blue-and-red jersey of a "first fifteen man" under my jacket, I found myself quite an object of veneration among the juniors who had lately been my compeers, and I accepted their homage with a vast amount of condescension. Nothing was talked of during the forenoon but the coming match. Would the Craven fellows turn up a strong team? Would that fellow Slider, who made the tremendous run last year, play for them again this? Would Wright select the chapel end or the other, if we won the choice? How were we off behind the scrimmage?

"Is Adams to be trusted?" I heard one voice ask.

Two or three small boys promptly replied, "Yes"; but the seniors said nothing, except Wright, who took the opportunity of giving me a little good advice in private.

"Look here, Adams; you are to play half-back, you know. All you've got to take care of is to keep cool, and never let your eyes go off the ball. You know all the rest."

A lecture half an hour long could not have made more impression. I remembered those two hints, "Keep cool, and watch the ball," as long as I played football, and I would advise every half-back to take them to heart in like manner.

At noon the Craven team came down in an omnibus, and had lunch in hall with us, and half an hour later found us all in a straggling procession, making for the scene of conflict in the Great Close. There stood the goals and the boundary-posts, and there was Granger, the ground-keeper, with a brand-new lemon-shaped ball under his arm.

"Look sharp and peel!" cried our captain.

So we hurried to the tent, and promptly divested ourselves of our outer garments, turned up the sleeves of our jerseys, and tied an extra knot in our bootlaces. As we emerged, the Craven men were making their appearance on the ground in battle array. I felt so nervous myself that I could not, for the life of me, imagine how some of them could look so unconcerned, whistling, and actually playing leapfrog to keep themselves warm!

An officer in the Crimean War once described his sensation in some of the battles there as precisely similar to those he had experienced when a boy on the football field at Rugby. I can appreciate the comparison, for one. Certainly never soldier went into action with a more solemn do-or-die feeling than that with which I took my place on the field that afternoon.

"They've won the choice of sides," said somebody, "and are going to play with the wind."

"Take your places, Parkhurst!" shouted our captain.

The ball lies in the centre of the ground, and Wright stands ten yards or so behind it, ready for the kick-off. Of our fifteen the ten forwards are extended in a line with the ball across the field, ready to charge after it the moment it goes flying. The two best runners of our team are stationed quarter-back, where they can skirmish on the outskirts of the scrimmage. I am posted a little in rear of them at half-back—an unusual post for so young a player, but one which was accorded to me by virtue of my light weight and not inconsiderable running powers. Behind me are the two backs, on whom, when all else fails, the issue of the conflict depends. The Craven players are similarly disposed, and waiting impatiently for our captain's kick.

"Are you ready?" he shouts.

Silence gives consent.

He gives a quick glance round at us, then springs forward, and in an instant the ball is soaring high in the direction of the Cravens' goal amid the shouts of onlooking friend and foe.

Our forwards were after it like lightning, but not before a Craven back had got hold of it and run some distance in the direction of our goal. He did not wait to be attacked, but by a clever drop-kick, a knack peculiar to all good backs, sent it spinning right over the forwards' heads into the hands of one of our quarter-backs. He, tucking it under his arm and crushing his cap on to his head, started to run. Going slowly at first, he steered straight for the forwards of the enemy till within a pace or two of them, when he doubled suddenly, and amid the shouts of our partisans slipped past them and was seen heading straight for the Craven goal. But although he had escaped their forwards, he had yet their rearguard to escape, which was far harder work, for was not one of that rearguard the celebrated Slider himself, who by his prowess had last year carried defeat to our school; and the other, was it not the stalwart Naylor, who only a month ago had played gloriously for his county against Gravelshire?

Yet our man was not to be daunted by the prestige of these distinguished adversaries, but held on his way pluckily, and without a swerve. It was a sight to see those two cunningly lay wait for him, like two spiders for a fly. There was nothing for it but to plunge headlong into their web in a desperate effort to break through. Alas! brave man! Naylor has him in his clutches, the Craven forwards come like a deluge on the spot, our forwards pour over the Craven, and in an instant our hero and the ball have vanished from sight under a heap of writhing humanity.

"Down!" cries a half-choked voice, from the bottom of the heap. It was rather an unnecessary observation, as it happens, but it served as a signal to both parties to rise to their feet and prepare for a "scrimmage."

Now, if truth must be told, our school always had the reputation of being second to none in "going through a scrimmage," so while the players are scrambling to their feet, and waiting for the ball to be "grounded," I will explain what our method of doing the thing was.

It was nothing more nor less than a carrying out of the principle of the wedge. The ball formed the apex; the fellows got up close to it, so as never to let it out of reach of their four feet. Behind these two came three with locked arms, and behind the three, four. The men in the middle pushed straight ahead, and those at the sides inwards towards the ball, while the two or three remaining forwards lent their weight to one side or other of the base, according as the exigencies of the scrimmage demanded. Thus our wedge, embodying a concentrated pressure in the direction of the ball, the farther it advanced the farther it scattered asunder the foe, who fell off from its gradually widening sides without hope of getting again within reach of the ball except by retreating to the rear and beginning the struggle over afresh. When this manoeuvre was well executed, it was almost certain to carry the ball through the scrimmage, and when that happened, then was the time for us half and quarter-backs to look out for our chance.

Our men went at it with their customary vigour and address, and presently the ball emerged on the far side of the scrimmage. In an instant it was caught up by one of the Craven quarter-backs, and in an instant our men were upon him again before he could get a start for a run. Scrimmage after scrimmage ensued, the ball was constantly in Chancery, but each crush brought us a yard or so nearer the enemy's goal than we had been before.

All this time I was little better than a spectator, for the ball never once came within reach of my fingers, and I was beginning to think that, after all, a big match was not so exciting a thing as one is apt to imagine.

At last, however, after one scrimmage more desperate than any that had gone before, the ball flew out suddenly, and bounded off one of the Craven men into my grasp. Now was my chance. "If only I could—"

The next thing I was conscious of was that about twenty people had fallen to the ground all of a heap, and that I and the ball were at the bottom.

"Down!" I cried.

"Pack up there, Parkhurst!" sang out Wright.

I extricated myself as quickly as I could, and got back to my place in the rear, thinking to myself, after all, there *was* some little excitement in football.

At last the ball got well away from the scrimmage, and who should secure it but the redoubtable Slider! I felt a passing tremor of deep despair, as I saw that hero spring like the wind towards our goal.

"Look out, Adams!" shouted Wright.

Sure enough he was coming in my direction! With the desperation of a doomed man I strode out to meet him. He rushed furiously on—swerving slightly to avoid my reach, and stretching out his arm to ward off my grasp. I flung myself wildly in his path. There was a heavy thud, and the earth seemed to jump up and strike me. The next moment I was sprawling on my back on the grass. I don't pretend to know how it all happened, but somehow or other I had succeeded in checking the onward career of the victorious Slider; for though I had fallen half stunned before the force of his charge, he had recoiled for an instant from the same shock, and that instant gave time for Wright to get hold of him, and so put an end for the time to his progress.

"Well played!" said some one, as I picked myself up. So I was comforted, and began to think that, after all, football was rather a fine game.

Time would fail me to tell of all the events of that afternoon—how Wright carried the ball within a dozen yards of our opponents' goal; how their forwards passed the ball one to another, and got a "touch-down" behind our line, but missed the kick; how Naylor ran twenty yards with one of our men hanging on his back; how our quarter-back sent the ball nearly over their goal with as neat a drop-kick as ever it has been my lot to witness.

The afternoon was wearing. I heard the time-keeper call out, "Five minutes more!" The partisans of either side were getting frantic with excitement. Unless we could secure an advantage now, we should be as good as defeated, for the Craven had scored a "touch-down" to our nothing. Was this desperate fight to end so? Was victory, after all, to escape us? But I had no time for reflection then.

"Now, Parkhurst," sang out Wright, "pull yourselves together for once!"

A Craven man is standing to throw the ball out of "touch," and either side stands in confronting rows, impatient for the fray. Wright is at the end of the line, face to face with Naylor, and I am a little behind Wright.

"Keep close!" exclaims the latter to me, as the ball flies towards us.

Wright has it, but in an instant Naylor's long arms are round him, bearing him down.

"Adams!" ejaculates out captain, and in a trice he passes the ball into my hands, and I am off like the wind. So suddenly has it all been done that I have already a yard or two start before my flight is discovered. There is a yelling and a rush behind me; there is a roar from the crowds on either side; there is a clear "Follow up, Parkhurst!" from Wright in the rear; there is a loud "Collar him!" from the Craven captain ahead. I am steering straight for their goal; three men only are between me and it—one, their captain, right back, and Slider and another man in front of him.

I see at a glance that my only hope is to keep as I am going and waste no time in dodging, or assuredly the pursuing host will be upon me. Slider and his companion are closing in right across my path, almost close together. With a bound I dash between them. Have they got me, or have I escaped them? A shout louder than ever and a "Bravo!" from Wright tell me I am clear of that danger, and have now but their last defence to pass. He is a tall, broad fellow, and a formidable foe to encounter, and waits for me close under their goal. The pace, I feel, is telling on me; the shouting behind sounds nearer, only a few yards divides us now. Shall I double, shall I venture a kick, or shall I charge straight at him?

"Charge at him!" sounds Wright's voice, as if in answer to my thought. I gather up all my remaining force, and charge. There is a flash across my eyes, and a dull shock against my chest. I reel and stagger, and forget where I am. I am being swept along in a torrent; the waters with a roar rush past me and over me. Every moment I get nearer and nearer the fatal edge—I am at it—I hang a moment on the brink, and then—

"Down!" shouts a voice close at my ear, and there is such a noise of cheering and rejoicing that I sit up and rub my eyes like one waking bewildered from a strange dream.

Then I find out what has happened. When I charged at the Craven captain the shock sent me back staggering into the very arms of Wright and our forwards, who were close at my heels, and who then, in a splendid and irresistible rush, carried me and the ball and the half of the other side along with them right behind the enemy's goal-line, where we fall *en masse* to the earth—I, with the ball under me, being at the bottom.

Even if I had been hurt—which I was not—there was no time to be wasted on condolences or congratulations. The time-keeper held his watch in his hand, and our goal must be kicked at once, if it was to be kicked at all. So the fifteen paces out were measured, the "nick" for the ball was carefully made, the enemy stood along their goal-line ready to spring the moment the ball should touch the earth. Wright, cool and self-possessed, placed himself in readiness a yard or two behind the ball, which one of our side held an inch off the ground. An anxious moment of expectation followed; then came a sharp "Now!" from our captain. The ball was placed cunningly in the nick, the Craven forwards rushed out on it in a body, but long before they could reach it, Wright's practised foot had sent it flying straight as an arrow over the bar, and my first football match had ended in a glorious victory for the Old School.

The terms used here describe the Rugby game as it used to be played prior to 1880.

Chapter Two
The Parkhurst Paper-chase

"The meet is to be at one o'clock, sharp, in the Dean's Warren—don't forget!"

So said Forwood, the "whipper-in" of the Parkhurst Hare and Hounds Club, to me, one March morning in the year 18—. I had no need to be reminded of the appointment; for this was the day of the "great hunt" of the year, always held by the running set at Parkhurst School to yield in interest to no other fixture of the athletic calendar.

In fine weather, and over good country, a paper-chase is one of the grandest sports ever indulged in—at least, so we thought when we were boys—and the "great hunt" was, of course, the grandest run of the year, and looked forward to, consequently, with the utmost eagerness by all lovers of running in our school.

This year, too, I had a special interest in the event, for it was my turn to run "hare"—in other words, to be, with another fellow, the object of the united pursuit of some twenty or thirty of my schoolfellows, who would glory in running me down not a whit less than I should glory in escaping them.

For some weeks previously we had been taking short trial runs, to test our pace and powers of endurance; and Birch (my fellow-"hare") and I had more than once surveyed the course we proposed to take on the occasion of the "great hunt," making ourselves, as far as possible, acquainted with the bearings of several streams, ploughed fields, and high walls to be avoided, and the whereabouts of certain gaps, woods, and hollows to be desired. We were glad afterwards that we had taken this precaution, as the reader will see.

I can't say if the Parkhurst method of conducting our "hunts" was the orthodox one; I know *we* considered it was, as our rules were our own making, or rather a legacy left to us by a former generation of runners at the school.

We were to take, in all, a twelve miles' course, of nearly an oval shape, six miles out and six miles home. Any amount of dodging or doubling was to be allowed to us hares, except crossing our own path. We were to get five minutes' clear start, and, of course, were expected to drop our paper "scent" wherever we went.

Luckily for me, Birch was an old hand at running hare, and up to all sorts of dodges, so that I knew all it was needful for me to do was to husband my "wind," and run evenly with him, leaving him to shape our course and regulate our pace.

It was a lively scene at the Dean's Warren, when we reached it a few minutes before the appointed time that afternoon. The "pack"—that is, the twenty or thirty fellows who were to run as "hounds"—were fast assembling, and divesting themselves of everything but their light flannels. The whipper-in, conspicuous by the little bugle slung across his shoulders, and the light flag in his hand, was there in all the importance of his office; and, as usual, the doctor and a party of visitors, ladies and gentlemen, had turned out to witness the start.

"Five minutes, hares!" shouts Forwood, as Birch and I came on the spot.

We use the interval in stripping off all unnecessary apparel, and girding ourselves with our bags of "scent," or scraps of torn-up paper, which we are to drop as we run. Then we sit and wait the moment for starting. The turf is crisp under our feet; the sun is just warm enough to keep us from shivering as we sit, and the wind just strong enough to be fresh. Altogether it is to be doubted if a real meet of real hounds to hunt real hares—a cruel and not very manly sport, after all—could be much more exciting than this is.

"Half a minute!" sings out the whipper-in, as we spring to our feet.

In another thirty seconds we are swinging along at a good pace down the slope of the warren, in the direction of Colven meadows, and the hunt has begun.

As long as we were in sight of the pack we kept up a good hard pace, but on reaching cover we settled down at once to a somewhat more sober jog-trot, in anticipation of the long chase before us.

We made good use of our five minutes' start, for by the time a distant bugle note announced that the hounds were let loose on our track we had covered a good piece of ground, and put several wide fields and ditches and ugly hedges between us and our pursuers.

Now it was that Birch's experiences served us in good stead. I never knew a fellow more thoroughly cunning; he might have been a fox instead of a hare. Sometimes he made me run behind him and drop my scent on the top of his, and sometimes keep a good distance off, and let the wind scatter it as much as it could. When we came to a gap, instead of starting straight across the next field he would turn suddenly at right angles, and keep close up under the hedge half-way round before striking off into the open. Among trees and bushes he zigzagged and doubled to an alarming extent, so that it seemed as if we were losing ground every moment. So we should have been if the chase had been by sight instead of by *scent*; but that would have been against all rules.

If the hounds were to see the hares twenty yards in front of them, and the scent lay half a mile round, they would be bound, according to our rules, to go the half-mile, however tempting the short cut might seem.

It was after a very wide circuit, ending up on the top of a moderate rise, that we first caught sight of our pursuers. As they were a full six minutes behind us, we agreed to sit down under cover for a minute and watch them.

At that moment they had evidently lost the scent, and were ferreting about among some low trees and bushes in search of it. We saw the flag of the whipper-in marking the spot where it was last visible, and round this, on all sides, the hounds were exploring busily in search of the "new departure." Then, presently, came a cry of "Forward!" and off they all started in our direction; and as the scent after that seemed to lie pretty clear we considered it high time for us to resume our flight.

So we made off again, and being refreshed by our brief halt, made over a couple of ploughed fields, which Birch suggested "would make a few of the hounds look foolish"; and so on till we reached the first water we had encountered since the start. This was a trout-stream, well known to some of us who were fond of fishing—nowhere more than half a foot deep, and in some places easily passable, dry shod, on stepping-stones. Birch, however, avoided these, and boldly splashing into the stream over his ankles, bade me follow.

"We'll soon dry up," he said, "and this will gain us a minute or two."

Instead of going straight across, the wily hare began to paddle up the middle of the stream for twenty or thirty yards, and, of course, in so doing our scent was soon drifted away down the current. So we flattered ourselves, when we at last did make the opposite bank, that our pursuers would be puzzled for a minute or two to know what had become of us.

After a further quarter of a mile we thought we might venture to take another brief halt on the strength of this last manoeuvre. We were unable to do so where we could command a view of the hounds, but as we reckoned we had at least gained three minutes, we felt we could quite afford to take it easy for that length of time.

Fancy, then, our horror when, after about a couple of minutes, we heard a cry of "Forward!" close to us, and evidently on this side of the stream.

Off we dashed like mad, in a regular panic, and never checked our pace till we had put three ploughed fields and a couple of wide ditches to our credit. We did not discover till it was all over how it was our cunning scheme to perplex the hounds had thus miscarried. Then we were told that some of the scent, instead of dropping into the water, as we intended, had lodged on the top of some stones in mid-stream, and this had at once betrayed our dodge to the practised eyes of the foremost hounds. It was a caution to be more careful another time.

We had to work hard to make up for the ground we had lost by this mistake, but our next sight of the hounds showed that we were fairly ahead again, and that the ploughed fields had (as Birch predicted) told on a good portion of the pack, who now (at least, those of them who were at all well up) scarcely numbered a dozen.

Half a mile farther brought us to Wincot village, down the main street of which we sped, greatly to the admiration of the inhabitants, who turned out in force to see the sport.

By this time we had fairly got our "second winds," and began to realise the benefit of the steady training of the past fortnight. At an ordinary pace, with the second wind well laid on, we felt we ought to be able to hold out for the run home, unless some very unexpected accident should intervene.

Past the village, we rattled on till we came to the railway embankment, across which we trespassed, not without some difficulty, as it was steep and railed off on either side by high palisades. Once over this, we turned at right angles, and ran for half a mile close alongside the line, and past Wincot station. Here it was necessary to recross the line (down a cutting this time), and as we were doing so we caught sight, on our left, of the leading hounds scrambling to the top of the embankment, which we had passed only a minute or two before.

Clear of the railway, there remained a good steady piece of work cut out for us to reach home, across an awful country, full of hedges and ditches, and as hilly as a pie-crust.

But Birch and I were well in the humour of the thing by this time, and determined it should not be our fault if the "great hunt" of this year ended in a victory for the hounds. So we spurted for nearly a mile, jumping most of the narrow ditches and low hedges that crossed our path, and making as straight a course as the hilly ground allowed of. But, despite all our efforts, the occasional glimpses which we caught of our pursuers showed us that we were unable to shake off four or five of the leading hounds, who, with Forwood at their head, were coming on at a great pace, and, if not gaining on us, at least not losing ground.

This would never do. It would be all up if things went on so, we could see; so the cunning Birch had once again to resort to his dodges to gain time.

Suddenly altering our track, and leaving the fields, he struck a dusty lane, which wound in and out in the direction of Parkhurst. Now, as this was a very dusty and a very chalky lane, and as the wind was blowing the dust about very freely, it was easy to see why the artful Birch made use of it on the present occasion. Our white scraps of paper, falling on the white road, and being fallen on by the white dust, had a good chance of escaping detection, unless looked after very carefully; and to make matters more secure, we dodged off into the fields, and back again into the lane, pretty often, leaving our pursuers a ditch to jump each time.

This manoeuvre answered fairly well, for the next time we saw the hounds they were searching about by the side of a ditch for our track, a good way to the rear.

We had now to face the hardest bit of work of the afternoon. The last two miles home were over a perfectly flat bit of country—so flat that the hounds would have us in view nearly all the way, and, consequently, to dodge or double would be simply useless. Our only course was a straight hard run for it, trusting to our legs and our wind to pull us through. So we settled down to the task with a will. Scarcely had we emerged into the open ground for a couple of minutes, when we saw a figure dash out of the lane in full cry after us.

It was Forwood, the whipper-in, a terrible "scud" across country, and he was only fifty yards or so ahead of three others, also celebrated for their pace. So we hares had our work cut out for us, and no mistake!

Next moment the splash of a double 'header.'

For a mile we ran as hard as we well could, turning neither to right nor left, and halting neither at ditch nor dyke. Parkhurst Towers rose before us in the distance, and more than one boy was already strolling out in our direction to witness the finish.

How we wished we were as fresh as they!

"Put it on, hares!" shouted the first who met us, "you'll do it yet."

"Hounds are gaining!" cried the next we passed—a young urchin sitting on a bank and eating toffee.

And now there met us not single spectators only, but groups, who cheered loudly, backing, some the hares and some the hounds, till we hardly knew where we were. Some even began to run along with us, at a respectful distance, in order to be "in at the death."

The playground wall was now visible only half a mile away, on the other side of the Gravelshire Canal, which had to be crossed by a bridge which we were fast approaching.

I gave a rapid look back. Forwood was now only a hundred yards behind us, with lots of running still in him. He would certainly run us down in the next half-mile.

"Birch," I said, as I ran beside him, "are you good for a swim?"

"Rather!" he exclaimed; "if you are. Quick!"

We swerved suddenly in our course, and, to the amazement of all spectators, left the bridge on our left. In another minute we were on the margin of the canal, and the next moment the splash of a double "header," and the shouts of the assembled onlookers, proclaimed that we had made a plunge for it. The canal was only about thirty feet wide, and we were across it in a twinkling, our light flannel clothes scarcely interfering with our swimming, and certainly not adding much to the weight we carried after being soaked through.

Three hundred yards now! Ah! that cheer behind means that Forwood has followed our plunge. What are they laughing at, though? Can he have foundered? No! Another shout! That means he is safe over, and hard at our heels.

For the last three hundred yards we run a regular steeplechase. The meadows are intersected with lines of hurdles, and these we take one after another in our run, as hard as we can. Only one more, and then we are safe!

Suddenly I find myself on my face on the grass! I have caught on the last hurdle, and come to grief!

Birch in an instant hauls me to my feet, just as Forwood rises to the leap. Then for a hundred yards it is a race for very life. What a shouting there is! and what a rushing of boys and waving of caps pass before our eyes! On comes Forwood, the gallant hound, at our heels; we can hear him behind us distinctly!

"Now you have them!" shouts one.

"One spurt more, hares!" cries another, "and you are safe!"

On we bound, and on comes the pursuer, not ten yards behind—not *ten*, but more than *five*. And that five he never makes up till Birch and I are safe inside the school-gates, winners by a neck—and a neck only—of that famous hunt.

The pack came straggling in for the next hour, amid the cheers and chaffing of the boys. Three of them, who had kept neck and neck all the way, were only two minutes behind Forwood; but they had shirked the swim, and taken the higher and drier course—as, indeed, most of the other hounds did—by way of the bridge. Ten minutes after them one other fellow turned up, and a quarter of an hour later three more; and so on until the whole pack had run, or walked, or limped, or ridden home—all except one, little Jim Barlow, the tiniest and youngest and pluckiest little hound that ever crossed country. We were all anxious to know what had become of this small chap of thirteen, who, some one said, ought never to have been allowed to start on such a big run, with his little legs. "Wait a bit," said Forwood; "Jim will turn up before long, safe and sound, you'll see."

It was nearly dusk, and a good two hours after the finish. We were sitting in the big hall, talking and laughing over the events of the afternoon, when there came a sound of feet on the gravel walk, accompanied by a vehement puffing, outside the window.

"There he is!" exclaimed Forwood, "and, I declare, running still!"

And so it was. In a minute the door swung open, and in trotted little Jim, dripping wet, coated with mud, and panting like a steam-engine, but otherwise as self-composed as usual.

"How long have you fellows been in?" he demanded of us, as he sat down and began to lug off his wet boots.

"Two hours," replied Birch.

The little hero looked a trifle mortified to find he was so far behind, and we were quite sorry for him.

"Never mind," he said, "I ran on the scent every inch of the way, and only pulled up once, at Wincot, for five minutes."

"You did!" exclaimed one or two voices, as we all stared admiringly at this determined young hound.

"Yes; and a nice dance you gave a chap my size over the railway and across those ditches! But I didn't miss a single one of them, all the same."

"But what did you do at the canal?" asked Forwood.

"Why, swam it, of course—obliged to do it, wasn't I, if the hares went that way? I say, is there any grub going?"

Plucky little Jim Barlow! After all, he was the hero of that "big hunt," though he did come in two hours late.

This was the last big "hare and hounds" I ever ran in. I have many a time since ridden with a real hunt over the same country, but never have I experienced the same thrill of excitement or known the same exultation at success as when I ran home with Birch, two seconds ahead of the hounds, in the famous Parkhurst Paper-chase of 18 hundred and something.

Chapter Three
The Parkhurst Boat-race

"Adams is wanted down at the boat-house!" Such was the sound which greeted my ears one Saturday afternoon as I lolled about in the playground at Parkhurst, doing nothing. I jumped up as if I had been shot, and asked the small boy who brought the message who wanted me.

"Blades does; you've got to cox the boat this afternoon instead of Wilson. Look sharp!" he said, "as they're waiting to start."

Off I went, without another word, filled with mingled feelings of wonder, pride, and trepidation. I knew Wilson, the former coxswain of the school boat, had been taken ill and left Parkhurst, but this was the first I had ever heard of my being selected to take his place. True, I had steered the boat occasionally when no one else could be got, and on such occasions had managed to keep a moderately good course up the Two Mile Reach, but I had never dreamed of such a pitch of good fortune as being called to occupy that seat as a fixture.

But now it wanted only a week of the great race with the Old Boys, and here was I summoned to take charge of the rudder at the eleventh hour, which of course meant I would have to steer the boat on the occasion of the race! No wonder, then, I was half daft with excitement as I hurried down to the boathouse in obedience to the summons of Blades, the stroke of the Parkhurst Four.

I should explain that at Parkhurst we were peculiarly favoured in the matter of boating. The River Colven flowed through the town only half a mile from the school boundaries, and being at that place but a short distance from the sea, it was some fifty yards broad, a clear, deep stream, just the sort of water one would choose for rowing. There was no lock for six miles or so up, and the few craft which came in from the sea rarely proceeded beyond Parkhurst; so that we had a long, uninterrupted stretch of water for our boats, which, as soon as ever the spring set in, and the weather became too hot for football and hare and hounds, appeared in force every half-holiday on its surface.

Some of the fellows on such occasions used to amuse themselves by starting off for a long, leisurely grind up-stream; or else with set sail to tack down the lower reaches towards the sea; but most of us who laid claim in any degree to the name of enthusiastic oarsmen, confined our operations mainly to the Two Mile Reach, on which most of the club races were rowed, chief of which was the Old Boys' Race, already referred to.

This race had been instituted some years before my time at the school, by an old Parkhurstian, who presented a cup, to be rowed for annually, between the best four-oared crew of the present school, and any crew of old pupils who had been at Parkhurst within two years.

This race was the all-absorbing topic in our boat-club for several weeks before the event. How carefully the crew were selected, how strictly they trained, how patiently Mr Blunt, one of the masters, and an old Cambridge oar, "coached" or tutored them; how regularly the boat went over the course morning after morning, before breakfast; how eagerly the fellows criticised or commended the rowers; how impatiently we all looked forward to the coming contest!

This year our prospects were doubtful. The Old Boys had got together a strong crew, who were reported by some who had been over to see them to be very fast, and in splendid form; while we, at the last moment, had had the disadvantage to lose our coxswain and have to fill his place with a less experienced hand. Still, the school "four" was a good one, carefully drilled, with plenty of power; one which Mr Blunt pronounced ought to hold its own with any other average crew. So, on the whole, there was no saying how the chances stood.

I found I had all my work before me to get accustomed to my new duties before the day of the race. Daily I was out with the four, and several times besides I was taken over the course in a punt, and carefully shown all the shallows, and bends, and eddies of the stream, and made familiar with the ins and outs of either bank.

Luckily, I was a light weight to begin with, so that I did not lose much by my limited period of training, being indeed not so heavy as the former coxswain of the boat, whom I had succeeded.

Well, the eventful day came at last. The Old Boys arrived the day before, and from the two trial rows which they took over the course, we could see they were a first-rate crew and formidable opponents. Still our "coach," who had watched them minutely, told us we had the better stroke of the two, and if we could only hold out, ought to win after all. This was comforting information, for the showy style of our opponents had struck terror into not a few of those whose sympathies were on the side of the present boys.

The school turned out in force to witness the event. The towing-path was lined with spectators, many of them from a distance, attracted by the prospect of an exciting race. A goodly muster of old fellows revisited the haunts of their school days, and congregated about the winning-post, while others, of a more athletic turn, prepared to run along with the race from beginning to end.

Meanwhile, in the boat-house, we had stripped for action and launched our boat. As we were ready to put off, and make for the starting-point, Mr Blunt came up and said to Blades, our "stroke",—

"Now remember, row a steady stroke all through. Don't be flurried if they get the best of the start. If you can stick to them the first half of the way, you ought to be able to row them down in the last; and mind, Adams," he said, addressing me, "don't let them force you out of your straight course, and don't waste time in trying to bother them. Keep as straight as an arrow, and you can't go wrong."

As our fellows put off for the starting-place, their long clean stroke elicited no little admiration from the onlookers, who saw much in it that augured well for the success of our boat. Thanks to Mr Blunt, our crew had learned to master that steady, strong sweep of the oars which is universally admitted to be the perfection of rowing style and the most serviceable of all strokes. Rowed well through from first to last, gripping the water the instant the oar is back and the body and arms forward, and dragged clean through without jerk or plunge, the swing of the bodies regular as clockwork, the feather clear and rapid—this essentially is the kind of rowing which not only puts most pace into the boat, but is capable of being sustained far longer than any other.

Not long after us our opponents embarked, and we had an opportunity of criticising their style as they paddled up to where we lay waiting for them. It certainly looked pretty and taking. The stroke was quicker than ours, and equally regular, but it seemed to end in a spasmodic jerk as the oars left the water, which, though it succeeded in making the boat travel quickly, appeared to try the powers of the rowers rather more than our style did. Still, there was no mistaking that they were a fast and a powerful crew, and I remember to this day the passing thought, "I wish we were at the end of it!" that flashed through my mind as I gathered my rudder lines together, ready for the start.

Mr Blunt is to act as starter, and is coming towards us in a boat, with his watch in his hand. Our rivals' boat is lying close beside ours, and I can see their stroke is leaning forward and saying something to the coxswain. I wonder it it's about me? Perhaps he is telling him to push me out of my course, or perhaps they are saying how nervous I am looking! Well, I *am* nervous. I begin to think I shall forget which way I have to go. Perhaps I shall pull the right-hand line instead of the left; or possibly I shall omit to pull either line at all! What lasting disgrace will then be mine! Then suddenly I remember what Mr Blunt said, that it's all up with a race if the "cox" loses his head, and by a violent effort I banish my qualms, and resolve, come what may, *nothing* shall unsteady me. Still, my hands tremble as I grasp the lines.

"Adams," says Blades, "make my stretcher fast, will you?"

The voice of a human being close to me, somehow, has the effect of helping me to recover my wits completely; and as I kneel and make fast the stretcher, and then once again take my seat in the stern of the boat, I feel quite myself again, and wonder at myself for being such an ass.

"Back water half a stroke!" calls out Mr Blunt to us from his skiff.

We obey him, and then find the other boat is a little in front of us. We therefore move a quarter of a stroke forward. Still the boats are not quite level. The other boat must come back a foot or two. Not quite enough; our boat must advance a few inches. There, now they are level.

"Are you ready?" No, our boat has drifted forward again, and must be moved back. All this takes time, but presently we are once again level, and the question is repeated—

"Are you ready?"

The only answer this time is the leaning forward of both crews, with arms stretched and oars well back, in readiness for the signal.

What ages it seems! And there I actually the wind has blown our rivals' bows across the stream, and before we start another two minutes must be spent in manoeuvring her back into position. Once again—

"Are you ready?"

No answer, save the quick reach forward and silent suspense.

"Then go!" and I feel the boat half lifted in the water under me. The first stroke is rather a scramble, and so is the second, but by the third the boat has begun to get its "way" on, and in a stroke or two more our men have settled down to their customary swing.

But what of our opponents? At the first stroke their boat had dashed away an inch or two in advance of ours, at the third that distance had become a foot, and presently they were far enough ahead to enable me to catch sight of their coxswain's back. As we both settled down to work, they were rowing at a considerably quicker pace than we, wrenching the boat forward at each stroke, and inch by inch improving their advantage.

All this I noticed before the shout with which the spectators hailed the start had died away. I had a dim vision of a body of runners starting along with us on the banks, and of eager cries to one crew or the other from sympathising onlookers; but I had enough to do to keep my eye fixed ahead, without gaping at the crowd.

Remembering Mr Blunt's advice, I selected a landmark in front, and steered our course direct for it; a plan of which I had cause to be glad pretty early in the race. For the Old Boys' boat, drawing steadily ahead to about half a boat's length, began very gradually to insinuate its nose a little over in our direction, so that, had I not had a fixed point on which to steer, I should have been strongly tempted to give way unwittingly before it, and so abandon an inch or two of the water that fairly belonged to our boat. As it was, however, I was able both to detect and defeat this manoeuvre, for, keeping on a perfectly straight course, the others were obliged to draw in their horns, and return to a straight course too, having lost some little ground in the process. Still, they seemed to be forging ahead, and the shouts from the banks announced that thus far, at any rate the Parkhurst boat was getting the worst of it.

I stole a look at Blades. His face was composed and unconcerned, and it was easy to see he knew what he was about. He kept up his long steady swing, being well backed up by the three men behind him, and lifted the boat well at the beginning of the stroke, never letting it down till the end. I could see that he knew exactly how far the others were ahead, and at what rate they were rowing; and yet he neither quickened nor altered his stroke, but plodded on with such a look of easy confidence that I at once felt quite satisfied in my own mind as to the result. It was not long before our opponents gave indication of abating somewhat the quick stroke they had hitherto maintained, and by virtue of which they had already got nearly a boat's length ahead. At the same moment Blades slightly quickened his stroke, and instantly our boat began to crawl up alongside that of our rivals, amid the frantic cheers of the onlookers. Slowly and surely we forged ahead, till our stroke's oar was level with their coxswain. Then a spurt from the Old Boys kept the two boats abreast for a few seconds, but it died away after a little, and once more their boat travelled slowly back, as we drew level, and began in our turn to take the lead. Now was our time to—

What is that ahead on the water, drifting right across the bows of our boat? A shout from the banks apprises me that others besides myself have taken the sudden alarm. An empty boat, insecurely moored to the bank, has got adrift, and is calmly floating up with the tide in mid-stream along our very course! What is to be done? The other boat, being on the opposite side, can easily clear the obstacle, but not so ours. Either we must put our bows across our enemy's water, and so run the risk of a "foul," and consequent defeat, or else we must lose ground by slackening our pace and going out of our course to avoid the unlucky boat. There are not ten seconds in which to decide; but that suffices me to choose the latter alternative, trusting to the rowing powers of our crew to make up the disadvantage.

"Look to your oars, stroke side!" I cry, and at the same time pull my rudder line quickly.

It was as I expected. The boat lost ground instantly, and I could see, out of the corner of my eye, the Old Boys' boat shoot forward with a quickened stroke, and hear the triumphant shouts of their partisans.

A second or two sufficed to get past the obstructing boat, our oars on the stroke side just scraping it as we did so; but as we headed again into our proper course, we saw our opponents two clear boats' lengths in front, their men pulling with all the energy of triumph and confidence.

It was a sight to make one despair. How were we ever to make up that tremendous gap?

"How much?" Blades inquires, as he swings forward towards me.

"Two!" I reply.

He sets his face determinedly, and quickens his stroke. The men behind him do not at first get into the altered swing, and for a moment or two the rowing is scrambling, and our boat rolls unsteadily, a spectacle hailed with increased joy by the partisans of the Old Boys' boat.

"Steady now!" cries Blades, over his shoulder, and next moment the boat rights itself; the four oars dip and feather simultaneously. I, sitting in the stern, can feel the swing as of one man, and the boat dashes forward like a machine. Our fellows on the banks mark the change and cheer tremendously.

"Well spurted, Parkhurst!" "Put it on now!" "You're gaining!" "Rowed indeed!" Such were the cries which, as I heard them, set my blood tingling with excitement.

It was a long time before any perceptible gain was noticeable from where I sat. The Old Boys had taken advantage of their lead to come across into our water, and all I could see of them was the blades of their oars on in front, which rose and fell swiftly and with a regular beat.

Still the shout from the bank was, "You're gaining!" and presently I saw their boat edging off again into their own water, by which I concluded we had pulled up sufficiently to make this necessary to avoid a foul.

Our men pulled splendidly. Cool, determined, and plucky, each rowed his best, his eyes fixed on the back of the man before him, keeping perfect time, and pulling each stroke through with terrible energy. I could see by their pale looks that they shared the common excitement, but there was no sign of flurry or distress, nothing but a quiet determination, which augured better for the result of their efforts than all the shouts of the onlookers.

Where are we now? Those willows on my left are, I know, just half a mile from the winning-post. Shall we, in that distance, be able to pull up the length which now divides us and our rivals? There is a chance yet! The leading boat is not going as fast as it was a minute ago. I can tell that by the eddies from their oars which sweep past.

"How much?" inquired Blades again, as he swung forward.

"One!" I replied.

I could see by the gleam in his eyes that he had hope still of making that one length nothing before the winning-post was reached.

That shout from the bank means something, surely!

"Well rowed indeed, Parkhurst!"

"They're overlapped!"

Yes, those who could see it were watching the little pink flag at the prow of our boat creeping, inch by inch, up the stern of our rivals'. The eddies from their oars came past nearer now, and the "thud" of their outriggers sounded closer.

Yes, we are gaining without doubt; but shall we overtake them in time to avoid defeat? I can see a mass of people ahead on the banks, and know that they are gathered opposite the winning-post. It can't be a quarter of a mile off now!

Again that shout from the bank. Ah, yes, our bow oar is level with their stroke. "Now you have it!" shout our fellows.

Blades turns his head for half a second, and cries to his men as he quickens up to his final spurt.

What a shout then rent the air! Our boat no longer crawled up beside the Old Boys, but began to fly. On, on! Their coxswain seems to be gliding backwards towards me. In vain they attempt to answer our spurt; they have not the rowing left in them to do it. Nothing can stop us! In another moment we are abreast, and almost instantly there come such cheers after cheers from the bank that even the dash of the oars was drowned in it.

"Parkhurst's ahead!"

"Ah, well rowed!"

"Now, Old Boys!"

"It's a win!"

On, on! What sensation so glorious, so madly exciting, as that of one of the crew of a winning boat within twenty yards of the goal? I am tempted to shout, to wave my hat, to do something ridiculous, but I set my teeth and sit still, holding my breath. Four strokes more will do it. One! I am level with the stroke of the Old Boys' boat. Two! Our fellows pull as if they had another half-mile to go still. Three! The judge at the winning-post is lifting his hand and cocking his pistol. Four! Crack goes the signal! and as our men cease rowing, and the boat shoots forward with the impetus of that last terrific stroke, amid the cheers and shouts of the assembled crowd, I breathe again, knowing that the Parkhurst boat has won, by three yards, the grandest race in which it was ever my lot to take part.

Chapter Four
Parkhurst versus Westfield

"Now, Parkhurst, turn out sharp! They are going in first." So shouted Steel, the captain of our eleven, putting his head in at the door of the tent in which we were arraying ourselves in flannels and spiked shoes, and otherwise arming for the great match against Westfield School, which was now about to commence.

We always looked upon these Westfield fellows as our most dangerous rivals on the cricket field (much in the light in which we esteemed Craven where football was concerned), and the match in which our respective pretensions were yearly settled was, I need hardly say, regarded as *the* match of the season, and made the object of untiring practice and feverish excitement.

Year after year, for twelve years, our rival elevens had met, always on the last Saturday of June, one year at Parkhurst and the next at Westfield, and so far the result had been that each school had won six matches. Fancy then the state of our feelings this year, as we started off in the early morning on our omnibus from Parkhurst, to engage in the decisive contest which (unless it ended in a draw) must turn the balance either in favour of our school, or to the glorification of our rivals. We could not bear to think of the possibility of a defeat; it would be too tragical, too shameful. So as we drove over to Westfield that morning, we talked of nothing but victory, and felt very like those determined old Spartans who, when they went to the wars, made a vow they would return either with their shields or on them.

Of course there was a regular swarm of people to see the match. Old Parkhurst "bats," who had played in the first match, thirteen years ago, were there, with big beards, and very majestic to look at; Old Boys, now settled in life, were there with their wives and children; carriages full of our own and Westfield's fathers and mothers; and shoals of young brothers and sisters, crammed the space beyond the flags; the "doctors," as usual, had driven over; and almost gave offence to some of our most enthusiastic partisans by "chumming up" publicly with the head master of our rivals! And then, besides, there was a host of outsiders, drawn together by simple curiosity or love of cricket; so that altogether, as we emerged from our tent in our snow-white flannels and pink belts, we felt that the eyes of the world were upon us, and were more convinced than ever that anything short of victory would be the most terrible of all calamities which could fall on our youthful heads.

Our great hope was in Steel, our captain, one of the best cricketers Parkhurst had ever produced; and for coolness and self-confidence without his equal anywhere. We all adored him, for he never snubbed youngsters, or made light of their doings. If, during practice, a fellow bowled, batted, or fielded well, Steel took care to encourage him; but if any one played carelessly, or bungled, Steel scowled, and that unlucky man's name disappeared for a season from the list of candidates for a place in the first eleven.

See him now stroll up to the wickets, with his wicket-keeping pads on, talking on the way to one of the two men who are to officiate first with their bats on behalf of Westfield.

We youngsters can't understand such coolness, and keep our eyes on him, as if every moment we expected to see him fell his rival to the earth. It's a great matter to be used to a thing. I, who was now making my first appearance in the first eleven, felt as if the world began, continued, and ended within the area of this Westfield meadow; but here was some one who, to all appearances, made no more of the great match than he would of his dinner.

But away now with all thoughts but cricket! The ball we have been tossing about idly is taken into custody by the umpire; Steel is behind the wickets, looking round to see if we fielders are all in our places, and motioning one or two of us to stand deeper or closer in, as he deems advisable. The Westfield batsman who is to receive the first over is getting "middle"; our bowler is tucking up his sleeves, and gripping the brand-new ball in his hand; the ground-keeper is chasing a few small boys back behind the ropes; and the scorers in the big tent are dipping their pens in the ink.

Altogether, it is a critical moment in my life—a moment that seems as long as a whole day.

"Play!" cries the umpire; and our bowler delivers his first ball—not a very alarming one, and evidently meant more as a test of the ball and the pitch than as a serious attack on the enemy's wicket. My readers of course do not expect me to give a full, true, and particular account of every ball bowled on that eventful day. That would be as tedious for them as for me. But I shall do my best to recall the chief features of the game as they presented themselves to me from my post, first at cover-point, and (while our side was batting) from the tent and the wickets.

The first few overs were not eventful. They rarely are. Our men had to get used to the ground and the ball; and the batsmen chose to be exceedingly careful how they hit out at first. In the third over a single run was made, and of course the Westfield fellows cheered as if the match were already won. Then gradually came one or two more singles, a two, another one, a three, and then, just as the two batsmen were getting into good humour and fancying they might lay about them a little more freely, down went the first wicket amid the cheers of our fellows, and we saw the figures 12 posted up on the telegraph, as indicating the score so far standing to the credit of Westfield.

We had not long to wait for the next man in, and still less long to see him out, poor fellow! for the very first ball sent his bails flying over Steel's head, and he had to trudge back to the tent and take off his pads almost before he had got used to the feel of them on his legs.

In the over following the arrival of his successor an easy catch by point disposed of another wicket.

"This is something like!" I exclaimed to myself. "Three men out for fourteen runs. If it goes on like this, we shall have it all our own way"; and in my satisfaction I ventured to communicate my ideas to the man fielding at point.

"Adams, will you attend to the game?" It was Steel who spoke, and at the sound of his voice I started like one shot, and discovered that the next man was in and ready to begin. I stepped back to my place in an instant, and would sooner have had one of Hurley's swiftest balls catch me on the bare shin than be thus publicly called to order before the whole field. I can safely say that never in my life since that moment have I caught myself talking during "play" in a cricket match.

I felt in disgrace, and got nervous; I dared not look at Steel, for fear of meeting his eye. I wished myself a mile away, and repented of my satisfaction of being in the first eleven. Most devoutly I hoped no ball would chance near me, as I should assuredly miss it. As the thought passed my mind the man who was batting cut a ball hard and low in my direction. It was so hard and so low that under any circumstances it would have been a most difficult ball to field, still more to catch. It flew towards me a few inches from the ground, and I was in despair. I knew every eye in the field was on me—Steel's in particular. Here would be some hundreds of witnesses to my utter imbecility! Would that the ground would swallow me! I sprang forward and tripped as I sprang. In my fall the ball dashed into my hand,

and fell from it to the earth. I had missed the catch, and my disgrace was complete. Fancy then my astonishment when I heard Steel's awful voice cry, "Well tried, sir!" and when a distant sound of clapping reached me from the tents! I could not understand it at first; but I afterwards found out that by my lucky trip I had more nearly succeeded in catching the ball than a more experienced player would have done had he kept his balance, and so I got credit for a good piece of play which I did not in the least deserve. However, it served to recover me from my nervousness and bad spirits, and incite me to a desire to accomplish something for which I could honestly take credit.

Never was such a determination more called for than now. Driver, the captain of the Westfield eleven, was at the wickets, a most tremendous hitter. All bowling came alike to him. The swifter the ball the happier he was; sending one over the bowler's head, another nearly into the scorers' tent, another among the spectators behind the ropes. The score, hitherto so slow, began to fly up. Forty, fifty, sixty, seventy we saw posted up in rapid succession, and wondered how it all would end. He seemed to have as many lives as a cat. Some easy catches were missed, and some "runs out" were only just avoided. Still he scored, no matter who his partner was (and one or two came and went while he was in); he hit away merrily, and the cheers of Westfield grew almost monotonous from their frequency.

We on the "off" side, however, had not much to do, for nearly all Driver's hits were to the "on," and, curiously enough, nearly all found their way between two of our men, the "mid-wicket on" and the "long on," just out of the reach of either. I could not help wondering why neither of these fellows altered his place, so as to guard the weak point.

It is curious how sometimes in cricket the same thing occurs to two people at the same time. While I was inwardly speculating on the result of this change of position, Steel appeared to become aware of the same necessity, for I saw him behind the batsman's back silently motioning "mid-wicket on" to stand farther back, and "mid on" to come round to a "square" position. This manoeuvre, however, did not escape the wily Driver, who sent his next ball to leg, and the next to the identical spot "mid-wicket on" had just quitted. Still, Steel motioned to them to remain in their new posts. He knew well enough that if a man has a habit of hitting in any one direction, however studiously he tries to avoid the place. Nature will sooner or later assert herself, and the ball will fly where it has been wont to fly. So it was in this case. He could *not* resist an impulse to lift one specially tempting ball in the direction of his old haunt, and sure enough in so doing he sent it clean into "long on's" hands, and with his own innings ended, to our great relief, the innings of his side, for a total score of 174, of which he had contributed quite the odd 74.

It was a good round score to overtake, and things did not promise cheerfully for us at the commencement of our innings. The Westfield men were happy in possessing two swift bowlers, who made havoc of the first two or three on our side who presented themselves. I was one of these.

When I started for the wickets, armed with pads and gloves and bat, I did not feel happy; still, I was in hopes I might at least succeed in "breaking my duck's egg," which was more than could be said for either of my predecessors.

I felt rather important as I requested the umpire to give me "middle," and hammered the mark a little with my bat. Still, my feet fidgeted; there was a sort of "cobwebby" feeling on my face, and a tickling sensation in the small of my back, as I stood ready for my first ball, which convinced me I was by no means at home in my new position.

"Play!" cries the umpire.

The bowler starts to run, with arm extended. He makes a sort of curve round the wicket, and balances himself on one foot as he discharges his ball. It comes like lightning, right on to my bat, twisting it in my grasp, and then is snatched up in an instant by "point," who tosses it to the wicket-keeper, who returns it to the bowler. All this is very alarming. Here are eleven men banded together with the one object of putting me out, and they are all so quiet and determined about it that I feel like a guilty thing as I stand there to defend my wicket.

The bowler starts again for his sinuous run, and again the ball whizzes from his hand. I lift my bat in an attempt to strike it; it slips under it; there is a little "click" behind my back, and then the ball flies aloft, and I discover that my services at the wicket are no longer required.

So ended my first innings. Happily for our side, some of the men who went in afterwards made a better show than we three unfortunates who had opened the ball had done. Steel made forty, and two others about twenty each, which, added to the odds and ends contributed by the rest of our side, brought the Parkhurst score up to 102—72 runs behind our competitors.

There was great jubilation among the Westfield partisans, as their heroes entered on their second innings under such promising auspices, especially when the redoubtable Driver went in first with the bat which had wrought such wonders in the former innings. There seemed every probability, too, of his repeating his late performance with even greater vigour, for the first ball which reached him he sent flying far and high right over the tents for six, a magnificent hit, which fairly deserved the praise it received, not from the Westfield fellows only, but from ours, who for a moment could forget their rivalry to admire a great exploit. The next three balls were delivered to his partner at the wickets, who blocked carefully, evidently bent on acting on the defensive while his companion made the running. From the fifth ball of that over a bye was scored, which brought Driver once again to the end facing the bowler. The next ball came slightly to the "off," and he tried to cut it. Either he miscalculated, or was careless about the direction he gave it, for he lodged it clean into my hands, a safe and easy catch, but a catch of enormous importance to our side, as it disposed once and for all of our most dreaded opponent.

Bereft of their champion, the Westfield fellows only succeeded in putting together the moderate score of fifty in their second innings, of which twenty-four were contributed by one man. So our spirits revived somewhat, as we discovered we had only 123 to make to win. That was indeed plenty against such bowling, but it was a good deal less than we had dreaded.

Well, the decisive innings began, as soon as we had fortified ourselves with lunch, provided for us by our hospitable rivals. The afternoon was getting on, but still the crowd of spectators kept together patiently, determined to see the end of the match.

"Shall we do it?" I heard some one ask of Steel.

"Do what?" was the evasive reply.

"Win," said the other.

"How do I know?" was our captain's curt answer.

If there was one thing that annoyed Steel above others, it was to be asked foolish questions.

He sent in two steady men first, with orders not to be in a hurry to score, but to "break the back" of the bowling. And this advice they faithfully acted upon. For over after over there was nothing but blocking. In vain the bowlers strained every nerve to get round or under those stubborn bats. They could not do it! Runs came few and far between—the field had nothing to do—and altogether the game became very monotonous. But those fellows did better service to our side than many who scored more and played in more brilliant style. We could see their prolonged stand was not without its effect on the Westfield bowlers. Their bowling became less and less steady, and their style seemed to lose its precision, as ball after ball fell hopelessly off those obstinate bats. This was evidently just what Steel wanted, and we could tell by his frequent "Played, sir!" how thoroughly he approved of the steady discipline of his men. After a time the very monotony of the game seemed to excite the spectators, who answered each neat "block" with a cheer, which showed they, too, could appreciate the tactics of our captain.

It was getting desperate for Westfield, and humiliating too, when one of their bowlers happened to change his style. Instead of the slashing round-arm balls which he had hitherto sent in, he suddenly and without warning put in an underhand lob—an easy, slow, tempting ball, apparently bound to rise exactly on the player's bat.

Our man fell into the snare. I could hear Steel, who was near me, groan, as we watched him lift the bat which had till now remained so well under control, and stepping forward prepare for a terrific "slog." Alas! the deceitful ball never rose at all, but pitching quietly a foot before the crease, shot forward along the ground, and found its way at last to the wicket, amid the tremendous shouts of all the crowd.

A parting being thus made between the two steady partners, the survivor, as is so often the case, did not long remain behind his companion, and when Steel went in, three wickets had already fallen with only fifteen runs.

Will our captain save us from defeat? See him stand coolly at the wicket—how sure of himself he seems!—how indifferent to that imposing combination of bowlers and fielders which surround him! He takes his time to get comfortably settled at his wicket, and kneels down to tighten a shoestring, as if nobody was waiting for him. Then pulling down the peak of his cap to shade his eyes from the sun, he leisurely turns his face to the bowler, and announces himself ready for the worst that desperate character can do to him.

We watched breathlessly the result of his first over, and with an excitement strangely in contrast with the indifferent and apparently careless demeanour of the batsman himself. It was soon apparent, however, that we might dismiss all anxiety from our minds as to his safety, for he set briskly to work, punishing every ball that came to him, yet never giving a single chance. I have rarely seen such good "all-round play." Unlike the Westfield captain, who was strong only on the leg side of the wicket, he was thoroughly at home from whatever side the attack was delivered. Some balls he hit to "leg," and some he cut with terrific force past "cover-point." No ball came amiss to him; he was up to "twisters," and "lobs," and "thunderbolts," and walked into them all with faultless dexterity.

Up went our score. Twenty grew to forty, and forty to fifty. It was all a matter of time now. If the five remaining men still to go in could together make a stand long enough to enable him to overtake the enemy's score, he would assuredly do it, unless some unforeseen accident prevented it. Of these five I was next in order; nor was it long before my turn arrived, and I found myself sallying forth to join my captain at the wickets. Remembering the poor figure I had cut in the first innings, I was not very sanguine of distinguishing myself on this occasion. Still, there was something in being opposite Steel which gave me confidence, and relieved me of the nervous sensations which marked my late *début*.

The first ball or two after my arrival fell to the lot of Steel, who sent them flying promptly, and gave me some running to do in consequence. This helped still more to make me comfortable, so that when at last my turn came to be bowled at, I experienced none of the desolate feeling which had rendered my former brief innings so unhappy.

I manage to block the first ball, and the second also. Then comes a third, under which I contrive to get my bat and send it flying.

"Come!" shouts Steel, and I run.

"Another!" he cries; and I run again, and am safe back before the ball returns to the wicket-keeper's hands.

Positively I had scored two! I felt as proud as if I had been elected an M.P. The next ball went for two more, and I could hear a cheer from the tent, which made me feel very valiant. I glanced to the signal-board; our score was ninety-six, only twenty-seven to win! Why should not I be able to hold out until Steel made up the figure, and so defeat Westfield by four wickets? At any rate I would try; and I sent my next ball for a single.

Then it was Steel's turn to bat. Of course he would send it flying.

Horrors! He has missed it! A deafening shout proclaims that his glorious innings is at an end, and I feel like an orphan as I watch him, with his bat under his arm, quitting the wicket at which he had put together sixty-six runs in as fine a style as any player ever did. It was good to hear the applause which welcomed him back to the tent.

But what was to become of us? Here were twenty-six runs to get, and the four weakest batsmen of our side to play. However, one can but do his best.

So I played as carefully as I could, becoming gradually accustomed to the bowling, and knocking an occasional one or two on to the score. My new companion, however, kept me company but a short time, and his successor shorter still. This fellow coming in now is our last man. Will he and I ever be able to stick together till these fifteen runs which are now required can be made up?

"Steady, Tom," I whisper, as he passes me on the way to his wicket. He winks his answer.

It is a responsible thing for us two youngsters, with the whole fate of the school depending on us. But we keep cool, and play our very best. One by one the score runs up. Ten to win—now eight, seven. It is getting exciting. The crowd hangs eagerly on the result of each ball. Another two from my companion. The Westfield fellows look nervously at the signal-board, as if by watching it they could make our figure grow less. But, no! Another two, from my bat this time, and then a single. Only two to win! The next ball gets past my comrade's bat, and skims within a hair's-breadth of his bails.

"Steady, now!" cries Steel, cheerily. "Mind what you're at!"

Steady it is. The next two balls are blocked dead.

Then my companion makes a single. Hurrah! We are equal now. At any rate defeat is averted! Now for victory! It is my turn to bat; but this ball is not the sort of one to play tricks with; so with an effort I keep my bat square, and stop it without hitting.

"Played, sir!" cries some one, approvingly, and I feel my self-denial rewarded.

But the next ball is not so dangerous. I can see it is a careless one, which I may safely punish. Punish it I will; so I step forward, and catching it on the bound, bang it I know not and care not where.

What shouting! what cheering as we run, one, two, three, four, five times across the wickets! The match is ours, with a wicket to spare; and as we ride back that evening to Parkhurst, and talk and laugh and exult over that day's victory, we are the happiest eleven fellows, without exception, that ever rode on the top of an omnibus.

Chapter Five
A Boating Adventure at Parkhurst

Once, and once only, did I play truant from Parkhurst, and that transgression was attended with consequences so tragical that to this day its memory is as vivid and impressive as if the event I am about to record had happened only last week, instead of a quarter of a century ago.

I shall recall it in the hope of deterring my readers from following my foolish example—or at least of warning them of the terrible results which may ensue from a thoughtless act of wrong-doing.

I have already mentioned that Parkhurst stood some two or three miles above the point at which the River Colven flows into the sea. From the school-house we could often catch the hum of the waves breaking lazily along the shore of Colveston Bay; or, if the wind blew hard from the sea, it carried with it the roar of the breakers on the bar mouth, and the distant thunder of the surf on the stony beach.

Of course, our walks and rambles constantly took the direction of the shores of this bay; and though, perhaps, a schoolboy is more readily impressed with other matters than the beauties of nature, I can remember even now the once familiar view from Raven Cliff as if my eyes still rested upon it.

I can see, on a hot summer afternoon, the great curve of that beautiful bay, bounded at either extremity by headlands, bathed in soft blue haze. I can see the cliffs and chines and sands basking, like myself, in the sun. On my right, the jagged outline of a ruined sea-girt castle stands out like a sentinel betwixt is land and water. On my left I can detect the fishermen's white cottages crouching beneath the crags. I can see the long golden strip of strand beyond; and, farther still, across the wide estuary of the Wraythe, the line of shadowy cliffs that extend like a rugged wall out to the dim promontory of Shargle Head.

Above all, I can see again the sea, bluer even than the blue sky overhead; and as it tumbles languidly in from the horizon, fringing the amphitheatre of the bay with its edge of sparkling white, my ears can catch the murmur of its solemn music as they heard it in those days long gone by.

Well I remember, too, the same bay and the same sea; but oh, how changed!

Far as the eye could reach the great white waves charged towards the land, one upon another, furious and headlong; below us they thundered and lashed and rushed back upon their fellows, till we who watched could not hear so much as our own voices. In the distance they leapt savagely at the base of the now lowering headlands, and fought madly over the hidden rocks and sands. They sent their sleet and foam-flakes before them, blinding us where we stood on the cliff-top; they seethed and boiled in the hollows of the rocks, and over the river bar they dashed and plunged till far up the stream their fury scarcely spent itself.

At such times no ship or boat ventured willingly into Colveston Bay; or if it did, it rarely, if ever, left it again.

But such times were rare—very rare with us. Indeed, I had been months at Parkhurst before I witnessed a real storm, and months again before I saw another. So that my acquaintance with the bay was almost altogether connected with its milder aspects, and as such it appeared both fascinating and tempting.

It was on a beautiful August holiday morning that four of us were lounging lazily in a boat down at the bar mouth, looking out into the bay and watching the progress of a little fishing smack, which was skipping lightly over the bright waves in the direction of Shargle Head. Her sails gleamed in the sunlight, and she herself skimmed so lightly across the waters, and bounded so merrily through their sparkling ripples, that she seemed more like a fairy craft than a real yacht of boards and canvas. "I'd give a good deal to be in her!" exclaimed Hall, one of our party, a sea captain's son, to whom on all nautical matters we accorded the amplest deference. "So would I," said Hutton. "How jolly she looks!"

"Ever so much more fun than knocking about on this stupid old river," chimed in I.

"I say, you fellows," cried Hall, struck by a sudden idea, "why shouldn't we have a little cruise in the bay? It would be glorious a day like this!"

"I'm not sure old Rogers," (that was the disrespectful way in which, I regret to say, we were wont to designate Dr Rogers, our head master) "would like it," I said; "he's got some notion into his head about currents and tides, and that makes him fidgety."

"Currents and fiddlesticks!" broke in Hall, with a laugh; "what does *he* know about them? I tell you, a day like this, with a good sailing breeze, and four of us to row, in case it dropped, there'd be no more difficulty in going over there and back than there would in rowing from here back to Parkhurst."

"How long would it take to get to Shargle?" inquired Hutton.

"Why, only two hours, and perhaps less. The wind's exactly right for going and coming back too. We can be back by four easily, and that allows us an hour or two to land there."

It certainly was tempting; the day was perfection, and Colveston Bay had never looked more fascinating. The headlands stood out so distinctly in the clear air that it was hard to imagine Shargle Head was five miles distant from where we sat.

When the proposition had first been made I had felt a passing uncomfortableness as to the lawfulness of such an expedition without the distinct sanction of the head master; but the more I gazed on the bay, and the more Hall talked in his enthusiastic manner of the delights of a cruise, and the longer I watched the fairy-like progress of the little white-sailed fishing-boat, the less I thought of anything but the pleasure which the scheme offered.

So when Hall said, "Shall we go, boys? What do you say?" I for one replied, "All serene."

All this while one of our party had been silent, watching the fishing-boat, but taking no part in our discussion. He was Charlie Archer, a new boy at Parkhurst, and some years our junior. But from the first I had taken a remarkable fancy to this clever, good-humoured, plucky boy, who henceforth had become my frequent companion, and with me the companion of the others who now composed our party. He now looked up and said, greatly to our surprise—

"I say, I don't want to go!"

"Why not?" we all asked.

"Oh, it doesn't matter," he replied, in evident confusion. "I don't want to spoil your fun, you know, but I'd rather not go myself."

"Why, what on earth's the matter with you, Charlie?" I asked. "I thought you were always ready for an adventure."

"I'd rather not go, please," he repeated. "You can put me ashore."

"Why not?" again inquired Hall, this time testily. He never liked Charlie quite as much as Hutton and I did, and was evidently displeased to have him now putting forward objections to a proposition of his own making. "Why not?"

"Because—because," began the boy hesitatingly—"because I don't want to go."

Hall became angry. Like most boys not sure of the honesty of their own motives, he disliked to have it suggested that what he was urging was wrong. He therefore replied, with a taunt keener than any persuasion—

"Poor little milksop, I suppose he's afraid of getting drowned, or of doing something his mamma, or his grandmamma, or somebody wouldn't like their little pet to do. We'd better put him ashore, boys; and mind his precious little boots don't get wet while we're about it!"

It was a cruel blow, and struck home at Archer's one weak point.

Plucky and adventurous as he was, the one thing he could not endure was to be laughed at. And his face flushed, and his lips quivered, as he heard Hall's brutal speech, and marked the smile with which, I am ashamed to say, we received it.

"I'm *not* afraid," he exclaimed.

"Then why don't you want to go?"

He was silent for some time. A struggle was evidently going on in his mind. But the sneer on Hall's face determined him.

"I do want to go. I've changed my mind!"

"That's the style," said Hutton, patting him on the back. "I knew you were one of the right sort."

Hall, too, condescended to approve of his decision, and at once began to busy himself with preparations for our immediate start.

I, however, was by no means comfortable at what had taken place. It was plain to see Charlie had yielded against his better judgment, and that with whatever alacrity he might now throw himself into the scheme, his mind was not easy. Had I been less selfishly inclined towards my own pleasure, I should have sided with him in his desire not to engage in a questionable proceeding; but, alas! my wishes in this case had ruled my conscience. Still, I made one feeble effort on Archer's behalf.

"Hall," whispered I, as I stooped with him to disengage the ropes at the bottom of the boat, "what's the use of taking Charlie when he doesn't want to go? We may as well put him ashore if he'd sooner not go."

"Archer," said Hall, looking up from his ropes, "did you say you wanted to go, or not?"

The question was accompanied by a look which made it hard for the boy to reply anything but—

"I want to go."

"And it's your own free will, eh?"

"Yes."

So ended my weak effort. If only I had been more determined to do right; if, alas! I had imagined a thousandth part of what that day was to bring forth, I would have set Archer ashore, whether he would or not, even if to do so had cost me my life.

But this is anticipating.

For half an hour we were busy getting our boat trim for her voyage. She was a somewhat old craft, in which for many years past we had been wont to cruise down the seaward reaches of the Colven, carrying one lug-sail, and with thwarts for two pairs of oars. She was steady on her keel, and, as far as we had been able to judge, sound in every respect, and a good sailor. Certainly, on a day like this, a cockleshell would have had nothing to fear, and we were half sorry we had not a lighter boat than the one we were in to take us across to Shargle.

Hall, who assumed the command from the first, impressed us not a little by the businesslike way in which he set to work to get everything ship-shape before starting. He knew clearly the use of each rope and pulley; he knew precisely the necessary amount of ballast to be taken, and the proper place for stowing it; he discoursed learnedly on knots and hitches, and aroused our sympathy by his laments on the absence of a bowsprit and foresail. Hutton was sent ashore to buy provisions. Charlie was set to baling out the boat. I occupied myself with mopping the seats, and generally "swabbing her up," as Hall called it, so that in due time we were ready to sail, well provisioned and well equipped, on our eventful voyage.

Up went the sail; we watched it first flap wildly, and then swell proudly in the wind as the sheet rope was drawn in, and Hall's hand put round the helm. Then, after a little coquetting, as if she were loth to act as desired without coaxing, she rose lightly to the rippling waves, and glided forward on her way.

"Adams," said Hall, "you'd better make yourself snug up in the bows; Hutton, sit where you are, and be ready to help me with the sail when we tack. Charlie, old boy, come down astern, beside me; sit a little farther over, Hutton. Now she's trim."

Trim she was, and a strange feeling of exhilaration filled my breast as we now darted forward before the steady breeze, dancing over the waves with a merry splash, tossing them to either side of our prow, and listening to them as they gurgled musically under our keel.

"There's Neil!" cried Charlie, as we passed the coastguards' boathouse, "spying at us through the telescope."

"Let him spy," laughed Hall; "I dare say he'd like to be coming too. It's slow work for those fellows, always hanging about doing nothing."

"What's he waving about?" inquired I from the bows, for we could see that the sailor had put down his glass, and was apparently trying to catch our attention by his gesticulations.

Hall looked attentively for a moment, and then said—

"Oh, I see, he's pointing up at the flagstaff to show us the wind's in the north-east. I suppose he thinks no one knows that but himself."

"Let's see," said Hutton, "we are going north-west, aren't we?"

"Yes, so we shall be able to make use of the wind both ways, with a little tacking."

"He's shouting something now," said Charlie, with his eyes still on Neil.

"Oh, he's an old woman," said Hall, laughing; "he's always wanting to tell you this and that, as if no one knew anything about sailing but himself." And he took off his hat and waved it ceremoniously to the old sailor, who continued shouting and beckoning all the while, though without avail, for the only words that came to us across the water were "fresh" and "afternoon," and we were not much enlightened by them.

"I'm afraid he's fresh in the morning," laughed Hutton.

A short sail brought us to the bar mouth, over which, as the tide was in and the sea quiet, we passed without difficulty, although Hall had bade us have the oars ready in case of emergency, should it be necessary to lower our sail in crossing. But of this there was no need, and in a minute we were at last in the bay, and fairly at sea.

"Do you see Parkhurst over the trees there, you fellows?" cried Charlie, pointing behind us. "I never saw the place from the bay before."

"Nor I," I answered; "it looks better here than from any other side."

We were all proud of the old school-house, and fully impressed with its superiority over any other building of the kind in the kingdom.

The view in the bay was extremely beautiful, Shargle Head stood out opposite us, distinct and grand, towering up from the water, and sweeping back to join the moorland hills behind. On our left, close beside the bar mouth, rose Raven Cliff, where we so often had been wont to lie and look out on this very bay; and one by one we recognised the familiar spots from our new point of view, and agreed that from no side does a grand coast look so grand as from the sea.

Our boat scudded along merrily, Hall keeping her a steady course, well up to the wind. After a few lessons we got to know our respective duties (so we thought) with all the regularity of a trained ship's crew. With the wind as it was, right across our course, we had not much need to tack; but when the order to "stand by" did arrive, we prided ourselves that we knew how to act.

Hall let go the sheet, and Hutton lowered the sail, Charlie put round the helm, and I in the bows was ready to aid the others in shifting the canvas to the other side of the mast and hauling up the sail again. Then Hall resumed charge of the helm and drew in the sheet, Charlie and Hutton "trimmed" over to the other side of the boat, and once again our little craft darted forward.

We were all in exuberant spirits that lovely summer morning; even Charlie seemed to have forgotten his uneasiness at first starting, for he was now the life and soul of our party.

He told us wonderful stories about this very bay, gathered from some of his favourite histories. How, after the defeat of the Spanish Armada, when the proud vessels of Spain were driven partly by tempest, partly by the pursuit of our admiral, headlong along this very coast, one of them had got into Colveston Bay, and there been driven ashore at the base of Raven Cliff, not one man of all her crew surviving that awful wreck. And he repeated one after another the legends connected with Druce Castle, whose ruined turrets we could discern away behind us, and of all the coves and crags and caves as we passed them, till, in our imagination, the bay became alive once more with ships and battle, and we seemed to watch the gleam of armour on the castle walls, and the glare of beacons on the headlands, and to hear the thunder of cannon from the beach; when presently Hall's cheery call to "stand by" wakened us into a sudden recollection of our present circumstances. And then what songs we sang! what famous sea stories Hall told us! how Hutton made us roar with his recitations! how the time seemed to fly, and the boat too, and we in it, until at last we found the Great Shargle towering over our heads, and knew we had all but reached our destination.

Hall looked at his watch.

"That was a good run, boys," said he; "not quite two hours—an uncommonly good run for an old tub like this. Now where shall we land?"

"I vote we land on Welkin Island," said Charlie.

Welkin Island was separate about three-quarters of a mile from the mainland, famous for its caves and shells.

"All serene," said Hall, putting the boat about; "stand by."

So we made our last tack, and very soon were close up at the island. After some cruising we selected an eligible creek for landing, into which Hall ran our boat as neatly as the most experienced helmsman in Her Majesty's Navy.

Then we landed, and dragging ashore our hamper of provisions, picnicked at the edge of the rocks, with the water on three sides of us, with Shargle Head across the narrow channel rising majestically above us, and the great amphitheatre of the bay extended like a picture beyond.

Need I say what a jovial repast it was; what appetites we had, what zest our situation lent to our meal, how each vied with each in merriment! But Charlie was the blithest of us all.

Then we wandered over that wonderful island. We waded into the caves, and climbed to the cliff tops; we filled our pockets with shells, we bathed, we aimed stones into the sea, we raced along the strand, we cut our names in a row on the highest point of the island, in commemoration of our expedition, and there they remain to this day.

"I say, I hope it's not going to rain," said Hutton, looking up at the clouds, which had for some time been obscuring the sun.

"Who cares if it does?" shouted Charlie. "Hullo, there goes my roof!" cried he, as a sudden gust of wind lifted his hat from his head, and sent it skimming down the rocks.

"I think it's time we started home," said Hall hurriedly.

There was something in the uneasy look of his face as he said this which made me uncomfortable.

So we turned to embark once more in our boat.

We could not conceal from ourselves, as we made our way to the creek where we had left her moored, that the weather, which had thus far been so propitious to our expedition, was not holding out as we could have wished. The wind, which had been little more than a steady breeze during the morning, now met us in frequent gusts, which made us raise our hands to our hats. A few ugly-looking black clouds on the horizon had come up and obscured the sun, threatening not only to shut out his rays, but to break over the bay in a heavy downpour of rain. Even on the half-sheltered side of the island where we were, the water, which had hitherto moved only in ripples, now began to heave restlessly in waves, which curled over as they met the breeze, and covered the sea with little white breakers. There was an uncanny sort of moan about the wind as it swept down the hollows of the rocks, and even the seagulls, as they skimmed past us on the surface of the now sombre water, seemed uncomfortable.

However, the sea was not rough, and though the sun happened to be hidden from us, we could see it shining brightly away in the direction of Parkhurst. The wind, too, though stronger than it had been in the morning, was still not violent, and we had little doubt of making as quick, if not a quicker passage back than we had already made.

So, although in our secret hearts each one of us would perhaps have preferred the weather of the earlier part of the day to have continued, we did not let our uneasiness appear to our fellows, or allow it to interfere with our show of good spirits.

"I tell you what," said Charlie, laughing, as we came down to our boat, "it would be a real spree to have a little rough water going back, just for the fun of seeing old Hutton seasick."

"I shall be very pleased to give you some amusement," replied Hutton; "and perhaps Adams will assist, for I saw him looking anxiously over the bows once or twice as we were coming."

"So did I," said Charlie; "he must have seen a ghost in the water, for he looked awfully pale."

"Shut up, you fellows," cried I, who was notoriously a bad sailor, and easily disturbed by a rough sea; "perhaps we shall all—"

"I say," called out Hall from the boat, where he was busy tying up a reef in our sail, "I wish you fellows would lend a hand here, instead of standing and chaffing there."

We obeyed with alacrity, and very soon had our boat ready for starting.

"Now, Adams and Hutton, take the oars, will you? and pull her out of this creek: we had better not hoist our sail till we are clear of these rocks."

As we emerged from our little harbour the boat "lumped" heavily over the waves that broke upon the rocks, and we had a hard pull to get her clear of these and turn her with her stern to Shargle.

"Now stand by," shouted Hall.

We shipped our oars, and in a moment the sail, shortened by one reef, was hauled up, and the boat began to scud swiftly forward.

"You'll have to sit right over, you two," said Hall to Hutton and me, "to keep her trim. Look sharp about it!"

As he spoke a gust took the sail, and caused the boat to heel over far on to her side. She righted herself in an instant, however, and on we went, flying through the water.

"How do you feel, Adams?" called out Charlie mischievously, from his end of the boat.

"Pleasant motion, isn't it?" put in Hutton, laughing.

"Look here, you fellows," said Hall abruptly, "stop fooling now, and look after the boat."

"Why, what's the row?" said Hutton, struck with his unusually serious tone. "It's all right, isn't it?"

"It's all right," said Hall curtly, "if you'll only attend to the sailing."

Our merriment died away on our lips, for it was plain to be seen Hall was in no jesting humour.

Then several things struck us which we had not previously noticed. One was that the wind had shifted farther north, and was blowing hard right into the bay, gathering strength every minute. Hall, we noticed, was sailing as close as possible up to it, thus making our course far wider than that which had brought us in the morning.

"Why are you steering out like that?" I ventured to ask.

"Because if I didn't— Look out!" he exclaimed, as a sudden gust caught the boat, making her stagger and reel like a drunken man. In an instant he had released the sheet rope, and the sail flapped with a tremendous noise about the mast. It was but an instant, however, and then we saw him coolly tighten the cord again, and put back the helm to its former course. After that I did not care to repeat my question.

Reader, have you ever found yourself at sea in an open boat, a mile or so from land, in a gathering storm; with the wind in your teeth and the sea rising ominously under your keel; with the black clouds mustering overhead, and the distant coastline whitening with breakers? Have you marked the headlands change from white to solemn purple? Have you listened to that strange hiss upon the water, and that moaning in the wind? Have you known your boat to fly through the waves without making way, and noted anxiously by some landmark that she is rather drifting back with the current, instead of, as it seems, tearing before the wind?

If so, you can imagine our feelings that afternoon.

It was useless to pretend things were not as bad as they looked; it was useless not to admit to ourselves we were fairly in for it now, and must brave it out as best we could; it was useless to maintain we had not been foolish, wickedly foolish, in starting on so venturesome an expedition; it was useless to deny that it would have been better had we remained at Shargle, or returned to Parkhurst by land.

We were in for it now.

The one thing which gave us confidence was Hall's coolness, now that the danger was unmistakable. He neither allowed himself to get flurried nor alarmed, but sat with closed lips watching the sail—one hand on the tiller and the other grasping the sheet, ready to let it go at a moment's notice.

As for us, we wished we could do anything more active than sit still and trim the boat. But even that was some use, and so we remained, watching anxiously the clouds as they rolled down the sides of the hills and half obscured Shargle Head from our view.

Presently, however, Hall said—

"Get the oars out, will you? we haven't made any way for an hour."

No way for an hour! Had we then been all that time plunging through the waves for nothing? With what grim earnestness we set to work to row through this unyielding current!

But to no effect—or scarcely any. The little white cottage on Shargle, which we looked round at so anxiously from time to time, to ascertain what progress had been made, remained always in the same position, and after twenty minutes' desperate pulling it seemed as if the total distance gained had been scarcely half a dozen yards.

It was disheartening work, still more so as the sea was rising every minute, and the rain had already begun to fall.

"We're in for a gale," said Hall, as a wave broke over the side, drenching Hutton and me, and half-filling the bottom of the boat with water. "Look sharp, Charlie, and bale out that before the next comes."

Charlie set to work with a will, and for a time we rowed steadily on, without saying a word.

"What's the time?" I asked presently of Hall, as I saw him take out his watch.

"Five," said he.

It was an hour after the time we had expected to be back at Parkhurst, and we were not yet clear of Shargle. The same thought evidently crossed the minds of the other three, for they all glanced in the direction of Raven Cliff, now scarcely visible through the heavy rain.

"I wish we were safe home," muttered Hutton, the most dispirited of our crew. "What fools we were to come!"

We said nothing, but pulled away doggedly at the oars.

Now it really seemed as if we were making some progress out of that wretched current, for the white cottage on the cliff appeared farther astern than it had done since we began to row, and we were beginning to congratulate ourselves on our success, when Hall, who had for some time been anxiously watching the shore, cried out—

"For goodness' sake pull hard, you fellows! we are drifting in fast. Here, Charlie, take the helm, and keep her the way she is, while I get down the sail. It's no use now. Mind your heads, but don't stop rowing," he shouted to us, as he let down the sail suddenly, and lowered the mast. "Keep her head out, Charlie, whatever you do. Let go that rope beside you. That's right. Now take hold of that end of the mast and slip it under the seat."

So saying he managed to get down the mast and stow it away without impeding either the rowing or the steering, and immediately the advantage of the step was manifest in the steadier motion of the boat, although we groaned inwardly at the thought of having now all the distance to row. At least I groaned inwardly. Hutton was hardly as reserved.

"I tell you what," he said to me, stopping rowing, "I don't know what you and the other fellows intend to do, but I can't row any more. I've been at it an hour together."

"What are we to do, then?" inquired I.

"Why shouldn't Hall take a turn? He's been doing nothing."

"He's been steering," replied I, "and he's the only fellow who knows how, and Charlie's not strong enough to row."

"Well, all I can say is, I don't mean to row any longer."

All this had been said in an undertone to me, but now Hall cried out—

"What are you shopping for, Hutton? Pull away, man, or we shall never get out of this."

"Pull away yourself!" said Hutton sulkily. "I've had enough of it. You brought us here, you'd better take us back!"

Hall's face at that moment was a study. I fancy if this had been a ship and he the skipper, he would not have hesitated an instant how to deal with this unexpected contingency. But now he did hesitate. It was bitter enough punishment to him to be there exposed to all the dangers of a sudden storm, with the safety, and perhaps the life, not only of himself, but of us whom he had induced to accompany him, on his hands; but to have one of those comrades turn against him in the moment of peril was more than he had looked for.

"I'll take an oar," said Charlie, before there was time to say anything.

"No," said Hall, starting up; "take the helm, Charlie. And you," added he, to Hutton, "give me your oar and get up into the bows."

The voice in which this was spoken, and the look of scorn which accompanied it, fairly cowed Hutton, who got up like a lamb and crawled into the bows, leaving Hall and me to row.

"Keep her straight to the waves, whatever you do! it's all up if she gets broadside on!" said the former to Charlie.

And so for another half-hour we laboured in silence; then almost suddenly the daylight faded, and darkness fell over the bay.

I rowed on doggedly in a half-dream. Stories of shipwrecks and castaways crowded in on my mind; I found myself wondering how and when this struggle would end. Then my mind flew back to Parkhurst, and I tried to imagine what they must think there of our absence. Had they missed us yet? Should I ever be back in the familiar house, or—but I dared not think of that. Then I tried to pray, and the sins of my boyhood came up before my mind as I did so in terrible array, so that I vowed, if but my life might be spared, I would begin a new and better life from that time forward. Then, by a strange impulse, my eyes rested on Charlie, as he sat there quietly holding the tiller in his hands and gazing out ahead into the darkness. What was it that filled me with foreboding and terror as I looked at the boy? The scene of the morning recurred to my mind, and my halfhearted effort to prevent him from accompanying us. Selfish wretch that I had been! what would I not now give to have been resolute then? If anything were to happen to Charlie, how could I ever forgive myself?

"I think we've made some way," he cried out cheerily. "Not much," said Hall gloomily; "that light there is just under Shargle Head."

"Had we better keep on as we are?" I asked. "I don't see what else is to be done. If we let her go before the wind, we shall get right on to the rocks."

"You've a lot to answer for," growled Hutton from where he lay, half-stupid with terror, in the bows.

Hall said nothing, but dashed his oar vehemently into the water and continued rowing.

"I wonder if that light is anywhere near Parkhurst?" presently asked Archer. "Do you see?"

We looked, and saw it; and then almost instantly it vanished. At the same time we lost sight of the lights on Shargle Head, and the rain came down in torrents. "A mist!" exclaimed Hall, in tones of horror. Well indeed might he and we feel despair at this last extinguisher of our hopes. With no landmark to steer by, with wind and sea dead in our teeth, with the waves breaking in over our sides, and one useless mutineer in our midst, we felt that our fate was fairly sealed. Even Hall for a moment showed signs of alarm, and we heard him mutter to himself, "God help us now!" Next moment a huge wave came broadside on to us and emptied itself into our boat, half filling us with water. In the sudden shock my oar was dashed from my hand and carried away overboard!

"Never mind," said Hall hurriedly, "it would have been no use; put her round, Charlie, quick—here, give me the tiller!"

In a moment the boat swung round to the wind (not, however, before she had shipped another sea), and then we felt we were simply flying towards the fatal rocks.

"Bale out, all of you!" shouted Hall; and we obeyed, including even Hutton, who seemed at last, in very desperation, to be awakening to a sense of his duty.

The next few minutes seemed like an age. As we knelt in our half-flooded boat scooping up the water there in our hats, or whatever would serve for the purpose, we could hear ahead of us the angry roar of breakers, and knew every moment was bringing us nearer to our doom.

By one impulse we abandoned our useless occupation. What was the use of baling out a boat that must inevitably in a few minutes be dashed to pieces on the rocks? Hutton crawled back into the bows, and Charlie and I sat where we were on the seat and waited.

I could not fail, even in such a situation, to notice and admire Hall's self-possession and coolness. Desperate as our case was, he kept a steady hand on the helm, and strained his eyes into the mist ahead, never abating for a moment either his vigilance or his courage. But every now and then I could see his eyes turn for a moment to Charlie, and his face twitch as they did so, with a look of pain which I was at no loss to understand.

"How far are we from the rocks?" asked Charlie.

"I can't say; a quarter of an hour, perhaps."

"Whereabouts are we?" I asked.

"When the lights went out we were opposite Raven Cliff," replied Hall.

We were silent for another minute; then Hall took out his watch.

"Eight o'clock," said he.

"They'll be at prayers at Parkhurst," said Charlie; and in the silence that followed, need I say that we too joined as we had never done before in the evening prayers of our schoolfellows?

"Charlie, old boy," said Hall, presently, "come and sit beside me, will you?"

Poor Hall! had it been only *his* own life that was at stake, he would never have flinched a muscle; but as he put his arm round the boy whom he had led into danger he groaned pitiably.

"I wonder if Neil's out looking for us," Hutton said from the bows.

"Not much use," said Hall. "If only this mist would lift!"

But it did not lift. For another five minutes we tore through the waves, which as we neared the shore became wilder and rougher. Our boat, half full of water, staggered at every shock, and more than once we believed her last plunge had been taken.

On either side of us, for the little distance we could see through the mist, there was nothing but white foam and surging billows; behind us rushed the towering waves, overtaking us one by one, tossing us aloft and dashing us down, till every board of our boat creaked and groaned. Above us the rain poured in torrents, dashing on to our bare heads, and blinding us whenever we turned our faces back.

Then Hall cried out, "Listen! those must be breakers behind us!"

Assuredly they were! On either side we could hear the deafening thunder of the surf as it dashed over the rocks.

"Then, thank God!" exclaimed Hall, "we must have got in between two reefs; perhaps we shall go aground on the sand!"

The next two minutes are past description. Hutton crawled down beside me where I sat, and I could feel his hand on my arm, but I had no eyes except for Charlie, who sat pale and motionless with Hall's arm round him.

"Now!" shouted Hall, abandoning the tiller, and tightening his hold on the boy.

There was a roar and a rush behind us, our boat swooped up with the wave, and hung for a moment trembling on its crest, then it fell, and in an instant we were in the water.

Hutton was beside me as the rush back of that huge wave swept us off our feet. I seized him by the arm, and next moment we were struggling to keep our heads up. Then came another monster, and lifted us like straws, flinging us before it on to the strand, and then rolling and foaming over us as we staggered to our feet.

Hutton, half stunned, had been swept from my hold, but mercifully was still within reach. Clutching him by the hair, I dragged him with all my might towards the land, before the returning wave should once more sweep us back into the sea. By a merciful Providence, a solitary piece of rock was at hand to aid us; and clinging to this we managed to support that terrific rush, and with the next wave stagger on to solid ground.

But what of Charlie? Leaving my senseless companion, I rushed wildly back to the water's edge, and called, shouted, and even waded back into the merciless surf. But no answer: no sign. Who shall describe the anguish of the next half-hour? I was conscious of lights and voices; I had dim visions of people hurrying; I felt something poured down my throat, and some one was trying to lift me from where I sat. But no! I would not leave that spot till I knew what had become of Charlie, and in my almost madness I shrieked the boy's name till it sounded even above the roaring waves.

Presently the lights moved all to one spot, and the people near me moved too. Weak as I was, I sprang to my feet and followed.

Good heavens! what did I see? Two sailors, half naked, stooped over something that lay on the sand between them, What, who was it? I cried; and the crowd made way for me as I fought my way to the place.

Two figures lay there; the smaller locked in the arms of his protector! But dead or living? Oh, if I could but hear some voice say they were not dead! Another person was kneeling over them beside me. Even in that moment of confusion and terror I could recognise his voice as that of the Parkhurst doctor.

"Look after this one here," he said; "he has a broken arm. Carry up the little fellow to the cottage."

Then I knew Charlie was dead!

It was weeks before I was sufficiently recovered in body or mind to hear more than I knew. Then the doctor told me:—

"Hall is getting better. He broke his arm in two places, trying to shield the boy from the rocks. He will not speak about it himself, and no one dares mention Archer's name to him. There was neither bruise nor scratch on the little fellow's body, which shows how heroically the other must have tried to save him."

I soon recovered, but Hall was ill for many weeks—ill as much from distress of mind as from the injuries he had received. He and I are firm friends to this day; and whenever we meet, we speak often of little Charlie Archer. Hall is a sea captain now, and commands his own vessel in distant seas; but though he has been through many a peril and many a storm since, I can confidently say he never showed himself a better sailor than he did the night we sailed back from the Shargle.

Chapter Six
"Fivers" versus "Sixers" at Parkhurst

"I tell you what it is, you fellows, I shall learn to swim!" The speaker was Bobby Jobson, a hero of some thirteen summers, who, in company with four of us, his schoolfellows, sat on the bank of the Colven, under some willows, dabbling his shins in the clear water of the river.

The summer had been tremendously hot. Cricket was out of the question, and boating equally uninviting. The playground had been left deserted to bake and scorch under the fierce sun, and the swings and poles in the gymnasium had blistered and cracked in solitude. The only place where life was endurable was down by the river, and even there it was far too hot to do anything but sit and dabble our feet under the shelter of the trees, and think of icebergs!

A few of the fellows, to our unbounded envy, bathed. They could swim, we could not; and if any rule at Parkhurst was strict, it was the rule which forbade any boy who could not swim to bathe in the river, except with special leave and under the care of a master. And so, like so many small editions of Tantalus, we sat on the bank and kicked our heels in the water, and bemoaned the fate which had brought us into the world without web-feet.

Young donkeys that we were! The idea of *learning* to swim had never occurred to any of us till Bobby Jobson, in a happy moment, gave birth to the idea in his ejaculation, "I tell you what it is, you fellows, I shall learn to swim!"

"How?" I inquired.

"How?" said Jobson; "why, you know, how does every body learn?" and then he was polite enough to call me a duffer.

"I'll tell you the way," said Ralley, one of our set. "Lie across a desk on your stomach, two or three hours every day, and kick out with your arms and legs."

"Corks and bladders," mildly suggested some one else.

"Get old Blades," (that was the boatman) "to tie a rope round your middle and chuck you into the Giant's Pool," kindly proposed another.

"Just tumble in where you are," said Ralley, "and see if it doesn't come naturally."

"Ugh!" said Jobson, with a grimace, giving a sidekick in the water in the direction of the last speaker. "I'm not sure that *that* dodge would pay."

While he spoke, to our unbounded horror, the bank on which he and his next neighbour were sitting suddenly gave way, and next moment, with a shout and a splash, our two comrades were floundering helplessly in five feet of water!

Help, happily, was at hand, or there is no saying what might have been the end of the adventure. We did all we could by reaching out our hands and throwing them our jackets to help them, while, with our shouts, we summoned more effective aid. Old Blades, who providentially happened to be passing, was with us in less than a minute, and fished out the two poor half-drowned boys, scarcely a moment before they needed it. They were more frightened, I fancy, than damaged; anyhow, we smuggled them home, dripping as they were, and helped them to bed; and when, next morning, they turned up as usual, nothing the worse for their first swimming lesson, we were, as you may imagine, infinitely relieved.

This little adventure was the origin of the Parkhurst Swimming Club. The doctor, on hearing of the affair, took the proper course; and, instead of forbidding us the river, he secured the services of one or two instructors, and had us all taught the art of swimming. For three months, every day of the week, the School Creek was full of spluttering, choking youngsters. Every new boy was hunted down to the river in turn, and by the end of the year there was hardly a boy at Parkhurst who could not keep his chin up in deep waters.

But this is a long introduction.

One day, two summers after that in which young Jobson and his friend had tumbled into the Colven, a large party of us were down at the bathing-place, indulging in what had now become a favourite summer pastime. It so happened that our party was made up entirely of boys in the two senior classes of the school—the fifth and the sixth. Most of us were landed and dressing, and while so occupied had leisure to watch the performances of those who still remained in the water.

Two of these specially interested us, who were swimming abreast about a hundred yards from the landing-place, evidently racing home. One of these chanced to be a sixth-form boy and the other a fifth, and a sudden impulse seized us of the latter class to cheer our man vehemently, and back him to be the first to reach home. The sixth-form fellows, thus challenged, became equally excited in backing *their* man, and so, without premeditation, a regular match was made. The two swimmers, hearing our shouts, entered into the spirit of the thing, and a desperate race ensued. They came on, neck and neck, towards us, cheered like mad by their respective supporters, both sides deeming the honour of his form at stake in the event. Within a yard or two of the finish they were still level, when the sixth-form man put on a terrific spurt, to our huge disgust, and just landed himself in a nose ahead.

Of course, we were not going to be beaten thus, and there and then demanded our revenge. Whereupon the company—half of them in a very elementary stage of dressing, and the other half in no stage at all—resolved itself into a meeting on the spot, and fixed that day week for a formal trial of prowess between the two classes. Three events were to be contested—a half-mile race, a hundred yards, and a duck hunt—and, of course, the winner of two out of the three would carry the day.

Then, in great excitement, we finished our toilets and hurried back to the school, where, naturally, the news of the coming contest spread like wildfire and caused a great commotion. The school divided itself forthwith into two factions, calling themselves the "fivers" and "sixers." The selection of representatives to compete in the races was a matter of almost as much excitement as the races themselves, and I need hardly say it was a proud day for me when I was informed I was to act in the capacity of "hunter" for the fifth in the duck hunt. I accepted the honour with mingled pride and misgivings, and spent a busy week practising for my arduous duties.

Well, the eventful day came at last, and nearly the whole school mustered at Cramp Corner to see the sport. For the half-mile race, which was to come off first, there were only two fellows competing. Our man was Barlow—of paper-chase celebrity—while the sixth were very confident of winning with Chesney, a hero nearly six feet high. Certainly, as the two stood on the spring-board waiting the signal to go, there seemed very little chance for the small Jim against his lanky antagonist, although some of us comforted ourselves with the contemplation of our man's long arms and the muscles in his legs. The course was to be once up Cramp Reach and back— just half a mile. The swimmers were at liberty to swim in any manner they chose, and bound only to one rule—to keep their right side.

They were not long kept waiting in their scanty attire on the planks. The doctor himself gave the signal to start, and at the word they darted with two "swishes" into the water. Jim's head was up first, and off he started at a steady chest-stroke, meaning business. Chesney's dive was a long one, and, considering he had a half-mile race before him, a foolish one, for he taxed his breath at the outset, which might have been avoided, had he thought less about elegance and more about the race. However, he did not seem at first to be any the worse off for he took a slight lead of Jim, going through the water swiftly and easily, with as pretty a side-stroke as any fellow's at the school. In point of style there was no comparison between the two. Jim pounded along monotonously, but steadily, with a square front, preserving all along the same regular stroke, the same pace, and the same dogged expression of countenance with which he had entered the water. His rival, on the other hand, delighted the spectators by all kinds of graceful variety. Now he darted forward on his side, now on his back. Sometimes he refreshed himself by a swift dive, and sometimes he swung his arms like a windmill. In fact, there was scarcely any accomplishment possible in rapid swimming which he did not give us the benefit of.

But it was evident some of his friends did not approve of his style. I heard one of them, running near me, growl, "I wish he would give over his capers and swim like a rational animal."

"Rational or not, he's keeping his lead," said another, and so he was. Plodding Jim, with his everlasting chest-stroke, was half a dozen yards or so behind, and did not look like picking up either. Nevertheless, we cheered him like mad, and kept up our hopes that he would "stay out" the better of the two.

When both turned at the top of the reach, Chesney gave up his fanciful swimming, and, to our alarm, settled down to a side stroke, which for a time looked powerful and effective. But he had been too confident all along, and now, when he reckoned on shaking off his opponent and getting a clear lead, he found out he was destined to do just the reverse. What long faces the "sixers" pulled as their man began to puff and slacken pace! A half-mile race is no joke, believe me; and so Chesney began to find out. Before half the distance back was covered he showed unmistakable signs of going to pieces, and—a very ominous sign—took to changing from one side to another at very frequent intervals.

Of course we "fivers" howled with delight! Our man had never turned a hair, and was now pulling up at every stroke. As he drew level, Chesney gathered up all his remaining strength for a spurt. But it came to nothing. Jim held on his way almost remorselessly, and headed his man fifty yards from the winning-post; and the next thing we saw was Chesney pulling up dead, and making for the bank in a very feeble condition. Jim quietly swam on amid our frantic plaudits, and landed pretty nearly as fresh as when he started.

So far so good. Loud and long were our exultations, for we had hardly expected to win this race; we had put our chief confidence on the hundred yards, which was to follow. In this race three a side were entered, and of our three we knew no one in the school who could beat Halley at a hundred yards. It was rumoured, indeed, that Payne, one of the three "sixers," had been doing very well in training, but the reports of him were not sufficiently decided to shake our faith in our own hero.

It was an anxious moment as they stood there waiting for the doctor's signal. If only we could win this race, we should have our two races out of the three in hand without further combat.

"Go!" cried the doctor; and at the word six youthful forms plunge into the water, and for a second are lost to sight. But the moral of the half-mile race has evidently been taken to heart by these six boys. They waste neither time nor wind under the surface, but rising quickly, dash to their work. After the first few strokes Payne showed in front, greatly to the delight of the "sixers," who felt that everything depended on their man. We, however, were glad to see our man sticking close up, and keeping stroke for stroke after his rival. Of the others, one only—little Watson—of the sixth seemed to hold his own, and that was a good three yards in the rear of Halley: while the three others fell off hopelessly from the very beginning.

The race was short, but eventful. To our delight, Halley overhauled Payne before half-way was reached, and we felt now absolutely sure of the race. It never occurred to us to think of young Watson at all. But all of a sudden it became apparent that that young man meant business. He changed his front, so to speak, in a very unexpected manner, and just as we were beginning to exult over our man's certain victory, he lay over on his side, and, with a peculiar, jerky side-stroke, began to work his little carcase through the water at a wonderful pace.

Before long he had overtaken his fellow-"sixer," and almost immediately drew up to our champion. We were in consternation. Twenty yards more would end the race, and if only our man could hold out and keep his lead, we were all right. At first it looked as if he would, for, encouraged by our cheers, and seeing his peril, he spurted, and kept a good yard ahead of this audacious young "sixer." But the latter put one spurt on to another, and drew up inch by inch. Ten yards from home they were level; then, for a stroke or two, there was a frantic struggle; then the "sixers" sent forth a shout that must have frightened the very fishes; and well they might, for their man had won the race, a yard and a half clear ahead of our champion.

One race each! And now for the "duck hunt" to settle the match. But before I go further I ought to explain, for the benefit of those who have not been initiated into the mysteries of the pastime, how a duck hunt was managed at Parkhurst.

The part of the river selected was close to the mouth, where the stream at high water is about a quarter of a mile broad. Two boundary boats, one above and one below, were anchored at half a mile distance, and between these limits the hunt was to take place. The "duck" was provided with a little punt, about five feet long and pretty wide, in which he was to escape as best he might from a cutter manned by four rowers and a coxswain, and carrying in its bows a "hunter." As long as he chose, or as long as he could, the duck might dodge his pursuers in his punt; but when once run down he would have to take to the water, and by swimming make good his escape from his pursuers, whose "hunter" would be ready at any moment to jump overboard and secure him. If, however, after twenty minutes the duck still remained uncaught, he was to be adjudged winner.

Such was the work cut out for us on this memorable afternoon. The duck on the present occasion was a sixth-form fellow called Haigh, one of the best divers and swimmers in the school, while, as I have already said, I had been selected to act as hunter on behalf of the fifth.

The duck, arrayed in the slightest of costumes, was not long in putting in an appearance in his little punt, which, being only five feet long, was so light that it seemed to jump through the water at every stroke of the oars; while a single stroke either way sufficed to change its course in a moment. The cutter, in the prow of which I (as slenderly attired as the duck) was stationed, was also a light boat, and of course, with its four rowers, far swifter than the punt; but when it came to turning and dodging, it was, because of its length, comparatively unwieldy and clumsy.

All now was ready for the chase. The duck was to get a minute's clear start, and at the signal off he darted up the stream. The minute seemed to us in the cutter as if it were never going to end, and we watched with dismay the pace at which our lively fugitive was "making tracks."

"Ready all, in the cutter!" cries the doctor. "Off!" and next moment we are flying through the water in full cry. As we gradually pull up to the duck he diminishes his pace, and finally lies on his oars and coolly waits for us.

"Put it on, now!" calls out our coxswain, and our boat shoots forward. When within a few yards, the duck, apparently alive to his danger, dashes his oars into the water and darts ahead. But we are too fast for him. Another two strokes and we shall row him down.

"Now then!" cries our coxswain.

Ah! At a tremendous pace our boat flew forward over the very place where, a second before, our duck had been. But where was he? By a turn of the hand he had twisted round his punt, and as our fellows dug their oars wildly into the water and tried to pull up, there was he, calmly scuttling away in an opposite direction, and laughing at us!

In due time we had swung round, and were after him again, the wiser for this lesson.

Next time we overhauled him we made our approach in a far more gingerly manner. We kept as little way as possible on our boat, determined not to lose time again by overshooting our mark. As long as he could, our duck led us down stream, then, when we had all but caught him, he made a feint of swooping off to the right, a manoeuvre which our coxswain promptly followed. But no sooner was our rudder round than the rogue deftly brought his punt sharp to the left, and so once more escaped us.

This sort of thing went on for a long time, and I was beginning to think the hunt was likely to prove a monotonous affair after all, when our coxswain suddenly called to me down the boat—

"Be ready, Adams."

Then it began gradually to dawn on me our coxswain after all knew what he was about. There was a rather deep bay up near the top of the course, bounded by two prominent little headlands, and into this bay the duck, in a moment of carelessness, had ventured. It was a chance not to be let slip. A few strokes brought our cutter up to the spot, and once there, our cunning coxswain carefully kept us pointed exactly across the bay. The duck, seeing his danger, made a dash to one corner, hoping to avoid us; but he was too late, we were there before him, and before he could double and make the other corner our boat had back-watered to the spot. Thus gradually we hemmed him in closer and closer to the shore, amid the cheers of our friends, until at last it was evident to every one the punt was no longer of use.

Still, he let us sidle close up to him before he abandoned his craft; then with a sudden bound he sprang overboard and disappeared from view.

It was no use going after him, I knew, till I could see where he would rise, and so I waited, ready for a plunge, watching the water where he would probably turn up. Several seconds passed, but there were no signs of him. He was a good diver, we all knew, but this was surely a very long dive. Had an accident happened to him? A minute elapsed, two, and yet he never appeared! We in the boat were aghast; he must have come to grief. Ah! what were the people on the bank laughing at? Could there be some trick? Next instant the coxswain called out, laughing—

"He's hanging on to the rudder; over you go, Adams!"

At the word I slipped overboard and gave chase. And now began an exciting pursuit. Haigh, though perfectly at home in the water, was not a rapid swimmer; but in point of diving and dodging he had a tremendous advantage over any of his pursuers. The moment I got near him, and just as I was thinking to grab him, he would disappear suddenly and come up behind me. He would dive towards the right and come up towards the left. He would dodge me round the boat, or swim round me in circles, but no effort of mine could secure him. The time was getting on, and I was no nearer having him than before. With all his dodges, too, he never seemed to take his eyes off me for an instant, either above or below the water.

Once, as I was giving him chase, he suddenly dived, and the next intimation I had of his whereabouts was a sly pinch of my big toe as he came up behind me. This was adding insult to injury, so I dashed round, and made at him. Again he dived; and this time, without waiting an instant, I dived too. I could see him distinctly under the water, scuttling away in a downward direction just below me. Shutting my lips tight, I dug my way down after him; but, alas! under water I was no match for Haigh. I felt an irresistible temptation to gasp; my nose smarted, and the water round my head seemed like lead. As quickly as possible I turned my hands up, and struck out for the surface.

What ages it seemed before I reached it! A second—half a second longer, and I should have shipped a mouthful, perhaps a chestful of water. I reached the surface at last, and, once above water, felt all right again. I looked about anxiously for my duck. But he was still down below. I reckoned, from the direction in which he had dived, that he would not be able to go far to either side, and therefore would rise close to me, probably exhausted, and if so, I had a good chance at last of catching him. So I waited and watched the place, but he never came.

Remembering my own sensations, and how nearly I had come to grief, I took a sudden fright, and concluding he must be in straits down below, shouted to the boat to come to the place, and then dived. I groped about, and looked in all directions, but saw no sign of him, and finally, in a terrible fright, made once more for the surface.

The first thing I was conscious of, on getting my head up, was a great shouting and laughing, and then I caught sight of that abominable duck, who had come up behind me, and had been laughing all the while behind my back, while I had been hunting for him in a far more serious way than I need ever have done!

Before I could turn and make towards him "Time!" was shouted from the bank; and so the Parkhurst Swimming Contest ended in a lamentable, though not disgraceful, defeat of the "fivers."

Chapter Seven
Athletic Sports at Parkhurst

The last Saturday before the summer holidays was invariably a great day at Parkhurst. The outdoor exercises of the previous ten months culminated then in the annual athletic sports, which made a regular field-day for the whole school. Boys who had "people" living within a reasonable distance always did their best to get them over for the day; the doctor—an old athlete himself—generally invited his own party of friends; and a large number of spectators from Parkhurst village and the neighbourhood were sure to put in an appearance, and help to give importance to the occasion. Athletic sports without spectators (at least, so we boys thought) would be a tame affair, and we were sure to get through our day's performances all the better for a large muster of outsiders on the ground.

The occasion I am about to recall was specially interesting to me, as it was the first athletic meeting in which I, a small boy just entering my teens, ever figured. I was only down to run in one of the races, and that was the three-legged race; and yet I believe there was not a boy in the school so excited at the prospect of these sports as I was. I thought the time would never come, and was in positive despair when on the day before it a little white cloud ventured to appear in the blue sky. A wet day, so I thought, would have been as great a calamity as losing the whole circle of my relatives, and almost as bad as having my favourite dog stolen, or my fishing-rod smashed; and I made a regular fool of myself in the morning of the eventful day by getting up first at two a.m., then at three, then at four, and four or five times more, to take observations out of the window, till at last my bedfellow declared he would stand it no longer, and that since I was up, I should stay up.

Ah! he was an unsympathetic duffer, and knew nothing of the raptures of winning a three-legged race.

Well, the day was a splendid one after all—a little hot, perhaps, but the ground was in grand order, and hosts of people would be sure to turn up. My race yoke-fellow and I went out quite early for a final spin over the course, and found one or two of the more diligent of our schoolfellows taking a similar advantage of the "lie-abeds." Of course, as *we* were of opinion that the three-legged race was the most important and attractive of all the day's contests, we paid very little heed to what others were doing, but sought out a retired corner for ourselves, where, after tying our inside legs together, and putting our arms round one another's necks in the most approved fashion, we set to and tore along as fast as we could, and practised starts and falls, and pick-ups and spurts, and I don't know what else, till we felt that if, after all, we were to be beaten, it would not be our faults. With which comfortable reflection we loosed our bonds and strolled back to breakfast.

Here, of course, the usual excitement prevailed, and one topic engrossed all the conversation. I sat between a fellow who was in for the Junior 100 yards, and another who was down for the "hurdles." Opposite me was a hero whom every one expected to win in throwing the cricket-ball, and next to him a new boy who had astonished every one by calmly putting his name down for the mile race before he had been two hours at Parkhurst. In such company you may fancy our meal was a lively one, and, as most of us were in training, a very careful one.

The first race was to be run at twelve, and we thought it a great hardship that the lower school was ordered to attend classes on this of all days from nine to eleven. Now I am older, it dawns on me that this was a most wholesome regulation; for had we small chaps been allowed to run riot all the morning, we should have been completely done up, and fit for nothing when the races really began. We did not do much work, I am afraid, at our desks that morning, and the masters were not particularly strict, for a wonder. The one thing we had to do was to keep our seats and restrain our ardour, and that was no easy task.

Eleven came at last, and off we rushed to the mysteries of the toilet. What would athletic sports be like without flannel shirts and trousers, or ribbons and canvas shoes? At any rate, we believed in the importance of these accessories, and were not long in arraying ourselves accordingly. I could not help noticing, however, as we sallied forth into the field, that fine feathers do not always make fine birds. There was Tom Sampson, for instance, the biggest duffer that ever thought he could run a step, got up in the top of the fashion, in bran-new togs, and a silk belt, and the most gorgeous of scarlet sashes across his shoulders; while Hooker, who was as certain as Greenwich time to win the quarter-mile, had on nothing but his old (and not very white) cricket clothes, and no sash at all. And there was another thing I noticed about these old hands: they behaved in the laziest of manners. They sprawled on the grass or sat on the benches, appearing disinclined for the slightest exertion; while others, less experienced, took preliminary canters along the tracks, or showed off over the hurdles. Fine fellows, no doubt, they thought themselves; but they had reason to be sorry for this waste of energy before the day was out.

Programmes! With what excitement I seized mine and glanced down it! There it was! "Number 12. Three-legged Race, 100 yards, for boys under 15. 1, Trotter and Walker (pink); 2, White and Benson (green); 3, Adams and Slipshaw (blue)." Reader, have you ever seen your name in print for the first time? Then you may imagine my sensations!

Things now begin to look like business. The doctor has turned up, and a party of ladies. The visitors' enclosure is fast filling up, and there is a fair show of carriages behind. Those big fellows in the tall hats are old Parkhurstians, come to see the young generation go through its paces, and that little knot of men talking together in the middle of the ground consists of the starter, judge, and umpire. Not a few of us, too, turn our eyes wistfully to that tent over yonder, where we know are concealed the rewards of this day's combats; and in my secret heart I find myself wondering more than once how it will sound to hear the names "Adams and Slipshaw" called upon to receive the first prize for the three-legged race.

Hark! There goes a bell, and we are really about to begin. "Number 1, Junior 100 yards, for boys under 12," and 24 names entered! Slipshaw and 1, both over 12, go off to have a look at "the kids," and a queer sight it is. Of course, they can't all, 24 of them, run abreast, and so they are being started in heats, six at a time. The first lot is just starting. How eagerly they toe the line and look up at the starter!

"Are " he begins, and two of them start, and have to be called back. "Are you ready?" he says. Three of them are off now, and can't understand that they are to wait for the word "Off!" But at last the starter gets to the end of his speech and has them fairly off. The little fellows go at it as if their lives depended on it. Their mothers and big brothers are looking on, their "chums" are shouting to them along the course, and the winning-post is not very far ahead. On they go, but not in a level row. One has taken the lead, and the others straggle behind him in a queer procession. It doesn't last long. Even a Junior 100 yards must come to an end at last, and the winner runs, puffing, into the judge's arms, half a dozen yards ahead of the next boy, and 50 yards ahead of the last. The other three heats follow, and then, amid great excitement, the final heat is run off, and the best man wins.

For the Senior 100 yards which followed only three were entered, and each of these had his band of confident admirers. Slipshaw and I were very "sweet" on Jackson, who was monitor of our dormitory, and often gave us the leavings of his muffins, but Ranger was a lighter-built fellow, and seemed very active, while Bruce's long legs looked not at all pleasant for his opponents. The starter had no trouble with them, but it was no wonder they all three looked anxious as they turned their faces to him; for in a 100 yards' race the start is everything, as poor long-legged Bruce found out, for he slipped on the first spring, and never recovered his lost ground. Between Ranger and Jackson the race was a fine one to within twenty yards of home, when our favourite's "fat" began to tell on him, and though he stuck gallantly to work he could not prevail over the nimble Ranger, who slipped past him and won easily by a yard.

This was a damper for Slipshaw and me, who, as in duty bound, attended our champion back to where he had left his coat, and so missed the throwing of the cricket-ball, which was easily won by the favourite.

But though we missed that event, we had no notion of missing the high jump, which promised to be the best thing (next to the three-legged race) that day. Four fellows were in for it, and of these Shute and Catherall were two of the best jumpers Parkhurst had ever had; and it was well known all over the school that in practice each had jumped exactly 5 foot 4 inches. Who would win now? The two outsiders were soon got rid of, one at 4 foot 10 inches, and the other at 5 foot; and the real interest of the event began when Shute and Catherall were left alone face to face with the bar. Shute was a tall fellow, of slight make and excellent spring. Catherall was short, but with the bounce of an india-rubber ball in him, and a wonderful knack of tucking his feet up under him in jumping. It was a pretty sight to watch them advance half-inch by half-inch, from 5 foot to 5 foot 3 inches. There seemed absolutely nothing to choose between them, they both appeared to clear the bar so easily. At 5 foot 3½ inches. Shute missed his first jump, greatly to the dismay of his adherents, who saw Catherall clear it with complete ease. If he were to miss the second time, he would be out of it, and that would be a positive tragedy. So we all watched his next jump with breathless anxiety. He stood looking at the bar for a second or two, as if doubting his own chance. Then his face cleared up, and he sprang towards it. To our delight he rose beautifully and cleared it easily. At 5 foot 4 inches both missed the first jump, but both cleared it at the second trial. And now for the tug of war. Both had accomplished the utmost he had ever hitherto achieved, and it remained to be seen whether the excitement of the occasion would assist either or each to excel himself. Shute came to grief altogether at 5 foot 4½ inches, and again, to our dismay, Catherall bounded over the bar at his first effort. Shute's friends were in despair, and if that hero had been a nervous fellow he might have been the same. But he was a very cool fish, and instead of losing his nerve, sat down on the grass and tightened the lace of his shoe. Then he slowly rose to his feet and faced his task. At that moment I forgot all about the three-legged race, and gave my whole heart up to the issue of this jump. He started to run at last, slow at first, but gathering pace for his final leap. Amid breathless silence he sprang forward and reached the bar, and then—then he coolly pulled up and walked back again. This looked bad; but better to pull up in time than spoil his chance. He kept us waiting an age before he was ready to start again, but at last he turned for his last effort. We could tell long before he got to the bar that this time, at any rate, he was going to jump, whether he missed or no. Jump he did, and, to our unbounded delight, just cleared the bar—so narrowly that it almost shook as he skimmed over it. That was the end of the high jump; for though both attempted the 5 foot 5 inches, neither accomplished it, and the contest was declared to be a dead heat.

After this several unimportant races followed, which I need hardly describe. Number 12 on the list was getting near, and I was beginning to feel a queer, hungry sort of sensation which I didn't exactly like. However, the mile was to be run before our turn came, and that would give me time to recover.

For this race we had many of us looked with a curious interest, on account of the new boy, of whom I have spoken, being one of the competitors in it. He didn't look a likely sort of fellow to win a race, certainly, for he was slightly bow-legged and thick-set, and what seemed to us a much more ominous sign, was not even arrayed in flannels, but in an ordinary white shirt and light cloth trousers. However, he took his place very confidently at the starting-post, together with three rivals, wearing respectively black, red, and yellow for their colours.

The start for a mile race is not such a headlong affair as for a hundred yards, and consequently at the word "Off!" there was comparatively little excitement among us spectators.

Yellow went to the front almost immediately, with red and black close behind, while the new boy seemed to confirm our unfavourable impression by keeping considerably in the rear. The mile was divided into three laps round the field, and at the end of the first the positions of the four were the same as at starting. But it was soon evident yellow was not destined to continue his lead, for before the half distance was accomplished, red and black, who all along had been neck and neck, were up to him and past him, and by the end of the lap the new boy had also overtaken him.

And now we became considerably more interested in the progress of this new boy, who, it suddenly occurred to us, seemed to be going very easily, which was more than could be said of red, who was dropping a little to the rear of black. A big boy near me said, "That fellow's got the wind of a balloon," and I immediately began to think he was not far wrong. For in this third lap, when two of the others were slacking pace, and when the third was only holding his own, the new boy freshened up remarkably. We could watch him crawl up gradually nearer and nearer to red, till a shout proclaimed him to be second in the running. But black was still well ahead, and in the short space left, as the big boy near me said, "He could hardly collar his man."

But see! The fellow is positively beginning to tear along! He seems fresher than when he started. "Look out. Black!" shout twenty voices. All very well to say, "Look out!" Black is used up, and certainly cannot respond to this tremendous spurt. Thirty yards from home the new boy is up to his man, and before the winning-post is reached he is a clear ten yards ahead.

"Bellows did it," said the big boy; "look at his chest"; and then for the first time I noticed where the secret of this hero's triumph lay.

But, horrors! the next race is Number 12, and Slipshaw and I scuttle off as hard as we can go, to get ready.

How miserable I felt then! I hated athletic sports, and detested "three-legged races." As we emerged from the tent, we and the other two couples, ambling along on our respective three legs, a shout of laughter greeted our appearance. I, for one, didn't see anything to laugh at, just then.

"Adams," said Slipshaw, as we reached the starting-place, "take it easy, old man, and mind you don't go over."

"All right," said I, feeling very much inclined to go over at that instant. Then that awful starter began his little speech.

"Are you ready?" he asked.

"Not at all," inwardly ejaculated I.

"Off!" he cried; and almost before I knew where I was, Slipshaw and I were hopping along on our three legs amid the cheers of the crowd.

"Steady!" said he, as I stepped out rather *too* fast.

Alas! we were last. The other two couples were pounding along ahead at a wonderful pace.

"Steady!" growled Slipshaw again, as I began to try to run, and nearly capsized him.

You may laugh, reader, but it was no joke, that three-legged race. The others ahead of us showed no signs of flagging; they were going hard, one couple close at the heels of the other, and we a full five yards behind. I was giving one despairing thought to the pots and prizes in the tent, when a great roar of laughter almost made me forget which foot to put forward.

What could it be?—and Slipshaw was laughing too!

"Steady, now," he said, "and come along!"

The laughter continued, and looking before me, I suddenly detected its cause. The leading couple in a moment of over-confidence had attempted to go too fast, and had come on their noses on the path, and the second couple, too close behind them, had not had time to avoid the obstacle, but had plunged headlong on to the top of them! It was all right now! Slipshaw and I trotted triumphantly past the prostrate heap, and after all won our prize! You may fancy I was too excited to think of much else after that, except indeed the hurdle race, which was most exciting, and won most cleverly by Catherall, who, though he came to grief at the last hurdle, was able to pick himself up in time to rush in and win the race by a neck from the new boy, whom we found to be almost as good at jumping as he was at running.

Then followed a two-mile race—rather dull to watch—and with that the sports were at an end.

Need I say how proudly Slipshaw and I marched up arm-in-arm to receive the prize for our race, which consisted of a bat for me and a telescope for my companion?—or how the new boy was cheered?—or how Shute and Catherall were applauded?

Before I left Parkhurst I was an old hand at athletic sports, but I don't think I ever thought any of them so interesting as the day on which Slipshaw and I, with our legs tied together, came in first in the three-legged race!

Chapter Eight
The Sneak

Sneak! It's an ugly name, but not ugly enough, believe me, for the animal it describes.

Like his namesake, the snake, he may be a showy enough looking fellow at first sight, he may have the knack of wriggling himself into your acquaintance, and his rattle may amuse you for a time, but wait till he turns and stings you!

I am at a loss how to describe in a few words what I—and, I expect, most of us—mean when we talk of a sneak. He is a mixture of so many detestable qualities. There is a large amount of cowardice in his constitution, and a similar quantity of jealousy; and then there are certain proportions of falsehood, ingratitude, malice, and officiousness to complete his ugly anatomy, to say nothing of hypocrisy and self-conceit. When all these amiable ingredients are compounded together, we have our model sneak.

How we detest the fellow! how our toes tingle when he comes our way! how readily we go a mile round to avoid him! how we hope we may never be like *him*!

Let me tell you of one we had at our school. Any one who did not know Jerry would have said to himself, "That's a pleasant enough sort of fellow." For so he seemed. With a knack of turning up everywhere, and at all times, he would at first strike the stranger as only an extremely sociable fellow, who occasionally failed to see he wasn't as welcome as one would think he deserved to be. But wait a little. Presently he'd make up to you, and become very friendly. In your pleasure at finding some one to talk to after coming away from home to a new and lonely place, you will, in the innocence of your heart, grow confidential, and tell him all your secrets. You will perhaps tell him to whom your sister is engaged; how much pocket-money your father allows you. You'll show him a likeness of the little cousin you are over head and ears in love with, and tell him about the cake your old nurse has packed up among the schoolbooks in your trunk. He takes the greatest interest in the narration; you feel quite happy to have had a good talk about the dear home, and you go to bed to dream of your little sweetheart and your new friend.

In the morning, when you wake, there is laughter going on in the beds round you. As you sit up and rub your eyes, and wonder where you are— it's all so different from home—you hear one boy call out to another—

"I say, Tom, don't you wish you had a nurse to make you cakes?"

That somehow seems pointed at you, though addressed to another, for all the other boys look round at you and grin.

"Wouldn't I?" replies the Tom appealed to. "Only when a chap's in love, you know, he's no good at cakes."

"Cakes!" "in love!" They must be making fun of you; but however do they know so much about you? Listen! "If *I* had a sister, I'd take care *she* didn't go and marry a butter-man, Jack, wouldn't you?"

It must be meant for you; for you had told Jerry the evening before that your sister was going to marry a provision merchant! Then all of a sudden it flashes upon you. You have been betrayed! The secrets you have whispered in private have become the property of the entire school; and the friend you fancied so genial and sympathising has made your open-hearted frankness the subject of a blackguard jest, and exposed you to all the agony of schoolboy ridicule!

With quivering lips and flushed face, half shame, half anger, you dash beneath the clothes, and wish the floor would open beneath you. When the getting-up bell sounds, you slink into your clothes amid the titters of your companions. It is weeks before you hear the end of your nurse, your pocket money, your sister, and your sweetheart; and for you all the little pleasure of your first term at school has gone.

But what of Jerry? He comes to you in the morning as if nothing had happened, with a "How are you, old fellow?"

You are so indignant you can't speak; all you are able to do is to glare in scorn and anger.

"Afraid you're not well," remarks the sneak; "change of scene, you know. I hope you'll soon be better."

Just as he is going you manage, though almost bursting with the effort, to stammer out—"What do you mean by telling tales of me to all the fellows?" He looks perplexed, as if at a loss for your meaning. "Tell tales of you?" says he. "I don't know what you mean, old chap."

"Yes, you do. How did they all know all about me this morning, if you hadn't told them?"

Then, as if your meaning suddenly dawned upon him, he breaks into a forced laugh, and exclaims—

"Oh, the chaff between Tom and Jack! I was awfully angry with Jack for beginning it—awfully angry. We happened to be talking last night, you know, about home, and I just mentioned what you had told me, never thinking the fellow would be such a cad as to let it out."

You are so much taken aback at the impudence of the fellow, that you let him walk away without another word. If you have derived no other advantage from your first day at school, you have at least learned to know the character of Jerry. And you find it out better as you go on.

If you quarrel with him, and threaten him with condign punishment, he will report you to the doctor, and you'll get an imposition. If you sit up beyond hours reading, he'll contrive to let the monitors know, and your book will be confiscated; if you happen to be "spinning a yarn" with a chum in your study, you will generally find, if you open the door suddenly, that he is not very far from the keyhole; if you get up a party to partake of a smuggled supper in the dormitory, he will conduct a master to the scene, and get you into a row. There's no secret so deadly he won't get hold of; nothing you want kept quiet that he won't spread all round the school. In fact, there's scarcely anything he does not put his finger into, and everything he puts his finger into he spoils.

If, in a weak moment of benevolence, you take him back into your confidence and friendship, no one will be more humble and forgiving and affable; but he will just use your new favour as a weapon for paying back old grudges, and sorely will you repent your folly.

In fact, there is only one place for Jerry—that place is Coventry. That city is famous for one sneak already. Let Jerry keep him company. There he can tell tales, and peep and listen and wriggle to his heart's content. He'll please himself, and do no one any harm.

A sneak has not always the plea of self-interest for his meanness. Often enough his tale-bearing or his mischief-making can not only do his victims incalculable harm, but cannot do him any possible good.

What good did the snake in the fable expect who, having been rescued, and warmed and restored to life by the merciful woodcutter, turned on his deliverer and stung him? No wonder the good fellow knocked him on the head! I knew another sneak once who seemed to make a regular profession of this amiable propensity. He seemed to consider his path in life was to detect and inform on whatever, to his small mind, seemed a culpable offence. In the middle of school, all of a sudden his raspy voice would lift itself up in ejaculations like these, addressed to the master,—

"Please, sir," (he always prefaced his remarks with "Please, sir"), "Please, sir, Tom Cobb's eating an apple!"

"Please, sir, Jenkins has made a blot!"

"Please, sir, Allen junior is cutting his name on the desk!"

Perhaps the indignant Allen junior would here take occasion to acknowledge his sense of this attention by a private kick under the desk. Then it would be—

"All right, Joe Allen; *I'll sneak of you*, you see if I don't!"

No one could do it better.

Amiable little pet, how we all loved him!

Sneaking seems to be a sort of disease with some people. There's no other way of accounting for it. It sometimes seems as if the mere sight of happiness or success in others is the signal for its breaking out. As we have said, its two leading motives are cowardice and jealousy. Just as the cur will wait till the big dog has passed by, and then, slinking up behind, give a surreptitious snap at his heels, so the sneak, instead of standing face to face with his rival, and instead of entering into fair competition with him, creeps up unobserved and inflicts his wound on the sly.

Thus it has been with all traitors and spies and deserters and mischief-makers since the world began. What a list one could give of the sneaks of history, beginning at that arch-serpent who marred the happiness of Eden, down to some of the informers and renegades of the present day!

Boys cannot be too early on their guard against sneaking habits. No truly English boy, we are glad to think, is likely to fall into them; still, even among our own acquaintance, it is sad to think how many there are who are not wholly free from the reproach.

The child in the nursery who begins to tell tales to his mother of his little brothers and sisters will, if not corrected, grow up to be just such another sneak as Jerry; and Jerry, unless he cures himself of his vice, will become a mere odious meddler and scandalmonger in society, and may arrive at the unenviable distinction of being the most detested man of his generation.

Every disease has its cure. Be honest, be brave, be kind, and have always a good conscience, and you *cannot* be a sneak.

Chapter Nine
The Sulky Boy

We all know him. He might be a good-looking fellow, perhaps, if it weren't for the scowl over his eyes and the everlasting pout about his lips. He skulks about with his hands in his pockets, and his head hung down. We all make room for him, and give him a wide berth; no one is anxious to be chosen upon the same side with him at chevy, or to get the desk next his in school. It's a fact we are all afraid of him, though we all despise him. He makes everybody unhappy, by being miserable himself for no reason at all.

Sometimes, indeed, he can be jolly enough—when he chooses. No one could tell at such times that there was anything queer about him; but then all of a sudden he shows in his true colours (and dingy enough colours they are), and then it is all up with enjoyment till he takes himself off, which he generally does before long.

All this is very sad; and if I say a word or two about sulkiness now, it will be in the hope of inducing my readers to give no encouragement to so ugly a vice.

There are two ways of showing anger, when one is unfortunate enough to be under the necessity of being angry. You can't always help it. Some people are never put out. However much you rile them, they are always good-humoured, always cool, always friendly. You might as well try to talk the sun behind a cloud as to get them in a rage. Happy the few who have this art! They always get the best of it, they always win the greatest respect, they always are the least likely people for any one to quarrel with.

I don't count these among the two classes of angry people, because they are not angry. But angry people are generally either in a rage or in the sulks. Neither is pleasant to meet, yet for my own part I would sooner have to do with the fellow in the rage. There's no deception about him; he's angry, and he lets you know it; he's got a grievance, and he blurts out what it is; he hits straight out from the shoulder, and you know what you've to expect. With such a one it is generally soon all over. Just as the April shower, sharp enough while it lasts, gives place in time to the sun, so Will Hothead generally gets all right as soon as he has let the steam off; and when he shakes hands and makes it up, you are pretty sure he thinks none the worse of you, and bears no malice.

Don't imagine I'm trying to justify exhibitions of temper. Far from it. I say every boy who can't control his temper has yet to learn one of the greatest lessons of life. What I want to show is that even passion, bad as it is, is not so bad as sulkiness.

For just consider what a miserable sort of boy this Tom Sulks, that we all of us know, is. Why, almost before he could speak he had learned to pout. If a toy was denied him, he neither bellowed like his little brother nor raved like his little sister, but toddled off and sulked in a corner all day long. When he grew a little older, if he was not allowed to play in the garden because it was damp, he refused to play in the nursery, he refused to come down to the dining-room, he refused to say his prayers at bedtime. When he was old enough to go to school, he would either play marbles the way he was used to (which was the wrong way), or not at all. If found fault with for not knowing his lesson, he pushed his books from him, and endured to be stood in the corner, or punished some other way, rather than learn his task. The vice only became worse and worse as time went on, and to-day Tom is an odious fellow. Look at him playing at cricket. He steps across the wickets to hit at a ball, but, instead, stops it with his foot. "How's that, umpire?" cries the bowler. "Out, leg before," is the answer.

Tom still keeps his place.

"Out, do you hear, leg before?"

"It wasn't!" growls Tom.

"The umpire gives it out," is the unanswerable reply.

Thereupon Tom's face clouds over, his eyebrows gather, and his lips shape themselves into a pout, as he drops his bat and walks from the wicket without a word. No one takes any notice of him, for the event is too common, alas, to occasion surprise. We know what his sulks mean. No one will get a word from him for hours, perhaps a day; no attempts at conciliation will tempt him back to the game, no friendly talk will chase the cloud from his face. There he goes, slouching up the playground into the house, and he will skulk upstairs to his study and slam the door, and that's all we shall see of Tom till suppertime.

Once, I remember, young Jim Friendly, a new boy, tried hard to coax Tom back into good humour. They had been having a match at something, I forget what, and Jim happened to say that something Tom did was against the rules. Tom, as usual, grew sulky and walked off.

"What, you aren't going in?" said Jim, disconcerted. No answer. "I didn't mean to offend you, old fellow; you may be right, after all." No answer. "I beg your pardon, Tom. I wouldn't have said it if I thought you'd have minded." No answer. "Don't be angry with a fellow, I didn't mean—"

No answer. And so Jim went on apologising, as if he had been all in the wrong and the other all in the right, and getting no word in reply, only the same scowl and uncompromising sullenness. "I'll take jolly good care not to stroke that fellow the wrong way again," said Jim, afterwards; "and if I should, I won't waste my time in stroking him the right way."

Just fancy what sort of man such a fellow as Tom is likely to turn out. Is he likely to have many friends? Unless he can get a few of his own sort, I'm afraid he'll be rather badly off in that respect. And then, oh, horrors! fancy half a dozen Tom Sulks together! What a happy family they would be! When Tom goes to business, he had better make up his mind to start a concern of his own, for I'm afraid he would have some difficulty in getting a partner, or, at any rate, keeping one. I could quite fancy some important question arising where Tom and his partner might hold different views. Tom insists he's right, the partner insists he's right. Tom consequently stays away for a week from the office, during which the poor partner has to manage as best he can.

Whatever Tom will do about marrying I don't know; and when he is married, what his wife will do, I know still less—it's no use speculating on such a matter. But now, letting Tom be, let us inquire whether the sulky boy is more to be blamed than pitied. That he is an odious, disagreeable fellow, there is no doubt. But perhaps it's not *all* his own fault. Some boys are of duller natures than others. The high-spirited, healthy, sanguine fellow will flare up at a moment's notice, and let fly without stopping to think twice of the injury done him, while the dull boy is altogether slower in his movements: words don't come to his lips so quickly, or thoughts don't rush into his mind as promptly as in others; he is like the snail who, when offended, shrinks back into its shell, leaving nothing but a hard, unyielding exterior to mark his displeasure. A great many boys are sulky because they have not the boldness to be anything else; and a great many others are so because to their small minds it is the grandest way of displaying their wrath. If only they could see how ridiculous they are!

I once knew two boys who for some time had been firm friends at school. By some unlucky chance a misunderstanding occurred which interrupted this friendship, and the grievance was, or appeared to be, so sore, that neither boy would speak to the other. Well, this went on for no less than six months, and became the talk of the whole school. These silly boys, however, were so convinced of the sublimity of their respective conducts that they never observed that every one was laughing at them. Daily they passed one another, with eyes averted and noses high in the air; daily they fed their memories with the recollection of their smart. For six months never a word passed between them. Then came the summer holidays, in the course of which it suddenly occurred to both these boys, being not altogether senseless boys, that after all they were making themselves rather ridiculous. And the more they thought of it, the more ashamed of themselves they grew, till at last one sat down and wrote,—

"Dear Dick, I'm sorry I offended you; make it up," to which epistle came, by return post, a reply,—

"Dear Bob, *I'm* sorry *I* offended you; let's be friends."

And the first day of next term these two met and shook hands, and laughed, and owned what fools they had both been.

A great many of the faults of this life come from the lack of a sense of humour. Certainly, if sulky boys had more of it, they would be inclined to follow the example of these two.

But, although there is a great deal about the sulky boy that merits pity rather than blame, there is much that deserves merciless censure. Why should one boy, by a whim of selfish resentment, mar the pleasure, not only of those with whom he has his quarrel, but with every one else he comes in contact with? "One dead fly," the proverb says, "makes the apothecary's ointment unsavoury"; and one sulky boy, in like manner, may destroy the harmony of a whole school. Isn't it enough, if you must be disagreeable, to confine your disagreeableness to those for whom it is meant, without lugging a dozen other harmless fellows into the shadow of it? Do you really think so much of your own importance as to imagine all the world will be interested in your quarrel with Smith, because he insisted a thing was tweedledum and you insisted it was tweedledee? Or, if you have the grace to confine your sulkiness to Smith alone, for his private benefit, do you imagine you will convince him of the error of his ways by shutting yourself up and never looking or speaking to him?

It used to be a matter of frequent debate at school what ought to be done to Tom Sulks.

"Kick him," said some. "Laugh at him," said others. "Send him to Coventry," put in a third. "Lecture him," advised others. "Let him alone," said the rest.

And this, after all, is the best advice. If a sulky fellow won't come round of his own accord, no kicks, or laughs, or snubs, or lectures will bring him.

Surely none of the readers of this chapter are sulky boys! It is not to be expected you will get through life without being put out—that is sure to happen; and then you've three courses open to you: either to take it like a man and a Christian, not rendering evil for evil, not carried away by revengeful impulse, but bearing what can honourably be borne with a good grace; and for the rest, if action is necessary, righting yourself without malice or vindictiveness; or else you can fly into a rage, and slog out blindly in wild passion; or you can sulk like a cur in a corner, heeded by no one, yet disliked by all, and without a friend—not even yourself.

You will know which of the three best becomes a British boy. Be assured, that which worst becomes him is *sulking*.

Chapter Ten
The Easy-going Boy

It is a common complaint in these degenerate days that we live harder than our fathers did. Whatever we do we rush at. We bolt our food, and run for the train; we jump out of it before it has stopped, and reach the school door just as the bell rings; we "cram" for our examinations, and "spurt" for our prizes. We have no time to read books, so we scuttle through the reviews, and consider ourselves up in the subject; we cut short our letters home, and have no patience to sit and hear a long story out. We race off with a chum for a week's holiday, and consider we have dawdled unless we have covered our thirty miles a day, and can name as visited a string of sights, mountains, lakes, and valleys a full yard long.

If such charges are just (and they are, we fear, not wholly unfounded), it is at least a satisfaction to know that there is one brilliant exception to the rule, and that is in the person of Master Ned Easy.

Whatever other folk do, *he* has no notion of hurrying himself. Some one once said of him that he was a fellow who looked as if he'd been born with his hands in his pockets. He takes his time about everything he does. If the breakfast bell rings before he is dressed, then—well, breakfast must wait. If breakfast is over before he has well begun, then everybody else must wait while he, in a leisurely way, polishes off his viands. In the classes, his is sure to be the last paper to be handed up; and when the boys are dismissed, he saunters forth to the playground in the rear of all the others. When he is one of a fishing-party, and everybody but he is ready, he keeps them all waiting till their patience is completely exhausted, while he gets together his tackle, laces his boots, and selects his flies.

"Come on! look alive!" is the cry that is for ever being hurled at him, "All serene, old fellow; what's the hurry?" is his invariable reply.

I well remember the first time I made Ned's acquaintance, and I will recall the incident, as giving a fair specimen of the fellow and his peculiarity.

It was a big cricket match, the afternoon was far advanced, the light was getting uncertain, and time was almost up. Our school's ninth wicket had fallen, and yet there were five runs to get to win, which we could just do, if our last man in was quick.

"Now, Ned!" calls out our captain, coming up to the tent; "look sharp in."

Ned coolly sat down on the bench in our tent and proceeded to put on a pad.

"Never mind about that! there's no time," said our captain impatiently, "and they are bowling slow."

"Oh, it won't take a minute," says Ned, discovering he had been putting the pad on upside down, and proceeding to undo it. We stood round in feverish impatience, and the minute consumed in putting on those miserable leg-fenders seemed like a year.

Ned himself, however, did not seem in the least flurried by our excitement.

"Pity they don't make these things fasten with springs instead of straps," he observed, by way of genial conversation.

Oh, how we chafed and fumed!

"*Will* you look sharp, if you're going to play at all?" howls our captain.

"All *right*, old chap; I can't be quicker than I am; where are the gloves?"

The gloves are brought like lightning, but not like lightning put on. No, the india-rubber gauntlets must needs be drawn with the greatest care and deliberation over his fingers, and even then require a good deal of shifting to render them comfortable. Then he was actually (I believe) going to take them off in order to roll up his shirt sleeves, had not two of us performed that office for him with a rapidity which astonished him.

"Upon my word, this is too bad," says our captain, flinging down the bat he was holding, and stamping with vexation. "We might as well give the whole thing up!"

"I'm awfully sorry," drawled Ned, in an injured tone; "but how could I help it? I'm ready now."

"Ready! I should hope you were. Off you cut now; it only wants five minutes to the time."

He starts to go, but turns before he has well left us, and says—

"Oh, I say, Jim, lend us your bat, will you? This one is sprung, and one of the—"

"Here you are," we shout, running to him with a dozen bats at once— "only look sharp."

"I only want one," he says. "Let me see this; no, this will do. Thanks, old man," and off he saunters again.

The other side is lying comfortably on the grass, very well satisfied at the delay which every moment adds to their chance of victory. What centuries Ned appears to be taking in strolling up to the wickets!

"I wish I was behind him with a red-hot poker," says one; "I'd make him trot!"

"Not a bit of it," growls our captain; "Ned would want more than that to start him."

Look at him now, getting "middle" as if he'd the whole afternoon before him! And that done, he slowly and deliberately taps the end of his bat on the place till we almost yell with rage.

"It's no use now!" groans our captain in absolute despair; and so, indeed, we and our smiling adversaries all thought.

"Play!" cries the bowler.

"Wait a bit," says the aggravating Ned, dipping his hands in the sawdust! "now!"

The ball comes at last, and Ned lets fly. It is a grand hit; the ball comes whizzing right past where we stand, and with delight as great as our previous agony we cheer till we are hoarse.

Three runs are added to our score, and now we only want one more to equal our opponents, and two to win; but we shall never do it in the time, unless fortune favours us strangely. For see, it is "over," and the fielders will consume half of the remaining two minutes in changing their position.

Then again "play" is called.

Would you believe it? Ned calls out for "middle" again at the new wicket, and repeats the same pottering operation when he has got it. "Well, if ever *I* saw—"

What our captain is about to say no one ever hears, for at that moment the ball is delivered, and Ned blocks it dead.

There is just time for one ball more, and on that all our hopes depend.

It comes, and Ned bangs at it! It's a run! No, it isn't! yes it is! The fielder has missed it. Hurrah! we are equal!

Actually they are running another! They won't do it. Up comes the ball to the wicket-keeper, and forward darts Ned's bat over the crease.

"How's that, umpire?" cries the wicket-keeper.

"Not out!"

"Time's up!"

Oh, how we cheer! How we rush forward and shoulder Ned home to the tent. Never was such a close shave of a match!

Ned himself by no means shares in the general excitement.

"Why, what a hurry you fellows were in!" he says. "Look here, George, I'll show you now what I meant about the springs on the pads."

Now you will understand what a very aggravating fellow this Ned Easy was; and yet he generally managed to come off best in the end. He generally managed to scrape in at the finish of whatever he undertook.

I am certain that if he were a prisoner of war *let* out on parole, with a pledge to return in one hour or suffer death, he would turn up cool and comfortable on the sixtieth tick of the sixtieth minute of that hour, and look quite surprised at the men who were loading their muskets for his execution.

But some day the chances are he will be late in earnest, and then he will have to repent in a hurry of his bad speed.

A fellow who is easy-going about his time is generally easy-going about his friends, his money, and his morals.

Not that Ned is the sort of fellow to turn out a rascal exactly. He has not the energy, even if he had the inclination. A rascal, to be at all successful, must be brisk, and an observer of times and seasons, and that is altogether out of Ned's line. No; he'll be careless about what he does, and about what people think of him; he will lend a sovereign with as little idea of getting it back as he has of returning the pound he himself had borrowed; he will think nothing of keeping a friend waiting half a day; neither will he take offence if his own good nature is drawn on to an unlimited extent.

He is, after his fashion, an observer of the golden rule, for although he is constantly annoying and exasperating people by his easy-going ways, he is never afflicted if others do *to him* as he does to them. He goes through life with the notion that every one is as complaisant and comfortable as himself. "Easy-going-ness" (if one may coin a word for the occasion) is, many people would say, a combination of selfishness and stupidity, but I think such people judge rather too hardly of Ned and his compeers. It's all very well for some of us, who perhaps are of an active turn of mind, to talk about curing oneself of this fault; but perhaps, if we knew all, we should find that it would be about as easy as for a fair-complexioned person to make himself dark. Ned's disposition is due more to his constitution than his upbringing, and those who are blindly intolerant of his ways do him a wrong. I'm sure he himself wishes he were as smart as some boys he sees, but he can't be, and you might just as well try to lash an elephant into a gallop as Ned into a flurry.

It is generally found that what he does he does well, which in a measure makes up for the length of time he takes in doing it; he is good-natured, brave, harmless, and cheery, and has lots of friends, whom he allows full liberty both to abuse and laugh at him (and what can friends want more?) and for the rest, he's neither vicious nor an idiot; and if nobody were worse than he is, the world would perhaps be rather better than it is.

An artificial "easy-going-ness" is undoubtedly a vice. It's a forgery, however, easily detected, and generally brings its own punishment. I advise none of my readers to try it on. If they are naturally energetic and smart, they have a much better chance of rising in the world than Ned has; but let them, when they laugh at Ned and abuse him, remember the fable of the hare and the tortoise.

I must just tell one more story of Ned in conclusion.

One night our whole school was startled by an alarm of "Fire!" We sprang from our beds, and, without waiting to dress, rushed to the quarter from which the cry had proceeded. It was only too true; a barn at one end of the buildings was in flames, and there seemed every prospect of the school itself catching fire.

We hurried back in a panic towards the staircase leading to the front door, and in doing so discovered Ned was not with us.

One of us darted off to the dormitory, where he lay in bed sound asleep.

A rough shake roused him.

"What's the row?" he drawled, stretching himself.

"Get up quick, Ned; there's a fire!"

"Where?" asked Ned, without stirring.

"In the doctor's wing."

The doctor's wing was that farthest removed from our dormitories.

Ned yawned.

"Then it couldn't possibly reach here for half an hour. Call us again in twenty minutes, Ben, there's a good fellow!"

Chapter Eleven
The Boy who is "Never Wrong"

One might fancy at the first blush, that such a boy is one to be envied, admired, and caressed above all others. Never wrong! What would not some of us give to have the same said of us? Aren't *we* always blundering and losing our way and making asses of ourselves every day of our lives? What wonder then if to us a being who is "never wrong" should appear almost superhuman in his glory?

But, so far from being the noble, delightful creature one would expect, the boy I am speaking of is an odious fellow, and as ridiculous as he is odious, and I will tell you why.

The principal reason is, because he requires us to believe, on his own unaided testimony, that he is the infallible being he professes to be; and the second and hardly less important reason is, that, so far from being always right, he is as often, if not oftener, wrong than other people; in short, he's a hum!

"Never wrong," indeed! If all the British Association were to declare as much of any one man, we should hardly be inclined to swallow it; but when our sole authority in the matter is Master Timothy Told-you-so himself, it becomes a joke, and a very poor joke too.

Let us just take stock of Timothy for a minute or two, to explain what we mean.

He's in class, and the lesson is history. He does not look happy, but of course that can't be because he doesn't know the lesson. Timothy not know a lesson indeed!

"Timothy," says the master, "tell me in whose reign the Reformation was introduced into England, will you?"

"James the First," replies Timothy.

"Next boy?"

"Henry the Eighth."

"Right; go up."

"Oh, sir," says Timothy, "that's what I meant; *I mistook the name* for a moment!" And he goes down with the air of an injured and resigned boy.

In the geography class which follows Tim has another opportunity of displaying his learning.

"On what river does Berlin stand?" is the question.

Tim hums and haws. "On the—oh—the—the, on the—er—the—"

"Next boy?"

"Berlin is on the Spree, sir."

"Ah, of course! It slipped me," mutters Tim with a thoughtful frown. "Any one knows Berlin is on the Spree!" And down he goes again, as if it were the common lot of all clever boys.

Arithmetic ensues. "Tell me, Timothy, if a man earns four shillings and sixpence halfpenny a day, how much does he make in a week of six days?"

This enormous problem Tim takes due time to cogitate. Of course he could tell you straight off if he chose; but as it is the practice to work out sums in the head, he condescends to the common prejudice. At length the oracle speaks.

"One pound three and two pence halfpenny."

"Quite wrong; what do you make it, Edward?"

"One pound four."

"Wrong. Next?"

"One pound seven and threepence."

"That's right."

"Oh yes, to be sure!" exclaims Tim, with the gesture of one who clutches at the very words of his own lips uttered by another; "of course, *that's what I meant!*"

"Timothy," says the master, gravely, "if you meant it, why did you not say it?"

Why not, indeed? That is one of the very few questions, reader, in all this world's philosophy which Timothy is unable to answer.

Of course every one laughs at Timothy, but that does not afflict him. So fortified is he in the assurance of his own infallibility, that the scorn of the ignorant is to him but as the rippling of water at the base of a lighthouse.

Do not mistake me, Tim is not a dunce. For every question he answers wrongly, perhaps he answers half a dozen correctly. If he chose to take his stand on his general proficiency, he would pass for a fairly clever fellow. But that will by no means satisfy him. He will never admit himself beaten. There is always some trivial accident, some unforeseen coincidence, without which his success would have been certain and recognised; but which, as it happens, slightly interfere with his triumph.

It is the same in games as in the class-room. If he is beaten in a race, it is because he has slipped in starting; if he is clean bowled first ball at cricket, it is because there was a lump in the grass just where the ball pitched; if he lets the enemy's halfback pass him at football, it is because he made sure Perkins had collared him—otherwise, of course, he would have won the race, made top score at the wickets, and saved his goal. As it happens, he does neither.

There is a touch of dishonesty in this, though perhaps Tim does not intend it. Why cannot he own he is "out of it" now and then? His fellows would respect him far more and laugh at him far less; he would gain far more than he lost, besides having the satisfaction of knowing he had not tried to deceive anybody. But I sometimes think, when Tim makes his absurd excuses, he really believes what he says; just as the ostrich, when he buries his head in the sand, really believes he is hidden from the sight of his pursuers.

It is natural in human nature not to relish the constant admission of error or failure. Who of us is not glad to feel at times (even if we do not say it) that "it's not our fault"? The person who is always making little of himself, and never admitting what small merit he might fairly claim, is pretty much the same sort of deception as Tim, and we despise him almost as much. We would all of us, in fact (and what wonder?) like to be "always right," and perhaps our tendency is to let the wish become father to the thought rather too often.

But to return to Timothy. Nothing, of course, could astonish him; nothing was ever news to him; nothing could evoke his applause. "Tim," perhaps some one would say, "do you know old Grinder (the head master) is going to be married, and we are to get a week extra holiday?"

"Ah," says Tim, to whom this is all news, "I always thought there was something of the kind up. For my own part, I thought we should get a fortnight extra."

"Buck made a good jump yesterday, Tim," says another. "Five feet and half an inch."

"Sure it wasn't three-quarters of an inch?" is Tim's provoking answer.

Of all irritating things, perhaps the most irritating is to have your big bundle of news calmly opened and emptied, and its contents appropriated without scruple or acknowledgment.

Tim this very day has the gratification of amazing half the school with the news of Dr Grinder's approaching marriage and the consequent extra holidays, and of seeing the enthusiastic astonishment of others to whom he retails the latest achievement of the athletic Buck.

But he did not always come off so easily. Once he was made the victim of a joke which, in any one less self-satisfied, might have effectually checked his foolish propensity. It was a wet day, and the boys were all assembled in the big play-room, not knowing exactly what to do, and ready for the first bit of fun which might turn up.

"Couldn't somebody draw Tim out?" one of us whispered.

The idea caught like wildfire, and after a brief pause Tidswell, the monitor, said, amid the hushed attention of the company—

"By the way, Tim, wasn't that a queer account of the sea-serpent in the paper the other day?"

"Awfully queer," replied the unsuspecting Tim; "I didn't know you had seen it."

"Fancy a beast a mile and a half long from head to tail!"

"It's a good size," said Tim, "but nothing out of the common for a sea-serpent, you know."

"Now I come to think of it, though," said Tidswell, "it didn't say that the *serpent* was a mile and a half long; it was a mile and a half from the ship when it was seen, wasn't that it?"

"Yes, a mile and a half from the ship. I *thought* you were drawing the long bow in saying it was so big as all that."

"They saw it a mile and a half off, and just fancy feeling its breath at that distance?"

"I'm not astonished at that," said Tim, "for all those beasts have enormous lungs."

"How absurd of me! I should have said it seemed to all appearances lifeless when they saw it," said Tidswell.

"Yes; dead, in fact," put in Tim, getting into difficulties.

"And then suddenly it stood erect on its tail, and shot forward towards the vessel."

"Shows the strength of their backs. I couldn't help thinking that when I saw the account."

"What am I talking about?" exclaimed Tidswell, hastily correcting himself; "it was the ship stood in towards the monster and shot at him."

"Ah, yes; so it was. I made the same mistake myself, see. Yes, they fired a broadside at him."

"No; only one shot at his head."

"That was all. Isn't that what you said?"

"And then he turned over in the water—"

"Dead as a leg of mutton!" put in Tim.

"No; the shot missed him, and he wasn't touched."

"No. I meant they all thought he was as dead as a leg of mutton; but he was not so much as grazed."

All this while the amusement of the listeners had been growing gradually beyond control, and at this point smothered explosions of laughter from one and another fell on Tim's ears, like the dropping of musketry fire. But he did not guess its meaning, and continued turning towards Tidswell, and waiting for the conclusion of the story.

"And the last they saw of him," resumed that worthy, his voice quailing with the exertion to keep it grave and composed—"the last they saw of him was, he was spinning away at the rate of twenty knots an hour, with his tail in his mouth, in the direction of the North Pole."

"I fancied it was only eighteen knots an hour," put in Tim seriously.

Another moment, and the laughter would assuredly burst upon him.

"Not in the account I saw. What paper did you see it in, Tim?"

"Eh? Why, the same as you," replied Tim hurriedly, beginning to suspect the crimson faces of his comrades meant something more than admiration of his wisdom. "Where did you get the tale from? I forget."

"I got the tale out of my head—like the serpent, you humbug!" roared Tidswell; and for the next five minutes Tim sat on his stool of repentance, amid the yells of laughter with which his companions hailed his discomfiture.

When silence was restored, of course he tried to explain that "he knew all along it was a joke, and only wanted to see how far he could gammon the fellows, and fancied he succeeded," and presently quitted the room, an injured but by no means humiliated boy.

One last word. Timothy and his friends are amusing up to one point, and detestable up to another point; but when they come to you in the hour of your deepest sorrow and distress, and, with bland smile, say to you, "I told you so!" they are beyond all endurance, and you hope for nothing more devoutly than that you may never see their odious faces again.

The best cure possible for Tim is a homoeopathic one. Find some other boy equally conceited, equally foolish, equally unscrupulous, and set him at Tim. I will undertake to say that—unless the two devour one another down to the very tips of their tails, like the famous Kilkenny cats—they will bring one another to reason, and perhaps modesty, in double-quick time.

The great and wise Newton once said of himself that, so far from knowing all things, he seemed to himself to be but as a boy gathering pebbles on the seashore, while the great ocean of truth lay all undiscovered before him.

Newton was, in his way, almost as fine a fellow as Timothy Told-you-so, and if Timothy would but stoop to have more of Newton's spirit, he might in time come to possess an atom or two of Newton's sense.

Chapter Twelve
The Untidy Boy

Look at him! You could tell he was an untidy fellow at a single glance. One of his bootlaces is hanging loose, and the band of his scarf has slipped up above his collar. Though it is a fine day, his trouser legs are splashed up to the knee; and as for a parting to his hair, you might as well expect an Indian jungle to be combed. His hands are all over ink, and the sticky marks about his mouth tell their own tale. In short, Jack Sloven is a dirty boy, and is anything but a credit to the school he belongs to.

I wish you could see his school books. The pages look like well-used drum parchments, and I am certain Jack must often find it hard to decipher the words upon them. His exercises look as if they had been left out in an ink shower, and the very pen he uses is generally wet with ink up to the very tip of the handle, which, by the way, he usually nibbles when he's nothing better to do. Who shall describe his desk? It is generally understood that a schoolboy's desk is the receptacle for a moderately miscellaneous assortment of articles, but Jack's seemed like a great pie, into which everything under the sun was crammed and stored up. The lid never shut; but if you were to open it, its contents would astonish you as much as the contents of that wonderful pie in the nursery rhyme astonished the king when he lifted the crust.

There were books, papers, hooks, balls, worms, stale sandwiches, photographs, toffee, birds' eggs, keys, money, knives, cherry stones, silkworms, marbles, pencils, handkerchiefs, tarts, gum, sleeve links, and walnut shells. Any one venturesome enough to take a header through these might succeed in reaching the layer of last year's apple peel below, or in penetrating to the crumb heaps in the bottom corners; but few there were who possessed that amount of boldness. Of course, Jack had no notion of what his worldly goods consisted. He had a way of shying things into his desk and forgetting them; and only when it became so full that the lid stood nearly wide open did he apprehend the necessity of a "clear-out."

But if there was ever anything more awful to behold than Jack's desk, it was one of these "clear-outs." The event generally got wind when it was about to happen, and never failed to create a sensation in the school. All who had a right took care to be present at the ceremony, and I do believe if Jack had had the sense to issue reserved seat tickets, he might have made a nice thing out of it. At any rate, he made a nice thing out of that desk.

Quite indifferent to our presence and laughter, he began leisurely to take out its contents and spread them in glorious array upon the floor, with a view (as he was kind enough to explain to some one who asked him) "to sort them up." The books and papers went in a pile by themselves; all loose papers were thrust inside the covers of the books; and all books without covers were jammed into all the covers without books that seemed likely to fit. Then all the pens and pencils were put into a pencil case, and if any happened to be too long, they were broken to the required shortness. This being satisfactorily done, Jack used next to turn his attention to the miscellaneous articles of food of which he found himself possessed. The sandwiches, if not more than a week old, he either ate or generously offered to some of us; the toffee he put into his pocket, and the tarts (if the jam were not already dried up) he put aside for private consumption hereafter. The shells, stones, peel, etcetera, he heaped up in one place on the floor, and trusted to Providence to dispose of them. The fish-hooks and baits, the birds' eggs that were not broken, the silkworms, the photographs, pencils, knives, and other articles of use or ornament, he sorted carefully, and then put back into the desk. By this time it would occur to him he had been long enough over this business, so he shovelled the books and papers in anyhow, and anything else which happened still to be left out, and then finding that the lid would shut within an inch, he sighed with the relief of a man who has well discharged a painful duty.

How was it to be expected Jack could ever find anything he wanted? Sometimes he would sit grubbing in his desk, or among his books, to find a certain exercise or paper for half an hour, and finally, when everything was upside down, he would remember he had it in his waistcoat pocket, from the recesses of which he produced it crumpled, greasy, and almost illegible. On Sundays he always had a hunt for his gloves; and at the end of the term, when he undertook his own packing, he generally first of all contrived to pack up his keys in the very bottom of the trunk, and so had to take everything out before he could get them, and then when (with the aid of some dozen of us sitting on the top of the unfortunate receptacle, to cram down the jumble of things inside to a shutting point) he had succeeded in triumphantly turning the lock, it was a wonder if he had not to open and unpack it all again to find his straps.

As to his dress, I can safely say that, though Jack always had good clothes, he always looked much less respectable than other boys whose parents could not afford them anything but common material. Not only did he lose buttons, and drop grease over his coat and trousers, but he never folded or brushed them, or had them mended in time, as a tidy boy would have done. We were quite ashamed to be seen walking with him sometimes, he looked so disreputable, but no reproofs or persuasions could induce him to take more pains about his appearance.

"A place for everything, and everything in its place," was a lesson Jack could not learn; the result was constant and incalculable trouble. If people could only realise the amount of time lost by untidiness, I think they would regard the fault with positive horror. Why, Jack Sloven, at the very mildest computation, must have lost half an hour a day. Half an hour a day, at the end of the year, makes a clear working fortnight to the bad, so that in twenty-five years, if he goes on as he has begun, he will have one year of which it will take him all his time to give an account.

But not only does untidiness waste time, and render the person who falls into it a disreputable member of society, but it seriously endangers his success in life. Jack Sloven was naturally a clever fellow. When he could find his books, he made good use of them; none of us could come up to him in translations, and he had the knack of always understanding what he read. If it had not been for this wretched habit, he might have got prizes at school, and still higher honours in after life; but as it was, he always came to grief. The notes he had made on his work were never to be found; he spent more time in collecting his materials than he had to spare for using them; most of his work had to be scrambled through at the last moment, and was accordingly imperfect. If Jack goes to business, he has a very poor chance of getting on, for untidiness and business will no more go together than oil and water. Few things are more against a man in business than untidiness; people fight shy of him. If his dress is untidy, his letters slovenly, his habits unpunctual, and his accounts confused, he will be regarded as a man not reliable, and not to be trusted, and people will refuse to transact with him. If he has a house of his own, he will never succeed in keeping his servants long, for they—so they say—have quite enough to do without unnecessary work. In fact, I don't see how Jack is to get on at all unless he mends his ways.

Is it possible for an untidy boy to become tidy? Try. And if at first you don't succeed—try again. You are sure to succeed if you stick to it. Don't aim at apple-pie order—everything in lavender—never to be touched, and all that sort of thing. That's as bad as the boy who once possessed a desk, which he would never use, for fear of marking the blotting-paper, and breaking the paper bands round the envelopes.

No; if you can get into the way of always putting the book you read back into its place on the shelf, and the paper you want where you will be certain to find it again—if you encourage a jealousy of rubbish, and a horror of dirt—if you take to heart the proverb I quoted just now, "A place for everything, and everything in its place"—you will be as tidy as you ever need be; and Jack Sloven's troubles and misfortunes will never be yours.

Chapter Thirteen
The Scapegrace

The fellow's always in a row! No matter what it's about; no matter whose fault it is; no matter how he tried to keep out of it; it's always the same—he's in a row.

To fancy him not in a row would involve a flight of imagination of which we, at any rate, are utterly incapable. He has lived in an atmosphere of rows—rows in the nursery, rows at the dinner table, rows in the schoolroom, rows in the playground. His hands are like leather, so often have they been caned; his ears are past all feeling, so often have they been boxed; and solitary confinement, impositions, the corner, and the head master's study, have all lost their horrors for him, so often has he had to endure them.

Sam Scamp of our school was, without exception, the unluckiest fellow I ever came across. It was the practice in the case of all ordinary offences for the masters of the lower forms to deal out their own retribution, but special cases were always reserved for a higher court—the head master's study. Hither the culprits were conducted in awful state and impeached; here they heard judgment pronounced, and felt sentence executed. It was an awful tribunal, that head master's study! "All hope abandon, ye who enter here," was the motto—if not written, at least clearly implied—over the door. The mere mention of the place was enough to make one's flesh creep. Yet, somehow or other, Sam Scamp, was always finding himself there. He must have abandoned hope once a week at least during his school life, and before he left school I am certain he must have worn that awful carpet threadbare, for all *his* offences were special offences. When half a dozen boys had spent one afternoon in throwing stones over a certain wall, the stone which broke the doctor's conservatory window was, as might be expected, Sam's. On the occasion of the memorable battle of the dormitories—that famous fight in which fifteen boys of Ward's dormitory, arrayed in their nightgowns and armed with bolsters, engaged at dead of night in mortal combat with twenty boys of Johnson's dormitory for the possession of a certain new boy who had arrived that day with a trunk full of cakes—when the monitors appeared on the scene, one boy, and one only, was captured, and that was Sam. When a dozen fellows had been copying off one another, the exercise book from which the discovery was made would be sure to be Sam's; and when, in the temporary absence of the master, the schoolroom became transformed into a bear-garden—as it sometimes will—if suddenly the door were to open the figure which would inevitably fall on the master's eye would be that of Sam, dancing a hornpipe in the middle of the floor, shouting at the top of his voice, and covered from head to foot with the dust he had himself kicked up.

On such occasions he was led off to the doctor's study. I happened to be there once when he was brought up, and so had an opportunity of witnessing a scene which, if new to me, must have been very familiar to my unfortunate schoolfellow. (By the way, the reason *I* was in the doctor's study was merely to return a book he had lent me, mind that, reader!)

"What, here again, Samuel?" said the doctor, recognising his too-well-known visitor.

"I'm very sorry, sir," says Sam, humbly. "I can't make out how it is. I try all I know—I do indeed—but somehow I'm always in trouble."

"You are," replies the doctor. "What is it about this time, Mr Wardlaw?"

"I can tell you, sir—" begins Sam eagerly.

"Be silent, sir! Well, Mr Wardlaw?"

"The boy has been very disrespectful, sir. When I came into the class-room this morning and opened my desk, I found it contained a guinea-pig and two white mice, who had—"

Here the unlucky Sam, after a desperate effort, in the course of which he has almost choked himself with a handkerchief, bursts into a laugh.

"What do you mean, sir?" thunders the doctor.

"Oh, sir, I couldn't help it—really I couldn't; I would rather have choked than do it—it's just like me!"

And he looks so distressed and humble that the doctor turns from him, and invites Mr Wardlaw to resume his impeachment.

"I have only to say that this boy, on being charged with the deed, confessed to having done it."

"Oh yes, sir, that's all right—I did it; I'm very sorry; somehow I can't make out how it is I'm so bad," says Sam, with the air of one suffering from the strain of a constant anxiety.

"Don't talk nonsense, sir!" says the doctor, sternly; "you can make it out as well as I can."

"Shall I hold out my hand, sir?" says Sam, who by this time has a good idea of the routine of practice pursued in such interviews.

"No," says the doctor. "Leave him here, Mr Wardlaw; and you," adds he, for the first time remembering that I was present—"you can go."

So we departed, leaving Sam shivering and shaking in the middle of the carpet. It was half an hour before he rejoined his schoolfellows, and this time his hands were not sore. But somehow he managed to avoid getting into scrapes for a good deal longer than usual. But there is no resisting the inevitable. He did in due time find himself in another row; and then he suddenly vanished from our midst, for he had been expelled.

Now, with regard to Sam and boys like him, it is of course only natural to hold them up as examples to others. No boy can be a scamp and not suffer for it some way or other; and as to saying it's one's misfortune rather than one's fault that it is so, that is as ridiculous as to say, when you choose to walk north, that it is your misfortune you are not walking south.

But, in excuse for Sam, we must say that he was by no means the worst boy in our school, though he did get into the most rows, and was finally expelled in disgrace. If he had been deceitful or selfish, he would probably have escaped oftener than he did; but he never denied his faults or told tales of others. We who knew him generally found him good-natured and jovial; he looked upon himself as a far more desperate character than we ourselves did, and once I remember he solemnly charged me to take warning by his evil fate.

Still, you see, Sam sinned once too often. Even though his crimes were never more serious than putting guinea-pigs into the master's desk, yet that sort of conduct time after time is not to be tolerated in any school. The example set by a mischievous boy to his fellows is not good; and if his scrapes are winked at always, the time will come when others will be encouraged to follow in his steps, and behave badly too. Sam, no doubt, deserved the punishment he got; and because one bad boy who is punished is no worse than a dozen bad boys who get off, that does not make him out a good boy, or a boy more hardly treated than he merited.

Scapegraces are boys who, being mischievously inclined, are constantly transgressing the line between right and wrong. Up to a certain point, a boy of good spirits and fond of his joke, is as jolly a boy as one could desire; but when his good spirits break the bounds of order, and his jokes interfere with necessary authority, then it is time for him to be reminded nothing ought to be carried too far in this world.

One last word about scapegraces. Don't, like Sam, get it into your heads that you are destined to get into scrapes, and that therefore it is no use trying to keep out of them. That would be a proof of nothing but your silliness. I can't tell you how it was Sam's stone always broke the window, or why the master's eye always fell on him when there was a row going on; but I can tell you this, that if Sam hadn't thrown the stone, the window would not have been broken; and that if he had behaved well when the master's eye was turned away, he would not have cut a poor figure when the door was opened. Some boys make a boast of the number of scrapes they have been in, and fondly imagine themselves heroes in proportion to the number of times they have been flogged. Well, if it pleases them to think so, by all means let them indulge the fancy; but we can at least promise them this—nobody else thinks so!

Chapter Fourteen
The Unoriginal Boy

It takes one a long time to discover that there is something wanting in the character of Ebenezer Ditto; and it takes a longer time still to make out exactly what that something is. He's an ordinary-looking and ordinarily-behaved boy. There's nothing amiss with the cut of his coat—it's neither extra grand nor extra shabby; there's nothing queer about his voice—he doesn't stammer and he doesn't squeak; there's nothing remarkable about his conversation or his actions—he's not a dunce, though he's not clever; he's not a scamp, though he's not goody; he never offends any one, though he never becomes great friends with any one. What is it makes us not take to Ebenezer? Why is it, on the whole, we rather despise him, and feel annoyed when in his society? For, it is the truth, we *don't* much care about him.

Well, the answer to this question may be, as I have said, not very readily discovered; but if you watch Master Ditto carefully, and make up your mind, you will get at the bottom of the mystery, you will find that it is this very "ordinary" manner about him to which you object. The fellow is dull—he is unoriginal.

You feel sometimes as if you would give a sovereign to see Ebenezer stand on his head, by way of variety. It annoys you when he sits there with his eyes on you, smiling when you smile, frowning when you frown, talking about the weather when you talk about the weather, and when you whistle "Nancy Lee" whistling his everlasting "Grandfather's Clock." It is a relief, by the way, even to hear him whistle a different tune, for it is about the only thing in which he does take an independent course. But, if truth were known, it would come out he only knows this one tune, and that is the reason. He has not originality enough in him to learn a second.

It *is* an annoying thing to be copied and imitated by any one, most of all by a fellow one's own age. We can understand the little child imitating its father, and we enjoy seeing what capers it sometimes cuts in the attempt, but there's nothing either interesting or amusing in the way Ebenezer goes on. When, for instance, by a sudden inspiration of genius, you take it into your head to shy a slice of apple across the room at Jack Sleepy just while he is in the act of yawning, with his mouth open wide enough to let a wheelbarrow down, it is not pleasant that immediately afterwards some one at your side should hurl a walnut at the same person and wound him seriously in the eye. Besides making a row, it takes away from the fun of your achievement, and makes the whole affair more than a joke. Or, being asked, let us suppose, to name your favourite hero in fiction, you are careful to select a somewhat out-of-the-way name, and reply, "Sidney Carton." You are rather pleased to think you have thereby not only named some one whom no one else is likely to hit upon, but also you have delicately let your master see you have lately read a very good book. It is rather vexing when Ebenezer replies to the same question, "Sidney Carton," in a knowing sort of manner, although you are positive he has never read the *Tale of Two Cities*, and doesn't even know that Dickens was its author. Of course, your distinction in the matter has gone, and if your answer is judged the best, you only get half the credit you deserve. Or, to take one more example, supposing one day, being utterly sick of Ebenezer's society, and longing to get a little time by yourself, you decline the tempting offer of a cricket match in which you know he also is likely to play. You mean to read this afternoon, you say. Well, isn't it too bad when next moment you hear that wretched Ebenezer saying, in answer to the same invitation, "Very sorry, but I mean to read this afternoon," and then have him come and sit down on a bench beside you with his book? And the worst of it is, you know if you now change your mind and go in for the match after all, he will change *his* mind and do the same.

The most aggravating thing about unoriginal fellows is that you cannot well get in a rage with them, for if you find fault with them, you find fault with yourselves.

"What a young ass you are not to play in the match!" you say to Ebenezer, hardly able to contain yourself.

"Why aren't *you* playing in it?" he replies.

"Oh! I've some particular reading I want to do," you say.

"So have I," replies he.

You cannot say, "You have no business to read when cricket is going on," nor can you say, "What do you mean by it?"

Clearly, if *you* do it, you are not the person to say *he* shall not.

I doubt if Ebenezer knows to what an extent he carries this trick of his. It is so natural for him to do as he sees others do that he fails to see how his actions appear in the same light as that in which others see them. Sometimes, indeed, he appears to be conscious of following his copy pretty closely, for we catch him trying to make some slight variation which will prevent it being said he does exactly the same. For instance, if you give a little select supper party in your study to two friends off roast potatoes and sardines, he will probably have three friends to breakfast off eggs and bread and jam; or if you hang up the portraits of your father and sister over your mantelpiece, he will suspend the likenesses of his mother and brother on his wall. He generally, you will find, tries to improve on you—which, of course, is not always hard to do. But sometimes he comes to grief in the attempt, as happened in the case of his wonderful "hanging shelves." Ted Hammer, quite a mechanical genius, had made to himself a set of these shelves, which for neatness, simplicity, and usefulness were the marvel of the school. Of course Ebby got to know of it, and was unhappy till he could cap it with something finer still. So he made all sorts of excuses for coming constantly into Ted's room and inspecting his work of art, till at last he felt quite sure he could make a set for himself. So he started to manufacture a set, twice the size, and with double the number of shelves. In due time he had it done and suspended on his wall, and it seemed as if Ted's nose was completely out of joint, for Ebby's shelves held not only his books, but his jam-pots and tumblers, and all sorts of odds and ends besides. But that very night there was a crash in his room, the like of which had never been heard before. We all rushed to the place. There were books, jam pots, ink pots, tumblers, in one glorious state of smash on the floor, and the unlucky shelves on the top of them; for Ebenezer had driven the small nail that supported the structure into nothing better than ordinary loose plaster. The only wonder was how the thing stayed up two minutes. So Ted Hammer's nose was not out of joint after all.

This reminds us of the story of the two rival shoemakers, who lived opposite one another, and always strove each to outdo the other in every branch of their trade. One day, one of the two painted over his door the highly appropriate Latin motto, "Mens conscia recti." His neighbour gnashed his teeth, of course, and vowed to improve on the inscription. And next day, when cobbler Number 1 and the world awoke, they beheld painted in huge characters over the fellow's shop-front the startling announcement, "*Men's and Women's* conscia recti."

It is the easiest thing possible (where the operator is not quite such a fool as this shoemaker) to improve on another's production. When some genius brings out a machine over the plans of which he has spent half an anxious lifetime, a dozen copyists will in a year have out a dozen "improved machines," each of them better than the first one, and therefore each helping to ruin the inventor. He had all the labour and all the knowledge. All the others did was to add a few slight improvements, for which they get all the credit due to the man without whom they would not have had an idea. This is, alas! very common, and cannot be avoided.

You can't make a law against one boy imitating another, or even against his stepping into the credit due to you.

It is as easy to be unoriginal as it is hard at times to be original. Everybody falls into the fault more or less. Why is it we can never find anything to begin a conversation with except the weather? Somebody, I suppose, began on that topic once. Why is it we always wear the shaped coats that everybody else does? Somebody must have astonished the world by setting the fashion in the first instance.

There is a touch of envy in Ebenezer, I'm afraid; but the kindest way of accounting for his annoying ways is to believe he is not clever. No more he is. If he were, he would at least see how ridiculous he sometimes makes himself. The original boys, on the other hand, *are* clever, and they are quick in their ideas, which Ebenezer is not. The great thing in originality is to have your idea out before any one else. As long as it's in your head and no one knows of it, you are no better off than the unoriginal many; but give your idea a shape and a name, and you are one of the original few. And the glory of being one of them is that you are sure to have one or two of Ebenezer's sort at your tail!

Unoriginality is more a failing than a crime. Sometimes it may lead to actions which do real injury to another, but injury is rarely intended. It is stupidity more than anything else. But there is a point at which unoriginality may become a sin. Every boy has in him the power to say "Yes" or "No," and he has also the conscience in him which tells him when he ought to say the one or the other. Now, when every one is saying "Yes" to a thing about which your conscience demands that you shall say "No," it becomes your positive duty for once in your life to be original, and say it.

After all, most of us are medium sort of fellows. We are not geniuses, and we trust we are not dolts. The best thing we can do is to look out that we don't lose all our originality while knocking through this world. The more we can keep of it, the more good we shall do; and if we find we have enough of it to entitle us to some "followers," let us see to it we turn them out, if anything, better fellows than they were when first they "jumped up behind."

Chapter Fifteen
The Duffer

What school is without its duffer, I wonder? Of course, none of us answer to the name, but we all know somebody who does, and it's a curious thing nobody ever thoroughly dislikes a duffer. Why? Well, one reason may be that there's nothing as a rule objectionable about such fellows, and another is that we are always ready enough to forgive one who makes us laugh; but I have an idea that the best reason why we are all so tolerant of duffers is that we are able to remind ourselves, when laughing at them, how very much the reverse of duffers we are ourselves.

However that may be, we had a glorious duffer at our school, who got himself and us into all sorts of scrapes, and yet was quite a favourite among his schoolfellows.

Billy Bungle (that was his name) was not by any means an idiot. He knew perfectly well that two and two made four, and yet, such a queer chap as he was, he would take any amount of pains to make five of it.

If there were two ways of doing anything, a right way and a wrong way, he invariably selected the latter; and if there seemed only one way, and that the right way, then he invented a wrong one for the occasion.

One day, one of the little boys in the school had a letter telling him to come home at once. He was not long in packing up his carpet bag, and getting the doctor's leave to depart. But the doctor was unwilling for such a little helpless fellow as he to undertake the long journey all alone. He came down to the playground where we were, and beckoning to Billy, who happened to be the nearest at hand, said, "Bungle, will you go with this boy to the station, and see him off by the twelve train to X—? Here is the money to get his ticket; and carry his bag for him, there's a man."

Billy readily accepted the commission, and we watched him proudly marching from the playground with his small charge on one side and the carpet bag on the other. The station was a mile off, and it was nearly one o'clock when he returned home. We were in class at the time.

"Well, did you see him off?" asked the doctor.

"Yes, sir, all right; we caught an earlier train than the one you said—at a quarter to," replied Billy, with the tone of a clever man.

"But the quarter to doesn't go to X—. Didn't I tell you to see him off by the twelve train?"

"I thought it would be all the better to catch the early one."

"Stupid boy, don't you know that train doesn't *go to* X—?"

"No one said it didn't, sir," put in Billy, with an injured face.

"Did any one say it did?"

"I didn't hear," said Billy; "shall I go back and ask?"

"That would not be the least use," said the master, too vexed almost to speak.

Billy stood before him, staring at him, and looking anything but cheerful.

"I shall have to go down to the station myself," said the doctor. "You are the stupidest boy I ever had to do with."

Billy looked resigned; then fumbling in his waistcoat pocket, he pulled out a bit of blue cardboard. "Oh, here's the ticket, sir."

"What! Wasn't it enough to send the poor boy off by a wrong train, without keeping his ticket? Go away, sir, this instant, to your room, and stay there till I give you leave to quit it!"

Billy obeyed, evidently unable to make the affair out.

By dint of telegrams and messengers, the missing boy turned up again; but it was a long time before Billy was allowed to forget the way he had "seen him off."

This is just one specimen of our unlucky schoolfellow's blunders. He was always in some trouble of the kind. He had to cease taking lessons in chemistry, because one time he nearly succeeded in blowing himself and three or four of us up by mixing certain combustibles together by mistake; and another time he upset a bottle of sulphuric acid over his clothes.

He was always very near the bottom of his class, because he *would* prepare the wrong lessons, or misunderstand the questions asked him. And yet he was always anxious to get on. Once, I remember, he confidentially asked me, if he were to learn Liddell and Scott's Lexicon by heart, whether I thought he would be able to get the Greek prize? But he bungled more in the playground than anywhere. Perhaps it was because we laughed at him and made him nervous.

It was rarely any one cared to have him on their side at cricket. He missed the easiest catches, he got leg before wicket, he stopped still in the middle of a run to see if he would have time to finish it, and whenever he did manage to score one he was sure, in his excitement, to knock down his own wicket with a flourish of his bat.

In football it's no exaggeration to say he was more often on the ground than the ball itself, and was invariably of more service to the other side than to his own. In fact, the possession of him got to be quite a joke.

"Who's going to win?" asks some one, before a match begins.

"Which side is Billy Bungle on?" is the counter question.

"Oh, he's on our side."

"Then of course the other fellows will win," is the uncomplimentary conclusion; and Billy, poor boy, who overhears it, half chokes with wounded feelings, and tucks up his sleeves and goes into the game, determined for once he will disappoint those who mock at him. Alas I scarcely has the ball been kicked off than he gets in the way of everybody he ought not to get in the way of, and lets the others pass him; he collars his own men, and kicks the ball towards his own goal, and falls down just in time to cause half a dozen of his side to tumble over him, and just as the ball rises, straight as an arrow, to fly over the enemy's goal, his unlucky head gets in the way and spoils everything. No wonder he is in very poor demand as an ally.

Now, the question is, is it altogether Billy's fault he is such a duffer? Of course it is, say nineteen out of every twenty of my readers. Any one with an ounce of brains and common sense could avoid such stupid blunders. But the twentieth is not quite so positive. "Perhaps it's not altogether Billy's fault," he says. And I must confess I am inclined to agree with this. Of course, a great deal of his "duffingness" (I believe that's the proper word) is due to his carelessness. If he took the trouble to think about what he was doing, he would never translate a French exercise into Latin, or learn his arithmetic by heart instead of his history; he would never mix together (under his nose) two chemicals that would assuredly explode and nearly blow his head off. For he has a few brains in that head, which makes such blunders all the less excusable. But I am not sure if a good deal of his bad luck is not due to the merciless way in which he was laughed at, and called "duffer," and taught to believe that he could no more do a thing right than a bull could walk through a china-shop without making a smash. He got it into his head he was a duffer, and therefore did not take the pains he might have done.

"What's the use of my bothering? I'm sure to make a mess of it!"

Fancy a boy saying this to himself at cricket, while a ball is flying beautifully towards him, an easy catch, even for a duffer. Do you suppose he will catch it? Not he. He will stand where he is, and put up his hands, and look another way. In fact, he won't do his best. And why? Because all of us never expect him to catch it; and if he did, we should probably call it a "fluke," and laugh at him all the more. Yes, it's our fault in a certain measure that Billy is the awful "duffer" he is.

Sometimes, as in the game of football we have referred to, he does make up his mind to do his best; but even then the idea that "destiny" is against him, and that everybody is expecting him to make a fool of himself, as usual, is enough to make any fellow nervous and a duffer.

However, whatever excuses we may make for Billy, he was undoubtedly a duffer. I have named one reason of his bad luck—want of thought—and another was hurry. In fact, the two reasons become one, for it was chiefly because Billy would never give himself time to think that he made so many mistakes. All his thinking came after the thing was done. As soon as the chemicals had blown up, for instance, it entered his head he had mixed the wrong ingredients, and as soon as the ball was flying to the wrong goal it occurred to him he had kicked it in a wrong direction.

And this really brings me to the moral of my discourse. Don't despair, if you are a duffer, for you may cure yourself of it, if you will only *think* and *take your time*. If we are not quick-witted, it does not follow we have no wits, and if we only use them carefully, we shall be no greater duffers than some of our sharp fellows.

The great philosopher Newton once appeared in the light of a great duffer. He had a cat, and that cat had a kitten, and these two creatures were continually worrying him by scratching at his study door to be let either in or out. A brilliant idea occurred to the philosopher—he would make holes in the bottom of his door through which they might pass in or out at pleasure without troubling him to get up and open the door every time. And thereupon he made a big hole for the cat and a little hole for the kitten, as if both could not have used the big hole!

Well, you say, one could fancy Billy Bungle doing a thing like that, but what an extraordinary error for a philosopher to fall into! It was, but the reason in both cases is alike. Neither thought sufficiently about what he was doing. Newton was absorbed with other things, and Billy was thinking of nothing, and yet both he and Newton were duffers, which goes to prove that without care any one may belong to that class.

How many men who have begun life as reputed "duffers" have turned out great men! but you will find that none of them ever did themselves any good till they had cured themselves of that fault. That's what you, and I, and Billy Bungle must all do, boys.

Just two words more about Billy. We all liked him, as I have said, for he was imperturbably good-tempered. He bore no malice for all our laughing, and now and then, when he was able to see the joke, would assist in laughing at himself.

And then he never tried to make himself out anything but what he was. Of all detestable puppies, the duffer who tries to pass himself off for a clever man is the most intolerable; for nothing will convince him of his error, and nothing will keep him in his place. He's about the one sort of character nobody knows how to deal with, for he sets everybody else but himself down as duffers. What can anybody do to such a one?

But there is another extreme. Billy's great fault was that he was too ready to believe others who called him a duffer. Don't take it for granted you are a duffer because any one tells you so. Find it out for yourself, and when you've found it out—"don't be a duffer!"

Chapter Sixteen
The Dandy

Fine feathers make fine birds. This is a proverb which a great many people in our country—especially young people—most devoutly believe in, and they show their belief in a very emphatic way. They rig themselves out in the height of the fashion, no matter how ridiculous it is, or how uncomfortable; they take airs upon themselves which do not properly belong to them; they try to pass for something finer than they are, and if they do not end by being laughed at it is no fault of theirs.

You never saw such a dandy as we had at our school. He rejoiced in the name of Frederick Fop, and seemed possessed of the notion that his dainty person was worthy of the utmost amount of decoration that any one person could bestow upon it. No one objects to a fellow having a good coat and trousers, and a respectable hat; but when it comes to canary-coloured pantaloons, and cuffs up to the finger ends, and collars as high as the ears, and a hat as shiny as a looking-glass, the fellow gets to be rather a nuisance. Indeed, we had just as much objection to walking out with Fred Fop as we had with Jack Sloven; one was quite as unpleasantly conspicuous as the other.

It was often a marvel to some of us how it came to be allowed for a boy to dress as Fred did. You should have seen him coming down the stairs on Sunday, as we were about to start for church, putting on a lavender glove, and taking a couple of minutes to adjust his hat to the proper angle on his head.

How he minced along the pavement, dreading to speck his exquisite boots, and how artlessly he would carry one glove in his hand, in order to show off his elegant ring. His umbrella was the size of an ordinary young lady's parasol, and as for his collars—of course it was impossible to turn his head one way or the other with those things sticking up on either side. He always insisted on having the inside of the pavement, in order to avoid the splashing of the cabs; and invariably entered church last, having occupied a certain time in the porch (so it was said) to make sure his necktie was properly tied, and that the corner of his handkerchief was hanging sufficiently far out of his breast-pocket, and that the expression of his countenance was sufficiently interesting. Having satisfied himself on these points, he advanced up the aisle in procession with himself, and scented the whole building in his triumphal progress.

It is hardly to be wondered at that Master Fop became the victim of all sorts of practical jokes. If by any chance one of the fellows should happen to be pitching water out of the window, it was an extraordinary coincidence that Fred in his grand hat was nearly always walking underneath. Another time, when some of the elder boys were allowed to attend a grand concert in the village, Fred of course was in his glory, and took every means to create a sensation by his elaborate toilet. And so he did! For as he sauntered beautifully up the hall to his seat in front, he was wholly unconscious that a startling label was hanging gracefully on the back buttons of his coat with this legend inscribed thereon—

"Look here! Our noted 50 shilling suit! A bargain!"

It was not till he went to sit down that he discovered the heartless joke, and then—but we may as well draw a veil over his confusion. Suffice it to say he did not enjoy the concert a bit.

But he was by no means cured of his vanity. No, not even by a subsequent and still more embarrassing adventure.

Several of the boys, among whom were Fred and Jack Sloven, were one day down at the river bathing, when a sudden thought seized certain of Fred's tormentors to play him a very unkind trick. So while he was swimming by himself some distance off, they scuttled ashore and made off, taking with them Jack Sloven dressed up in Fred's clothes, and, of course, leaving that disreputable young gentleman's garments behind for the dandy. They made home as fast as they could, and Jack, as quickly as possible, divested himself of his unwonted finery, and put on another of his own suits. Then the conspirators assembled in the playground with as many of us as had heard what was going on, and awaited the return of poor Fred. He was a long time coming, and before he arrived the head master and two ladies had appeared on the scene.

But the end came to our suspense at last, and we saw our hero march home in state. Such a spectacle you never saw! being rather tall, Sam's greasy and ink-stained breeches came down only half-way below his knees, and fitted as tight as gloves. The elegant wrists, usually shrouded beneath their snowy cuffs, now stuck out like skewers from two very short, very tight, and very shabby sleeves. Fred had not attempted to don the shirt and collar which had been left for him, and it was pretty evident by the way he shivered that if any one had unbuttoned the coat and grimy waistcoat he would not have discovered much more in the shape of vestments. But he had Jack's great muddy boots on, and his disgracefully caved-in hat. In this guise he had to perambulate the village, and now, worst of all, he found himself face to face not only with a whole body of his schoolfellows, but with the doctor and two ladies!

If the whole scene had not been so ludicrous, one would have felt sympathy for the poor fellow; as it was, every one burst out laughing the moment he appeared. Even the doctor had to turn suddenly and walk towards the house.

But we heard of the affair again presently; for the doctor always visited severely any act of unkindness done even in joke, and the offenders in this case were duly punished. To his credit be it said, Fred did not exult over his vindication; the only revenge he took was when he had arrayed himself once more in his usual faultless get-up. He came down to the schoolroom where we were all assembled, and walking up to Jack Sloven, drawled out in a voice which everybody could hear, "Oh, you'll find your things in the bath-room—all but your shirt. I really couldn't touch *that*, so it's lying on the river bank still, where you left it!"

There is one peculiarity about dandies. They are hardly ever persons of great minds. When the exquisite, on being asked how on earth he came by the wonderful necktie he had got on, replied, "Well, you see, I gave my whole mind to it!" he probably spoke the truth. But then you know a mind that exhausts all its energy in the production of a "choker," however remarkable, cannot be a great one.

I should be sorry to hurt any one's feelings, but it is nevertheless a fact that an unhealthy craving after finery is very often a symptom of something not very far short of idiocy. I do not mean to say Fred Fop was an idiot. He had a certain amount of sense; but he would have had a vast deal more if he had not given so much of his mind to the decoration of his person. And with it all he never succeeded, at school at any rate, in passing himself off for any one more important than he was. It is as much a sign of being no gentleman to over-dress as to dress like a sloven, but, as in every other case, the secret is to find the golden mean. I have often seen working-men dressed in a more gentlemanly way than certain gorgeous snobs of my acquaintance; not that their clothes were grander or cost more, but because they were *neat*. That really is the secret. It always seems to me a sign of a man being well dressed when one never notices how he is dressed at all. If he were badly dressed, or if he were over-dressed, one would notice it; and it is a sure sign of his having hit the happy mean when his dress leaves no impression on your mind at all.

But I am not going to set up as a tailor, and so I will bring this paper to a close with this one piece of advice; when there is nothing else left to think about, then by all means let us give our whole mind to the cut of our coats.

Chapter Seventeen
The Growler

Who doesn't know Growler, of our school? He was a sort of fellow nothing and nobody could satisfy. If Growler were a week in an African desert without a drop of water to drink, and some one were then to come and offer him a draught, you may depend upon it the fellow would have something to find fault with. The rim of the bowl would be too thick, or there would be a flavour of sand in the water, or the Good Samaritan who held it to his parched lips wouldn't tilt it up exactly when he ought to do so. If his rich uncle were to give him a splendid gold hunter watch and chain, he would growl because there wasn't a seal hanging on the latter. If he were to succeed in getting a third prize, he'd growl because he had not got the second. If he got the second, he'd growl because he had not got the first. And if he should win the first prize of all, then he would growl because there was not a higher one possible. Was ever such a hopeless fellow to have to deal with!

I dare say you have heard the story of the Scotch elder who, on the question being raised what service he could render at the church meetings, replied briskly, "I can always object." Well, Growler's one strong point was his talent for objecting, and gallantly he used it.

He was one of those fellows who think a great deal more about the thorn of the rose than the flower, and who, feeing quite sure that nothing under the sun is perfect, set themselves to discover the imperfections in all things.

I remember once a lot of us had planned a most delightful picnic for a certain holiday. We were to take two boats some miles up the river to a certain little island, where we proposed to land and erect a tent. Each fellow was to bring some contribution to the picnic, which we were to partake of with grand ceremony under the willows. Then we were to have some music, and generally take it easy. Afterwards we were to bathe, and then row some mile or two farther up to the woods, and have a squirrel hunt; and towards evening, after a picnic tea, drift down with the stream in time for the nine o'clock bell. It seemed a perfect plan, and as we sat and discussed it our spirits rose, and we found ourselves already enjoying our picnic in prospect. But presently Growler came into the room, and as he was to be one of the party, we had to go over all the plans again to him. Well, it was too bad! Not a single detail in our programme pleased him.

"Row?" he said; "don't we get enough rowing, without having to give up holidays to it? besides, what's the fun of sitting in a tent, or eating your food among all the wasps and gnats up in that place? You surely aren't going to take that wretched concertina; that'll be enough to give us the blues, even if it doesn't rain, which it's pretty sure to do. I suppose you know the island's about the worst place for bathing—"

"Come, now, old man, it's a first-rate place."

"Well, you may think so; I don't. In fact, I don't see the fun of bathing after dinner at all. You don't expect *me* to make a fool of myself hunting squirrels, do you, in those horrid woods? And you'll have to have tea, as you call it (though you might as well make one meal do for both), jolly early if you expect to drift down here by nine. Why, you won't do it in anything like the time, and fine fun it will be, sitting like dummies in a boat going at a mile an hour."

This was cheerful, and no amount of argument would do away with our desirable friend's objections. The result was, we went, but tried to alter our programme in some points to please him: But he growled all the more, and would not enjoy the day himself, nor let us do so; and our grand picnic, thanks to him, was quite a failure.

It wouldn't have been so bad if the result of Growler's grumblings had been to give us something better in place of what he wanted us to give up. But that is a thing he never did. He could pick holes to any extent, but he couldn't fill them up. There was no scheme or project he couldn't pull to pieces with the utmost industry, but I never remember his originating any scheme of his own to take its place. This was hardly fair. If you take something away from a person, and give him nothing in exchange, it is robbery, and in this respect Growler was an awful thief.

Isn't it true that if you set yourself to it, you could find fault with nearly everything? But in order to do it, you would have to be very selfish in the first place, and very hard-hearted in the next. The dog in the manger is a good type of this happy combination. He trampled on the hay that the cows thought so sweet, and wouldn't touch it himself, and he wouldn't let them touch it either; and that is precisely the charge to which Growler lays himself open. Let us hope he is not quite such a bad sort as this dog. He had got into a regular habit of growling, and it would be against his nature altogether to praise anything cordially.

Supposing Growler to be grown to a man, now; what a desirable creature he must be! What a fine man to get on to a committee, or into parliament! What a delightful partner to have in business! Why, he'd wear out an ordinary man in a month. What complainings, and questionings, and disapprovals, and censures would he ever be loading on the head of his colleagues!—how ready people would be to avoid him and give him a wide berth! For, assuredly, if in anything there was to be found a fault, Growler was the boy to find it. I remember a fairy tale about some folk who wanted to find out if a certain lady were a fairy princess or not; and the way they did it was to lay a pea on the floor of her room, and cover it with twenty feather beds one on the top of the other. Next morning they asked how she slept.

"Not at all," said she, "for there was a dreadful lump in the bed."

Then they knew she must be a fairy! Perhaps it would be a little too much to compare Growler with a fairy; but he certainly had a wonderful knack of discovering peas under the bed; and where there were none to discover, he found out something else. Now, you and I, I expect, in talking of the sun, would speak of it as a glorious light and heat-giving orb, without which we could none of us get on for a moment. But Growler's version of the thing would be quite different.

"A thing full of great ugly spots, that goes scorching up one part of the earth and leaving another in the cold, and is generally hidden by clouds from all the rest."

Such is the genial, bright view of things taken by our old schoolmate.

There are two sorts of growlers. There is the man who honestly attacks what is really wrong for the sake of making it right, and there is the man who instinctively grumbles at everything for the mere sake of growling. The former class is as useful as the latter is tiresome, and if we must growl, by all means let us find out some real grievance to attack. Grumbling is a habit that grows quickly and with very little encouragement, and those who go in for it must make up their minds to have to do with very few friends. For who would consent to be the friend of a growler? It would be as bad as becoming the servant of a man who kept an electrical machine—he would always be trying it on you! And he must be content also to find that very few people sympathise with him. For when a man is a confirmed grumbler at everything, no one afflicts himself much about his lamentations, but puts it all down to his infirmity.

"Poor fellow, his digestion isn't good, or his liver's out of order!" they will say, and think no more about it.

Growler of our school was an able fellow in his way; and successful, too, but he wasn't liked. Some were afraid of him, some detested him, and most cared very little about him. I don't suppose he will ever do much good in the world, for this reason—his influence is so small. One would like to know if he is really as unhappy as he would make every one believe. I have a notion he is not, but is the victim of a habit which he has allowed to grow on him till it is past shaking off. Moral, boys: When you catch yourselves grumbling, make sure the grievance is a real one. If it is, don't be content with grumbling, but follow it up till the wrong is put right. But if you find yourself growling merely because it sounds a fine thing to do, then let growl number one be not only the first but the last performance of the kind; and no one then will be able to growl at you.

Chapter Eighteen
The Bully

There are bullies and bullies. There is the big brother, for instance, who considers it as much part of his duty to administer an occasional cuff to his youthful relative, as he does to stroke his own chin for the first sign of a beard, or to wear his tall hat on Sundays. That is not the sort of bullying any one complains of. Pretty sort of fellows some of us would have turned out if we hadn't come in for a little wholesome knocking about in our day! What's the use of big brothers, we should like to know, if it's not to chastise youngsters! and what are younger brothers made for, if they are not to be occasionally "whopped!"

When I first reached a "bullyable" age, I found myself number three of a set of five boys. I had looked on in awe at the discipline inflicted by my eldest brother on number two; I had been a trembling spectator of scuffles and tears, and pulled ears and sore knuckles, and knew my turn for the same hardships was coming. And so it did. Number one went to college, and then number two was cock of the walk, and didn't I catch it then? The ears that had recently smarted between another's finger and thumb were now deaf to my lamentations, and the knuckles that I had seen bruised and sore now played on my poor countenance as if it had been a tambourine. It wasn't pleasant while it lasted, of course; but then it was all in the regular course of things, and had to be grinned at and borne; and besides it was a splendid training for me, when I came to be left ruler of the roost with young number four at my mercy. Poor number four! he had a hard time of it. He was a meek sort of fellow, and took a lot of bullying. I've a broken-backed lexicon to this day which often used to fly across the room at his devoted head, and which he as regularly picked up and handed back to me.

Never was a czar more absolute than I during the brief years of my supremacy.

But it was monotonous work bullying a fellow who never showed fight; and one day, in reply to a touching lamentation on his part, I demanded, "Why don't you say you won't, then, and stick to it?" Would you believe it? the ungrateful fellow took me at my word! Next time I issued a decree, he made my hair stand on end by shouting, "Shan't!" I could not believe my wits; and when he not only refused, but (in accordance with my own unlucky advice) positively defied me, I was fairly nonplussed! In vain the lexicon performed its airy flight; in vain my ruler flourished over his knuckles; in rain I stormed and raged. No martyr at the stake was ever more sublimely firm; and from that day my reign was over.

It was over as far as he was concerned; but as he resolutely declined to do his duty in knocking about number five, I had to sacrifice myself for the family good, and take that young scamp in hand too, and as he was the youngest, he had nothing to do but wait till he grew up, and then—when he suddenly discovered he was six feet high—he took a turn at bullying me, who by that time was a married man with a family.

Now, perhaps, this sort of bullying within ordinary bounds does no great harm. In our case we almost seemed to like one another the better for it, though each in his turn rent the air with his howls and lamentations. Perhaps, however, we were exceptional boys, and I am not going to recommend the system.

The dog mother who routs up her little pup from his comfortable nap, and shakes him with her teeth, and knocks him down and rolls him over and worries him till he yaps and yelps as if his last day had come, is not such a bully as the cat who holds a mouse under his paw, and plays with it and torments it previous to making a meal of it.

In one case the discipline is salutary and serves a good end; in the other it is sheer cruelty.

Just let me introduce you to a bully of the true sort—one whom we might call a *professional* bully—as contrasted with the *amateur* big-brother bullies of whom I have been speaking.

Bob Bangs of our school was a big, ill-conditioned, lazy, selfish, cross-grained sort of fellow. He was nearly the tallest fellow in the fifth form, but by no means the strongest. He was narrow across the chest, and shaky about the knees, though we youngsters held him too much in awe to take this into account at the time. To the big boys of the sixth form Bob was cringing and snivelling; nothing was too menial, so only as he could keep in their good graces. If he had known how, I dare say he would have blacked their boots or parted their hair; as it was, he laid himself out to fetch and carry, to go and come just as their lordships should direct; and their lordships, I have a notion, winked at one another and gave him plenty to do.

But to us youngsters Bob was wholly different. For one of us to come so much as across his path was sufficient provocation to his spite. Like a spider in its web, he would waylay and capture the wretched small fry of our school and haul them away to his den. There he would screw their arms and kick them, just for the pleasure of seeing their faces and hearing their howls. Generally, indeed, he managed to invent some pretext for his chastisement. This one had made a grimace at him across the room yesterday; that one had spilt some ink on his desk; poor Jack Flighty had had the cheek to laugh outside his door while he was reading; or Joe Tyler had bagged his straw hat instead of his own.

One day, I remember, I, a little unfortunate of ten summers, fell into his awful clutches.

"Come here, you young beggar!" I heard him call out.

I dared not disobey, and stood before him shaking in my shoes.

"What are you laughing at?" he says.

"I'm not laughing," I said, feeling anything but in the humour for jocularity.

"Yes, you are, I tell you—take that!" and a smart box on the ear followed.

I writhed, but tried hard to suppress my ejaculation of pain.

"What's that you called me?" demanded the bully.

"Nothing," I faltered, rubbing my head.

"Yes, you did," he said; "take that for telling a cram, and that for calling me names!" and suiting the action to the word he bestowed one cuff and one kick on my unoffending person, each of which I acknowledged by a howl.

"Now then," said he, "what did you mean by borrowing Tom Groby's *Gulliver's Travels* yesterday when you knew I wanted to read it, eh?"

And he caught hold of my hand and gave my arm a suggestive preliminary screw.

"I didn't," I said.

"Yes, you did," said he, tightening the pressure, so as to make me catch my under lip in my teeth. "You knew well enough I was half through it."

"I mean, I *didn't* borrow it. I never saw the book," I shrieked, truly enough too, for this was clearly a case of mistaken identity.

"Yes, you did, for I was told so."

"I didn't; oh, let me go!" I cried, twisting under the torture; "it wasn't me!"

"I tell you it was;" another screw, and another dance and howl from me; "and what's the use of you saying it wasn't?"

"Indeed it wasn't!" I yelled, for by this time I was on my knees, and half dead with agony. "Oh! You'll break my arm! Oh! Oh!"

"Say you took it, then," replied my tormentor.

"It wasn't me," I shrieked. "Oh! *Yes it was!* Let go!"

Then he let go, and catching me by the collar of my coat with one hand, pulled my ear with the other, saying—

"What do you mean by telling lies, you young cub?"

"I only said I took it," whimpered I, nursing my sore arm, "because you made me."

"Then you mean to say you didn't, do you?" cried the bully, with another grab at my hand.

What would have become of me I don't know, had not a sixth-form fellow come by at that moment, at the sight of whom Master Bangs let go my arm, smiled benevolently on me and cringingly on him, and then slunk away to his den, never to find me again within reach of his ten fingers if I could help it.

It would be hard to say what object Bob had in this conduct. He certainly had not much to gain. Sometimes, indeed, he succeeded in compelling his victims to empty their pockets to him, and hand over the little treasures in the way of eatables, penknives, or india-rubber to which he might take a fancy, but this was comparatively rare. Nor was his bullying actuated by the lofty motive of administering wholesome discipline on his young schoolfellows. In fact, so far from doing them good, he made sneaks and cowards of a good many of them, and, as happened in my case, led them to tell falsehoods in order to escape his clutches.

I should be sorry to think that Bob Bangs was influenced by sheer spite and cruelty of heart, or by a wanton delight in witnessing and contributing to the suffering of others; yet so one was often forced to believe. It is bad enough when one fellow stands by and, without lifting a finger to help, lets another suffer; but when, instead of that, he actually makes himself the instrument of torture, he is nothing short of a brute.

Perhaps, however, it would hardly be fair to say that Bob was quite so bad as this. We are bound to give the worst characters their due; and without attempting to excuse or justify a single blow the Bully ever struck, we must bear in mind this one thing.

There is a certain class of people to whom power becomes a ruling passion. Somebody must be made to feel, and somebody must be brought to acknowledge it. These people are generally those who have the greatest possible aversion to enduring oppression in their own persons, or who have themselves in their time been roughly handled. They love to see others quail before them, as they themselves would be ready to quail before those they hold in awe; and it is no small set-off against their own terrors to feel themselves in turn objects of terror to others. People of this sort are of course generally cowards and toadies, and in bullying they find the fullest gratification of their craving for power.

Bob may sometimes feel a passing pity for the poor little wretch he is tormenting; but until that poor little wretch consents to knuckle under, to apologise, to obey, to accuse himself, in the manner Bob selects, he must not be spared.

Boys who want to understand what real bullying is, should call to mind that parable about the servant who, having quailed and cringed and implored before his lord until he was forgiven his huge debt, forthwith pounced on a poor fellow-servant who happened to owe him a few shillings, and, deaf to the very entreaties which he himself had but a minute before used, haled him off to gaol till the last farthing should be paid.

He was bad enough; but the wolf in Aesop's fable was still worse. The poor lamb there owed nothing; it only chanced to be drinking of the same stream.

"What do you mean by polluting my water?" growls the wolf.

"I am drinking lower down than you," replies the innocent, "and so that cannot be."

"Never mind, you called me names a year ago."

"Please, sir, a year ago I wasn't born."

"Well, then, it was your father, and it's all the same thing; and, what's more, you need not think I'm going to be done out of my breakfast by your talk—so here goes!" And we all know what became of the poor lamb. A gentleman cannot be a bully, and a bully cannot be a gentleman. By gentleman I mean not the vulgar use of the word. The rich snob who keeps his carriages, and counts his income with five or six figures, and considers that sufficient title to the name, may be, and often is, a bully. His servants may lead the lives of dogs, his tradesmen dread the sound of his voice, and his dependants shake in their shoes before him. But a gentleman—a man (or boy) of honour, kindliness, modesty, and sense—could no more be a bully than black could be white.

Bullying is essentially vulgar, and stamps the person who indulges in it as ill-conditioned and stupid. He tries to pass off his lack of brains with bluster, and to make up by tyranny for the contempt which his ill-bred manners would naturally secure for him. But he deceives nobody but himself. The youngsters tremble before him; but they despise him; in a year or two they will laugh at him, and after that—thrash him.

Yes; I am sorry to counsel that physic for anybody, but really it is the only one which can possibly cure the bully. The time must come when the little boy will find himself grown up and possessed of a muscle, and then the bully will find, to his astonishment, that he has tried his art once too often.

So it was with Bob Bangs. He found himself on his back one day with a small army of youngsters executing a war dance round him. He got roughly used, poor fellow, and at last changed his tune from threats to whines, and eventually, with the aid of a few parting kicks, was permitted to depart in peace. And he never tried on bullying with us again, except indeed when he was fortunate enough to get hold of one of us singly in a lonely comer. And even then he generally heard of it afterwards.

But, boys, mind this. There's nothing more likely than that in your struggle for independence you will, if victorious, be tempted to become bullies yourselves. In your anxiety to "pay out" your old enemy, you may forget that you are yourselves falling into the very transgression for which you have chastised him. That would be sad indeed. A boy that can bear malice, and refuse quarter to a fallen foe, is very little different from a bully himself.

Rather be careful to show yourselves Christians and gentlemen, even in the way you rid yourselves of bullies. It is one thing, in self-defence, to right yourself, and it is another to return evil for evil. The best revenge you can have is, instead of dancing on his prostrate body, to set him an example of forbearance and self-control in your own conduct, which shall point him out a surer road to respect and authority than all the bullying in the world could ever give him.

Chapter Nineteen
William the Atheling; or, The Wreck of the "White Ship"

The eager crowd thronged the little Norman seaport of Barfleur. Knights in armour, gay ladies and merry children mingled in the narrow streets which led down to the bustling harbour, in which lay at anchor a gay fleet of ships, decked with pennons and all the marks of festivity and rejoicing. One man's name was on every lip, and in expectation of that man's arrival this brave company lined the seashore and its approaches. Presently was heard a distant trumpet note, and then a clatter of many horses.

"He comes!" shouted the crowd. "Long live our Duke Henry!" And at the shout there appeared the royal troop, with King Henry of England at its head, followed by his sons and daughter and nobles, amid the plaudits of the loyal crowd.

"All bids fair," said the king to one who was near him, as he rode slowly towards the harbour; "the sea is calm and the wind is propitious; an emblem of the happy peace we have concluded with France, and the prosperous years that he before us."

"Long live Henry of England!" shouted the crowd again. With that the troop reached the sunny harbour.

Here ensued all the bustle and confusion of an embarkation. Baggage and horses and armour were transferred speedily from the shore to shipboard. Henry himself inspected the vessel which was to convey him and his household across the sea, while the loyal Norman crowd pressed round, eager to bid their liege good speed on his voyage.

The afternoon was advancing, and the order had already been given to embark, when, through the crowd which thronged King Henry, there struggled forward a man dressed in sailor guise, who advanced and fell on one knee before his sovereign.

"My liege," said he, "a boon for me!"

"Who art thou?" inquired the king.

"My lord duke, Stephen, my father, served thy father, William of Normandy, all his life. He it was who steered the vessel which carried the duke to the conquest of England. Permit me, my lord, a like honour. See where my 'White Ship' waits to receive her captain's noble sovereign."

Henry looked in the direction pointed, and saw the gallant vessel, gleaming like silver with its white poop and oars and sails in the sun; surely as fair a ship as ever crossed the sea.

"Brave son of a brave father," replied the king, "but that my word has been given, and my baggage is already embarked on another's vessel, thy request should not have been in vain. But, to show that I hold thy father's son worthy of his name, see, I entrust to thee my son William, heir to my throne, in all confidence that thou wilt conduct him safely over. Let him go with thee, while I myself do set sail in the vessel I had chosen."

Fitz-Stephen bowed low, and the young Prince William, a lad of eighteen years, stepped forward gaily towards him, and cried—

"Come, comrade! thou shalt find a king's son as good company as his father. In token of which, bid thy brave men feast at my charge with as much to eat and drink as they have a fancy to. Then, when that is done, we will start on our merry voyage."

Almost immediately afterwards King Henry embarked, leaving the Prince William, and two other of his children, Richard and Adela, to follow that same night in the "White Ship."

"Farewell, my father!" shouted the young prince, as the oars of the king's vessel struck the water; "perchance I shall be on the farther side before thee!"

So the king started.

It was late before the merrymakers on board the "White Ship" set their faces seaward. The prince himself had honoured the feast, and bidden every man to fill his cup and drink deep and long. So when about midnight they addressed themselves to the voyage, the rowers splashed wildly with their oars, and the crew pulled at the ropes with unsteady hands.

Far across the calm waters might have been heard the song and the laughter of the two hundred voyagers. In a few hours, thought they, we shall be across, and then will we renew our feast in England.

"Fitz-Stephen!" cried the prince, flushed with wine himself, and in a tone of excitement—"Fitz-Stephen, how far say you is my father's ship before ours?"

"Five leagues," replied the sailor, "or more."

"Then may we not overtake him before the night is past? You know this coast; can we not steer closer in, and so gain on them?"

"My lord," said Fitz-Stephen, "there are many sunken rocks on this coast, which the mariner always avoids by keeping out to sea."

"Talk not to me of rocks on a night when the sea is calm and the wind so gentle it scarce fills the sails, and the moon so clear we can see a mile before us! What say you, my men? Shall we overtake the king? Fitz-Stephen," he added, "thou earnest a king's son to-night. If thou and thy men can set me on English ground before my father, I will never sail more, as long as I live, save in thy ship."

The sailor yielded, and turned his helm nearer to the coast, and the crew, clamouring loudly with excitement, pulled wildly at the oars, while the prince and the nobles, with song and laughter, made the quiet night to resound. So they went for two hours. Then the prince's sister Adela, Countess of Perche, stepped up to him timidly, and said—

"My brother, what sound is that, like the roar of distant thunder?"

"It is nothing, my sister; go down again and sleep."

"It sounds like the breaking of wares on the rocks."

"How can that be, when the sea is scarcely ruffled?"

"I fear me we run a risk, sailing so close to shore," said the maiden. "I myself heard Fitz-Stephen say that the currents ran strong along this coast of Normandy."

"Be easy, sister; no danger can befall a night like this."

Louder and louder rose the shouting and the revelry. The rowers sang as they rowed. And the knights and nobles, who made merry always when the prince made merry, sang too.

But all the while the maiden, as she lay, heard the roar of the breakers sound nearer and nearer, and was ill at ease, fearing some evil.

"Now, my merry men," shouted the prince, "row hard, for the night is getting on!"

Fitz-Stephen at that instant uttered an exclamation of horror, and wildly flung round his helm. There was a sudden roar ahead, and a gleam of long lines of broken water.

"Pull for your lives!" shouted the captain, "or we shall be on the Ras de Catte!"

It was too late. The treacherous current swept them on to the reef. There was a sudden tossing of the "White Ship," then a great shock as she struck— then a cry of terror from two hundred lips.

King Henry in his vessel, three leagues away, heard that sudden awful cry across the still waters. But little guessed he that it was the death cry of his own beloved children.

Every man on board the "White Ship" was startled by that shock into instant sobriety. The brave Fitz-Stephen left the now useless helm, and rushed to where the prince, entrusted to his care, was clinging to the mast of the fast-filling vessel. With his own hand he cut loose the small boat which she carried, and by sheer force placed William in it, and a few of the crew.

"Row for the shore!" he shouted to the men, waving his hand; "lose not a moment!"

William, stupefied and bewildered, sat motionless and speechless.

The men had already dipped their oars, and the frail boat was already clear of the sinking vessel, when there fell on the prince's ear the piercing shriek of a girl.

Looking behind him, he saw his poor sister clinging to the deck of the doomed ship, and stretching a hand appealingly in the direction of his boat.

In an instant his senses returned to him.

"Put back, men!" he cried, frantically.

"It is certain death!" cried one of the crew.

"Must William the Atheling order a thing twice?" thundered the prince, in a tone so terrible, that the men immediately turned and made for the wreck.

"My sister!" shouted William, as they came under the spot where Adela clung; "throw yourself into my arms!"

She did so; but, alas! at the same moment, fifty more, in the desperation of terror, jumped too, and the little boat, with all that were in her, turned over, and was seen no more.

Then the waters poured over the "White Ship," and with a great plunge that gallant vessel went down.

With her went down all the souls she carried save three. One of these was the brave Fitz-Stephen. Rising to the surface, he saw the two others clinging to a spar. Eagerly he swam towards them.

"Is the prince saved?" he asked.

"We have seen nothing of him," replied they.

"Then woe is me!" exclaimed he, as he turned in the water and sank beneath it.

Of the other two, one only, a butcher, survived to carry the dreadful news to England.

For many days, Henry, impatient for his son's arrival, waited in ignorance of his sad fate.

Then went to him a little child, who, instructed what to say, told him in his own artless way the whole story; and King Henry the First, so they say, after he had heard it, was never seen to smile again.

Chapter Twenty
John Plantagenet, the Boy who broke his Father's Heart

A youth was pacing restlessly to and fro in a wood bordering on the old town of Tours, in France. He was scarcely twenty years of age, and of a forbidding countenance. Cruelty and cunning were stamped on his features, and as he strode aimlessly among the trees, muttering to himself, and striking often with his sheathed sword at the bushes and twigs in his path, he seemed to be the victim of an evil passion, with nothing to make a man love him or desire his acquaintance.

His muttering not unfrequently rose to the pitch of talking aloud, when one might have heard sentences like these.

"Why should I longer delay? Am not I John, the son of Henry of England, a man? and shall I submit to be treated for ever as a child? Are my brothers, who have rebelled against their father, to have ah the spoil, and I, who have remained obedient, to go portionless and penniless? What means my father's meeting here with the King of France, who has espoused the cause of Richard, my brother, in his rebellion, if it be not to yield to the traitor the kingdoms *I* have earned by my obedience? But I will delay no longer. I have been obedient too long! Henceforth this sword shall be my obedience!"

And as he spoke he unsheathed his weapon, and struck savagely at the graceful branch of a fir tree before him, and brought it down crashing at his feet. At the same instant there appeared coming towards him a man of middle age, clad like a soldier, who saluted respectfully the young prince.

"Whence come you, Ralph Leroche?" inquired John.

"From the meeting of the Kings of France and England."

"And what went forward there?" asked the prince, leading his companion in among the trees.

"I know only what I am told," said the knight, "for the meeting of your father and King Philip was secret."

"And what have you been told?" inquired John, impatiently, and with clouding brows.

"I have been told that the King of France demanded that your father should do him homage, and should acknowledge your brother Richard as King of England."

"And what said my father?" broke in John.

"He said that Richard, by his conduct, deserved only the death of a traitor, but—"

John's brow darkened as he seized Ralph's arm, and ejaculated, "But what? did he yield? Speak!"

"But for the sake of peace he would receive him back to the heart which he by his disobedience had wellnigh broken, and make him heir to his crown."

"He said so, did he?" almost shouted the prince, his face livid with fury.

"I am told so by one who knows," replied the other.

"And did he say more?"

"He blessed heaven before them all that he had one son left him who was true to him, and in whose love he might end the shattered remnant of his life."

Loud and cruelly laughed Prince John at those words, till the woods echoed again. "Is it thus you comfort yourself, my father?" he exclaimed. "Ralph," added he, in tones thick with passion, "all my life till now I served my father, and never failed in my duty to him. Henry, my brother, rebelled, and died in his rebellion while I was a child. Geoffrey rebelled too, and is dead. Richard for years has been in arms against his parent. I, of all his sons, have never lifted hand against him. Had not I a right to look for my reward? Had not I a right to count upon the crown which my brothers' disobedience had forfeited? Had not—"

He stopped, unable from the vehemence of his passion to proceed, and Ralph Leroche answered calmly: "Obedience is its own reward, and worth more than a kingdom. It is not obedience that calculates on profit. But you know not, prince, what your father may yet have in store for you."

"Speak not to me of my father," exclaimed John; "I hate him!"

"Heaven forgive you that word!" replied the fearless knight. "Be advised, I entreat; and repent—"

"Dotard!" exclaimed the prince, as in blind rage he struck him in the mouth with his clenched fist. "Keep thy advice for dogs, and not for princes!"

How the scene would have ended, one cannot say. At that moment a flourish of trumpets raised the echoes of the wood, and a gay procession passed down the forest road towards Tours.

Alas, for Prince John! He recognised in the two men who rode at its head, Philip of France, his father's enemy, and Richard, his own rebel elder brother. Goaded by passion, burning with resentment towards his father for the supposed injustice he had suffered, he rushed recklessly into the arms of this sudden temptation. Striding through the thickets, and heedless of the warnings of the loyal Ralph, he emerged on to the road in front of the cavalcade.

The leaders halted their horses in sudden surprise.

"What brave lad have we here?" asked Philip, perplexed.

John stepped forward, and answered for himself.

"I am John Plantagenet, once son of the King of England, but now vassal to the King of France!"

Great was the astonishment on every face, and on none more than on those of Philip and Richard.

The latter flushed, half in anger, half in shame, as he exclaimed, "Boy, thou art mad!"

"Nay," said Philip, "the lad is a lad of sense, and bears a worthy name that will serve our cause exceedingly."

So saying, he summoned one of his knights, and bidding him dismount, gave the young prince his horse, and made him ride beside him.

"But tell us, lad," he said, when they had proceeded a little way, "how is it thy father's dutiful and cherished son (for so I have heard him speak of thee) comes thus among the ranks of his foemen, and that at a time like this, when peace has been almost completed?"

"Ask me no questions," replied the prince, gloomily; "I am here because I choose."

And so they rode into Tours.

A few days later, a silent group was standing round the sickbed of the King of England, listening to the broken utterances which fell from the lips of that old and wellnigh worn-out warrior. Those who thus stood round him were his favourite knights and barons, not a few of whom were moved to tears as he spoke.

"I have sinned, and I have had my punishment. My kingdom is gone, and my glory. Henceforward Henry Plantagenet will be the name but of a vanquished and feeble old man. The one whom I loved, and would have forgiven as many times as they had asked forgiveness, have all, save one, left me and turned against me. I am like a man, wrecked and tempest-tossed, clinging for hope to a single spar. Yet I bless Heaven for that. Ruin I can submit to, dishonour I can survive, defeat I can endure, while yet there is one child left to me of whom it can be said, 'He loved his father to the end.' And such a son is John. I charge you all, honour him as you honour me, for though I have sworn to yield the crown of England to his brother, Normandy, and all I possess besides, belongs to *him*. But where is he? Why tarries he? A week has passed since he was here. Where stays he?"

Before any of the attendants could reply, a knocking was heard without, and entrance demanded for the messengers of Philip of France. "We are come," said they, "from our sovereign with the articles of treaty between yourself and him, arranged at your late conference, and which now await your ratification."

Henry motioned to them to proceed to business; and as each article was read—declaring his allegiance to the crown of France and his cession of his own crown to Richard—he inclined his head mechanically in token of his assent, manifesting little or no interest in the proceeding. But his attention became more fixed when the article was read which provided for the free pardon of all who had in any way, secretly or openly, been engaged in the cause of his rebel son.

He turned in his bed towards the reader, and said: "A king must know the names of his enemies before he can pardon them. Read me, therefore, the list of those who have rebelled, that I may forgive them each and all, beginning with the noblest, down to the meanest."

He lay back on his bed, and half closed his eyes as he listened.

The messenger of Philip then said, "The first and foremost of your majesty's enemies is John Plantagenet, your youngest son."

He sprang with a sudden cry of pain into a sitting posture, and trembling in every fibre, and with a voice half choked, cried, "Who says that?" Then glaring wildly at the envoy, he whispered, "Read it again!"

"The first and foremost of your majesty's enemies is John Plantagenet, your youngest son."

"Can it be true?" gasped the poor father, in helpless despair. "Has he also deserted me? Then let everything go as it will; I care no more for myself, nor for the world."

So saying, with his heart broken, he sank back upon the bed, from which he never rose again.

Chapter Twenty One
Arthur of Brittany, the Boy who should have been King of England

The fierce storm beats down on the gloomy Norman Castle of Falaise, in a deep dungeon of which lies imprisoned the boy Prince Arthur, lawful heir to the crown of England, but now, alas! a helpless victim of the cruelty and injustice of his bad uncle, John Plantagenet, the usurper of his throne. The thunder peals so loudly, and the wind rages so angrily, that Hubert de Burgh, the warden, does not for a long time distinguish the sound of a knocking and shouting at the outer gate of the castle. Presently, however, in a lull of the wind, his ears catch the noisy summons, and he instantly gives orders to his men to let down the drawbridge, and admit the new-comers. These were three in number: one attired as a king's messenger, and mounted on a richly caparisoned horse; the other two in the garb of common men, and on foot. When they had come into the presence of the warden, the king's messenger said—

"I am charged by His Majesty King John of England to deliver to you this letter, and require your faithful discharge of its commands."

So saying, he handed to Hubert de Burgh a sealed letter, which the latter eagerly broke open and read. As he read, his face clouded. It was a long letter, and couched in vague terms, but its substance was this. That whereas the peace of England and of King John's possessions in France was constantly being disturbed by the partisans of the young Prince Arthur, desiring to see him king instead of his uncle, and taking up arms to enforce their claim, it was necessary, in order to put an end to this rebellion, that the young prince should be rendered unfit for governing; and as no people would be likely to choose a blind boy for their king, Hubert de Burgh was instructed to have Arthur's eyes put out; and the two men who had arrived with the king's messenger were come, so the letter said, to carry out this design.

Hubert de Burgh said nothing as he put by the letter, and dismissed his three visitors from his presence. Cruel man as he had been, his heart had still some pity left, and he shrank from obeying his master by so brutal an act of cruelty upon the innocent boy in his charge.

However, the order of the king was peremptory; and if the deed must be done, thought he, the sooner the better.

So he ordered the two villains to get ready their instruments, and follow him to the dungeon.

"Stay here," said he, as they reached the young prince's door, "while I enter alone and prepare him for his fate."

So those two set down their fire and the red-hot irons, and waited outside for their summons.

When Hubert entered the dungeon, the poor boy was just waking from a sleep. He sat up and rubbed his eyes, being dazzled by the light which Hubert carried in his hand.

"You are welcome," said he (for Arthur, with so few to love him, loved even his surly, though not unkind, jailor). "I have been in my dreams away in merry England, where I thought I was living in a beautiful palace, with food and servants, and rich clothing, and that there was a crown on my head. And so it shall be some day, Hubert, when I get my rights; and then because you have not been as unkind to me as some in my adversity, you shall be a great and rich man. But why look you so solemn? What ails you?"

The warden stood silent for some moments before he spoke, and then his voice was thick and hoarse.

"Prince," he said, "take your last look on the light, for you may never see it again."

The boy sprang from his bed, and seized Hubert by the knees.

"What! Are they going to kill me? Must they take away my life?"

"Not so," said Hubert; "it is not thy life that is required, but thine eyes." And as he spoke he stamped on the floor, as the signal to those two who waited without to enter.

At sight of their horrid instruments, the cords which were to bind him, and the cruel faces of the executioners, Arthur fell on his knees and implored mercy of the stubborn Hubert.

It was a strange and pitiful sight to see that weak and helpless boy kneeling, and with tears entreating that stout old warrior, whose bosom heaved and whose ringers twitched, and whose face winced, as he listened; while the two others stood motionless, grasping their irons and cords, ready for the word of command to step forward and do their cruel deed.

But the cries and entreaties of the helpless and beautiful prince prevailed. Hubert wavered and hesitated; he bade the men advance, and then bade them withhold; he looked at the prince, and he looked at the glowing irons; he pushed the suppliant from him, and then suffered him to cling to him. The executioners themselves were moved to pity, and lay down their instruments. Finally, with a mighty effort, the warden yielded, and said, "Retire, men, and take with you your tools, till I require you." Then turning to Arthur, he said, "Prince, thou shalt keep thy sight and thy life while I am by to protect thee." And the rough hand of the old warrior stroked the hair of the weeping boy as it might have been his own son's.

The answer that Hubert de Burgh sent back that day by the king's messenger was an earnest appeal for mercy on behalf of his young and now beloved charge.

But King John was a stranger to all feelings of pity, and his vengeance was quick and dreadful. Foiled of his cruel design upon the eyesight of his hapless nephew, he determined now to have his life. So he ordered him to be removed from Falaise, and the custody of the humane De Burgh, to the castle of Rouen, under whose walls flowed the waters of the River Seine. But the prince did not remain long there. One night a jailor entered his dungeon, and, waking him from his sleep, ordered him to follow him. The boy obeyed in silence, as the jailor conducted him down the winding staircase which led to the foot of the tower, beside which the Seine flowed. A boat was waiting at the bottom, in which sat two men. The torch of the jailor cast a sudden glare over the dark waters, and by its light Arthur recognised, with horror and despair, in one of the two the cruel features of his Uncle John. It was useless for him to pray and entreat; it was useless for him to struggle or cry out. They dragged him into the boat, and held him fast as she drifted under the shadow of those gloomy walls into mid stream. What happened then no one can tell; but had any listened that still, dark night, they might have heard a boy's wild cry across the waters, and then a dull, heavy splash—and that was all.

The story is that of those two, King John with his own hand did the foul deed. However that may be, Arthur of Brittany was never even heard of more.

Chapter Twenty Two
Richard the Second, the Boy
who quelled a Tumult

A vast, disorderly rabble thronged the great open space of Smithfield, in London, on one side of which stood the venerable Abbey of Saint Bartholomew, now occupied by the hospital of that name. The men who composed it were rough and wild, and, for the most part, shouted and clutched their clubs and bows in a meaningless sort of way, which plainly showed that they were not very clear in their own minds as to the object of their assembling together, but that they came and shouted and threatened because their leaders did so.

These leaders were few in number, and but that they were mounted, and armed with swords and daggers, not to be distinguished from their followers, for they were rough, wild men—men too whose occupation seemed to be more in the way of herding cattle and plying their hammers than leading an army of 20,000 rioters, or brandishing their swords against a government.

Yet, though many of these rebels seemed not to comprehend the why and the wherefore of their demonstration, there were not a few who looked very much—nay, cruelly—in earnest, who talked vehemently and scowled, and seemed, by the way they gripped their arms, determined to enforce their demands against any man, be he noble, or baron, or king. From some of the groups one might have heard excited utterances like the following:—

"We will have our rights or die! Why do our leaders halt?"

"The king is expected!"

"Nay, then, let us slay him, who is the head of all our wrongs!"

"Not so; the king has already granted what we first demanded; and we are gathered now because Wat Tyler demands yet more."

"God save Wat Tyler! Was it not he who struck the first blow against the tyrant?"

"It was. The nobles demanded a poll tax on every man, woman, boy, and girl in the land; and when one of their collectors would exact it from Wat Tyler, at his place in Dartford, and (disbelieving his word concerning the age of his young daughter) vilely insulted the maiden, he arose and slew the wretch with his hammer. And so this business began."

"Huzzah for Wat Tyler! Down with the tyrant!"

"Nay, friend; our cause was a good one when it began, but since then Wat and his friends have, to my mind, done us and themselves damage by their bloodthirstiness and their unreasonableness. Have they not demolished palaces and temples? Have they not butchered an archbishop and nobles and harmless citizens? Have they not insulted noble ladies? And now, when their demands have all been satisfied by the young king, they demand yet more, and become themselves the tyrants."

"A traitor!—a traitor! Who speaks against our brave Wat Tyler? Kill the traitor! Down with tyranny! Death to the king! God save the people!"

With such clamour and angry talk did the crowd agitate itself, till suddenly there arose a cry. "The king comes!"

And there rode up fearlessly, at the head of sixty men, a boy, only fifteen years old, at sight of whom these rebels hung their heads and let their wild clamour die on their lips. A few of the most determined looked black as they regarded the royal boy, and noted the effect his frank carriage had on their followers.

"I am come," said King Richard, rising on his horse at a few paces from the front of the crowd, "as I promised, to confer with my subjects and hear their grievances. Let your leader advance and speak with me."

Then Wat Tyler turned to his followers and said to them, "I will go speak with him; do you abide my signal, then come on and slay all save the young king; he will serve us better as a humble captive in our hands, to lead through the land and bring all men to our service, than as a slaughtered tyrant at our feet."

So he put spurs to his horse and advanced towards the king, whom he approached so close that the flank of the horse touched that of the king's. Richard, nothing daunted by this threatening demeanour, turned courteously towards him and waited for him to speak.

"Do you see this concourse of people?" began Wat, rudely, pointing towards the now silent crowd.

"I see them," said the boy. "What have you to ask on their behalf?"

"These men," said Tyler, "have sworn, one and all, to obey me in all things, and to follow in whatever enterprise I shall lead them, and they will not go hence till you grant us our petition."

"And I will grant it," replied the boy, frankly, for the demands to which Wat Tyler now alluded had reference to the rights of the people to hunt and fish on common lands. "I will grant it."

What followed history does not very clearly record. Among the followers of the king, Wat, it is said, caught sight of a knight whom for some reason he hated. Turning his attention from the king, he glared angrily at his enemy, and, putting his hand on the hilt of his dagger, exclaimed, "By my faith, I will never eat bread till I have thy head!" At that same instant up rode Sir William Walworth, the Lord Mayor of London, who, seeing the menacing gesture of the insurgent leader, and hearing his threatening speech, immediately concluded he was about to attack the person of the young king. Quick as thought, Sir William drew his dagger, and before any one could interpose or hold him back, he struck Wat Tyler in the throat, and his attendants following with repeated blows, the leader of the people fell from his horse a dead man! All this was so suddenly done, and so astonished the onlookers, that Wat Tyler was already dead before a hand was moved or a voice raised on either side. Then there rose an angry shout from those twenty thousand rebels, as they saw their leader down. "We are betrayed!" they cried; "they have killed our leader!" And with that they raised their bows and pointed their shafts at the heart of the young king.

But they lowered them in amazement when, instead of shrinking and cowering behind his knights, they saw the lad put spurs to his horse and gallop, all by himself, up to the very place where they stood. "Men," he cried, "follow me; I am your king, and I will be your captain! Wat Tyler was a traitor; no ill shall befall you if you make me your leader."

The brave words disarmed that great crowd as if by magic; the men who had just now shouted, "Long live Wat Tyler!" now shouted with a mighty shout, "Long live our King Richard!"

The insurrection was at an end, the confidence of the people returned once more to their rulers, and they marched that day from Smithfield, under the leadership of their young king, as far as the country hamlet of Islington, there quietly to disperse to their own homes and resume once again their ordinary pursuits.

Chapter Twenty Three
Richard Whittington, the Scullery Boy who became Lord Mayor

A poor boy, meanly clad, and carrying in his hand a small bundle, trudged sadly along the road which led over the moor of Finsbury to Highgate. The first streak of dawn was scarcely visible in the eastern sky, and as he walked, the boy shivered in the chill morning air. More than once he dashed from his eyes the rising tears, and clutched his little wallet and quickened his pace, as if determined to hold to some desperate resolve, despite of all drawings to the contrary. As the road rose gradually towards Highgate, the sun broke out from behind the clouds on his right, and lit up fields and trees and hills with a brightness and richness which contrasted strangely with the gloom on the boy's face, and the poverty of his appearance. The birds in the hedges began to sing, and the cattle to low and tinkle their bells; the whistle of the herdsmen came up from the valley, and all nature seemed to wake with a cry of gladness to greet the new day.

Even poor Dick Whittington could not wholly resist the cheering influence of that bright summer morning. It was impossible to believe that everything was miserable in the midst of so much gladness, and Dick's face brightened and his step became brisker almost without his knowing it, as he trudged higher and higher up that steep road. His thoughts, too, took a less desponding turn.

"After all," said he to himself, "perhaps I am foolish to be running away from my master's house. I had better be the scullery boy of good Master Fitzwarren, although his cook does ill-treat me and lead me a dog's life, than the vagabond idle boy which I am now. And yet I cannot endure the thought of returning to that cruel woman. Would that I knew what to do!"

Thus he thought and questioned with himself, when he came to a stone set by the wayside; and here he sat to rest, and ruminate further upon his evil fortune.

"If some voice would but say 'Return,' I would return," said he, "even though she scold and beat me, for I know not what to do, without a friend in the world. Was ever such a wretched boy as I?"

And he buried his face in his hands and gave himself over to his misery. Suddenly in the quiet morning air there came to his ears a wonderful sound, up from the valley, where, in the sun, shone the towers and steeples of London town.

It was the sound of distant bells, and as the boy listened, it came clearer and clearer, and seemed to fill the air with the very voice for which he had but a minute since been longing. But what a strange voice and what a strange story the bells told! —

Turn again, Whittington, Thrice Lord Mayor of London!

Over and over again they said the same words. Over and over again Dick persuaded himself he was dreaming, yet felt sure he was awake. "Turn again!" that was plain enough, and he could believe it, even though Bow Bells said it. But—"Thrice Lord Mayor of London!" what could that mean? That was never meant for the poor ill-used scullery boy of Master Fitzwarren, the mercer in the Minories! And yet what could be more distinct than the voice of those bells?

He sprang from his seat, turned his face in the direction of that wonderful sound, and ran. And that morning, when the family of Master Fitzwarren assembled for their early meal, and the scolding cook took possession of the kitchen, Dick Whittington was in his place, scouring the pots and pans in the scullery, singing to himself a tune no one had ever heard before.

Only a few days after this adventure of Dick's, news came of the arrival in port of one of Master Fitzwarren's vessels with a valuable cargo on board. Now it was the custom in those days, in some houses, for all the servants of a family to invest something in the fortunes of any vessel their master might send out; and when, many months before this, Master Fitzwarren had been equipping the vessel now in question, he had summoned all his servants together, and beginning with the chief, had called upon them to put their savings into his venture, promising each a fair return of whatever profit his share should entitle him to at the end of the voyage.

Dick, poor boy, had no money; nothing in the world but a cat, whom he loved as his only friend, and to whom he owed no common gratitude for the manner in which she had protected him against the rats that infested his garret. When it came to his turn to put his share into the voyage, he had not the heart to offer this companion—and he had nothing else he could call his own—so he begged to be excused. His master, however, insisted that, as his servant, he must put down whatever he had, however little, and even though this cat had cost only a penny, to sea she must go, and Dick should have full value for her when the voyage was over.

Dick wept at this, and the young daughter of Master Fitzwarren, being moved to pity, offered from her own money what would preserve to the lad his four-footed friend. But not even this would the stern merchant allow, and Dick therefore had to bid a tearful farewell to his favourite, and resign himself to his loss.

All this had taken place many months ago.

Now when the "Unicorn"—that was the name of the vessel—returned to port, great was the astonishment of everybody (and no one's greater than Dick's) to find that the principal portion of the treasures on board belonged to the little scullery boy of Master Fitzwarren.

The very first day of its arrival there was brought to the house a cabinet of jewels, forming part of the boy's share, which was considered too precious to be left on board ship. And the men who brought it told this marvellous story:

When the ship reached Algiers, in Africa, the ruler of the land ordered all the crew to wait upon him with presents, which accordingly they did, after which he prepared a feast, and invited them all to partake. But no sooner were the covers removed then a swarm of rats, attracted by the scent of the good things, came and devoured all the victuals before their very faces. This, the governor told them, was no unusual thing, for rats were the plague of his land, and he would give any price to know of a means to be rid of them. Then one of the sailors bethought him of Dick Whittington's cat—who had already distinguished herself on shipboard by her industry in her art—and accordingly next day, when the feast was served, and the rats, as usual, prepared to make away with it, puss was produced, and not only drove away the pest, but killed a considerable number. This happening for several days, his highness was so delighted that he instantly offered an enormous sum for the possession of so remarkable an animal, and loaded the crew with presents, in token of his joy and gratitude.

Such was the story of the men, which explained this wonderful prize which fell to the share of the fortunate Dick Whittington.

He, poor lad, could not understand it all, and went on with his drudgery in the scullery as if nothing had happened, until his master compelled him to quit it, and from being his boy-of-all-work made him his partner in business.

Then Dick remembered the words the bells had sung to him a while ago, and rejoiced that he had obeyed their call.

He rejoiced at another thing too, which was that the kind young daughter of Master Fitzwarren, who had pitied him in his poverty, did not avoid him in his prosperity, but smiled happily upon him when he took his seat at the family table to eat out of the dishes he had so recently scoured.

So this scullery boy became a rich merchant, and being just and honourable as well as wealthy, he gained the respect and love of all with whom he had to do. When he grew to be a man, he married the kind Miss Fitzwarren, which made him happier than all his wealth.

Not only did merchants look up to him, but nobles and even kings came to him in their money difficulties, and he was the same upright gentleman to all men. Honours increased, and at last the prophecy of Bow Bells came true, and Sir Richard Whittington was made Lord Mayor of London.

In that capacity he grew still in riches and fame; and when his first term was expired, his admiring fellow-citizens, after a few years, made him Lord Mayor for a second time, and when the second term was past, for a third. His third mayoralty happened in 1419, when King Henry the Fourth was on the throne of England; and then it was his honours rose to their highest pitch, for he entertained at his own table the king and queen of the land in such grand style that Henry said of him, "Never king had such a subject."

And never poor had such a friend. He never forgot the little forlorn boy on Highgate Hill, and it was his delight to his latest day to make the hearts of the needy glad, and show to all that it is not for money nor grandeur but for an honest soul and a kind heart that a man is to be loved and honoured by his fellows.

Chapter Twenty Four
Edward the Black Prince, the
Boy who won a Battle

The sun rose brightly over the little village of Creçy on the morning of Saturday, August 26, 1346. The golden corn was standing in the fields, the cattle were quietly grazing in the meadows, the birds were twittering in the woods, and in the still morning air rose the gentle murmur of a joyous stream. Everything spoke of peace that bright summer morning; little could one have dreamed that before that sun should have set in the west the din and thunder of battle would wake the echoes of those quiet woods, or that those sunny fields would be torn and desolated by the angry tread of thousands of feet, or strewn with heaps of dead or dying! Yet so it was to be. A large army was even then halting in the cover of the forest over against the village, and far, far away, if any one had listened, might have been heard, mingling with the voices of the morning, the sound of a great host of horsemen and soldiers advancing in hot pursuit, with now and then a trumpet blast which echoed faintly among the hills.

The English soldiers, as they rose from their beds of turf and grass, heard those far-off sounds, and knew—who better?—they must fight like men to-day or perish.

So they sprang to their feet and seized their arms and armour, ready at any instant to obey the summons to action.

Suddenly along the ranks came the cry, "The king and the prince!" and directly afterwards appeared the great King Edward the Third of England riding slowly down the line of his army, and at his side a stately boy of sixteen years, dressed in black armour and mounted on a black horse. Never was king more honoured or king's son more loved than were these two as they passed with cheery word and dauntless bearing among their loyal and devoted soldiers.

The king stopped when he had reached a spot from which a good portion of his host could hear him, and raised his hand.

Every man stood silent as he spoke.

"My loyal subjects, we must meet to-day a host greater than we in number, but not greater in valour. Fight, I charge you, for the honour of your country. My son here leads the first division of my army. This is his first battle, and sure I am he will quit himself like a man. Do you the same, and God will give us the victory."

With such encouraging and confident words the king addressed his men, who cheered him and the brave prince long and loud.

Then every man took his helmet and his bow, and waited for the enemy.

The morning passed, but still no foe appeared. But the distant murmur was now grown to a loud and ever-increasing din; and as they sat the English could hear shouts and the neighing of horses and the tumult of many voices, which betokened the near approach of the host of King Philip of France.

It was not till about three in the afternoon that the French army came in sight of Creçy. They had had a rapid and fatiguing march since daybreak, and were now in no condition, even with their vastly superior numbers, to grapple with the refreshed and inspirited Englishmen. So thought and said many of Philip's officers, and did their best to persuade him to put off the encounter till next day.

But however much Philip might have been inclined to adopt this good advice, his army was in such a state of confusion and disorder, owing to their rapid march, that they were quite unmanageable. When the officers bade those in front to halt, those behind, shouting and impatient, still pressed on, so much so that the king and all his nobles were carried along with them into the very face of the English, who stood awaiting the attack.

When Philip saw the collision could not be put off, that the battle was inevitable, he shouted loudly, "Bring forward the Genoese bowmen!"

Now these bowmen, 15,000 in number, on whom Philip depended to scatter and drive from the field the main portion of his enemy's force, were in no sort of condition for beginning a battle after their long, fatiguing march, and with the strings of their crossbows all loose with damp, and with a dazzling sun now glaring full in their eyes. But Philip, too confident to heed any such trifles, impatiently, nay, angrily, ordered them to the front, and bade them shoot a volley against the English archers, who stood opposite.

So these foreigners stepped forward, and, as their manner was, gave three leaps in the air, with the idea of terrifying the foes, and then raised their bows to their cheeks, and let fly their arrows wildly in the direction of the English.

The trusty English archers, with the sun behind them, were not the men to be intimidated by leapings into the air, nor panic-struck by a discharge so ill-aimed that scarce one arrow in ten even grazed their armour.

Their reply to the Genoese was a sudden step forward, and a sharp, determined twang of their bow-strings. Then the air was white with the cloud of their arrows, and next moment the foremost ranks of the Genoese were seen to drop like one man.

This was enough for those already dispirited hirelings. They fell back in panic disorder; they cut their bow-strings; they rushed among the very feet of the horsemen that Philip, in his rage, had ordered "to ride forward and cut down the cowardly villains!" Then the confusion of the French army was complete.

The English followed up their first advantage steadily and quickly. Knight after knight of the French dropped from his horse, troop after troop fell back, standard after standard tottered.

Nowhere was the fight fiercer than where the young Black Prince led the van of the English; and from a windmill on a near hill, the eager eyes of King Edward watched with pride that figure clad in black armour ever in the thick of the fight, and never halting an instant where danger or duty called.

It would be too long to tell of all the fighting that day. Philip, with his great army, could not dislodge his compact foe from their position; nor could he shelter his men from the deadly flight of their arrows. Bravely he rushed himself into the fray to rally his men, but to no avail. Everywhere they fell back before their invincible enemy.

Once, indeed, it seemed as if his brave knights would surround and drive back the division of which the boy prince was leader. An English noble sent post-haste a message to Edward to say, "Send help; the prince is in danger."

But Edward knew more of battles than most of his officers. He replied coolly—

"Is the prince slain?"

"No."

"Is he wounded?"

"No."

"Is he struck down?"

"No."

"Then go, tell him the battle he has won so far shall be his, and his only. To-day he must win his own spurs."

The words flew like wildfire among the English ranks, and our brave men fought with renewed valour.

That evening, as the sun was getting low in the west, Philip and his host turned their backs on Creçy and fled—all that were left of them—anywhere to be out of the reach of the army of that invincible boy. Horsemen and footmen, bag and baggage, they fled, with the English close at their heels, and never drew rein till night and darkness put an end to the pursuit.

Meanwhile, there were rejoicing and thanksgiving on the field of Creçy. The English king hastened from his post of observation, and, in the presence of the whole army, embraced his brave son, and gave him the honours of that glorious victory, wherein two kings, eleven princes, 1,200 knights, and 30,000 men had fallen. A sad price for glory! "Sweet son," said he, "God give you good perseverance. You are my true and valiant son, and have this day shown yourself worthy of a crown."

And the brave boy bowed low before his father, and modestly disclaimed the whole glory of the victory.

Loud and long did the loyal knights and soldiers cheer their brave king and their heroic prince; and when they saw the latter bind on his helmet the plume of three ostrich feathers, worn by the most illustrious of his slain foemen, John, King of Bohemia, with the noble motto *Ich dien* ("I serve") beneath, their enthusiasm knew no bounds. And the motto has descended from prince to prince since then, and remains to this day as a glorious memorial of this famous boy, who earned it by doing his duty in the face of danger, and setting an example to all about him that "he who serves rules."

Chapter Twenty Five
Henry of Monmouth, the Prince whom a Judge sent to Prison

A strange crowd thronged the Court of King's Bench one memorable day four and a half centuries ago. Nobles and commoners alike jostled their way into the sombre hall, every one intent on securing a good place, some talking loudly, others arguing angrily, all highly excited and impatient. It was evident that the trial about to take place was one of unusual interest and extraordinary importance, for the gloomy court was not used to be so crowded, and seldom attracted so mixed and so eager a throng as that which now filled it.

Suddenly a lull fell on the scene, heads were uncovered, the jostling and wrangling ceased, and order prevailed.

The judge, Lord Justice Gascoigne, entered and took his seat. He was a grave, quiet man, but there was something in his look so dignified and so firm, that it awed into respectful silence all within that place as if by a spell. Then he said—"Bring hither the prisoner."

All eyes turned now to the door by which the officer of the court went out to obey the order.

Presently it swung back, and there entered, between two jailors, a man of dissipated appearance and reckless demeanour, whose flushed cheeks and extravagant attire told only too plainly their own sad tale of intemperance and debauchery.

He regarded with an indifferent look judge, jury, and the crowd which his trial had drawn together, and took his place at the bar rather with the air of a man harassed and ill-used than of one guilty and overawed.

The trial began. The story of the man's crime was a short and simple one. He had been ringleader in a highway robbery lately committed, and taken in the very act, with the booty upon his person. The evidence was clear as daylight; no one attempted to dispute it or deny the accusation.

Was this, then, all that had brought the assembly together? The man was of a name known to comparatively few of those present. His crime was an ordinary felony, and his defence appeared to be hopeless. It was evidently something else than this for which these onlookers had crowded into court, and it was not long before their curiosity was satisfied.

A witness stood forward to be questioned as to the associates of the prisoner. He gave several names, and then stopped.

"Have no others joined him in these expeditions?" inquired the judge.

The witness hesitated.

"The law requires that you shall tell the whole truth," calmly said the judge. "Have no others joined the prisoner in these expeditions?"

Then the truth came out.

"The Prince Henry of Wales has borne the prisoner company on divers occasions."

What! A Prince of Wales, the coming King of England, implicated in a disgraceful, discreditable highway robbery! Though the crowd had heard of it already, a buzz of astonishment passed through their midst, as the fact was thus clearly and indisputably established.

"Was the prince concerned in the robbery for which the prisoner is now charged?"

Witness could not say.

In reply to further questions, however, it was stated that the prince frequently formed one of the party which indulged in these illegal practices; that he was as lawless and desperate as the worst of them; and that he was known to boast among his boon companions of his exploits as a common highwayman, and to exhibit proudly the plunder he had thus acquired.

It was enough. The judge reminded the court that they were met to try, not the prince, but the prisoner at the bar; and painful as the fact was, it was no affair of theirs at that time to investigate the conduct of another man, except in as far as it threw light on the present case.

The good judge was not the only man in England who had watched the dissipated career of the young prince with sorrow and concern. All to whom the honour of their country was dear bewailed the wasted youth and misused talents of this boy, whom his father's jealousy and illiberality had driven into courses of riot and debauchery. They longed for the time to come, ere it was too late, when the serious duties of the camp or the throne would call out those better traits of his disposition which at present lay hidden beneath what was discreditable and wretched. They saw in him a nobility disfigured and a chivalry marred, still capable of asserting itself, but which as yet every rebuke and every warning had failed to arouse; and on this account the good people of England sorrowed with a jealous sorrow over their "Prince Hal," and looked forward with trembling to see how all this would end.

But to return. The case against the prisoner was full and complete, and nothing now remained but to pronounce him guilty, and sentence him to the penalty his crime required. This duty the judge was proceeding to discharge, when at the door of the court was heard a commotion. For a moment the judge's words were drowned in the shuffling of feet and the sound of voices; then the door opened, and in walked a youth, scarcely more than a boy, tall, slender, and handsome, with flushed cheeks and wild eye, fashionably dressed, with a sword at his side and a plumed hat upon his head.

"The Prince of Wales!" broke from the lips of a score of onlookers, as they recognised in that youth the heir to the crown, towards whose delinquencies their thoughts had that moment been turned.

He advanced gaily and recklessly to the bench, the crowd falling back on either side to give him passage. As he passed the bar at which the prisoner stood awaiting his sentence, he stopped, and, nodding familiarly, exclaimed—

"What ho, comrade! I heard thou wast in trouble, and have come myself to ease thee; so cheer up, lad!" Then approaching the judge, he said, "Good Master Gascoigne, your prisoner is a friend of mine, too gay a comrade to languish in bonds for a trifling scrape like this. Spare yourself, therefore, further pains on his account, and come, solace your gravity with a party of boon companions who assemble to-night to celebrate their hero's emancipation from your clutches!"

Gravely and sorrowfully the judge regarded the prince who thus flippantly defied the law of which he was the guardian, but his face was firm and his voice authoritative as he replied—

"Prince, my duty is to defend the laws of the king, your father, not to break them. As you entered, I was passing the sentence of imprisonment on the prisoner which he has merited by his evil deeds. That sentence must now be put in force."

Prince Henry's face clouded, and he scowled as he exclaimed—

"What I would you defy the Prince of Wales to his very face? Liberate my comrade, I charge you, at once, or it shall be the worse for you!"

"Be warned, prince. They who obstruct the law incur the penalties of the law, be they princes or peasants. Officers, remove the prisoner."

Henry flushed angrily, and his eyes glared like fire. Advancing a step, he laid his hand on the hilt of his sword, and drew it from its scabbard.

The judge rose quietly to his feet, and laying his hand gently on the foolish boy's shoulder, said, in a voice calm and clear, which all could hear—

"Henry, Prince of Wales, I arrest thee in the name of the king, your father, whose laws you have defied, and whose court you have insulted! Officers, remove the prince in custody."

There was a strange and solemn pause as the judge resumed his seat, and all eyes turned on Henry. The firmness of the judge had touched the right chord at last. The sword dropped back into its sheath, the scowl of passion gave place to the flush of shame, the wild eyes sought the ground, and the haughty head hung down in confusion. Without a word he submitted to the officers of the court, and accompanied them to the place of his confinement, humble and repentant.

Years after this a gay throng of courtiers were assembled at court to do homage to King Henry the Fifth of England on his accession to the throne. There were there princes and nobles and ladies—some the friends of the late king, some the friends of the new. In the faces of not a few of the former might be detected traces of uneasiness and anxiety; while the latter talked and looked, for the most part, confident and triumphant. It was easy to guess the cause of this strange variety of feeling. The gay young reveller was now king. There were some there who had made no secret of their disapproval of his wild courses as a prince. How would he regard them now the crown was on his head? Others there were who had borne him company in his excesses, drinking from the same bowl, and sharing in all the lawlessness of his lawless youth. Was not the time for their advancement come, now that the fountain of honour was in the person of their own boon companion and comrade?

Amid waving and acclamation, the young king stepped into the presence chamber to receive the homage of his subjects.

In general appearance he was not much changed from the tall, handsome youth who, a few years ago, had openly defied the law and insulted its dignity; but the more serious expression of his face, and the more sedate pose of his lips, betokened an inward change of no small importance. And now that the whole court was eagerly looking for some indication of his conduct under the new honours and duties which had this day devolved upon him, he was not long in satisfying their curiosity in a decided and significant manner.

Glancing for a moment among the gay throng which surrounded him, his eye lit on a grave, dignified man, with clear eye and firm mouth, now advanced in years, and clad in the robes of a judge.

King Henry stepped towards him, and, with a friendly smile, took him by the hand.

"Good Master Gascoigne," he said, "I know you of old. What my father said of you, let me say too, in the hearing of all these people. *Happy is the king that has such a man who dares to execute justice even on the king's son.* You did well by me when you once committed me to prison; you shall still be my councillor and the trusted guardian of my laws."

The judge bowed low as he replied, "My lord, your father added yet another word to that you have yourself recalled. *Happy,* said he, *the king that has such a son, who will submit even his princely self to the hand of justice.*"

And a tear stood in the grave man's eye as he kissed the hand of him who had once been his prisoner, but was now his king and his friend.

Chapter Twenty Six
Lambert Simnel, the Baker's Boy
who pretended to be a King

A scene of unwonted excitement was being enacted in Dublin. The streets were thronged with people, the houses were gay with flags, soldiers lined the paths, and nobles in their grand carriages went by in procession. The common folk shouted till they were hoarse, and pressed forward on every hand towards the great church of the city, to witness the ceremony which was taking place there.

Whence was all this excitement? How came the Irish capital into such a state of festivity and holiday-making? The story is a short one and a strange.

Some weeks before, a man in the dress of a priest, accompanied by a good-looking boy, had landed in Dublin, and made his way to the residence of the governor of the place, with whom he sought an interview. On being admitted, he much astonished that nobleman by the tale he told.

It was well known that Richard the Third had during his lifetime shut up in prison the young Earl of Warwick, his nephew, whose title to the crown was better than his own. The cruel uncle, who seemed unable to endure the presence of any of those whom he had so basely robbed of their inheritance, had already, as is well known, murdered those other two nephews whose claims were most prominent and unmistakable. The young Earl of Warwick, however, was allowed to keep his life, but remained a close prisoner in a castle in Yorkshire.

When Henry the Seventh took the crown from Richard and became king, he was by no means disposed to liberate a prince who was clearly nearer to the throne than himself. So he had him removed from Yorkshire to the Tower of London, where he remained almost forgotten amid the bustle of coronation festivities of the new king.

Now the story told by the priest was that this prince had succeeded in escaping from the Tower, and indeed was none other than the lad who now stood at his side, having made his way to Ireland in the company of his tutor and friend, to beg the aid of the Governor of Dublin in an effort to recover his lawful inheritance.

The Earl of Kildare (that was the governor's name) looked in astonishment from one to the other, and bade them repeat their story, asking the boy many questions about his childhood and the companions of his youth, which the latter answered so glibly and unhesitatingly that the foolish governor was fully persuaded this was no other than the rightful King of England.

He caused the lad to be treated with all the honour due to royalty; he gave him a guard of soldiers, he showed him to the populace, who welcomed him with enthusiasm, and he set to work to organise an army which should follow to enforce his claim to the throne of England.

The boy took all this sudden glory in a half-bewildered manner, but adhered so correctly to his plausible story that none of those generous Irish folk doubted that he was any other than the disinherited prince he professed to be.

Had they only known that the youth about whom they were so enthusiastic was no better than a baker's son, named Lambert Simnel, they might have been less pleased.

Well, in due time it was decided to crown the new king with all honour. And this was the occasion about which, as we have seen, Dublin was in such a state of festivity and holiday.

The boy was conducted with great pomp to church, amid the shouts of the people, and there crowned with a diadem taken from a statue of the Virgin Mary. Afterwards, according to custom, he was borne on the shoulders of a huge Irish chieftain back to the castle, where he lived as a king for some time.

All this while the real Earl of Warwick was safe in the Tower, and now when the rumour of Lambert Simnel's doings in Ireland reached King Henry, he had him brought out from his prison and exhibited in public, so that every one might be convinced of the imposture of the boy who set himself up to be the same person.

But though the people of England were thus kept from being deceived, as the Irish had been, there were a good many of them who heartily disliked King Henry, and were ready to join in any movement against him, irrespective of right or wrong. The consequence was, Lambert Simnel—or rather the people who instigated him in his falsehood—found they might count on a fair amount of support even from those who discredited their story; and this encouraged them to attempt an invasion of England, and venture their scheme on the field of battle. So, with a force of about 8,000 men, they landed in Lancashire. There is no need to tell the result of this expedition. After many disappointments occasioned by the reluctance of the people to join them, they encountered the king's army near Newark, and after a desperate battle were defeated, and lost all their leaders. Lambert Simnel and the priest were taken prisoners, and for a time there was an end of this silly attempt to deceive the nation.

In the following years of Henry's reign, any one entering the royal kitchens might have observed a boy, meanly dressed, following his occupation as a turnspit; and that boy, had he felt disposed to give you his history, would have told you how once upon a time he was crowned a king, and lived in a palace, how nobles bowed the knee before him, and troops fought at his bidding. He would have told how people had hailed him as King Edward of England, and rushed along beside his carriage, eager to catch so much as a glance from his eye. And then he would go on to tell how all this was because designing men had put into his head foolish ambitions, and taught him to repeat a likely-looking story. And if one had questioned him further, doubtless he would have confessed that he was happier far now as a humble turnspit than ever he had been as a sham king, and would have warned one sadly that cheats never prosper, however successful they may seem for a time; and that contentment with one's lot, humble though it be, brings with it rewards infinitely greater than riches or power wrongly acquired.

Chapter Twenty Seven
Edward and Richard Plantagenet, the Boys who were murdered in the Tower

A horseman stood at the gate of the Tower of London, and demanded entrance in the name of the king, Richard Iii.

On hearing the summons, and the authority claimed by the stranger, the governor, Sir Thomas Brackenbury, directed that he should be admitted, and deliver his message.

"Read this," said the man, handing a missive sealed with the royal seal.

Sir Thomas read the document hastily, and as he read his face grew troubled. For a long time he was silent; then addressing the king's messenger, he said —

"Know you the contents of this letter?"

"How should I know?" replied the other evasively.

"The king directs me here," said Sir Thomas, "to do a deed horrible and unworthy of a man. He demands that I should rid him of the two lads now lying in this Tower in my custody."

"And what of that?" said the king's messenger. "Is it not necessary to the country's peace? And will *you*, Sir Thomas, render so base an ingratitude for the favours you have received at the king's hands by refusing him this service?"

"Not even with the sanction of a king will Thomas Brackenbury hire himself out as a butcher. My office and all I have," he added, "I hold at His Majesty's pleasure. He may take them from me if he will, but my hands shall at least stay free from innocent blood!"

With that he bade the messenger return to his master and deliver his reply.

When Richard, away in Gloucestershire, heard of the refusal of the Governor of the Tower to execute his commands, he was very wroth, and vowed he would yet carry out his cruel purpose with regard to his two helpless nephews.

These two boys, the sons of Edward the Fourth, were the principal obstacles to Richard's undisturbed possession of the throne he had usurped. The elder of them, a boy of thirteen, had already been crowned as Edward the Fifth, but he was a king in name only. Scarcely had the coronation taken place when his bad uncle, under the pretence of offering his protection, got him into his power, and shut him up, with his young brother Richard, in the Tower, while he himself plotted for the crown to which he had neither right nor title.

How he succeeded in his evil schemes history has recorded.

By dint of falsehood and cunning he contrived to make himself acknowledged king by an unwilling people; and then, when the height of his ambition had been attained, he could not rest till those whom he had so shamefully robbed of their inheritance were out of his path.

Therefore it was he sent his messenger to Sir Robert Brackenbury.

Foiled in his design of making this officer the instrument of his base scheme, he summoned to his presence Sir James Tyrrel, a man of reckless character, ready for whatever might bring him profit or preferment; and to him he confided his wishes.

That same day Tyrrel started for London, armed with a warrant entrusting him with the Governorship of the Tower for one day, during which Sir Robert Brackenbury was to hand over the fortress and all it contained to his keeping.

The brave knight had nothing for it but to obey this order, though he well knew its meaning, and could foretell only too readily its result.

In a lofty room of that gloomy fortress, that same summer evening, the two hapless brothers were sitting, little dreaming of the fate so nearly approaching.

The young king had indeed for some time past seemed to entertain a vague foreboding that he would never again breathe the free air outside his prison. He had grown melancholy, and the buoyant spirits of youth had given place to a listlessness and heaviness strangely out of keeping with his tender years. He cared neither for talk nor exercise, and neglected both food and dress. His brother, two years younger than himself, was of a more hopeful demeanour, perhaps realising less fully the hardships and dangers of their present imprisonment. As they sat this evening in their lonely chamber, he tried to rally his elder brother from his melancholy.

"Look not so black, brother; we shall soon be free. Why should we give up hope?"

The young king answered nothing, and apparently did not heed his brother's words.

"Nay," persisted the latter, "should we not be glad our lives are spared us, and that our imprisonment is made easy by the care of good Sir Robert, our governor?"

Still Edward remained absorbed in his own gloomy reflections, and the younger lad, thus foiled in his efforts at cheerfulness, became silent too, and sad, and so continued till a warder entered their chamber with food, and remained to attend them to bed.

They tasted little that evening, for the shadow of what was to come seemed already to have crept over their spirits.

"Will Sir Robert come to see us, as is his wont, before we retire to rest?" inquired Richard of the warder.

"Sir Robert is not now Governor of the Tower," curtly replied the man.

Now indeed they felt themselves utterly friendless, and as they crept to their bed they clung one to the other, in all the loneliness of despair.

Then the warder took his leave, and they heard the key turn in the lock behind him, and counted his footsteps as he descended the stairs.

Presently sleep mercifully fell upon their weary spirits, and closed their weeping eyes with her gentle touch.

At dead of night three men stole up the winding staircase that led to their chamber, armed, and carrying a light. The leader of these was Sir James Tyrrel, and his evil-looking companions were the men he had hired to carry out the cruel order of the king. The key turned in the door, and they entered the apartment.

It was a sight to touch any heart less hard than those of the three villains who now witnessed it, to see those two innocent boys sleeping peacefully in each other's arms, dreaming perhaps of liberty, and forgetting the sorrow which had left its traces even yet on their closed eyes. But to Tyrrel and his two assassins, Forest and Deighton, the spectacle suggested neither pity nor remorse.

At a signal from Tyrrel, who remained outside the room while the deed was being done, the ruffians snatched the pillows from under the heads of the sleepers, and ere they could either resist or cry out the poor lads were stifled beneath their own bedclothes, and so perished.

Then these two murderers called to Tyrrel to enter and look on their work, and bear witness that the king's command had been faithfully executed.

The cup of Richard's wickedness was now full. He concealed for some time the fate of his two victims, and few people knew what had become of their rightful king and his brother. But the vengeance of Heaven fell on the cruel uncle speedily and terribly. His own favourite son died, his family turned against him, his people rebelled: the kingdom so evilly gained was taken from him, and he himself, after months of remorse, and fear, and gathering misfortunes, was slain in battle, lamented by none, and hated by all.

Two centuries later, in the reign of King Charles the Second, some workmen, digging in the Tower, discovered under the stairs leading to the chapel of the White Tower a box containing the bones of two children, corresponding to the ages of the murdered princes. These were found to be without doubt their remains, and in a quiet comer of Westminster Abbey, whither they were removed, a simple memorial now marks their last resting-place, and records the fact of their cruel murder by perhaps the worst king who ever sat upon the throne of England.

Chapter Twenty Eight
Edward of Lancaster, the Boy whose Life a Robber saved

A terrible scene might have been witnessed near the small town of Hexham, in Northumberland, one May afternoon in the year 1464. A great battle had just been fought and won. Civil war, with all its hideous accompaniments, had laid desolate those fair fields where once cattle were wont to browse and peasants to follow their peaceful toil. But now all was confusion and tumult. On the ground in heaps lay men and horses, dead and dying—the vanquished were crying for mercy, the victors were shouting for vengeance. The country for miles round was alive with fugitives and their pursuers. Women, children, and old men, as well as soldiers, joined in that panic flight; and shrieks, and shouts, and groans told only too plainly of the slaughter and terror of the pursuit. To slaughter the victors added robbery and outrage. Far and wide they scoured the country in quest of victims and booty; houses were burned, villages were desolated, fields were laid bare, nor till night mercifully fell over the land did that scene of terror end. War is indeed a terrible scourge, and civil war the most terrible of all.

But while many of those who pursued did so in a blind thirst after plunder and blood, there were others more determined in their going, whose object was rather to capture than to slay, who passed without heeding the common fugitives, and gave chase only to such parties as seemed to be covering the flight of persons of distinction from the scene of their disaster. Of such parties one was known to contain the King of England, nobles, and officers, whom the victors desired to make captive and get into their power; while it was also rumoured that the Queen herself, with her youthful son, was among the fugitives. The soldiers of the Duke of York would indeed have been elated, had they succeeded in getting into their power the king and his son, whose throne they had seized for their own leader, and so they followed hard after the flying host in all directions.

That same evening, as the sun was sinking, and the distant sounds of battle were growing faint in the air, a tall, stately woman, leading by the hand a boy of scarcely six years, walked hastily in the direction of a wood which skirted the banks of the River Tyne. It was evident from her dress and the jewels she wore that she was a lady of no ordinary importance, and a certain imperious look in her worn face seemed to suggest that she was one of those more used to ruling than obeying, to receiving honour rather than rendering it. The boy who accompanied her was also richly dressed, and reflected in his handsome face the proud nature of his mother, as this lady seemed to be. Just at present, however, his expression was one of terror. He clung eagerly to the hand of his protectress, and once and again cast a frightened look behind, as if expecting to get sight of the pursuers, from whose clutches they were even now seeking shelter.

"Mother," said the lad, as they entered the wood, and for the first time abated somewhat of their hurried progress, "I am weary and hungry. May we not rest here awhile and eat something?"

"My child," said the lady, "there is naught here to eat, and we must go farther ere we are safe from our cruel foes."

So they went on, deep into the gloomy shade of the wood, till they were far beyond the sight of the outer world, and where the rays of the setting sun scarce gave the feeblest light.

"Mother," said the boy presently, "this is an awful place; we shall die here."

"Fear not, my child," replied the lady bravely. "Heaven will protect us when none else can."

"But do not robbers abound in these woods? Have I not heard you say so?"

"It is true; but they will not hurt thee or me. Remember whose son thou art."

"Ay, I am the king's son; but I would fain have a morsel to eat."

Just then there was a crackling among the underwood, and a sound of voices approaching the spot.

The boy clutched his mother's hand and trembled. She stood pale and motionless.

The sound of feet grew nearer, and presently the voices of those who spoke became distinguishable.

"Some will be sure to find their way to this wood," said one.

"I hope such as do may have full purses," said another. "I have taken nothing these three days."

"Ay, truly, and these wars have made folk so poor, they are not worth robbing when we do find them."

"Soft! methought I heard a voice!" suddenly said one of the speakers.

The band halted and listened, and then, hearing nothing, pushed on.

"It's as likely as not we might fall in with royalty itself this night, for I hear the king's rout has been complete at Hexham."

"And more than that, he has fled from the field in one direction, while his queen and son have sought another!"

"Hist!" again cried he who had spoken before. "I certainly heard a voice. This way, my men; follow me."

And advancing at as rapid a pace as the wooded ground allowed of, he conducted them in the direction of the voices. Suddenly they emerged into a clearing, where confronted them the lady and her boy.

Loud laughed these greedy robbers, for they spied the jewels on the lady's person and the rich robes on her and her son.

Like cowardly ruffians, as *they* were, they rushed forward, heedless of the sex or age of their victims, and threatening to slay them should they resist, tore away jewels, and gold, and silk—all that was of value, roughly handling the two in so doing, and meeting every attempt to speak or resist with the menace of a drawn sword.

It was a rich plunder, for the lady's jewels were large and precious, and, besides, she bore about her no small quantity of gold and other treasure. When they had taken all they could lay their wicked hands on, the men fell to dividing among themselves their ill-gotten booty, glorying as they did so in their crime, and laughing brutally at the expense of their two defenceless victims.

As might be supposed, the task of dividing the spoil was one not quietly accomplished. The robbers began to argue as to the division, and from arguing they went on to disputing, and from disputing they came to fighting, in the midst of which the lady and her boy took an opportunity to escape unobserved into the thicket, and hasten as best they might from the reach of their plunderers.

Thus they fled, robbed and penniless, exposed to the cold evening air, famishing for lack of food, smarting under insult and wrong, and not knowing where next to turn for shelter or safety.

The courage of the lady, hitherto so conspicuous, now fairly gave way. She sat down on the ground, and taking her boy to her arms, abandoned herself to a flood of tears. "My son," she cried, "better if we had died by the sword of our enemies, than die a shameful death in these woods! Alas! was ever woman so miserable as I?"

"But, mother," said the boy, who now in turn took upon him the office of comforter, "the robbers left us with our lives, and we shall surely find some food here. Cheer up, mother; did you not tell me God would take care of us when no one else could?"

The mother's only answer was to take her boy in a closer embrace and kiss him passionately.

Suddenly there appeared before them a man of fierce aspect, holding in his hand a drawn sword.

Escape was impossible; robbed as they already were, they had nothing but their lives to offer to this wild ruffian. And would he scruple to murder where he could not rob?

The courage of the lady, in this desperate case, returned as quickly as it had lately deserted her.

A sudden resolution gleamed in her face; then, rising majestically to her feet, and taking by the hand her trembling boy, she advanced proud and stately towards the robber. The man halted wonderingly. There was something in the imperious bearing of this tall, beautiful lady—something in the appealing looks of the gallant boy—which for a moment cowed his lawless resolve, and made him hesitate.

Noticing this, the lady advanced close to him, and said in clear, majestic tones,—

"Behold, my friend, I commit to your care the safety of your king's son!"

The man started back in astonishment, the sword dropped from his hand, and a look, half of alarm, half of perplexity, took possession of his face.

Then he fell on one knee, and respectfully bowed almost to the earth.

"Art thou, then, our good Queen Margaret?"

"I am she."

"And this youth, is he indeed our royal master's son?"

"Even so."

Once more the wild man bowed low. Then the queen bade him arise, told him how she and the young prince had come into the plight, and ended by asking if he could give them food and shelter for a short time.

"All I have is your majesty's," said the man, "even my life. I will at once conduct you to my humble dwelling." And he lifted the weary boy tenderly in his arms, and led the queen to his cottage in the wood, where they got both food and shelter, and every care and attention from the robber's good wife.

"Mother," said the young prince that night, "thou saidst right, that Heaven would protect us."

"Ay, my boy, and will still protect us!"

For some days they rested at the cottage, tended with endless care by the loyal robber and his wife, until the pursuit from the battle of Hexham was over. Then, with the aid of her protector, the queen made her way to the coast, where a vessel waited to convey her and the prince to Flanders. Thus, for a time they escaped from all their dangers. Had the young prince lived to become King of England, we may be sure that the kind act of the robber would not have been suffered to die unrewarded. But, alas! Edward of Lancaster was never King of England.

The Wars of the Roses, as we all know, resulted in the utter defeat of the young prince's party. He was thirteen years old when the rival Houses of York and Lancaster fought their twelfth battle in the meadow at Tewkesbury. On that occasion Edward fought bravely in his own cause, but he and his followers were completely routed by the troops of King Edward the Fourth. Flying from the field of battle, he was arrested and brought before the young king.

"How dared you come here?" wrathfully inquired the usurper.

"To recover my father's crown and my own inheritance," boldly replied the prince.

Whereat, the history says, Edward struck at him with his iron gauntlet, and his attendants fell upon him and slew him with their swords.

Chapter Twenty Nine
Edward the Sixth, the good King of England

It was a strange moment in the history of England when the great King Henry the Eighth. ("Bluff King Hal," as his subjects called him) breathed his last. However popular he may have been on account of his courage and energy, he possessed vices which must always withhold from him the name of a *good* king, and which, in fact, rendered his reign a continuous scene of cruelty and oppression. People were sick of hearing of the king and his wives—how he had beheaded one, and put away another, and ill-treated another, for no reason at all but his own selfish caprice. And men trembled for their lives when they remembered how Wolsey, and More, and Cromwell, and others had been sacrificed to the whimsical temper of this tyrannical sovereign. England, in fact, was tired out when Henry the Eighth died.

It was, at any rate, a change for them to find that their new king was in every respect the opposite of his father. Instead of the burly, hot-headed, self-willed, cruel Henry, they were now to be ruled by a frail, delicate, mild boy of nine, inheriting neither his father's vices nor his faults, and resembling him as little in mind as in body. But the chief difference of all was this—that this boy-king was *good*.

A *good* King of England. It was indeed and, alas! a novelty. How many, counting back to the day when the country first knew a ruler, could be so described? Had not the sceptre of England passed, almost without exception, down a line of usurpers, murderers, robbers, and butchers, and was it not a fact that the few kings who had not been knaves had been merely fools?

But now England had a good king and a clever king, what might not be expected of him?

On the day of his coronation all sorts of rumours were afloat respecting young Edward. Boy though he was, he was a scholar, and wrote letters in Latin. Young in years, he was mature in thought, he was a staunch Protestant, an earnest Christian. Tudor though he was, he loved peace, and had no pleasure in the sufferings of others. Was ever such a king?

"Alas," said some one, "that he is but a boy!"

The sight which presented itself within the walls of that gloomy fortress, the Tower of London, on the day of Edward the Sixth's proclamation, was an impressive one. Amidst a crowd of bishops and nobles, who bowed low as he advanced, the pale boy-king came forward to receive the homage of his new subjects.

Surely, thought some, as they looked, that little head is not fitted to the wearing of an irksome crown. But, for the most part, the crowd cheered, and shouted, "God save the king!" and not one was there who found it in his heart to wish young Edward Tudor ill.

The papist ceremony which had always before accompanied the coronation of English kings was now for the first time dispensed with. With joy the people heard good old Archbishop Cranmer urge the new king to see God truly worshipped, according to the doctrines of the Reformed religion; and with joy they heard the boy declare before them all his intention to rule his country according to the rules of God's Word and the Protestant faith.

Still, as we have said, many in the midst of their joy sighed as they looked at the frail boy, and wondered how so young a head would bear up amid all the perils and dangers of kingship; and well they might pity him.

The reign of Edward the Sixth is chiefly a history of the acts of his uncle, the Duke of Somerset, the Protector, and of the dissensions which embittered the government of that nobleman, leading finally to his death on the scaffold. Of Edward himself we do not hear much. We have occasional glimpses of him at his studies, under tutors chosen and superintended by Cranmer; but he does not seem to have taken much part—how could a boy of his age be expected to do so?—in the active duty of governing.

We know that such acts as the removal of popish restrictions from the clergy and people, the publication of the Book of Common Prayer, and the discouragement of all idolatrous and superstitious practices, had his hearty sympathy. In these and in such-like useful measures he interested himself, but as for the troubles and commotions of his reign, he had nothing to do with them.

His nobles, on the other hand, were by no means so passive. They made war in the king's name on Scotland, to capture a baby-wife for the poor boy, who was scarcely in his teens; they—accused and impeached one another; they brought their death warrants to Edward to sign, whether he liked or no (and he never did like); they persecuted those who disagreed with them; they goaded the common people into rebellion; they schemed how they should make their own fortunes after the young invalid was dead, and to that end worked upon his weakness and his timidity actually to disinherit his own sisters.

In the midst of all this disturbance, and scheming, and distress, we can picture the poor, confused, sickly boy seeking refuge in his books, shrinking from the angry bustle of the court, and spending his days with his grave tutors in quiet study. Reluctantly, once and again, he was forced to come out from his retreat to give the sanction of his authority to some act of his ambitious nobles. With what trembling hand would he sign the death warrants they presented! with what weariness would he listen to their wrangles and accusations! with what distress would he hear discussions as to who was to wear that crown of his when he himself should be in the grave!

That time was not long in coming. He was not fifteen when an attack of smallpox laid him on his deathbed; and while all the court was busy plotting and counterplotting as to the disposal of the crown, the poor boy-king lay there almost neglected, or watched only by those who waited the moment of his death with impatience. As the disease took deeper and fatal hold of him, all forsook him save an incompetent quack nurse; and how far she may have helped on the end no one can tell.

But for him death was only a happy release from a world of suffering. A few hours before his end he was heard to speak something; and those who listened discovered that the boy, thinking himself alone, was praying. One has recorded those closing words of that strange, sad life: "Lord, deliver me out of this wretched and miserable life, and take me among Thy chosen: howbeit not my will, but Thine be done. Lord, I commit my spirit to Thee. O Lord, Thou knowest how happy it were for me to be with Thee; yet, for the sake of Thy chosen, send me life and health, that I may truly serve Thee. O my Lord God, bless Thy people, and save Thine inheritance. O Lord God, save Thy chosen people of England. O my Lord God, defend this realm from papistry, and maintain Thy true religion, that I and my people may praise Thy holy name, for Thy Son Jesus Christ's sake."

And with these words on his lips, and these prayers for England in his heart, the good young king died. Who knows if by his piety and his prayers he may not have brought more blessing to his country than many a battle and many a law of less Godfearing monarchs?

What he would have done for England had he been spared to manhood, it is not possible to say. A diary which he kept during his life affords abundant proof that even at his tender age he possessed not a little of the sagacity and knowledge necessary to good kingship; and a manhood of matured piety and wisdom might have materially altered the course of events in the history of England of that time.

One boon at least he has left behind him, besides his unsullied name and example. Scattered about the counties of England are not a few schools which bear his name. It is possible that a good many of my readers are to be found among the scholars of the Bluecoat School, and of the King Edward Grammar Schools in various parts of the country. They, at least, will understand the gratitude which this generation owes to the good young king who so materially advanced the learning of which he himself was so fond, by the establishment of these schools. He was one of the few of his day who saw that the glory of a country consists not in its armies and exchequers, but in the religious and moral enlightenment of its people; and to that glory his own life was, and remains still, a noble contribution.

Chapter Thirty
Henry Stuart, the Boy whom a Nation loved

In the courtyard of a Scottish castle, over which floated the royal banner, a curious scene might have been witnessed one morning nearly three centuries ago. The central figures of the scene were a horse and a boy, and the attendant crowd of courtiers, grooms, lackeys; while from an open window, before which every one in passing bowed low, an ungainly-looking man watched what was going on with a strangely anxious excitement. The horse was saddled and bridled, but, with an ominous roll of his eyes, and a savage expansion of his nostrils, which bespoke only too plainly his fierce temper, defied every attempt on the part of the grooms to hold him steady. The boy, scarcely in his teens, was evidently a lad of distinction, as might be inferred from his gallant dress, and the deferential demeanour of those who now advanced, and endeavoured to dissuade him from a rash and perilous adventure.

"Beware, my lord," said one, "how you peril your life in this freak!"

"The animal," said another, "has never yet been ridden. See how even now he nearly pulls the arms of the grooms from their sockets."

"Lad," cried the ungainly man from the window, "dinna be a fool, I tell ye! Let the beast be."

But the boy laughed gaily at them all.

"Such a fuss about an ordinary horse! Let him go, men, and leave him to me."

And he advanced and boldly took the rein, which the grooms unwillingly relinquished.

There was something about the resolute bearing of the boy which for a moment seemed to impress the horse himself, for, pricking his ears and rolling his bloodshot eyes upon him, he desisted from his struggles and stood still.

The lad put out a hand and patted his neck, and in doing so secured a firm clutch of the mane in his hand; the next instant his foot was in the stirrup, and the next he had vaulted into the saddle, before the horse had recovered from his astonishment.

Once in, no effort of the untamed beast could succeed in ousting him from his seat. In vain it reared and plunged; in vain it pulled and careered round the yard; he stuck to his seat as if he grew there, and with cool eye and quiet smile seemed even to enjoy his position. After many unavailing efforts the horse seemed to yield his vicious will to the stronger will of his rider, and then the boy, lashing him into a gallop, fairly put him through his paces before all the spectators, and finally walked him quietly up to the window at which the ungainly man, trembling, and with tears in his eyes, had all the while watched his exploit. Here he halted, and beckoning to his attendants, dismounted and gave back the horse to their charge, saying as he did so—

"How long shall I continue a child in your opinion?"

Such is one of the recorded characteristic anecdotes of Prince Henry Stuart, eldest son of James the First of England.

Henry was only nine years old when a certain event entirely changed the prospects and circumstances of his early home. Instead of being the poor king of a poverty-stricken country, his father suddenly became monarch of one of the richest and most powerful countries of Europe. In other words, on the death of Queen Elizabeth James the Sixth of Scotland found himself James the First of England.

He came to the throne amid the mingled joy and misgivings of his new subjects. How soon he destroyed the one and confirmed the other, history has recorded, and we are not going to dwell upon that here, except to say that one of the few redeeming points about James the First in the eyes of the people was that he had a son who promised to make up by his virtues for all the vice and silliness of his father. They could endure the whims of their ill-conditioned king all the better for knowing that after him was to come a prince after their own heart, one of English sympathies and English instincts; one who even as a boy had won their hearts by his pluck, his frankness, and his wit, and who, as he grew up, developed into a manhood as vigorous and noble as that of his father was mean and imbecile.

Henry was, as we have said, emphatically an English boy—not in birth, for his father was Scotch and his mother a Dane—but in every other respect in which an English boy has a distinctive character. He was brave and honest, and merry and generous; his delight was in athletic exercise and manly sports; the anecdote we have quoted will testify to his skill and pluck. We read of him living at one time at Richmond, and swimming daily in the Thames; of his riding more than 100 miles in one day; of his hunting, and tennis playing, and shooting. The people could not fail to love one who so thoroughly entered into their sports, or to admire him all the more for his proficiency in them.

But, unlike some boys, Henry did not cultivate physical exercises at the expense of his mind. Many stories are related of his wit and his learning. A joke at his expense was generally a dangerous adventure, for he always got the best at an exchange of wit. Among his friends were some of the greatest and best men of the day, notably Raleigh; and in such society the lad could not fail to grow up imbued with principles of wisdom and honour, which would go far to qualify him for the position he expected to hold.

His ambition was to enter upon a military career, such as those in which so many of his predecessors had distinguished themselves. In this he received more encouragement from the people than from his own timid father, who told him his brother Charles would make a better king than he, unless Henry spent more time at his books and less at his pike and his bow. The people, on the other hand, were constantly comparing their young prince with the great Henry the Fifth, the hero of Agincourt, and predicting of him as famous deeds as those recorded of his illustrious namesake. However, as it happened, there was no war into which the young soldier could enter at that time, so that he had to content himself with martial exercises and contests at home, which, though not so much to his own taste, made him no less popular with his father's subjects.

In Henry Stuart the old school of chivalry had nearly its last representative. The knightly Kings of England had given place, after the Wars of the Roses, to sovereigns whose strength lay more in the council chamber than on the field of battle; but now, after a long interval, the old dying spirit flickered up once more in the person of this boy. Once again, after many, many years, the court went to witness a tournament, when in the tiltyard of Whitehall, before king and queen, and lords and ladies, and ambassadors, the Prince of Wales at the head of six young nobles defended the lists against all comers. There is something melancholy about the record—the day for such scenes had gone by, and its spirit had departed from the nation. The boy had his sport and his honestly earned applause; but when it was all over the old chivalry returned to the grave, never to appear again.

Henry himself only too soon, alas! sunk into that grave also. The closing years of his life leave many a pleasing trace of kindness, and justice, and earnestness. The boy was no mere boisterous schoolboy. He pondered and prepared himself for what he thought was his path in life; he foresaw its responsibilities, and he faced its duties, and set himself like a man to bear his part as a true king should.

It was not to be. Suddenly his health failed him—the tall boy had overgrown his strength before he knew it. Heedless of fatigue and exposure, he pursued his vigorous exercises, and what had been his life became his death. A cold taken during a game of tennis, when he was in his eighteenth year, developed into a fever, and for days he lay between life and death. The nation waited with strange anxiety for the issue, and a cloud seemed to fall over the length and breadth of the land.

Then he became worse.

"My sword and armour!" he cried; "I must be gone!" and after that the brave boy died.

The people mourned him as their own son; and years after, when England was plunged deep in the miseries and horrors of civil war, many there were who cried in their distress,—

"If but our Henry had lived, all this had not been!"

Chapter Thirty One
The Troubles of a Dawdler

I was born a dawdler. As an infant, if report speaks truly, I dawdled over my food, over my toilet, and over my slumbers. Nothing (so I am told) could prevail on me to stick steadily to my bottle till it was done; but I must needs break off a dozen times in the course of a single meal to stare about me, to play with the strings of my nurse's cap, to speculate on the sunbeams that came in at the window; and even when I did bring myself to make the effort, I took such an unconscionable time to consume a spoonful that the next meal was wellnigh due before I had made an end of a first.

As to dressing me in the morning, it took a good two hours. Not that I rebelled and went on strike over the business, but it was really too much of an effort to commit first one foot and then the other for the reception of my socks, and when that operation was accomplished a long interval always elapsed before I could devote my energy to the steering of my arms into sleeves, and the disposal of my waist to the adjustment of a sash. Indeed, I believe I am doing myself more than justice when I put forward two hours as the time spent in personal decoration during those tender years.

But of all my infant duties the one I dawdled over most was going to sleep. The act of laying me in my little cot seemed to be the signal for waking me to a most unwonted energy. Instead of burying my nose in the pillows, as most babies do, I must needs struggle into a sitting posture, and make night vocal with crows and calls. I must needs chew the head of my indiarubber doll, or perform a solo on my rattle—anything, in fact, but go to sleep like a respectable, well-conducted child.

If my mother came and rocked my cradle, I got alarmingly lively and entered into the sport with spirit. If she, with weary eyes and faltering voice, attempted to sing me to sleep, I lent my shrill treble to aid my own lullaby; or else I lay quiet with my eyes wide open, and defied every effort to coax them into shutting.

Not that I was wilfully perverse or bad—I am proud to say no one can lay that to my charge; but I was a dawdler, one who from my earliest years could not find it in me to settle down promptly to anything—nay, who, knowing a certain thing was to be done, therefore deferred the doing of it as long as possible.

Need I say that as I grew older and bequeathed my long clothes and cot to another baby, I dawdled still?

My twin brother's brick house was roofed in before my foundations were laid. Not that I could not build as quickly and as well as he, if I chose. I could, but I never chose. While he, with serious face and rapt attention, piled layer upon layer, and pinnacle upon pinnacle, absorbed in his architectural ambition, I sat by watching him, or wondering who drew the beautiful picture on the lid of my box, or speculating on the quantity of bricks I should use in my building, but always neglecting to set myself to work till Jim's shout of triumph declared his task accomplished. Then I took a fit of industry till my tower was half built, and by that time the bricks had to be put away.

When we walked abroad with nurse I was sure to lag behind to look at other children, or gaze into shops. Many a time I narrowly escaped being lost as the result. Indeed, one of my earliest recollections is of being conducted home in state by a policeman, who had found me aimlessly strolling about a churchyard, round which I had been accompanying the nurse and the perambulator, until I missed them both, a short time before.

My parents, who had hitherto been inclined to regard my besetting sin (for even youngsters of four may have besetting sins) as only a childish peculiarity, at last began to take note of my dawdling propensities, and did their best to cure me of them. My father would watch me at my play, and, when he saw me flagging, encourage me to persevere in whatever I was about, striving to rouse my emulation by pitting me against my playmates. For a time this had a good effect; but my father had something better to do than always preside at our nursery sports, and I soon relapsed into my old habits.

My mother would talk and tell stories to us; and always, whenever my attention began to fail, would recall me to order by questions or direct appeals. This, too, as long as it was fresh, acted well; but I soon got used to it, and was as bad as ever. Indeed, I was a confirmed dawdler almost before I was able to think or act for myself.

When I was eight, it was decided to send me and Jim to school—a day school, near home, presided over by a good lady, and attended by some dozen other boys. Well, the novelty of the thing pleased me at first, and I took an interest in my spelling and arithmetic, so that very soon I was at the top of my class. Of course my father and mother were delighted. My father patted me on the head, and said, "I knew he could be diligent, if he chose."

And my mother kissed me, and called me her brave boy; so altogether I felt very virtuous, and rather pitied Jim, who was six from the top, though he spent longer over his sums than I did.

But, alas! after the first fortnight, the novelty of Mrs Sparrow's school wore off. Instead of pegging along briskly to be in time, I pulled up once or twice on the road to investigate the wonders of a confectioner's window, or watch the men harness the horses for the omnibus, till suddenly I would discover I had only five minutes to get to school in time, and so had to run for my life the rest of the way, only overtaking Jim on the very doorstep. Gradually my dawdling became more prolonged, until one day I found myself actually late. Mrs Sparrow frowned, Jim looked frightened, my own heart beat for terror, and I heard the awful sentence pronounced, "You must go to the bottom of the class."

I made up my mind this should be the last occasion on which such a penalty should be mine. But, alas! the very next day the confectioner had a wonderful negro figure in his window made all of sweets, his face of liquorice and his shirt of sugar, his lips of candy and his eyes of brandy-balls. I was spellbound, and could not tear myself away. And when I did, to add to my misfortunes, there was a crowd outside the omnibus stables to watch the harnessing of a new and very frisky horse. Of course I had to witness this spectacle, and the consequence was I got to school half an hour late, and was again reprimanded and stood in the corner.

This went on from bad to worse. Not only did I become unpunctual, but I neglected my lessons till the last moment, and then it was too late to get them off, though I could learn as much in a short time as any of the boys. All this grieved poor Mrs Sparrow, who talked to my parents about it, who talked very seriously to me. My father looked unhappy, my mother cried; Mrs Sparrow (who was present at the interview) was silent, and I wept loudly and promised to reform—honestly resolving I would do so.

Well, for a week I was a model of punctuality and industry; but then the confectioner changed his sugar negro for an elephant made all of toffee, and I was once more beguiled. Once more from top of my class I sank to the bottom; and though after that I took fits and starts of regularity and study, I never was able for long together to recover my place, and Mrs Sparrow fairly gave me up as a bad job.

What was to be done? I was growing up. In time my twelfth birthday arrived, and it was *time* I went to boarding school.

I could see with what anxiety my parents looked forward to the time, and I inwardly reproached myself for being the cause of their trouble. "Perhaps," thought I, "I shall get all right at Welford," and having consoled myself with that possibility I thought no more about it. My father talked very earnestly to me before I left home for the first time in my life. He had no fears, he said, for my honesty or my good principles; but he had fears for my perseverance and diligence. "Either you must conquer your habit of dawdling," he said, "or it will conquer you." I was ready to promise any sacrifice to be cured of this enemy; but he said, "No, lad, don't promise, but remember and do!" And then he corded up my trunk and carried it downstairs. I cannot to this day recall my farewell with my mother without tears. It is enough to say that I quitted the parental home determined as I never was before to do my duty and fight against my besetting sin, and occupied that doleful day's journey with picturing to myself the happiness which my altered habits would bring to the dear parents whom I was leaving behind.

I pass over my first week at Welford. It was a new and wonderful world to me; very desolate at first, but by degrees more attractive, till at last I went the way of all schoolboys, and found myself settled down to my new life as if I had never known another.

All this time I had faithfully kept my resolution. I was as punctual as clockwork, and as diligent as an ant. Nothing would tempt me to abate my attention in the preparation of my lessons; no seductions of cricket or fishing would keep me late for "call over." I had already gained the approval of my masters, I had made my mark in my class, and I had written glowing letters home, telling of my kept resolutions, and wondering why they should ever before have seemed difficult to adhere to.

But as I got better acquainted with some of my new schoolfellows it became less easy to stick steadily to work. I happened to find myself in hall one evening, where we were preparing our tasks for next day, seated next to a lively young scapegrace, whose tongue rattled incessantly, and who, not content to be idle himself, must needs make every one idle too.

"What a muff you are, Charlie," he said to me once, as I was poring over my *Caesar* and struggling desperately to make out the meaning of a phrase—"what a muff you are, to be grinding away like that! Why don't you use a crib?"

"What's a crib?" I inquired.

"What, don't you know what a crib is? It's a translation. I've got one. I'll lend it to you, and you will be able to do your *Caesar* with it like winking."

I didn't like the notion at first, and went on hunting up the words in the dictionary till my head ached. But next evening he pulled the "crib" out of his pocket and showed it to me. I could not resist the temptation of looking at it, and no sooner had I done so than I found it gave at a glance the translation it used to take me an hour to get at with the dictionary. So I began to use the "crib" regularly; and thus, getting my lessons quickly done, I gradually began to relapse into my habits of dawdling.

Instead of preparing my lessons steadily, I now began to put off preparation till the last moment, and then galloped them off as best I could. Instead of writing my exercises carefully, I drew skeletons on the blotting-paper; instead of learning off my tenses, I read *Robinson Crusoe* under the desk, and trusted to my next-door neighbour to prompt me when my turn came.

For a time my broken resolutions did not effect any apparent change in my position in the classes or in the eyes of my masters. I was what Evans (the boy who lent me the "crib") called lucky. I was called on to translate just the passages I happened to have got off, or was catechised on the declensions of my pet verb, and so kept up appearances.

But that sort of thing could not go on for ever, and one day my exposure took place.

I had dawdled away my time the evening previously with one thing and another, always intending to set to work, but never doing so. My books had lain open before me untouched, except when I took a fancy to inscribing my name some scores of times on the title-page of each; my dictionary remained shot and unheeded, except when I rounded the corners of the binding with my penknife. I had played draughts clandestinely with Evans part of the time, and part of the time I had lolled with my elbows on the desk, staring at the head of the fellow in front of me.

Bedtime came, and I had not looked at my work.

"I'll wake early and cram it up," thought I, as I turned in.

I did wake up, but though the book was under my pillow I let the half-hour before getting up slip away unused. At breakfast I made an effort to glance at the lesson, but the boy opposite was performing such wonderful tricks of balancing with his teaspoon and saucer and three bread-crusts, that I could not devote attention to anything else. The bell for classes rang ominously. I rushed to my place with *Caesar* in one hand and the "crib" in the other. I got flurried; I could not find the place, or, when I found the place in the *Caesar*, I lost it in the "crib."

The master, to add to my misery, was cross, and began proceedings by ordering Evans to learn twenty lines for laughing in school-time. I glanced at the fellows round me. Some were taking a last peep at their books. Others, with bright and confident faces, waited quietly for the lesson to begin. No one that I could see was as badly off as I. Every one knew something. I knew nothing. Just at the last moment I found the place in the "crib" and in the *Caesar* at the same time, but scarcely had I done so when the awful voice of the master spoke:

"Stand up!" All dictionaries and notes had now to be put away; all except the Latin books.

I had contrived *to get* off the first two lines, and only hoped the master might pitch on me to begin. And he did pitch on me.

"Charles Smith," I heard him say, and my heart jumped to my mouth, "stand forward and begin at '*jamque Caesar.*'"

"Please, sir, we begin at '*His et aliis,*'" I faltered.

"You begin where I tell you, sir," sternly replied he.

A dead silence fell over the class, waiting for me to begin. I was in despair. Oh, if only I had not dawdled! I would give all my pocket-money for this term to know a line of that horrid *Caesar*.

"Come, sir, be quick," said the master.

Then I fetched a sigh very like a sob, and began—

"*Que*, and—" I heard the master's foot scrape ominously on the floor.

"*Que*, and—" I repeated.

"*And* what, sir?" thundered the master, rising in his seat and leaning across his desk towards me. It was awful. I was never more miserable in my life.

"*Caesar*, Caesar," I stammered. Here at least was a word I could translate, so I repeated it—"*Que*, and—*Caesar*, Caesar."

A dead silence, scarcely broken by a titter from the back desks.

"*Jam*," I chokingly articulated, and there stuck.

"Well, sir, and what does *jam* mean?" inquired the voice, in a tone of suppressed wrath.

"*Jam*"—again I stuck.

Another dead silence.

"*Que*, and—*Caesar*, Caesar; *jam*"—It was no use; the only jam I knew of I was certain would not do in this case, so I began again in despair; "*Que*, and—*Caesar*, Caesar; *jam—jam—jam.*"

The master shut his book, and I knew the storm had burst.

"Smith, have you prepared this lesson?"

"No, sir," I replied, relieved to be able to answer any questions, however awful.

"Why not, sir?"

Ah! that I could not answer—not to myself, still less to him. So I was silent.

"Come to me after school," he said. "The next boy come forward."

After school I went to him, and he escorted me to the doctor. No criminal at the Old Bailey trembled as I did at that interview. I can't remember what was said to me. I know I wildly confessed my sins—my "cribbing," my wasting of time—and promised to abjure them one and all.

The doctor was solemn and grave, and said a great deal to me that I was too overawed to understand or remember; after which I was sent back to my class—a punished, disgraced, and marked boy.

Need I describe my penitence: what a humble letter I wrote home, making a clean breast of all my delinquencies, and even exaggerating them in my contrition? With what grim ceremony I burned my "crib" in my study fire, and resolved (a resolution, by the way, which I succeeded in keeping) that, come what might, I would do my lessons honestly, if I did them at all!

I gave Evans to understand his company at lesson times was not desirable, and was in a rage with him when he laughed. I took to rising early, to filling every spare moment with some occupation, and altogether started afresh, like a reformed character, as I felt myself to be, and determined *this* time, at any rate, my progress should know no backsliding. How soon I again fell a victim to dawdling the sequel will show.

I had a long and painful struggle to recover my lost ground at Welford.

When a boy has once lost his name at school, when his masters have put him on the black book, when his schoolfellows have got to consider him as a "fellow in a row," when he himself has learnt to doubt his own honesty and steadiness—then, I say, it is uphill work for him to get back to the position from which he has fallen. He gets little sympathy, and still less encouragement. In addition to the natural difficulty of conquering bad habits, he has to contend against prejudices and obstacles raised by his own former conduct; no one gives him credit for his efforts, and no one recognises his reform till all of a sudden, perhaps long after its completion, it makes itself manifest.

And my reform, alas! consequently never arrived at completion at Welford.

For a few weeks all went well enough. My lessons were carefully prepared; my exercises were well written, and my master had no more attentive pupil than I. But, alas! I too soon again grew confident and self-satisfied. Little by little I relaxed; little by little I dawdled, till presently, almost without knowing it, I again began to slip down the hill. And this was in other matters besides my studies.

Instead of keeping up my practice at cricket and field sports, I took to hulking about the playground with my hands in my pockets. If I started on an expedition to find moths or hunt squirrels, I never got half a mile beyond the school boundaries, and never, of course, caught the ghost of anything. If I entered for a race in our school sports, I let the time go without training, and so was beaten easily by fellows whom I had always thought my inferiors. The books I read for my amusement out of school hours were all abandoned after a chapter or two; my very letters home became irregular and stupid, and often were altogether shelved.

And all this time (such is the blindness of some people) I was imagining I had quite retrieved my lost reputation! I shall never forget, however, how at last I discovered that my time at Welford had been wasted, and that, so far from having got the better of my enemy, I had become a more confirmed dawdler than ever.

I had come to my last half-year at school, being now seventeen. My great desire was to go to Cambridge, which my father had promised I should do if I succeeded in obtaining a scholarship, which would in part defray the cost of my residence there. On this scholarship, therefore, my heart was bent (as much as a dawdler's heart can be bent on anything) and I made up my mind to secure it.

The three fellows who were also going in for it were all my juniors, and considerably below me in the doctor's class; so I had little anxiety as to the result.

Need I say that this very confidence was fatal to me? While they were working night and day, early and late, I was amusing myself with boxing-gloves and fishing-rods. While they, with wet towels round their heads, burnt the midnight oil, I sprawled over a novel in my study. Of course, now and then I took a turn at my books, and each inspection tended to satisfy me with myself better than ever. "Those duffers will never be able to get up all that Greek in the time," I said to myself, "and not one of them knows an atom of mechanics."

Well, the time drew near. My father had written rejoicing to hear of my good prospects, and saying how he and mother were constantly thinking of me in my hard work, and so on.

"Yes," thought I, "they'll be pleased, I know." About a week before the examination I looked at my books rather more frequently, and, now and then (though I would not acknowledge it even to myself), felt my confidence a trifle wavering. There were a few things I had not noticed before, that must be got up with the rest of the subjects, "However, a day's work will polish them off," said I; "let's see, I've promised to fish with Wilkins to-morrow—I'll have a go in at them on Thursday."

But Thursday found me fishing too, and on Friday there was a cricket-match. However, the examination was not till Tuesday, so there was half a week yet.

Saturday, of course, was a half-holiday, and though I took another look at some of my books, and noted one or two other little things that would have to be got up, I determined that the grand "go in" at, and "polishing off" of, these subjects should take place on Monday.

On Monday accordingly I set to work.

Glancing from my window—as I frequently did while I was at work—whom should I see, with a fly-net over his shoulder, but Wilton, one of the three fellows in against me for the scholarship! And not long after him who should appear arm-in-arm in cricket costume, but Johnson and Walker, the other two!

"Ho! ho!" said I to myself, "nice boys these to be going in for an exam.! How can they expect to do anything if they dawdle away their time in this way! I declare I quite feel as if I were taking an unfair advantage of them to be grinding away up here!"

Had I realised that these three fellows had been working incessantly for the last month, and were now taking a breath of fresh air in anticipation of the ordeal of the following day, I should have been less astonished at what I saw, and more inclined to work, at any rate this day, like mad.

But I allowed my benevolent desire not to take an unfair advantage to prevail, and was soon far up the stream with my fishing-rod.

So Monday passed. In the evening I had another turn at my books, but an unsatisfactory one.

"What's the use of muddling my brain? I had better take it easy, and be fresh for to-morrow," thought I, as I shut them up and pushed my chair back from the table.

Next morning brought me a letter from my father:

"This will reach you on the eventful day. You know who will be thinking of their boy every moment. We are happy to know your success is so sure;

but don't be *too* confident till it's all well over. Then we shall be ready to rejoice with you. I have already heard of rooms at Cambridge for you; so you see mother and I are counting our chickens before they are hatched! But I have no fears, after what you have told me."

This letter made me unhappy; the sight of my books made me unhappy; the sight of Wilton, Johnson, and Walker, fresh and composed, made me unhappy; the sight of the doctor wishing me good morning made me unhappy. I was, in fact, thoroughly uncomfortable. The list of those one or two little matters that I had intended to polish off grew every time I thought of them, till they wellnigh seemed to eclipse the other subjects about which I felt sure. What an ass I had been!

"The candidates for the Calton Scholarship are to go to the doctor's class-room!"

To the doctor's class-room we four accordingly proceeded.

On the way, not to appear nervous, I casually inquired of Wilton if he had caught any specimens yesterday.

"Yes," he said gaily. "I got one splendid fellow, a green-winged moth. I'll show him to you in my study after the exam, is over."

Here was a fellow who could calmly contemplate the end of this day's ordeal. I dared not do as much as that!

The doctor affably welcomed us to his room, and bade us be seated. Several quires of blank paper, one or two pens, a ruler, and ink, were provided at each of our four desks.

Then a printed paper of questions was handed to each, and the examination began.

I glanced hurriedly down my paper. Question 1 was on one of those subjects which had escaped my observation. Question 2 was a piece of translation I did not recognise as occurring in the Greek book I had got up, and yet I thought I had been thoroughly through it. Question 3—well, no one would be able to answer that. Question 4—oh, horrors! another of those little points I had meant to polish off. Thus I glanced from top to bottom of the paper. Here and there I fancied I might be able to give some sort of answer, but as for the rest, I was in despair. I dashed my pen into the ink, and wrote my name at the head of a sheet of paper, and ruled a line underneath it. Then I dug my fingers in my hair, and waited for an inspiration. It was a long time coming. In the meantime I glanced round at the other three. They were all writing hard, and Wilton already had one sheet filled. Somehow the sight of Wilton reminded me of the moth he had spoken of. I wondered if it was a finer specimen than I had got at home—mine had blue wings and a horn. Funny insects moths were! I wondered if the doctor used to collect them when he was a boy. The doctor must be nearly sixty now. Jolly to be a doctor, and have nothing to do but examine fellows! I wondered if Walker's father had written him a letter, and what sort of nib he (Walker) must be writing with, with such a peculiar squeak—rather like a frog's squeak. I wouldn't mind being a frog for some things; must be jolly to be equally at home on dry ground or in water! Fancy eating frogs! Our French master was getting more short-tempered than ever.

And so I rambled on, while the paper in front of me remained empty.

The inspirations never came. The hours whizzed past, and my penholder was nibbled half away. In vain I searched the ceilings, and my thumb-nails; they gave me no help. In vain I read over the examination paper a score of times. It was all question and no answer there. In vain I stared at the doctor as he sat quietly writing; he had no ideas for me. In vain I tried to count, from where I sat, how many sheets Johnson had filled; that did not help to fill mine. Then I read my questions over again, very closely, and was in the act of wondering who first decided that p's should turn one way in print and q's another, when the doctor said, "Half an hour more!"

I was electrified. I madly began answering questions at random. Anything to get my paper filled. But, fast as I wrote, I could not keep pace with Wilton, whose pen flew along the paper; and he, I knew, was writing what would get him marks while I was writing rubbish. Presently my attention was diverted by watching Walker gather up and pin together his papers. I looked at my watch. Five minutes more. At the same time the doctor took out his. I could not help wondering if it was a Geneva or an English watch, and whether it had belonged to his father before him, as mine had. Ah! my father, my poor father and mother!

"Cease work, please, and hand in your papers."

I declined Wilton's invitation to come and see his moth, and slunk to my room miserable and disgusted.

Even now I do not like to recall the interval which elapsed between the examination and the declaration of the result. To Johnson, Wilton and Walker it was an interval of feverish suspense; to me it was one of stolid despair. I was ashamed to show my face among my schoolfellows; ashamed to write home; ashamed to look at a book. The nearer the day came the more wretched I grew; I positively became ill with misery, and begged to be allowed to go home without waiting for the result.

I had a long interview with the doctor before I quitted Welford; but no good advice of his, no exhortations, could alter my despair.

"My boyhood has been a failure," I said to him, "and I know my manhood will be one too."

He only looked very sorrowful, and wrung my hand.

The meeting with my parents was worst of all; but over that I draw a veil.

For months nothing could rouse me from my unhappiness, and in indulging it I dawdled more than ever. My prospects of a college life were blighted, and I had not the energy to face business. But, as was always the case, I could not for long together stick to anything; and in due time I emerged from my wretchedness, an idle, dawdling youth, with no object in life, no talents to recommend me, nothing to do.

It was deplorable, and my father was nearly heart-broken. Heroically he strove to rouse me to activity, to interest me in some pursuit. He did for me what I should have done for myself—sought occupation for me, and spent days and days in his efforts to get me settled in life. At last he succeeded in procuring a nomination to a somewhat lucrative government clerkship; and, for the first time since I left Welford, my father and mother and I were happy together. Despite all my demerits, I was now within reach of a position which many a youth of greater ability and steadier character might well have envied; and I believe I was really thankful at my good fortune.

"I will go with you to-morrow," said my father, "when you have to appear before the head of the department."

"All right," said I; "what time is it?"

"Half-past eleven."

"Well, I must meet you at the place, then, for I promised to see Evans early in the morning."

"Better go to him to-day," said my mother; "it would be a thousand pities to be late to-morrow."

"Oh, no fear of that," said I, laughing; "I've too good an eye to my own interests."

Next morning I went to see Evans, and left him in good time to meet my father at the stated hour. But an evil spirit of dawdling seized me as I went. I stopped to gaze into shops, to chat with a passing acquaintance, and to have my boots blacked. Forgetting the passage of time altogether, I strolled leisurely along, stopping at the slightest temptation, and prolonging my halts as if reluctant to advance, when suddenly I heard the deep bell of Westminster clock chime a quarter. "A quarter past eleven," thought I; "I must look sharp." And I did look sharp, and reached the place of appointment out of breath. My father was at the door. His face was clouded, and his hand trembled as he laid it on my shoulder, and said, "Charlie, will *nothing* save you from ruin?"

"Ruin!" said I, in amazement; "what do you mean? What makes you so late?"

"Late! it's not half-past yet; didn't you tell me half-past eleven was the time?"

"I did; and it is now just half-past twelve! The post you were to have had was filled half an hour ago by one of the other applicants."

I staggered back in astonishment and horror. Then *it* flashed on me that I had dawdled away an hour without knowing it, and with it the finest opening I ever had in my life.

I must pass over the next two years, and come to the conclusion of my story. During those two years I entered upon and left no less than three employments—each less advantageous than the former. The end of that time found me a clerk in a bank in a country town. In this capacity my besetting sin was still haunting me. I had several times been called into the manager's room, and reprimanded for unpunctuality, or cautioned for wasting my time. The few friends who on my first coming to the town had taken an interest in me had dropped away, disgusted at my unreliable conduct, or because I myself had neglected their acquaintance. My employers had ceased to entrust me with any commissions requiring promptitude or care; and I was nothing more than an office drudge—and a very unprofitable drudge too. Such was my condition when, one morning, a telegram reached me from my mother to say—"Father is very ill. Come at once."

I was shocked at this bad news, and determined to start for London by the next train.

I obtained leave of absence, and hastened to my lodgings to pack up my few necessaries for the journey. By the time I arrived there, the shock of the telegram had in some way abated, and I was able to contemplate my journey more calmly. I consulted a time-table, and found that there was one train which, by hurrying, I could just catch in a quarter of an hour, and that the next went in the afternoon.

By the time I had made up my mind which to take, and inquired where a lad could be found who would carry down my portmanteau to the station, it was too late to catch the first train, and I therefore had three hours to spare before I could leave. This delay, in my anxious condition, worried me, and I was at a loss how to occupy the interval. If I had been wise, I should never have quitted that station till I did so in the train. But, alas! I decided to take a stroll instead. It was a sad walk, for my father's image was constantly before my eyes, and I could hardly bear to think of his being ill. I thought of all his goodness and forbearance to me, and wondered what would become of us if he were not to recover. I wandered on, broken-hearted, and repenting deeply of all my ingratitude, and the ill return I had made him for his love to me, and I looked forward eagerly to being able to throw myself in his arms once more, and beg his forgiveness.

Thus I mused far into the morning, when it occurred to me to look at my watch. Was it possible? It wanted not half an hour of the time for the train, and I was more than two miles from the place. I started to walk rapidly, and soon came in sight of the town. What fatal madness impelled me at that moment to stand and look at a ploughing match that was taking place in a field by the roadside? For a minute or two my anxiety, my father, the train, all were forgotten in the excitement of that contest. Then I recovered myself and dashed on like the wind. Once more (as I thought but for an instant) I paused to examine a gipsy encampment on the border of the wood, and then, reminded by a distant whistle, hurried forward. Alas! as I dashed into the station the train was slowly turning the corner and I sunk down in an agony of despair and humiliation.

When I reached home at midnight, my mother met me at the door.

"Well, you are come at last," she said quietly.

"Yes, mother; but father, how is he?"

"Come and see him."

I sprang up the stairs beside her. She opened the door softly, and bade me enter.

My father lay there dead.

"He waited for you all day," said my mother, "and died not an hour ago. His last words were, 'Charlie is late.' Oh, Charlie, why did you not come sooner?"

Then she knelt with me beside my dead father. And, in that dark lonely chamber, that night, the turning-point of my life was reached.

Boys, I am an old man now; but, believe me, since that awful moment I have never, to my knowledge, dawdled again!

Chapter Thirty Two
A Night on Scafell Pike

Off at last! Hard work to get off, though; as if a fellow of fifteen wasn't old enough to take care of himself. Mother cut up as much as if I'd asked leave to go to my own funeral—said I was too young, and knew nothing of the world, and all that sort of thing. But I don't see what knowing the world has to do with a week's tramp in the Lakes; not much of the world there—anyhow, where I mean to go.

I've got it all up in the guide-book, and written out my programme, and given them my address for every day, and promised to keep a diary, and always sleep between blankets, for fear the sheets shouldn't be aired—and what more can a fellow do?

Well, then mother said I must promise to keep in the valleys, and not attempt to climb any of the mountains. Oh, ah! lively work that would be. I might just as well stay at home and walk round Russell Square fifty times a day; and I said so, and repeated off from memory what the guide-book says about the way up Helvellyn. This last fetched them rather, and convinced them I wasn't undertaking what I didn't know all about. So at last father said, "Let the boy go, it may do him good and teach him self-reliance."

"But what'll be the good of that," sobs mother, "if my Bartholomew falls over a precipice and never comes home?"

"Oh, I'll promise not to fall over a precipice," said I.

And at last it was settled, and here I am in the train, half-way to Windermere.

Just been looking through my knapsack. Frightful nuisance! Had it weighed at Euston, and it weighs 4 pounds 8 ounces. I wanted to keep it under 4 pounds! Must be the spare shirt the girls insisted on my bringing, as if I couldn't wash the one I've got on in half a dozen waterfalls a day, and just run myself dry afterwards! Don't see what I can throw out. Must take the guide-book, and boot-laces, and needle and worsted for my blisters, and a collar for Sunday, and a match-box, and this diary book and a night-shirt. Bother that extra eight ounces.

I'm certain it will drag me down. By the way there are the sandwiches and apples! Suppose I eat them now, that'll make it all right. Good thought that. Here goes!

Getting near Windermere now—be there in an hour. May as well put on my knapsack, so as to be ready. By the way, I hope my money's all right, and I hope father's given me enough. He paid for my return ticket down here, and he's given me 6 shillings a day for the rest of the time. Says he did the Lakes once on 5 shillings a day when he was a boy. Somehow don't fancy there'll be much change for me out of the 6 shillings, if the guide-book says right; but you won't catch me spending more! Shan't ride anywhere where I can walk, and don't mean to tip any waiters all the time! Shall have to shut up now and look at the scenery at page 52 of the guide-book.

8 p.m., Ambleside.—The "Green Unicorn." Here at last, very fagged. I mean to have a row with the shoemaker when I get home about the hobs on my boots. Two of them are clean out, and all the rest are beginning to get worn already. Anyhow, I sold the coach people by walking. They thought I was bound to drive, but I didn't. Wouldn't have minded it, though, once or twice between Windermere and here, for of course I'm not in training yet.

Hope this inn isn't a dear one. It's the smallest I could find in the place, and I don't think they're likely to charge for attendance; if they do, it'll be a swindle, for I ordered eggs and bacon an hour ago, and they've not come yet. I wonder what they'll charge for the eggs and bacon. Suppose there are two eggs, that'll be 2 pence; and a slice of bacon, 2 pence; bread, 1 penny; tea, 1 penny; that's 7 pence; oughtn't to be more than 10 pence at the outside.

Ah, here it comes.

Good supper it was, too, and not much left at the end.

Mean to do Scafell to-morrow. Highest mountain in England, guide-book says. Two fellows in the inn are going, too; but I don't intend to hang on to them, as they seem to think no end of themselves. They're Cambridge fellows, and talk as if they could do anything. I'd like to take the shine out of them.

Tuesday, 8 a.m.—Just fancy, the swindlers here charged me 2 shillings for that tea, 2 shillings 6 pence for my bed, and 1 shilling for attendance—5 shillings 6 pence! I call it robbery, and told them so, and said they needn't suppose they could take *me* in. They said it was the usual charge, and they didn't make any difference for small boys, as they found they ate quite as much as grown-up people. The two Cambridge fellows seemed to find something to laugh at in this, and one of them said I didn't mind being taken in, but I didn't like being taken in and done for. I suppose he thought this was a joke. Some idiots can grin at anything.

I told the hotel people I should certainly not pay for attendance, as I didn't consider I had had any. The waiter said very well, my boots would do as well, and they would keep them till I settled the bill, and they had no time to stand fooling about with a whipper-snapper. Of course I had to shell out, as my boots were worth more than the whole bill—although my bootmaker has taken me in pretty well over the hobnails. I told them I should take good care to tell every one what sort of people they were, and I wouldn't have any breakfast there to pay them out.

Fancy this made them look rather blue, but the lesson will be good for them. Catch me getting done like that again! I'm going to start now, 8 a.m., as I want to get ahead of the Cambridge idiots. Page 54 of the guide-book has all about the scenery at Ambleside.

12 o'clock, Dungeon Ghyl.—Stopping here for lunch. Awful grind up the valley in the sun with an empty stomach. Going in for a 9 pence lunch here. The fellow says the weather is going to break this afternoon, and I'd better mind what I'm up to, going up Scafell Pike. He wants me to take a guide, that's his little dodge. As if I couldn't take care of myself! I've got it all up in the guide-book, and guess I could find the top blindfold. I'll laugh if I get up before the Cambridge fellows. They'll probably funk it, though, or miss the way, and have to get me to give them a leg up. It'll be a good lesson for them.

Don't think much of the inn here, so I'm glad I shan't be putting up here for the night. The waiter looks as if he expects to be tipped for everything. He seemed regularly cut up when I told him I was going on to Wastdale Head from the top, and shouldn't be staying here. Of course he tried to get me to come back, and said I could never get over to Wastdale this night. All stuff, I know, for it's no distance on the map. "Oh," he said, "don't you believe in the maps; they're no guide. Take my advice, and don't try to go to Wastdale, my boy." I was a good mind to be down on him for being so familiar, but what was the use? As if he knew better than the guide-books! Ah! here comes my lunch.

4 p.m., top of Rosset Ghyl.—Had to pay 1 shilling for that 9 pence lunch after all, as they charged 3 pence for attendance in the bill. Didn't care to have a row, as the Cambridge fellows turned up just that minute. Beastly the way they always grin when they see me. As if they couldn't grin at one another. I cleared out as soon as they came, and started up here.

There was a mile or so of pretty level path to the bottom of this ravine, and then it was a tremendous climb up to the top. You have to scramble nearly straight up among the rocks on each side of the waterfall, and if one of my hobnails went off, I'm certain half a dozen did. I'll tell my father not to pay that cobbler at all. I can't make out how the sheep manage to go up and down this place as they do. I know I'm glad I'm not coming back this way. I thought I was over once or twice as it was, owing to those wretched boots.

The Cambridge duffers caught me about half-way up, trying to look as if they weren't fagged. I knew better—never saw fellows so blown. They appeared to be greatly amused because I happened to slip backwards down a grass slope just as they passed, as if there was anything funny in that. One of them called out, "It's the other way up, youngster," and the other said, "We'll tell them you're on the way at the top." I was a good mind to shut them up, but I got some earth in my mouth at the moment, and as they didn't wait, it wasn't any use going after them. However, I expect I shall find them regularly done up when I get a little higher, and then perhaps they'll be sorry they cheeked me. All about the view from Rosset Ghyl in page 72 of the guide-book. Awful sell; it's coming on to rain, and quite misty, too. I'd better go on, or I shan't get the view from the top.

6 o'clock.—Don't exactly know where I am. Regular Scotch mist come down over the hills, and I can't see twenty yards. Only sitting down now because I'm not quite sure whether I'm right or wrong. Been looking it up in the guide-book, but there's not much to guide you there when you can't see your way. The only thing is, it says there are little cairns marking the way up to the top, every fifty yards or so. It would be rather a tip to find one of them.

The wind is making a noise, exactly like the sea, against the side of the mountain. I saw the side a little while ago, like a great black cliff, but it's too misty to see it now. Hope it'll clear up soon, or I may be late getting down to Wastdale. By the way, I wonder if they call this heap of stones I'm sitting on one of the cairns? Good idea! it must be.

Yes, it's all right; I left my traps here and went fifty yards further on up the slope, and there's another cairn there—very lucky! I had a job to find my way back here in the mist, though. However, I'm on the right track now. Wonder what's become of those Cambridge fellows. They're sure not to be up to my tips, and most likely they're wandering about lost. Poor duffers!

7 o'clock.—Hope I'm right, but it's getting more misty than ever, and I can hardly stand up in the wind. It's an awful job, too, feeling one's way along by these cairns; for you can't see one from the other, and the chances are you may now and then lose sight of both, and then you're lost. I've been lost several times, but luckily I've got into the track again. Fancy I must be getting on towards the top, for the rocks are getting bigger and tumbled

about in all directions, and the guide-book says that's what the top of Scafell Pike is like. Shan't I be glad to get to the top! I'm frightfully cold and wet here, and there's scarcely a hob left on my wretched boots. I wish I had that cobbler here!

All about the view going up to the top of Scafell Pike on page 76 of the guide-book. Sounds rather like a joke when you can scarcely see your hand in front of you, to read that behind you stretches the beautiful vista of the Langdale Valley, with Wansfell in the distance, and an exquisite glimpse of the waters of Windermere sparkling in the sun; to your right Helvellyn towers amidst its lesser brethren, while to the left the gloomy dome of Coniston lends a serious grandeur to the scene. Sounds all very fine, but it's a pity they don't put in the view on a day like this as well.

I quite miss the dashing of the wind against the cliffs. They're far behind now, and the wind seems to dash against me instead. Whew! I'd better peg on, or the tea will be cold at Wastdale Head! No sign of the Cambridge fellows. Wonder where they are. Half wish I was with them—idiots as they are.

8:30 o'clock.—Top at last! I'm black and blue all over, with tumbling among those brutal rocks. Don't know however I got up, and now I'm up, don't know how I shall get down. It's just dark now, and I can scarcely see the paper I'm writing on. Jolly fix I'm in. Can't positively see the big cairn, though I'm sitting on it, and haven't a notion which way I came up to it, or which way I have to go down to Wastdale.

I wish those Cambridge fellows would turn up. They weren't bad fellows after all. In fact, I rather liked one of them. Don't know what to do. By the way, may as well eat one of the biscuits I have in my knapsack. Think of sitting up here on the highest spot of England eating a biscuit, and not knowing how to get home! Enough to make any one feel down in the mouth. Wish I was down in the valley. All about the view from the top on page— Bah! that's too much of a joke. Wish I could see anything! Only thing I can see is that I'm stuck here for the night, and shall probably be found frozen to death in the morning. What an ass I was to snub those jolly Cambridge fellows! Fancy how snug it would be to be sitting between them now. I suppose they're down at the hotel having a good tea before a blazing fire. My word, it makes one blue to—

11 o'clock.—Just had the presence of mind to wind up my watch. Had to sit on my hands a quarter of an hour before I could feel the key in my waistcoat pocket. Ugh! wish the wind would shut up. Never felt so up a tree all my life. Those Cambridge fellows will be curling up in bed now, I expect. Can't write more.

12 o'clock.—It suddenly occurred to me there was no absolute necessity, if I must stick up here all night, to stick at the tip-top. So I crawled down gingerly among the rocks on the side away from the wind and looked, or rather felt, for a sheltered place. Presently I slipped and toppled down between two great boulders and nearly killed myself. However, when I came to, it struck me I might as well stay here as anywhere else. It's right out of the wind and pretty dry, as the mist doesn't seem to be able to get down into it. Then the lucky idea occurred to me I had two candles in my knapsack and a box of matches, and I might as well light up. So I lit one of the candles, and I've been warming my fingers and toes at it for the last half-hour; also been reading the guide-book, and find that the Isle of Man is visible from this place. Jolly comforting to know it, when I can't even see the tip of my own nose. Got sick of the guide-book after that, and thought it would warm me to say over my Greek irregular verbs. Been through them once, but not quite successful 4,000 feet above the level of the sea. They remind a fellow rather too much of home. Wonder what they'd think there if they saw me up here. Wish I saw them, and could get a blanket! I promised them to sleep between blankets every night. It's awful not being able to keep one's promise.

The one thing that does comfort me is, I shan't have to pay anything for attendance to-night. In fact, I never spent such a cheap night anywhere... Booh! had to stop just now and sit on my hands again. Find it warmer even than the candle. How I wish those two Cambridge fellows were here! We could be quite jolly in here, and play round games, and that sort of thing. I've been trying one or two songs to pass the time, but they didn't come off. Made me homesick to sing, "Here in cool grot" and "Blow, gentle gales." That reminds me, the wind's dropped since I got in here. Sorry for it. It was some company to have it smashing all round one. Now it's so quiet it makes a fellow quite creepy. They do talk of mountain-tops being haunted. I know Scafell Pike is, and I'm the haunter. Wonder if there's any chance of anybody turning up? I've a good mind to go on to the cairn and howl and wave my candle about for a bit; it might fetch some one. The only thing is, it might frighten them away. I'll try it, anyhow, and I hope whoever comes will have some grub in his pocket and a pair of gloves.

1:30.—No go. Been howling like a hyena for half an hour till I've no voice left, and I'm all over spots of wax with the waving of my candle. Heard nothing but my own voice. Not an echo, or a dog barking, or anything. The mist lifted a bit, but I don't suppose any one could see the candle down at Wastdale. Ugh! ugh! Perhaps there'll be an article in a scientific paper about a curious phenomenon on the top of Scafell Pike. Wish I knew how to warm phenomenons! I've put on the spare shirt over my coat, and stuffed my feet into my knapsack, and wrapped last Friday's *Daily News* round my body and legs. Oh–h–h! why *did* I make a beast of myself to those two dear Cambridge fellows? Think of them now, with blankets tucked round their chins, and their noses in the pillow, snoring away; and their coats and bags lying idle about in the room. I do believe if I had their two suits on over my own I might keep warm. Hullo, what's that!

Never got such a fright. Thought it was thunder, or an earthquake, or the cairn coming down on the top of me, or something of that sort. Turned out to be the *Daily News* crackling under my clothes. Everything's so quiet, it startles one to move a foot. I'll give it up—I'll—there goes my last candle!

3:30.—Actually been asleep—at least, I don't know what's been going on the last two hours. That *Daily News* was rather a tip, after all. I might have been frozen to death without it. Hurrah for the Radicals! Rather crampy all the same about the joints, and must get up and shake myself, or I shall be no good for the rest of the day. Ugh! What a state my mother would be in if she heard that cough! I'm certain I hadn't caught it before I went to sleep.

Just been up to the top and had a look round. Mist is nearly all away, and there are some streaks in the sky that look like the beginning of morning. May hold out, after all. Never know what you can do till you try. I'll just put on my *Daily News* again and wait here another half-hour, and then try out again. Wish it was daylight. Mustn't go to sleep again if I can help it, as I might catch cold.

4:30.—Hurrah! Just seen the sun rise! No end of a fine show. Long bit of poetry about it in the guide-book, cribbed from Wordsworth or somebody. Can't say the page, as I tore out the leaf last night to put inside my boot, to help to keep my toes warm. Never expected to see the sun rise from the highest spot in England. Awful good score for me, though—very few do it, I fancy. Think of those lazy Cambridge fellows curled up in bed and missing it all; just the way with these fellows, all show off.

The sun's warm already, and I've left off my *Daily News* and spare shirt, and I'm just going to take the paper out of my boots; that is, if I can ever get down to my toes—but I'm so jolly stiff.

Never mind, I've done it, and—bother that cough, it's made me break the point of my pencil.

5 a.m.—Been sharpening the pencil with my teeth. Rather a poor breakfast; never mind, I shall have a rousing appetite when I get to the bottom. May tip that waiter possibly, if he brings the grub up sharp. Now I'm starting down. I shall go down to Dungeon Ghyl the way I came, I fancy. If I went down to Wastdale, I might meet those Cambridge fellows again,

and I wouldn't care for that. It would mortify them too much to know what they've missed. Ta! ta! Scafell Pike, old man, keep yourself warm. I'll leave you my *Daily News*, in case you want it.

8 a.m.—Been all this time getting half-way down. Can scarcely crawl. Going up hill's nothing, but the bumping you get coming down, when you're as stiff as a poker, and coughing like an old horse, is a caution. Had a good mind to ask a shepherd I met half an hour ago to give me a leg down, but didn't like to; so I told him I'd just been to the top to see the sunrise, and it was a fine morning. All but added, "I suppose you haven't got a crust of bread in your pocket?" but pulled up in time. Pity to spoil my appetite for breakfast at Dungeon Ghyl. Ugh! if I sit here I shall rust up, and not be able to move. *Must* go on.

10 a.m.—Top of Rosset Ghyl. Not very swell time to get from the top of the Pike here in five hours. All a chance whether I get down at all, now—I'm about finished up. Wish those Cambridge fellows—

Here the diary ends abruptly; but, in case our readers are curious to know the end of our hero's adventure, they will be interested to learn that at the identical moment when the writer reached this point in his diary, the Cambridge fellows *did* turn up. They had, indeed, been out searching the hills from very early morning for the wanderer. As he did not arrive the night before at Wastdale, they had concluded he had given up the ascent, and returned to Dungeon Ghyl. But when early that morning a guide had come over from Dungeon Ghyl, and reported that the young gentleman had certainly not returned there, the two 'Varsity men became alarmed, and turned out to search. There was no sign of him on the Wastdale side of the mountain; and, getting more and more alarmed, they went on to the summit. There they discovered a crushed-up *Daily News* and two or three stained pages of a guide-book. Glad of any clue, they followed the track down towards Dungeon Ghyl, and at last came upon the poor fellow, fairly exhausted with hunger, fatigue, and rheumatism. They gave him what partially revived him, and then with the care and tenderness of two big brothers carried him down the steep side of Rosset Ghyl, and so on to the hotel. There they kept him under their special care, day and night, and never left him till he was well enough to return home to his anxious family.

Since then Bartholomew Bumpus has made several ascents of Scafell Pike, but he has never again, I believe, stayed up there all night to see the sunrise. Nor has he, when he could possibly help it, gone up unaccompanied by at least one Cambridge fellow.

Chapter Thirty Three
Very much abroad

Being the impressions of foreign travel, communicated chiefly to a particular friend by Thomas Hooker, minor, of Rugby, during the course of a Continental tour in France and Switzerland in the company of his brother, James Hooker, major, also of Rugby.

London, *July* 31.

Dear Gus,—Here's a spree! The pater's got an idea into his head that young fellows ought to see something of foreign parts, and store their minds with the beauties of Nature in her grandest—I forget what—anyhow, we backed him up; and Jim and I are to start abroad on our own hooks on Friday. How's that for luck? The pater has settled what hotels we go to in Paris and Switzerland, and he's sketched out a route for us every day we're away. The grind is, he's awfully particular we should write home every day and keep accounts. Jim will have to do that, and I'll keep you up. It really is a very good thing for fellows to travel and expand their minds, you know. We're starting from Holborn Viaduct at 9:30 on Friday. I'll write and let you know my impressions, as the pater calls it; and you might let your young sister see them too, if you like.

Yours truly, T. Hooker.

Paris, *August* 3.

Dear Gus,—We had an awful squeak for the train at Holborn, owing to Jim's hatbox falling off the cab and his insisting on going back to pick it up. It seems to me rather humbug taking chimneys at all, but he says that's all I know of foreign travel; so I caved in and brought mine too.

Another thing that nearly lost the train was a row about the luggage. The fellows wanted to do me out of two bob because they said my portmanteau was four pounds overweight! There was nearly a shindy, I can tell you, only Jim said we'd better walk into the chap on our way back. Anyhow, I wasn't going to be done, so I unlocked my portmanteau and took out my spare jacket and a pair of bags, and carried them over my arm, and that made the weight all right. The fellows tried to grin, of course, but I fancy they were rather blue about it.

Our tickets cost 45 shillings 6 pence each, not counting grub on the way, which about finished up a £5 note for the two of us.

Jim and I had a stunning time in the train. There was only one other old chap in the carriage. When the fellow came for the tickets outside Dover, Jim happened to be up on the luggage rack, and the fellow would never have spotted him if the rack hadn't given way. Then he got crusty, and we all but got left behind by the steamer.

Beastly tubs those steamers are! I wonder why they don't make some that go steady. And they ought to make the seats facing the side of the vessel, and not with your back to it. You miss such a lot of the view. I sat with my face to the side of the vessel most of the way. I don't exactly know what became of Jim. He said afterwards he'd been astern watching the English coast disappear. I suppose that accounted for his looking so jolly blue. We weren't sorry to clear out of that boat, I can tell you.

Jim was first up the gangway, and I was third, owing to dropping my spare bags half-way up and having to pick them up. There was an awfully civil French fellow at the top of the gangway, who touched his hat to me. I couldn't make out what he said, but I fancied he must be asking for a tip, so I gave him a copper. That seemed to make him awfully wild, and he wanted to know my name. I had to tell him, and he wrote it down; but as he didn't get my address, I hope there won't be a fuss about it. I didn't see any harm in tipping him, but I suppose it's against French law, and I don't mean to do it any more.

There was an awfully rum lot of chaps in our carriage between Calais and Paris. You'd have thought they had never seen a pair of bags before in their life; for they stared at mine all the way from Calais to Amiens, where we got out for refreshment. I thought it best to take my bags with me to the buffet, as they might have humbugged about with them if I'd left them in the carriage.

They ought to make English compulsory in French schools. The duffers in the buffet didn't even know what a dough-nut was! Not even when Jim looked it up in the dixy and asked for *noix à pâté*. The idiot asked us if we meant "rosbif," or "biftik," or "palal"—that's all the English they seemed to know, and think English fellows feed off nothing else. However, we did get some grub, and paid for it too. When we got back to the carriage I took the precaution of sticking my bags on the rack above Jim's head; so all the fellows stared at him the rest of the way, and I got a stunning sleep.

We had an awful doing, as Bunker would call it—by the way, did he pull off his tennis match against Turner on breaking-up day?—when we got to Paris. The row at Holborn was a fool to it. Just fancy, they made Jim and me open both our portmanteaux and hat-boxes before they would let us leave the station! I can tell you, old man, I'm scarcely cool yet after that disturbance, and if it hadn't been for Jim I guess they'd have found out how a "Rug" can kick out! Jim says it's the regular thing, and they collar all the cigars they can find. All I can say is, it's robbery and cool cheek, and I wish you or some of the fellows would write to the *Times* or the *Boy's Own Paper* and get it stopped. We had to turn every blessed thing out on the counter, and pack up again afterwards. It's a marvel to me how the mater stowed all the things away. I couldn't get half of them back, and had to shove the rest into my rug and tie it up at the corners like a washerwoman's bundle. Jim's too easy-going by half. I'm certain, if he'd backed me up, we could have hacked over the lot of them; and I shouldn't have lost that spare pair of bags, which I forgot all about in the shindy. I hope there'll be a war with France soon. We were jolly fagged when we got to the inn, I can tell you. The old woman had got the pater's letter, so she expected us. She's rather an ass, and must have been getting up her English for our benefit, for she's called us "nice young Englese gentilman" about a hundred times already.

I don't think Jim's got over the blues he had watching the English coast yesterday. He's asleep still, so I'm writing this while I'm waiting for him to come to breakfast. I shall not wait much longer, I can tell you. Ta-ta! Remember me to any of the old crowd you see; also to your young sister.

Yours truly, Thomas Hooker.

P.S.—By the way, see what your French dixy says for doughnut, and let me know by return. We're going on to Switzerland in a day or two.

Paris, *August* 6.

Dear Gus,—The dictionary word of yours won't wash here. We've tried it all round Paris, and you might as well talk Greek to them. I don't believe there's any word in the language for dough-nut. Jim's not bad at French, either. We should be regularly floored if it wasn't for him. And I expect they guess by his accent he comes from Rugby, for fellows all touch their hats to him.

You know the pater gave us a list of places to go and see in Paris—the Louvre and the Luxembourg, and all that. Well, he never stuck down where they were, and we've had to worry it out for ourselves. Jim stopped a fellow this morning and asked him, "Où est la chemin pour Luxembourg?" The fellow took off his hat and was awfully civil, and said, "Par ici, messieurs," and took us a walk of about three miles, and landed us at a railway station. He thought we wanted to go to Luxembourg in Germany, or wherever it is—fare about three cool sovs. The fellow hung about us most of the rest of the day, expecting a tip. Likely idea that, after the game he'd had with us! We couldn't shake him off till we bolted into one of the swimming baths on the river. That smoked him out. Most of these chaps draw the line at a tub. Would you believe it? at our inn, they never seem to have heard of soap in their lives, and we got quite tired of saying "savon" before we found some in a shop. Jim thinks they use it all up for soup. What we get at the inn tastes like it.

Jim is rather a cute beggar. We went to a café yesterday to get some grub, and he wanted a glass of milk. We had both clean forgotten the French for milk, and we'd left the dixy at the inn. We tried to make the fellow understand, but he was an ass. We pointed to a picture of a cow hanging on the wall and smacked our lips; and he grinned and rubbed his hands, and said, "Ah, oui. Rosbif! jolly rosbif!" Did you ever hear of such a born idiot? At last Jim had an idea and said, "Apportez-nous du café-au-lait sans le café." That fetched it. The fellow twigged at once. Not bad of Jim, was it?

Jolly slow place Paris. The swimming baths are the only place worth going to. Jim went in off the eight-foot springboard. You should have seen the natives sit up at the neat dive he made.

I hope the pater's not going to ask too much about the Louvre, because we scamped it. The fact is, there was a little unpleasantness with one of the fellows, owing to Jim's cane happening to scratch one of the pictures by a chap named Rubens. It was quite an accident, as we were only trying to spike a wasp on the frame, and Jim missed his shot. The fellow there made a mule of himself, and lost his temper. So we didn't see the fun of staying, and cut.

Montreux, Lake of Geneva, *August* 10.

Couldn't finish this before we left Paris. We meant to start for here on Friday, but settled to come on on Thursday night after all. You needn't go telling them at home, but between you and me it was a bit of a bolt.

The fact was, we went to a church called Nôtre Dame in the morning— not nearly such a snug place as Rugby Chapel, and they charge a penny apiece for the chairs. So we cut the inside and thought we'd go up to the top. It wasn't a bad lark, and you get a stunning view. The swimming baths looked about the size of a sheet of school paper. There was a door open into the belfry, and as nobody was about, we never thought it would be any harm to have a ring up. We couldn't get the big bell to go, but most of the others did, and it was enough to deafen you.

I suppose they must have heard the row below, for when we looked down we saw a regular crowd of fellows in the square underneath looking up our way. After that we thought we might as well shut up, and were just going to cut down, when a fellow belonging to the place, who had been somewhere on the top, came rushing round the parapet, flourishing a stick and yelling like a trooper in awfully bad French. We had a good start of him, especially as we shut the door at the top of the stairs behind us. Besides he was fat; so we easily pulled it off.

There was an old woman at the bottom who kept the ticket place. She twigged *it* was a bolt, and tried to stop us; but she couldn't *get* out of her box. So we strolled out easily and cabbed it back to the inn. It was an awful game to see the crowd still staring up at the tower as we drove off. The fat fellow got down just as we were turning the corner. I don't think he guessed we were cabbing it. Anyhow, we didn't see any one chasing the cab. Jim said we were rather well out of it; and we settled we might as well drive on to the swimming baths and stay there for an hour or so till things had quieted down, and then go on to Switzerland by the evening train, especially, Jim said, as the pater might not like to get his name mixed up in a French row.

Beastly uncomfortable carriages on the Swiss railway from Paris. There was the same humbug about the luggage at a little station in the middle of the night, but we were too fagged to cut up rough. We were jolly glad to get here at last, I can tell you.

I must shut up now, as I've got to write to pater. It's a regular go. We forgot he'd be sending the money to Paris, and now we've only got about half-a-sov. between us! Remember me to your young sister.

Yours truly, T. Hooker.

Montreux, *August* 10.

Dear Father,—We didn't see the Luxembourg, as a fellow directed us to the wrong place. We had several bathes in the Seine. Jim got on very well with his French, and I think we are both improved. We should be glad of some more money, as we are nearly out. I bought a present for you in Paris, which I think you will like when you see it. If you could send the money here by return it would do. I suppose what you sent to Paris missed us, as we came here a day sooner than we expected.

We went up Nôtre Dame the last day we were in Paris. There is a fine view from the top. It is surprising how few of the French you meet in the swimming baths. We had the place to ourselves one day. It's eight feet at the deep end. Jim and I both think foreign travel is good for a fellow, and we shall hope to have a reply to this by return.

Your loving son, Tom.

Montreux, *August* 11.

Dear Gus,—We're regularly stuck up, as the money hasn't come yet. I hope it will come soon, or the old girl at the inn here will think we're cadgers. We had a stunning row on the lake yesterday; the boats are only a bob an hour, so we thought we might go in for it. We raced a steamer for about half a mile, and weren't done then, only Jim's oar came off the pin (they haven't such things as row-locks here), and that upset us.

Of course it didn't matter, as we could swim; but the fellows in the steamer kicked up an awful shine about it, and came and hauled us up, boat and all. It was rather awkward, as we had nothing to tip them with. We got out at a dismal sort of place called Chillon. We told the captain if he was ever in London the pater would be glad to see him.

We had a grind getting back here with the boat, as it came on dark and misty, and we couldn't see where Montreux had got to. Jim got rather chawed up too by the cold, so I sculled. The wind was against us, and it was rather a hard pull, especially when you couldn't see the land at all. I managed to keep pretty warm with rowing, but old Jim's teeth chattered like a steam-engine. It came on a regular squall, and I didn't see the fun of sculling after about a couple of hours. So Jim and I huddled up to keep warm, and let her drift. We were jolly glad to see a light after a bit, and yelled to let them know where we were. They didn't hear, though, so we just stuck on and chanced it. The old tub drifted ashore all right, side on, though she upset just as we got to land. It was lucky the water was shallow, as we were too cold to swim. As it was, old Jim nearly came to grief. It was no end of a job hauling in the boat. She was rather knocked about. We had drifted back to Chillon, exactly where we started from.

The keeper of the castle put us up for the night and was no end of a brick. There was rather a row with the boat fellow when we got back to Montreux. He got crusty about the boat being damaged, and wanted about two sovs! As it happened, we hadn't got anything, as we gave the fellow at the castle five francs, and that cleared us out. We told the boat fellow to call at the inn to-morrow, and I hope to goodness the money will have turned up, as it's a bit awkward. Jim has a cold.

Yours truly T. Hooker.

Please remember me to your young sister.

Montreux, *August* 13.

Dear Father,—Thanks awfully for the money; it was jolly to get it, and mother's letter. It is very hilly about here. Jim's cold is getting better. Would you mind telegraphing to us who is the winner of the Australian cricket match to-morrow, and how many Grace scored? In haste, Your loving son, Tom.

Riffel Hotel, *August* 18.

Dear Gus,—We're awfully high up here—awful rum little inn it is. It was chock full, and Jim and I have to sleep under the table. There are about a dozen other fellows who have to camp out too, so it's a rare spree.

We're going to have a shot at the Matterhorn to-morrow if it's fine. It looks easy enough, and Jim and I were making out the path with a telescope this afternoon. It's rather a crow to do the Matterhorn. Some muffs take guides up, but they cost four or five pounds, so we're going without.

That boat fellow at Montreux got to be a regular nuisance. In fact, that's why we came on here a day earlier. He came up twice a day to the inn, and we couldn't shake him off. We gave him a sov., which was twice what he had a right to. He swore he'd have two pounds or bring up a policeman with him next time. So we thought the best way was to clear out by the early train next morning, and I guess he was jolly blue when he found us gone. I send with this a faint sketch of some of the natives! What do you say to their rig?

It was a pretty good grind up to Zermatt, and we walked it up the valley. There wasn't much to see on the way, and it's a frightfully stony road. There were some fellows playing lawn-tennis at the hotel at Zermatt. One of them wasn't half bad. His serves twisted to the leg and were awfully hard to get up. Jim and I wouldn't have minded a game, only the fellows seemed to think no one wanted to play but themselves. We may get a game to-morrow on our way to the Matterhorn. It was a tremendous fag getting up here from Zermatt. I don't know why fellows all come on, as there's no tennis court or anything up here.

There's an ice-field up here called a glacier, but it's an awful fraud if you want skating—rough as one of Bullford's fields at Rugby. A fellow told me it bears all the year round, but it's got a lot of holes, so we don't think we'll try it. I expect we shall be home next week, as the pater thinks we've run through our money rather too fast. Remember me to your people and your young sister.

Yours truly, T. Hooker.

Zermatt, *August* 20.

Dear Gus,—We didn't do the Matterhorn after all, as Jim screwed his foot. He's awfully unlucky, and if it hadn't been for the accident we might have got to the top; and of course it stops tennis too. We did get one game before we started up. Jim gave me fifteen in two games each set. I pulled off the first, but he whacked me the other two. It's a beastly rough court, though, and the mountain was awfully in the light.

We hadn't much difficulty finding the way to the Matterhorn, as there was a sign-post at the end of the village. We thought we might as well take the easy side, as the front of the hill is pretty stiff. Of course we had to take a good long round, which was a nuisance, as we meant to be back for *table d'hôte* at seven. When we got properly on to the side we put it on, but it was a good long grind, I can tell you. We weren't sorry to get up to a snow slope and cool ourselves.

They ought to sweep a path across the snow, or fellows are very likely to lose their way. We lost ours, but we had a good lark on the snow snowballing. It got deep in one part, so we had to clamber up the rocks at the side to get to the top of the slope. It's rather deceptive, distance, on the snow, for it took us an hour to do what seemed only a few yards. We got on to a flat bit after awhile, and had another turn on the snow.

It was rather a game rolling things down the slope. They went at an awful pace. The nuisance is the snow has a way of slipping from under you, and that's how Jim and I came to grief. We were sitting on the edge of the slope watching a boulder slide, when we began to slide ourselves. We hadn't our spikes on, or we might have pulled up. As it was, we got up no end of a speed down that slope. It was no joke. I yelled to Jim to lie flat, and not sit up, or he might pitch on his head. I don't remember how we got on after that; I must have bumped my head, for when I pulled myself together I found I was sitting in the middle of a grass field with a jolly headache, and pretty well black and blue.

I was able to get up though, and looked about for old Jim. I can tell you it was no joke. I couldn't see him anywhere, and thought he must have been buried in the snow. I can tell you, old man, it was rough on me for a quarter of an hour or so. But I found him at last, about a quarter of a mile down the field. He rolled, he said; he couldn't get up, as his foot was screwed. So it was a pretty go, as I couldn't carry him. If I hadn't been quite so knocked about I might have tried; but Jim's a good nine stone, so I might have dropped him. Luckily, some fellows came—they'd come to look for us, in fact, as we'd told the waiter we were going up the Matterhorn, and might not be back in time for dinner; and when we didn't turn up, they guessed, I suppose, we might have come to grief. It was a good job they came, as Jim's foot was rather bad. All the hotel turned out to see us get back. I had to be carried too, the last bit of the way, as I got fagged. It's a sell we couldn't get to the top, as it's rather a crow to do the Matterhorn.

Jim's foot is better to-day, but he'll have to shut off tennis the rest of this season. I wish mother was here. She could look after Jim better than I can. In fact, the doctor here, rather a jolly fellow, says she and the pater had better come at once. I got him to write to the pater himself, as I was afraid it might make them think something was wrong if I did.

Please to remember me to your young sister.

T. Hooker.

Zermatt, *August* 22.

Dear Gus,—There's a telegram from the pater to say they'll be here to-morrow night. I'm rather glad, as Jim is feverish. The pater will have a good deal of tipping to do, as everybody here's no end civil. Can't write more, as I'm fagged. Remember me to your young sister.

T.H.

P.S.—I fancy we shall spend next summer in England—Jim and I. We don't either of us think much of Switzerland.

Chapter Thirty Four
Bilk's Fortune—A Ghost Story

Chapter I. Superstition

We had a fellow at Holmhurst School who rejoiced in the name of Alexander Magnus Bilk. But, as sometimes happens, our Alexander the Great did not in all respects resemble the hero to whom he was indebted for his name. Alexander the Great, so the school-books say, was small in stature and mighty in mind. Bilk was small in mind and lanky in stature. They called him "Lamp-post" as a pet name, and as regarded his height, his girth, and the lightness of his head, the term conveyed a very fair idea of our hero's chief characteristics. In short, Bilk had very few brains, and such as he had he occupied by no means to the best advantage. He read trashy novels, and believed every word of them, and, like poor Don Quixote of old, he let any one who liked make a fool of him, if he only took the trouble to get at his weak side.

I need hardly say the fellows at Holmhurst were not long in discovering that weak side and getting plenty of fun out of Alexander Magnus. He could be gammoned to almost any extent, so much so that after a term or two his persecutors had run through all the tricks they knew, and the unhappy youth was let alone for sheer want of an idea.

But one winter, when things seemed at their worst, and it really appeared likely that Bilk would have to be given up as a bad job, his tormentors suddenly conceived an idea, and proceeded to put it into practice in the manner I am about to relate in this most veracious history.

The neighbourhood of Holmhurst had for some weeks past been honoured by the presence of a gang of gipsies, who during the period of their sojourn had rendered themselves conspicuous by their diligence in their triple business of chair-mending, fowl-house robbing, and fortune-telling. In the last of these three departments they perhaps succeeded best in winning the confidence of their temporary neighbours, and the private séances they held with housemaids, tradesmen's boys, and schoolgirls had been particularly gratifying both as to attendance and pecuniary result.

It had at length been deemed to be for the general welfare that these interesting itinerants should seek a change of air in "fresh fields and pastures new," and the police had accordingly hinted as much to the authorities of the camp, and given them two hours to pack up.

More than ever convinced that gratitude is hopeless to seek in human nature, the gipsies had shaken the dust of Holmhurst from the soles of their not very tidy feet, and had moved off, no one knew whither.

These proceedings had, among other persons, interested Alexander Magnus Bilk not a little, and no one mourned the rapid departure of the gipsies more than he. For Bilk had for some days past secretly hugged the idea of presenting himself to the oracle of these wise ones and having his fortune told. He had in fact gone so far as to make a secret observation of their quarters one afternoon, and had resolved to devote the next half-holiday to the particular pursuit of knowledge they offered, when, lo! cruel fate snatched the cup from his lips and swept the promised fruit from his reach. In other words, the gipsies had gone, and, like his great namesake, Alexander, Magnus mourned.

Among those who noticed his dejection and guessed the cause of it were two of his particular persecutors. Morgan and Dell had for some months been suffering affliction for lack of any notion how to get a rise out of their victim. But they now suddenly cheered up, as they felt the force of a mighty idea moving them once more to action.

"Old chap," said Morgan, "I've got it at last!"

"What have you got?" asked "the old chap"; "your back tooth, or measles, or what?"

"I've got a dodge for scoring off the Lamp-post."

"Have you, though? You are a clever chap, I say! What is it?"

What it was, Morgan disclosed in such a very low whisper to his ally that the reader will have to guess. Suffice it to say, the two dear lads put their heads together for some time, and were extremely busy in the privacy of their own study all that evening.

Bilk, little dreaming of the compassion and interest he was evoking in the hearts of his schoolfellows, retired early to his sorrowful couch, and mourned his departed gipsies till slumber gently stepped in and soothed his troubled mind. But returning day laid bare the old wound, and Alexander girded himself listlessly to the duties of the hour, with a heart far away.

He was wandering across the playground after dinner, disinclined alike for work and play, when Dell accosted him. Bilk might have known Dell by this time, but his memory was short and his mind preoccupied, and he smelt no rat, as the Irish would say, in his companion's salutation.

"Hullo! where are you off to, Lamp-post? How jolly blue you look!"

"I'm only taking a walk."

"Well, you don't seem to be enjoying it, by the looks of you. I've just been taking a trot over the common."

"I suppose the gipsies have all gone?" inquired Bilk, as unconcernedly as he could.

"Yes, I suppose so," answered Dell, offhand. "Anyhow, they've cleared off the common."

"But I was told," said Bilk rather nervously, "they'd gone quite away."

"Not all of them, anyhow," said Dell. "But of course they can't now show up the way they used to."

"Where are they, then?" asked Magnus, with a new hope breaking in upon him.

"How can I tell? All I know is there are some hanging about still, and I shouldn't wonder if they weren't far from here."

"Really, I say! I wonder where?"

"I'd as good as bet you'd come across one or two of them after dark in Deadman's Lane, or up at the cross roads, any evening for a week yet. They don't clear out as fast as fellows think. But I must be off now, as I've a lot of work to do. Ta, ta!"

Alexander stood where the other left him, in deep meditation. Those few casual observations of his schoolfellow had kindled anew the fire that burned within him. Little could Dell guess how interesting his news was! After dark! The afternoon was getting on already. The school clock had struck half-past four nearly a quarter of an hour ago, and by five it would be quite dark. Tea was at a quarter-past five, and for half an hour after tea boys could do as they liked. Yes, it would be foolish to throw away such a chance. At any rate, he would take the air after tea in Deadman's Lane, and if there he should meet—oh! how he wondered what his fortune would be! Tea was a feverish meal for Bilk that evening. He spoke to no one, and ate very little; and as the hand of the clock worked round to a quarter to six he began to feel distinctly that a crisis in his life was approaching. He was glad neither Dell nor Morgan, whose studies probably kept them in their study, were at tea. They were such fellows for worrying him, and just now he wanted to be in peace.

The meal was over at last, and the boys rushed off to enjoy their short liberty before the hour of preparation. Bilk, who had taken the precaution to put both a sixpence and a cricket-cap in his pocket, silently and unobserved slid out into the deserted playground, and in another minute stood beyond the precincts of Holmhurst.

Deadman's Lane was scarcely three minutes distant, and thither, with nervous steps, he wended his way, fumbling the sixpence in his pocket, and straining his eyes in the darkness for any sign of the gipsies. Alas! it seemed to be a vain quest. The lane was deserted, and the cross roads he knew were too far distant to get there and back in half an hour. He was just thinking of giving it up and turning back, when a sound behind one of the hedges close to him startled him and sent his heart to his mouth. He stood still to listen, and heard a gruff voice say—or rather intone—the following mysterious couplet:

Ramsdam pammydiddle larrybonnywigtail
Wigtaillarrybonny keimo.

This could be no other than an incantation, and Bilk stood rooted to the spot, unable to advance or retreat. He heard a rustling in the hedge, and the incantation suddenly ceased. Then a figure like that of an old man bent with age and clad in a ragged coat which nearly touched the ground advanced slowly, saying in croaking accent as he did so—

"Ah, young gentleman, we've waited for ye. We couldn't go till we'd seen ye; for we've something to tell ye. Come quietly this way, and say not a word, or the spell's broken—come, young gentleman; come, young gentleman;" and the old man went on crooning the words to himself as he led the way with tottering steps round the hedge, and discovered a sort of tent in which sat, with her face half shrouded in a shawl, an old woman who wagged her head incessantly and chattered to herself in a language of her own. She took no notice of Bilk as he drew near tremblingly, and it was not until the old man had nudged her vehemently, and both had indulged in a long fit of coughing, that she at last growled, without even lifting her head—

"I see nothing unless for silver."

It said a great deal for Bilk's quickness of apprehension that he at once guessed this vague observation to refer to the sixpence he had not yet offered. He drew it out and handed it to the old woman, and was about to offer an apology at the same time, when the man put his hand to his mouth and snarled—

"Not a word."

The old woman took the coin in her trembling hand, and bent her head over it in silence. Bilk began to get uneasy. The time was passing, and he would have to start back in a very few moments. Could it be possible these gipsies, now they had his sixpence, were going to refuse to tell him the fortune for which he had longed and risked so much?

No! After a long pause the old woman lifted up her hand and said something in gibberish to her partner. It was a long time coming, for they both coughed and groaned violently during the recital. At length, however, the old man turned to Bilk and said gruffly—

"Kneel."

The boy obeyed, and the old man proceeded.

"She says a great danger threatens you this night. If you escape it, you will live to be a baronet or member of parliament, and perhaps you will marry a duke's daughter; but she can't be certain of that. If you don't escape it, you will be in a lunatic asylum next week, and never come out. Not a word," added he, as Bilk once more showed signs of breaking silence. "Wait till she speaks again."

Another long pause, and then another long recital in gibberish by the old woman, broken by the same coughing and groaning as before. Then the man said—

"Stand up, and hold your hands above your head."

Bilk obeyed.

"You want to know how to escape the peril?" said the man.

Bilk, with his hands still up, nodded.

"To-night at nine o'clock you will hear a bell."

Again Bilk nodded. Fancy the gipsies knowing that!

"You will go up to a small room with a chair and a bed in it, and undress."

A pause, and another nod from the astonished Bilk.

"You will put on a long white robe coming down to your ankles. At half-past nine the place will be dark—as black as pitch."

Bilk shuddered a little at the prospect.

"Then will be the time to escape your peril, or else to fall a victim. To escape it you must go quietly down the stairs and out of the house. The being who rules your life will be away for this one evening, and you will escape through his room by the window, which is close to the ground."

Bilk started once more. *He* knew the doctor was to be out that evening, but what short of supernatural vision could tell the gipsies of it?

"You must escape in the long white robe, and run past here on to the cross roads. No one will see you. At the cross roads there is a post with four arms. You must climb it and sit on the arm pointing this way until the clock strikes twelve. The peril will then be past, and your fortune will be made. Not a word. Go, and beware, Alexander Magnus Bilk!"

The legs of the scared Alexander could scarcely uphold him as he obeyed this last order, and sped trembling towards the school. The gipsies sat motionless as his footsteps echoed down the lane and died slowly away into silence.

Then they rose to go also; but as they did so other footsteps suddenly sounded, approaching them. With an alacrity astonishing in persons of their advanced age they darted back to their place of retreat; but too late. The footsteps came on quickly, and followed them to their very hiding-place, and next moment the light of two bullseyes turned full upon them, and the aged couple were in the hands of the police.

Chapter Two. Science

De Prudhom did not often allow himself the luxury of an evening out during term time. But on this particular evening he was pledged to fulfil a long-standing engagement with an old crony and fellow-bachelor, residing about two miles from the school. By some mysterious means the worthy dominie's intentions had oozed out, and Bilk was by no means the only boy who had heard of it. Mice seem to find out by instinct when the cat is away, and fix their own diversions accordingly.

I merely mention this to explain that as far as Alexander Magnus was concerned no night could have been more favourable for carrying out the intricate series of instructions laid down by the gipsy for the making of his fortune. With this reflection he consoled himself somewhat as he ran back to the school.

The doctor had already started for his evening's dissipation, if dining with Professor Hammerhead could be thus described. This eccentric old gentleman combined in one the avocations of a bachelor, a man of science, and a justice of the peace. He rarely took his walks abroad, preferring the solitude of his library, and the occasional company of some old comrade with whom to talk over old times, and unburden his mind of the scientific problems which encumbered it. On the present occasion he had lit upon a congenial spirit in worthy Dr Prudhom, and the two spent a very snug evening together over the dessert, raking up memories of the good old days when they lived on the same staircase at Brasenose; and plunging deep into abstruse questions of natural and physical science which even the sherry could not prevent from being dry.

The professor's present craze was what is commonly termed ethnology. Anything connected with the history and vicissitudes of the primitive races of mankind excited his enthusiasm, and he was never tired of inquiring into the languages, the manners, the customs, the dress, the ceremonies, and the movements generally of various branches of the human family, of whom the most obscure were sure to be in his eyes the most interesting.

It was only natural, therefore, that when Dr Prudhom made some casual reference to the recent incursion of gipsies, his host should seize the occasion to expatiate on the history of that extraordinary race; tracing them from the Egyptians downwards, and waxing eloquent on their tribal instincts, which no civilisation or even persecution could eradicate or domesticate.

"Fact is," said he, with a chuckle, "they had me to thank that they were allowed here so long. Police came to me end of first week and said they were a nuisance. I told the police when I wanted their opinion I'd ask it. End of second week police came again and said all the farmyards round had been robbed. I said I must inquire into it. He! he! All the time I was making glorious observations, my boy; a note-book full, I declare. End of third week inspector of police came and said he should have to apply at head-quarters for instructions if I wouldn't give them. Not a place was secure as long as the vagabonds stayed. Had to cave in then, and issue a warrant or so and get rid of them. Sorry for it. Much to learn ye: about them, and the few specimens brought before me weren't good ones. Young gipsies, you know, Prudhom, aren't up to the mark. You only get the true aboriginal ring about the old people. Yes, I'm afraid they're breaking up, you know. Sorry for it."

Dr Prudhom concurred, and mentioned as a somewhat significant fact that very few old gipsies had accompanied the late visitation, which consisted almost altogether of the young and possibly degenerate members of the tribe.

The discussion had reached this stage, and the professor was about to adduce evidence from history of a similar period of depression in the race, when there came a ring at the front bell, followed by a shuffling of feet in the hall, which was presently explained by the appearance of the servant, who announced that there were two constables below who wished to see his worship.

Now his worship was anything but pleased to be interrupted in the midst of his interesting discussion by a matter of such secondary importance as an interview with the police.

"Can't see them now," said he to the servant; "tell them to call in the morning." The servant retired.

"Strange thing," observed the justice of the peace; "you can shut up your school at five o'clock every night, and every cheesemonger and tinker in the place can do the same; but we've got no time we can call our own. Pull your chair up to the fire, old fellow. Let's see, what were we saying?" The servant appeared again at this point, and said—"Please, sir, they've got a couple of the gipsies, and want—"

"Eh, what!" exclaimed the professor, jumping up. "Why didn't you say so before? Gipsies! Why, Prudhom, my boy, could anything be more opportune? Show them into the library, and set a chair for the doctor. Do you hear? How fortunate this is! Now while I'm examining them, watch closely, and see if you do not observe the peculiar curve of the nostril I was speaking to you about as characterising the septentrional species of the tribe. Come away, doctor!"

And off trotted the man of science to his library, closely followed by the scarcely less eager dominie.

At the far end of the dimly-lighted room stood the constables, on either side of an aged couple of vagabonds. The old man was arrayed in a long coat which nearly reached the ground, leaving only a glimpse of a stained and weather-beaten pair of pantaloons and striped parti-coloured stockings beneath. The old woman wore a shawl, gipsy fashion, over her head, and reaching to her feet, which were shod in unusually large and heavy hob-nailed boots. The faces and hands of both were black with dirt, and bronzed with heat, and as they stood there trembling in the grasp of the law, with chattering teeth and tottering knees, they looked a veritable picture of outcast humanity.

"Prudhom, my boy," whispered the magistrate to his guest, with a most unjudicial nudge, to emphasise his remarks, "they're old ones. Was ever such luck! Knowing ones, too, I guess: they'll try to trick us with their gammon, you see. He! he! Now, constable, what have you got here?"

For the first time the elderly couple lifted their heads and looked towards the Bench. As they did so they uttered an incoherent ejaculation, and attempted to spring forward. But the active and intelligent servants of the law checked them by a vigorous grip of their arms, and crying "Silence!" in their most majestic and menacing tones, reduced them at last to order.

"See that?" whispered the professor to the doctor; "most characteristic. Simulation is of the very essence of their race. Oh, this is beautiful! Did you catch what they said just then? It was an expression in the Maeso-Shemitic dialect, still to be found in the south of Spain and on the old Moorish coast of Africa. I know it well. Well, constable?"

"If you please, your honour, I was passing near the school about half-past five this afternoon along with my brother officer when I observe the defendants crawling along beside the wall. I keeps my eye on them, and observe them going in the direction of Deadman's Lane. I follows unobserved, and observes them crawl behind a hedge. I waits to observe what follows, and presently I observe a young gentleman walking down the lane. As I expects, the male defendant comes out and offers to tell him his fortune, and I observes the young gentleman give the parties money. I waits till he leaves, and then with my brother officer we arrest the parties. That's all, your worship. Stand still, you wagabone you; do you hear?"

This last observation was addressed, not to his worship, but to the female prisoner, who once more made an effort to step forward and speak. The grip of the constable kept her where she was, but, heedless of this threatening gesture, she cried out, in a shrill, trembling voice—

"Please, sir—please, doctor, we're two of your boys."

The doctor, who had been intently looking out for the curved nostril alluded to by his host, started as if he had been shot.

"Eh, what?" he gasped; "what was that I heard?"

"Why," said the professor, in ecstasy, "it's just as I told you. Dissimulation is second nature to the tribe. No he is too big for them. The old lady says she and the other rogue are your children. Doctor, there's a notion for you!—an old bachelor like you, too! He! he!"

"We are indeed!" cried the old man, echoing the shrill tones of his helpmeet. "I'm Morgan, Dr Prudhom, and he's Dell. Indeed, we're speaking the truth. We only did it—"

"There, you see," once more observed the delighted professor; "it's the very thing I knew would happen. They know you are a schoolmaster, and they want you to believe— Oh, this is really most interesting."

The doctor seemed to find it interesting. He changed colour several times, and looked hard at the two reprobates before him. But their weather-and-dust-beaten countenances conveyed no information to his mind. Their voices certainly did startle him with something like a familiar sound; but might not this be part of the deep dissimulation dwelt upon with so much emphasis by his learned friend?

"I wouldn't have missed this for twenty pounds," said the magistrate, beaming on his guest; "my theories are confirmed to the letter."

"We only did it for a lark, sir, and we're awfully sorry," cried the old man. "We really are, aren't we, Dell?"

"Yes, sir," cried the old lady; "please let us off this time."

"Upon my word," said the doctor, getting up and advancing towards the prisoners. "I don't know—"

"Don't be a fool, Prudhom; I know them of old. Sit down, man. Constable, I shall commit the prisoners. Where are my papers?"

"Oh, doctor, please save us!" cried the old lady again. "We are speaking the truth. Let us wash our faces and take off our cloaks, and you'll see we are. Oh, we'll never do it again!"

And before the doctor could reply, or the scandalised constables could prevent it, the two gipsies cast off their outer garments, and presented themselves to the bewildered spectators in the mud-stained jerseys and knickerbockers of the Holmhurst football club! I draw a veil over the explanations, the lectures, and the appeals which followed, as also I forbear to dwell upon the consternation of the man of science, and the cruel disorganisation of all his cherished theories. It is only fair to say that the professor bore no malice, when once he discovered how the matter stood, and used his magisterial influence with the doctor to procure at any rate a mitigated punishment for the culprits.

The delinquents were ordered off to the lavatory, and left there with a can of hot water and a cube of soap, to remove the wrinkles and sunburn from their crestfallen countenances. Which done, they humbly presented themselves in the library, where the doctor, looking very stern, stood already accoutred for the journey home. The leave-taking between the two old gentlemen was subdued and solemn, and then in grim silence Dr Prudhom stalked forth into the night, followed at a respectful distance by his trembling disciples.

Till that moment the thought of Bilk had never once crossed the minds of the agitated amateur gipsies, but it flashed across them now as the doctor strode straight for the cross roads. What if the miserable Alexander Magnus should have swallowed the absurd bait laid for him, and be in the act of making his fortune on the very spot they were to pass!

They held a hurried consultation in whisper on this terrible possibility. "We shall be expelled if it comes out!" groaned Dell. "Yes; we may as well tell him at once," said Morgan. "He may not be there, you know; perhaps we'd better wait and see, in case."

So they went on in the doctor's wake, nearer and nearer to the fatal cross roads at every step.

Suddenly, as they came within a hundred yards of the signpost, the doctor stood still and uttered an exclamation, the meaning of which they were able to guess only too readily. Straining their eyes in the direction indicated, they could discern a white shadowy form hovering in the road before them. "What's that?" exclaimed the doctor in a whisper. Dell was conscious of a secret nudge as Morgan gasped—"Oh, it looks like a ghost! Oh, doctor!" and the two boys clung wildly to the doctor's arm, trembling and gasping with well-feigned terror.

Dr Prudhom trembled too, but his agitation was unfeigned. The three stood still breathless, and watched the dim figure as it hovered across their path, and then vanished into the darkness.

"What can it be?" said the doctor, bracing himself up with an effort, and preparing to walk on.

"Oh, please, sir," cried the boys, "don't go on! do let us turn back! Oh dear! oh dear!"

"Foolish boys!" said the doctor; "haven't you sense enough to know that no such thing as—ah! there it is again!"

Yes, there it was again. A faint beam of the moon broke through the clouds, and lit up the white figure once more where it stood close to the sign-post. And as they watched it seemed to grow, rising higher and higher till its head nearly touched the cross-bars. Then suddenly, and with a groan, it seemed to drop into the earth, and all was darkness once more. The boys clung one on each side to the doctor, who trembled hardly less than themselves. No one dared move, or speak, or utter a sound.

Again the moon sent forth a beam, as the figure once more appeared and slowly rose higher and higher. For a moment it seemed as if it would soar into the air, but again with a dull crash it descended and vanished.

"Boys," said the doctor hoarsely, "I confess I—I am puzzled!"

"I—I wonder," said Dell, "if I ever dare go and see what it is. I say, M—m—organ, would you g—g—go with me—for the d—d—doctor's sake?"

"Oh, Dell! I'm afraid. But—yes, I'll try."

"Brave boys!" said the doctor, never taking his eyes off the spot where the ghost last vanished.

The two boys stole forward on tiptoe, holding one another's arms; then suddenly they broke into a rush straight for the sign-post.

There was a loud shriek as the white figure rose up to meet them.

"Bilk, you idiot, cut back for your life! here's the doctor! We were only having a lark with you. Do cut your sticks, and slip in quietly, and it'll be all right. Look alive, or we're all three done for!"

The ill-starred Bilk needed no further invitation. He started to run as fast as his long legs would carry him, his night-gown flapping in the evening breeze, and his two persecutors following him with cries of "Booh!"

"Scat!"

"Shoo!" and other formulae for exorcising evil spirits.

After a hundred yards or so the two heroes gave up the chase, and returned to the slowly-reviving doctor.

"Come along, sir," said Dell; "there's nothing there; it vanished as soon as we got to it. Let us be quick, sir, in case it comes back."

The remainder of the walk home that evening, I need hardly observe, was brisk; but it was not so brisk as the same journey accomplished by Alexander Magnus Bilk, who had reached the school a full quarter of an hour before his pursuers, and was safe between his blankets by the time that they peeped into his room on their way to bed, and whispered consolingly, "It's all up with the duke's daughter now, old man!"

The doctor may have had some dim suspicion of the real state of affairs; but if so, he gave no sign, and the boys, happy in their escape from what might have proved a grave matter, were content to forego all further practical jokes of the kind for the rest of the session.

Chapter Thirty Five
A Night in the Dreadnought

Chapter One. Stowaways

We were spending the winter of 185—, my young brother Jack and I, with our grandfather at Kingstairs, a quiet little seaside village not a hundred miles from the Nore.

I am not quite clear to this day as to why we were there—whether we were sent for a treat, or for a punishment, or whether I was sent to take care of Jack, or Jack was sent to take care of me. I can't remember that we had committed any unusually heinous offence at home. Indeed, since our attempt a week or two previously to emulate history by smothering the twins, after the manner of the princes in the Tower, we had been particularly quiet, not to say dull, at home. For the little accident of the squib that went off in the night nursery in the middle of the night counted for nothing, nobody being hurt, and only the head nurse and our aunt having hysterics.

So that when, the day after we had broken up for the holidays, our father told us we were going to spend Christmas at grandfather's, there was nothing in our past conduct to suggest that the step was to be regarded in the light of a punishment.

All the same, it was no great treat. At least it would have been far more of a treat to spend Christmas at home, and carry out our long-cherished design of digging at the bottom of the garden till we reached the fire in the middle of the earth, an operation which we reckoned would occupy at least a week; to say nothing of the usual Christmas parties, which we did not see the fun of missing, and the visits to the Tower and the Monument, which always seemed to be part of every Christmas holiday.

However, as it was all settled for us, and everybody seemed to think it a great treat for us, and further, as Jack had a boat which wanted sailing, we yielded to the general wish, and reminding everybody that the presents could be sent down in a trunk a day or two before the 25th, we took our leave and repaired to Kingstairs.

Our father came with us, just to see us settled down, and then returned to town. And it was not till after he had gone that we began to think it rather slow to be left alone down there with only grandfather and Jack's boat for company.

Grandfather was very old. We always used to put him down at a round hundred years, but I believe he was only seventy-five really. However, he was not as young as we were, and being rather infirm and subject to rheumatism, he preferred staying indoors near the fire to coming with us over the rocks and sailing Jack's boat in mid-December.

He little knew the pleasure he missed, of course! Happily, he did not insist on our staying indoors with him, and the consequence was we managed to do pretty much as we liked, and indeed rather more so than he or any one else interested in our welfare supposed.

Kingstairs, as any one who has been there knows, is not a very exciting place at the best of times. In summer, however, it is a pleasant enough retreat, where family parties come down from town for a week or so, and spend their days boating in the pretty bay, or else basking on the sands under the chalk cliffs, where the children construct fearful and wonderful pits and castles, and arm-chairs for their mothers to sit in, or canals and ponds in which to sail their craft. In fine weather nothing is so enjoyable as a day on the rocks, hunting for crabs and groping for "pungars," or else strolling about on the jetty to watch the packet-boat go out to meet the steamer, or see the luggers coming in after a week's fishing cruise in the German Ocean.

All this is pleasant enough. But Kingstairs in July and Kingstairs in December are two different places.

The lodging-houses were all desolate and deserted. The boats were all drawn high and dry up on the jetty. The bathing-machines stood dismally in the field behind the town. Not a soul sat in an arm-chair on the sands from morning to night. No one walked along the cliffs except the coastguardsmen. The London steamer had given up running, and no one was to be seen on the jetty but an occasional sailor, pipe in mouth and hands in pockets, looking the picture of dismalness.

You may fancy Jack and I, under these depressing circumstances, soon got tired of sailing the boat. And when one day, after we had waited a week for the water to calm down, we started it, with all sail crowded, before half a gale of wind, from the jetty steps, and watched it heel over on to one side and next moment disappear under the foam of a great wave which nearly carried us off our feet where we stood, we decided there was not much fun to be had out of Kingstairs in December.

It was often so rough and stormy that it was impossible to get to the end of the jetty; and on these occasions we were well enough pleased to take shelter in the "look-out," a big room over the net-house, reached by a ladder, where there was generally a fire burning, and in which the sailors and boatmen of the place always congregated when they had nothing else to do.

We struck up acquaintance with one or two of these rough tars, who, seeing perhaps that we were in rather a dismal way, or else glad of anything in the way of a variety, used to invite us up to warm ourselves at the fire. We very soon got to feel at home in the "look-out," and found plenty of entertainment in the yarns and songs with which the men whiled away the time.

A great deal of what we heard, now I remember it, was not very improving; the songs, many of them, were coarse, and as for the yarns, though we swallowed them all at the time, I fancy they were spun mostly out of the fancy of the narrators. Wonderful stories they were, of shipwreck, and battle, and peril, over which we got so excited that we lay awake at night and shuddered, or else dreamed about them, which was even worse.

One man, I remember, told us how he fought with a shark under water in the South Seas, and stabbed it with the knife in his right hand, just as the monster's teeth were closing on his other arm. And to make his story more vivid he bared his great shaggy arm, and showed us an ugly white scar among the tattoo marks above the elbow. Another man told us how he had stood beside Nelson on the "Victory," just as the admiral received his death-wound; and it never occurred to us to wonder how a man of not more than thirty-five could have been present at that famous battle, which took place fifty years ago! But the yarn that pleased us most was the one about the wreck of the "Wolf King," when the Kingstairs lifeboat, the "Dreadnought," put out in a tremendous gale, and reached her just as she was going down, and rescued sixteen of her crew. This story we called for over and over again, till we knew it by heart. And many a time, as we lay awake at night, and heard the wind whistling round the house, we wondered if it was a storm like this when the "Wolf King" went down, or whether any ship would be getting on to the Sands to-night.

It was Christmas Eve—a wild, blustering night. It had been blowing up hard for several days now, and we were used to the howling of the wind and the roar of the waves on the beach. We had gone to bed tired and excited, for the promised hamper had arrived that afternoon, and we had been unpacking it. What a wonderful hamper it was! A turkey to begin with, and a *Swiss Family Robinson*, and a tool-box, and a telescope, and a pair of home-made socks for grandfather. We were fain to take possession of our treasures at once, but the old gentleman forbade it, and made us put them all back in the hamper and wait till the morning.

So we went to bed early, hoping thereby, I suppose, to hasten the morning. But instead of that, the hours dragged past as though the night would never go. We heard nine o'clock strike, and ten, and eleven. We weren't in the humour for sleeping, and told one another all the stories we knew—finishing up, of course, with the wreck of the "Wolf King." Then we lay for a long time listening to the storm outside, which seemed to get wilder and wilder as the night dragged on. The tide, which had been only just turned when we went to bed, sounded now close under the house, and the thunder of the great waves as they broke on the sand seemed to make the very earth vibrate.

Surely it must have been a night like this when the "Wolf King"—

"Tom!"

"What?"

"Are you awake?"

"Yes."

"It's a storm, isn't it?"

There was a silence for some time, and I supposed Jack had dozed off, but he began again presently. "Tom!"

"What?"

"Hadn't we better go on the jetty?"

"Why?"

"There might be a wreck, you know."

"So there might."

Next moment we were out of bed and dressing quietly.

We need not have minded about the noise, for the roar of the storm outside would have prevented any one from hearing sounds twenty times louder than those we made, as we crept into our clothes and pulled on our boots.

"All ready, Jack?"

"Yes; mind how you go down."

We crept downstairs, past grandfather's room, where a light was burning, down into the hall, and through the passage to the back door. We pulled the bolts and opened it carefully. Fortunately, it was on the sheltered side of the house. Had it been the front, the blast that would have rushed in would certainly have discovered our retreat.

We stepped cautiously out and closed the door behind us. We were surprised to find how still it seemed at first, compared with what we had imagined. But next moment, as we got past the back of the house and came suddenly into the full force of the wind, we knew that the storm was even fiercer than we supposed. At first we could barely stand, as with heads down and knees bent we struggled forward. But we got more used to it in a little while, and once in Harbour Street we were again in shelter.

Harbour Street was empty. No one saw us as we glided down it towards the jetty. We heard the church clock strike half-past eleven, the chimes being swept past us on the wind.

As we turned out of Harbour Street on to the jetty the force of the gale once more staggered us, and we had almost to crawl forward. There were lights and the cheery glow of a fire in the "look-out," and we knew there must be plenty of sailors there. But somehow at this time of night we did not care to be discovered even by our friends the sailors. So we kept on, holding on to the chains, towards where the red light burned at the jetty-head.

We were too excited to be afraid. One of those strange spirits of adventure had seized upon us which make boys ready for anything, and the thought of standing alone at midnight at the pier-head in a storm like that did not even dismay us.

But before we were half-way along we found that it was not the easy thing we imagined. A huge wave struck the jetty behind the wall under which we crept, and next moment a deluge of spray and foam shot up and fell, drenching us to the skin. And almost before we knew what had happened another and another followed.

We turned instinctively towards the "look-out," but as we did so a fourth wave, huger than all the rest, swept the jetty from end to end, and but for the chain, on to which we clung, we should have been washed off.

Our only chance was to run for the nearest shelter, and that was the lee of the tarpaulin-covered lifeboat, which lay up on its stocks, out of the reach of the spray, and seeming to us to offer as much protection ashore as it could do afloat.

Half a dozen staggering steps brought us to it. But even in this short space another wave had drenched us. We were thankful to creep under its friendly shelter, and once there we wondered for the first time how we were ever to get back. Our hearts were beginning to fail us at last. We were cold and shivering, and wet through, and now the rain came in gusts, to add to our misery.

"Couldn't we get inside?" said Jack, with chattering teeth.

As he spoke a shower of salt spray leapt over the boat and deluged us. Yes; why not get inside under the tarpaulin, where we could shelter at once from the cold, and the wet, and the wind? Nobody could see us, and if any one came we could jump out, and presently, perhaps, the storm might quiet down, and we could get back to bed.

Jack had already clambered up the side, and lifted a corner of the tarpaulin. I followed, and in a minute we were snugly stowed away, in almost as good shelter as if we had never left our bedroom.

Then we sat and listened drowsily to the wind raging all round, and heard the spray falling with heavy thuds on the tarpaulin above us.

"It must be past twelve, Jack," said I; "a Merry Christmas to you."

But Jack was fast asleep.

Chapter Two. The Rescue

How long Jack and I had lain there, curled up under the bows of the "Dreadnought" that stormy Christmas morning, I never knew. For I, like him, had succumbed to the drowsy influence of the cold and wet, and fallen asleep.

I remember, just before dropping off, thinking the storm must be increasing rather than otherwise, and vaguely wondering whether the wind could possibly capsize the boat up here in the top of its runners. However, my sleepiness was evidently greater than my fears on this point, and I dropped off, leaving the question to decide itself.

The next thing I was conscious of was a strange noise overhead, and a sudden dash of water on to the floor of the boat just beside me. Then, before I could rub my eyes, or recollect where I was, the "Dreadnought" seemed suddenly alive with people, some shouting, some cheering, while the loud bell at the pierhead close by mingled its harsh voice with the roar of the storm.

"Stand by—cut away there!" shouted a hoarse voice from the boat. Then it flashed across me! The "Dreadnought" was putting out in this fearful storm to some wreck, and—horrors!—Jack and I were in her!

"Wait, I say, wait! Jack and I are here. Let us out!" I cried.

In the noise, and darkness, and confusion, not even the nearest man noticed me as I sprang up with this terrified shout.

I shook Jack wildly and shouted again, trying at the same time to make my way to the stern of the boat.

But before I had crossed the first bench, before the two men seated there with oars up, ready for the launch, perceived us, there was a cheer from the jetty, the great boat gave a little jolt and then began to slide, slowly at first, but gaining speed as she went on, and I knew she was off.

That short, swift descent seemed to me like an eternity. The lights on the jetty went out, the cheers were drowned, and—

A rough hand caught me where I stood half across the bench and drove me back down beside Jack, who was yet too dazed to stir. Next instant with a rush and a roar we plunged into the tempest, and all was blackness!

It seemed to me as if that first plunge was to be the last for the gallant boat and all in her. The bows under which we crouched, clinging for dear life to a ring on the floor, were completely submerged. The water rushed over us and around us, nearly stunning us with its violence and deafening us with its noise.

But presently we rose suddenly, and the boat shot up till it seemed to stand on end, so that, where we sat, we could see every inch of it from stem to stern, and the dim outline of Kingstairs jetty behind. At the same moment the ten oars dropped into their rowlocks, the coxswain, with his sou'-wester pulled down tight on his head, and a hand raised to screen his eyes from the sleet, shouted something—the boat soared wildly up the wave, and once again all was darkness for us.

How the brave boat ever got through that first half-mile of surf is a mystery to me. Every wave seemed as though it would pitch it like a plaything across to the next. Now we shot up till we looked down on the coxswain below us as from the top of a mast, and next instant we looked up at him till it seemed a marvel how he held to his place, and did not drop on to us. All the while the men tugged doggedly at the oars, heeding neither the waves that broke over them and flooded the boat, nor the surf that often nearly knocked the oars from their hands.

And what of Jack and me? We crouched there, close together, clutching fast at the friendly ring, looking out in mute terror on to this fearful scene, too stupefied to speak, or move, or almost to think. Had any one seen us? or had the hand which drove me down at the launch saved me from my danger by accident? I began to think this must be so, when the man nearest us, whom even in his cork jacket and sou'-wester I recognised as the hero of the shark story in the "look-out," turned towards us.

He was not one of the rowers, but had been busily drawing in and coiling a line close beside us during those first terrific plunges of the boat after she had taken the water. But now he turned hurriedly to where we sat, and without a word seized me roughly by the arm and drew me to my feet. I made sure I was to be cast overboard like Jonah into that fearful sea. But no. All he did was to throw a cork jacket round me, and then thrust me down again to my old place, just as a great wave broke over the prows and seemed almost to fill the boat. As soon as this had passed and the water swirled out from the boat, he seized Jack and equipped him in the same way. Then throwing a tarpaulin coat over us, he left us to ourselves, while he mounted his watch in the bows and kept a look-out ahead.

The cork jackets, if of no other use, helped to warm us a bit, as also did the coat, and thankful for the comfort, however small, we settled down to see the end of our adventure and hope for the best.

Settled down, did I say? How could any one settle down in an open boat on a sea like that, with every wave breaking over our heads and half drowning us, and each moment finding the boat standing nearly perpendicular either on its stem or its stern? How the rowers kept their seats and, still more, held on to their oars and pulled through the waves, I can still scarcely imagine. But for the friendly ring on to which Jack and I held like grim death, I am certain we should have been pitched out of the boat at her first lurch.

The "Dreadnought" ploughed on. Not a word was spoken save an occasional shout between the coxswain and our friend in the bows as to our course. I could see by the receding lights of Kingstairs, which came into sight every time we mounted to the top of a wave, that we were not taking a straight course out, but bearing north, right in the teeth of the wind; and I knew enough of boats, I remember, to wonder with a shudder what would happen if we should chance to get broadside on to one of these waves. Presently the man by us shouted—"You're right now. Bill!"

The coxswain gave some word of command, and we seemed to come suddenly into less broken water. The men shipped their oars, and springing to their feet, as if by one motion, hoisted a mast and unfurled a triangular sail.

For a moment the flapping of the canvas half deafened us. Then suddenly it steadied, and next minute the boat heeled over, gunwale down on the water, and began to hiss through the waves at a tremendous speed.

"Pass them younkers down here!" shouted Bill, when this manoeuvre had been executed.

Jack and I were accordingly sent crawling down to the stern under the benches, and presented ourselves in a pitiable condition before the coxswain.

He was not a man of many words at the best of times, and just now, when everything depended on the steering, he had not one to waste.

"Stow 'em away, Ben," he said, not looking at us, but keeping his eyes straight ahead.

Ben, another of our acquaintance, dragged us up beside him on the weather bulwarks, and here we had to stand, holding on to a rail, while the boat, with her sail lying almost on the water, rushed through the waves.

We were no longer among the breaking surf through which we had had to straggle at starting, although the sea still rolled mountains high, and threatened to turn us over every moment as we sailed across it. But the gallant boat, thanks to the skilful eye and hand of the coxswain, kept her head up, and presently even we got used to the situation, and were able to do the same.

Where was the wreck? I summoned up courage to ask Ben, who, no longer having to row, was standing composedly against the bulwarks by our side.

"Not far now. Straight ahead."

We strained our eyes eagerly forward. For a long time nothing was visible in the darkness, but presently a bright flash of light shot upward, followed almost immediately by a blaze on the surface of the water and a dull report.

"They're firing again!" said Ben; "we'll be up to them in a jiffey!"

"What are we to do?" asked Jack dismally.

"Hold on where you are," said Ben; "and if we upset stay quiet in the water till you're picked up."

With which consoling piece of advice Jack and I subsided, and asked no more questions.

The sight of a column of lurid flame and smoke made us wonder for a moment whether the vessel in distress was not on fire as well as wrecked. But I recollected that the "Wolf King" had burned tar-barrels all night long as a signal of distress, and this we rightly concluded was what was taking place on board "our" wreck.

Ben's "jiffey" seemed a good while coming to an end, and long before it did we passed once more into broken water, and the perils of the start were repeated, with the aggravation that we were now across the wind instead of being head on. Wave after wave burst over us, and time after time, as we hung suspended on the crest of some great billow, it seemed as if we never could right ourselves. But we did.

"Stand by!" cried the coxswain, when at last a great dim black outline appeared on our starboard.

Instantly the men were in their seats; oars were put out; the mast and sail came down, and the clank of the anchor being got ready for use fell on our ears from the bows.

The wreck was now right between us and the shore, we being some distance to the windward of it. My knowledge of the story of the wreck of the "Wolf King" gave me a pretty good notion of what was going on, and even in the midst of our peril I found myself whispering to Jack—

"They're going to drop the anchor, you know, and blow down on to her—"

"Hope they've got rope enough," said Jack. For in the case of the "Wolf King" it took three attempts to get within the right distance. The coxswain of the "Dreadnought" was evidently determined not to fall into his old error this time, and, with her head to the wind and the oars holding the water, he allowed her to drift to within about eighty yards of the wreck. Then he shouted—

"Pay away, there!" and instantly we heard the cable grinding over the gunwale.

Would it hold? Even to inexperienced boys like Jack and me the suspense was dreadful as the cable ran out, and the rowers kept the boat's head carefully up.

The grinding ceased. There was a moment's pause, then came a welcome "Ay, ay!" from the bows, and we knew it was all right.

It didn't take the wind long to drive us back on our cable, stern foremost, on to the wreck, which now loomed out huge and ghostly on the wild water.

As we drifted down under her stern we were conscious, amidst the smoke of the burning tar-barrels and the spray of the waves which broke over her, of a crowd of faces looking over her sides, and fancied we heard a faint cheer too. Our men still kept their oars out, and when, always holding on to our cable, we had drifted some twenty yards or so on to the lee side of the wreck, the order was given to pull alongside.

It was no easy task in the face of the wind; but the men who had taken the "Dreadnought" through the surf off Kingstairs jetty were not likely to fail now. A few powerful strokes brought us close under the lee of the wreck, ropes were thrown out fore and aft, and in a few minutes we lay tossing and kicking, but safely moored within a yard or two of the ill-starred vessel.

Half a dozen of our men were up her sides and on board in a moment, and we could hear the cheers with which they were greeted as they sprang on deck. No time was to be lost. The wreck was creaking in every timber, and each wave that burst over her, deluging us on the other side, threatened to break her in pieces. One mast already was broken short, and hung helplessly down, held only by her rigging to the deck. The other looked as though it might go any moment, and perhaps carry the wreck with it.

If she were to capsize now, what would become of us?

It seemed ages before our men reappeared.

One of them shouted down—

"There's twenty. Germans."

"Any women?"

"Two."

"Look sharp with them."

We could see a cloaked figure lifted on to the bulwarks of the wreck and held there. A wave had just passed. As the next came and lifted us up with a lurch towards her, some one cried "Jump!" and she obeyed wildly—almost too wildly, for she nearly overleaped us. Mercifully there were stout arms to catch her and place her in safety. The other woman followed; and then one after another the crew, until, with thankful hearts, we counted twenty on board.

Our work was done. No! There was a report like a crack of thunder over our heads, a shout, a shriek, as the mainmast of the wreck gave way with a crash, and swayed towards us.

"Jump!" shouted the coxswain to our men, who were waiting for the next wave to bring the boat to them. "Cut away for'ard, there!"

Another moment and the mast would be on us and overwhelm us! They jumped, although we were down in the trough of the wave, yards below them. At the same moment the rope in the stern was cut loose, and the boat swung round wildly, just in time to clear the mast as it fell with a terrific crash overboard. But our men? Four of them landed safely in our midst; but the others? Oh! how our hearts turned cold as we saw that two were missing, and knew that they mast be in that boiling, furious water! We sprang wildly to the side, in the mad hope of seeing them, or perhaps even reaching them a hand but a stern order from the coxswain sent us back to our places.

A minute of awful suspense followed. The oars were put up, and, still held by her stern cable, the boat was brought up again alongside. In a minute a shout from the prow proclaimed that one at least of the missing ones was discovered, and presently a dripping form clambered over the side of the boat close to us and coolly sat down to his oar, as if nothing had happened.

Another shout—this time not from the boat, but from the water. Our other man had been carried the wrong side of us by the wave, and could not reach us. But a rope dexterously pitched reached him where he floated, and we had the unspeakable joy of seeing him at last hauled safely on board, exhausted, but as unconcerned as if drowning were an ordinary occurrence with him.

How thankfully we saw the last cable which held us to the wreck cast loose, and found ourselves at length, with our twenty rescued souls on board, heading once more for Kingstairs! Little was said on that short voyage home. Sail and oar carried us rapidly through the storm. The waves that broke over us from behind were as nothing to those that had broken over us from in front. And as if in recognition of the gallant exploit of the tough old "Dreadnought," the very surf off Kingstairs beach had moderated when we reached it.

As we sighted the jetty we could see lights moving and hear a distant shout, which was answered by a ringing cheer from our men, in which Jack and I and the eighteen Germans and the two women joined. What a cheer it was! At the jetty-head we could see a large crowd waiting to receive us, and as we passed a stentorian voice shouted, "Ahoy! Have you got them two boys on board?"

"Ay, ay!" cried the coxswain; "safe and sound—the rascals!"

Rascals, indeed! As we clambered up the ladder, scarcely believing that we touched *terra firma* once more, and found our poor old grandfather almost beside himself with joy and excitement at the top, we considered we deserved the title.

"Thank God you're safe!" he cried, when at last he had us before a blazing fire and a hot breakfast in his dining-room. "Thank God, you rascals!"

We had done so long ago, and did it again and again, and thanked Him, not only for ourselves, but for the brave old "Dreadnought" too, so true to her name and the work she had done that night.

Before we went to bed Jack said, "Same to you, Tom." I knew what he meant. I had wished him a "Merry Christmas" at five minutes past twelve that morning, and this was his answer six hours after. What a lot may happen in six hours!

Chapter Thirty Six
Hannibal Trotter the Hero—A
Chapter of Autobiography

We know that it always is, or should be, embarrassing to a hero to recite the history of his own exploits. So if this simple narrative strikes the reader as defective, he must excuse it for that reason. For I am in this painful position, that as no one else will recount my adventures for me, I have nothing left but to do it myself. It has surprised me often that it should be so, for there have been times when I have even pictured myself reading the twentieth edition of my own memoirs, and the reviews of the Press on the same. I am not offended, however, but I am sorry, for it would have been good reading.

Without appearing immodest, may I say that the reader has really no idea what a hero the world has possessed in the person of me, Hannibal Trotter? It has been my misfortune never to be anything else. How often have I sighed for an unheroic half-hour!

I was born a hero. Glory marked me for her own from the first hour of my career. I wish she had let me alone. Had I captured a city, or rescued a ship's crew, I could not have been made more of than I was for the simple exploit of being a baby. Nobody else was thought of beside me; everybody conspired to do me honour. A fictitious glory settled upon me then, from which I have never escaped. They called me Hannibal. I was not consulted, or I should have opposed the name. It confirmed me in a false position. There was no chance of not being a hero with such a name, and I was in for it literally before I knew where I was.

The day I first walked, General Havelock was a fool to me. I must have been eighteen months at the time, but when the word went forth, "Hannibal walks!" I was simply deafened by the applause which greeted my feat. It wasn't much better when, at the very unprecocious age of two, I gave vent to an inarticulate utterance which, among those who ought to have known better, passed for speech. I assure you, reader, for the next few months I had the whole family hanging on my lips. How would you like your whole family hanging on your lips? But then you weren't born a hero.

Well, it went on. My infancy was one sickening round of glory. Did I build a house of bricks four courses high? Archimedes wasn't in it with me. Did I sing a nursery rhyme to a tune all one note? Apollo was a dabbler in music beside me. Did one of my first teeth drop out without my knowing it? Casabianca on the burning deck couldn't touch me for fortitude. Did I once and again chance to tell the truth? Latimer, Ridley, George Washington, and Euclid might retire into private life at once, and never be heard of again!

It was a terrific *rôle* to have to keep up, and as I gradually emerged from frocks into trousers, and from an easy-going infancy into an anxious boyhood, the true nature of my affliction began to dawn upon me. Hannibal Trotter, through no choice of his own, and yet by the undoubted ordering of Fate, was a hero, and he must act as such. He must, in fact, keep it up or give it up; and a fellow cannot lightly give up the only *rôle* he has.

In due time, after heroic efforts, I was, at about the age of ten, able to read to myself, and my attention was at once directed to a class of stories congenial to my reputation. It would hardly be fair to inflict upon the patient reader a digest of my studies, but the one impression they left upon my mind was that a young man, if he is to be worth the name, must on every possible occasion both be a hero and show it.

This conclusion rather distressed me; for while the first condition was easy and natural enough, the second was no joke. I knew I was a hero; I could not doubt it, for I had been brought up to the business, and to question it would be to question the veracity of every relative I had. But try all I would I couldn't manage to show it.

After a considerable amount of patient study, my conceptions of a hero had resolved themselves into several leading ideas, which it may be of use to the reader if I repeat here:—

1. He must save one life or more from drowning.

2. He must stop runaway horses.

3. He must rescue people from burning houses.

4. He must pull some one from under the wheels of a train.

5. He must encounter and slay a mad dog in single combat.

6. He must capture a burglar; and 7. He must interpose his body between the pistol of the assassin and the person of some individual of consequence.

In my researches I had collected a mass of information under each of these heads, and was perfectly acquainted with what was becoming in a hero in each emergency.

But, as I have said, try all I would the chance never came.

I was full of hopes when we went to the seaside that emergency number one at least might make an opening for me. I spent hours every morning on the beach watching the bathers, and longing to hear the welcome shout of distress. I sat with my boots unlaced and my coat ready to fling off at a moment's notice. I tempted my sisters to go and bathe where the shore shelved rapidly and the ebb washed back strongly. They went, and to my chagrin were delighted with the place, and learned to swim better than I could.

There was a man who went out every morning to bathe from a boat. I was always at the pier-head watching him, but he went into the water and scrambled out of it again over the stern of the boat with ruthless regularity, and quite mistook my interest in him for admiration, which was the very last sentiment I harboured.

Once I made sure my chance had come. It was a warm day, and the shore was crowded. Most of the people had finished bathing, and were spread about the sands drying their back hair and reading their papers. One adventurous bather, however, remained in the water. I had anxiously watched him swim round the pier-head and back, ready—longing—to see him cast his hands above his head and hang out other signals of distress. But it seemed I was again to be disappointed. He came in swimming easily, and mightily pleased with himself and his performance. He was about twenty yards off his machine and I was beginning to give him up, when to my delight I saw his hands go up and his head go down, and heard what I fondly hoped was a yell of despair.

In a moment—two moments, I should say, for one of my boots was not quite enough unlaced—I was floundering in the water in my flannel shirt and trousers, striking out wildly for the spot where he had disappeared. I had gathered from the authorities I had consulted that heroes, under these circumstances, got over distances in a shorter time than it takes to record it. This was not my experience. It took me a long time to get half the way, and by that time my clothes were very heavy and I was very tired. Moreover, my man was still invisible.

Of course I could not turn back. Even if I did not succeed in fishing him out, it was a "gallant attempt," which would be almost as good. Partly to see how the crowd was taking it, and partly to rest myself, I turned over on my back and floated. This do doubt was a tactical error; for as a rule a hero does not float out to save any one's life. In my case it did not much matter, for the first thing I perceived as I turned was my drowning man's head bobbing up merrily between me and the shore, having enjoyed his long dive and wholly unaware of the "gallant attempt" which was being made to rescue him from a watery grave.

As he caught sight of me, however, floundering on my back, and scarcely able to keep my head up for the weight of my clothes, his face became alarmed. "Hold up a second!" he shouted. Half a dozen strong strokes brought him to my side, and before I could explain or decline, he had gripped me by the two shoulders and was punting me ignominiously towards the shore.

It was a painful situation for me; the more so that I was quite done up and scarcely able to stagger out of the water into the arms of my affrighted relatives.

"Lay him on his back and work his arms up and down till you get all the water out of him, and then put him between hot blankets," cried my preserver, "and he'll be all serene. They ought to make a shallow place somewhere for these kids to bathe, where they won't get out of their depths. Bless you, ma'am," added he, in reply to my mother's thanks, "it's not worth talking of. It all comes in a day's work, and you're very welcome."

I was rather glad to leave the seaside after that; and whenever in the course of my future readings I came upon any further reference to emergency number one, I discreetly passed it over.

But hope springs eternal in the human breast, and the resources of heroism were by no means exhausted.

The drowning business had missed fire. I would go into the runaway-horse line, and try how that would stand me for glory.

So after a careful study of the theory of the art from my books, I took to haunting Rotten Row in my leisure hours with a view to business. I must confess that it is far easier to stop a runaway horse on paper than on a gravel drive. I speculated, as one or two specially reckless riders dashed past me, on what the chance would be of making a spring at the bridle of a horse going half as fast again as theirs, and bringing him gracefully on to his knees. I didn't like the idea. And yet had not a fellow done it in one of Kingsley's novels, and another in one of Lever's?

At last I screwed myself up to it. I had worked the thing out carefully, and arranged my spring and everything. But I was unlucky again when the time came.

I remember the occasion well—painfully well. It was a bright May afternoon. I had given the carriages up as hopeless—they drove far too soberly—and was taking a forlorn glance up and down the ride at the equestrians, when I perceived a youth approach on a very dashing animal, which, if it was not bolting, was sailing remarkably close to the wind in that direction. The ride was pretty clear, and the few seconds I had in which to make up my mind were enough for me. I heard some one say close beside me, "He'll be chucked!"

Instantly I dived under the rail and dashed out into the road. There was a shout and a yell, and the young gentleman had to pull his mare up on her haunches to avoid riding me down. Before I could act under these circumstances a mounted policeman dashed up, and collaring me by the coat, swung me along beside him a yard or two, and then, with a box on the ears, pitched me back in among the crowd.

I should have liked to explain, but he did not give me time.

"Young fool!" said one of the crowd; "you might have killed him. Do you know who that was?"

"Who?" I gasped, for I was out of breath. "That young man who—"

"Yes—that young man's the Prince of Wales."

It's twenty-six years ago since it happened, and probably the King has forgotten the adventure. I haven't. I retired from the runaway-horse business that very afternoon.

Another door was shut against me. Still there were others left, and the house-on-fire line had a good deal to recommend it. It was a thing in which one could not well make a mistake. It had been possible, as I had found out by painful experience, to mistake the pranks of a lively swimmer for drowning, and the capers of a lively mare for bolting. But there was no mistaking a house on fire when you saw one. People in a burning house, moreover, would be likely to give every facility possible for their own rescue, and the chances were one would not find many competitors to deprive one of the glory. On the whole, I warmed up to this new opening considerably.

Of course one never has the good fortune to have a fire in one's own house when it is wanted. It would have been exceedingly convenient for me to have to rescue my own family from the flames. As it was, I had to spend a good many dreary nights in the street in the neighbourhood of the fire alarms before I so much as smelt fire.

It was a good one when it came. A great warehouse in the City was gutted, and those who saw the blaze are not likely to forget it in a hurry. I saw it. I had scampered with all my might after one of the engines, but only to find a dense crowd on the spot before me. There was a wide circle kept round the place, and never did circus-goers fight for a front row in the gallery as did that crowd fight for a front place at this grand show.

It was nearly an hour before, by dint of squeezing, sneaking, fighting, and beseeching, I could get to the front. By that time the fire had done its worst. Still I had noted with satisfaction that no fire-escapes had yet been brought up, so that any unfortunate inmates were sure to be still safe for me. The firemen were playing on the flames with their hoses, and every now and then an alarm of a tottering wall sent them flying back to a safe distance. It was a grand opportunity for me to brave these poltroons on their own ground, and show them how a hero behaves at a fire.

So I took advantage of a policeman turning another way, to break bounds and run into the open space.

"Come back!" shouted the policeman.

"Come back!" yelled the mob.

"Mind the wall!" cried a fireman.

I was delighted, and already glowed with glory.

Alas! how soon our brightest hopes may be damped!

The fireman, seeing that I still advanced on the burning ruin, wheeled round on me with his hose, and before I could count five had drenched me through and through, and half-stunned me with the force of the water into the bargain.

The crowd screamed with laughter; the police seized me by all fours; the fireman executed a final solo on my retreating person, and the next thing I was aware of was being delivered at my own door from a four-wheeled cab, with my interest in conflagrations completely extinguished.

My faith in the history of heroism began to be a trifle shaken after this adventure. However, I was committed to a course of gallant action; and it were cowardice to lose heart after a rebuff or two. I must at any rate try my hand at a railway rescue before giving in.

In my studies I had only met with one successful case of extracting individuals from between the wheels of locomotives in motion, and therefore entered upon this branch of my experiments with considerable doubt. Nor did anything occur to remove that doubt. I watched the trains carefully for a month; and whenever I saw any one place himself near the edge of the platform as a train came up, I made a point of placing myself hard by. But we never got beyond the platform; and, indeed, the whole course of my experiments in this department resulted in nothing beyond my one day being knocked down by the unexpected opening of a carriage door; and on another occasion being nearly placed under arrest for clutching a man's arm as the train came up, he said with intent "to chuck him on the line," but as I told him, and unsuccessfully tried to explain to him, because he seemed to me to be about to be swept over by the engine.

It was on the whole a relief to me, when, in order to extricate myself from the serious consequences of this last adventure, I was obliged to promise never to do such a thing again. That settled the locomotive business. As a man of honour I was forced to quit it, and cast about me for a new road to glory.

Now, I think it argues considerably for my heroism that after the unfortunate result of so many adventures I should still persist in keeping up my struggle after Fame. I might fairly have given her up after the honest endeavours I had made to win her. But, whatever others might do, as long as a chance remained everything combined to keep Hannibal Trotter at his post.

So, with not a little searching of heart, I turned my attention to mad dogs. I must confess that my heart did not go out towards them, and I could have wished that that mark of heroism had been omitted by the authorities. But, on the contrary, it was insisted upon vehemently, and there was no getting out of it. So, like another Perseus, I choked down my emotion and girded myself for the new fray.

I knew the authorities, as a rule, were silent as to any precautions which their heroes may have taken for this particular service. Still, as they said nothing against it, I did the best I could by means of my unaided genius.

I contrived a pair of secret zinc leggings to wear under my trousers. They hurt me, it is true, and impeded my movements; still, I felt pretty safe in them. I also adopted the habit of wearing stout leather driving-gloves on every occasion, besides concealing an effective life-preserver about my person. Nothing, in short, was wanted to complete my equipment but the mad dog; and he never turned up.

One day I saw by the paper that there was one at large in Hackney, and thither I repaired, in greaves and gauntlets, with my life-preserver in my bosom. But though I met many dogs, they were all of them sane. Not one of them foamed at the mouth or looked out of the corner of his eyes.

There was one collie certainly who appeared to me more excited than the rest, and who by his proceedings seemed to menace the safety of a small group of children who were taking their walks abroad with their nurse. Not to be precipitate, I watched him for some time, to make quite sure I was right. Then, when one of the children uttered a scream, I felt my hour was come. So I drew my life-preserver and advanced boldly to the rescue. At the sight of me in this threatening attitude the children and nurse all set up a scream together, and the dog, showing his teeth and uttering a low growl, caught me by the fleshy part of my leg above the zinc and held me there until his little masters and mistresses, having recovered their wits and heard my scarcely articulate explanations, called him off, and allowed me to go in peace—I might almost say in pieces.

I was a good deal discouraged after this unfortunate affair, and might have postponed indefinitely my further experiments, had not fortune unexpectedly placed in my way what appeared to be an opportunity of dealing with a burglar after the most approved fashion of heroism. I was on a visit to an uncle who lived in rather a grand house at Bayswater, and kept up what people are wont to call a good deal of style. This "style" always rather depressed me, for it left me no opening for distinguishing myself on the heroic side of my character, and after a week I was beginning to get home-sick, when a curious incident occurred to break the monotony of my visit.

I was put to sleep in a sort of dressing-room immediately over the drawing-room, and here one night—or rather one dark winter morning—I was suddenly awakened by the sound of voices in the room below. I lay, as people are apt to lie under such circumstances, stiff and still for five minutes, listening with all my ears. There came into my mind while thus occupied all that the authorities had said in reference to burglars; and when, after a lapse of five minutes, the voices again became audible, I knew exactly what was expected of me.

I looked at my watch. Five o'clock. I was certain it could not be the servants; besides, even through the floor I could tell the voices were male. I glided from my couch, and pulled on my nether garments, and then warily set my door ajar. I could see a light through the chink of the door in the landing below, and heard a stealthy footstep. So far, so good. I returned to my room, seized the poker and the water-bottle, and then cautiously descended to the drawing-room door.

Here I once more listened carefully. The keyhole was not eligible for observation, but my sense of hearing was acute. I heard—and this rather surprised me—some one in the room whistle softly to himself, then a gruff, typical burglar's voice said, "Now, then, with that there sack! Fetch 'im 'ere, or I'll warm yer!"

I heard the whistling cease, as something was dragged across the floor. "Now, then," said the first voice, "wake up, Jemmy." That was enough for me. I recognised in this last name a term inseparably connected with burglary; and, not waiting longer, I flung open the door, and with a shout, as much to keep up my own courage as to alarm the enemy, I hurled first my poker, then my water-bottle, then myself in the direction of the voices, and felt that at last I was a hero indeed.

I retain but a dim idea of what followed. I recollect a sooty sack being drawn over my head, just as a general rush of servants and male members of the family, alarmed by the hideous noise of the water-bottle and fire-irons, rushed into the room. Then there was a pause, then a babel of voice, and then, with a cuff on the outside of the sack next to where my head was, the first burglar made a speech:—"I'm bust if I sweeps yer chimbleys any more! This 'ere lunertick was handy the death of Jemmy with his missals. Bust me! I'll summons the lot of yer, see if I don't."

I will not pursue this melancholy episode, and as a veil was drawn over me at the time, I will also draw a veil over what immediately ensued. My visit to my uncle's terminated that day, and a few weeks later I saw in the paper that he had been fined £5—for an assault committed by one of his household on two sweeps.

After this I had not the heart to proceed to the last desperate expedient for acquiring immortal fame. As long as my endeavours had hurt only myself, it was not so bad, but when they recoiled on the heads of my most important relatives I felt it time to draw the line. The bullet may not yet be cast which my heroic bosom is to receive in the stead of royalty, but I shall be ready for it when it is.

Meanwhile I have been cultivating the quieter graces of life, where, if I may not be a hero, I may at least do my duty without making a noise. I am not sure, when all is said and done, whether the two things are not sometimes pretty much the same after all.

Chapter Thirty Seven
The Heroes of New Swishford. A School Episode In Four Chapters

Chapter One. Consultation

The autumn term at Swishford School was more than half over, and boys were waking up to the hope that after all the Christmas holidays, which seemed such a way off six weeks ago, might yet arrive during their lifetime. It was already rumoured that Blunt, the captain, had been invited to spend Christmas at Walkenshaw's, the mathematical Dux's, and every one knew how well Miss Walkenshaw and Blunt had "hit it" the last prize day, and prophecies were rife accordingly. More than that, Shanks, of the Fifth, had whispered in the ear of one or two bosom friends, and thus into the ear of all Swishford, that he was going into "swallows" this winter, and he had got down a book from town with instructions for self-measurement, and was mysteriously closeted in his own study every other evening with a tape. Other boys were beginning to "sit up" a little in the prospect of the coming examination, and generally there was an air of expectation about the place which was prophetic of the coming event.

On the afternoon, however, on which my story opens, two boys as they walked arm-in-arm along the cliffs towards Raveling, appeared to be engrossed in consultation, which, to judge by their serious faces, had nothing to do with Christmas. Let me introduce them to the reader. The taller of the two is a fine, sturdy, square-shouldered youth of fifteen or thereabouts, whose name in a certain section of Swishford is a household word. He is Bowler, the cock of the Fourth, who in the football match against Raveling a fortnight ago picked up the ball at half-back and ran clean through the enemy's ranks and got a touch-down, which Blunt himself acknowledged was as pretty a piece of running as he had seen in his time. Ever since then Bowler has been the idol of the lower school.

His companion is a more delicate-looking boy, of about the same age, with a cheery face, and by no means unpleasant to look at. He is Gayford, as great a favourite in his way as Bowler, a boy whom nobody dislikes, and whom not a few, especially Bowler, like very much.

These are the two who walked that afternoon towards Raveling.

"Are you sure the fellow in the book doesn't make it all up?" said Bowler dubiously.

"Not a bit of it," replied his companion. "My uncle's a captain, you know, and he says there are hundreds of islands like it, the jolliest places you ever saw, any amount of food, no wild animals, splendid weather all the year round, magnificent mountains and valleys and woods and bays, gorgeous fishing and hunting, oceans of fruit trees, everything a fellow could wish for, and not a soul on one of them."

"Rum," said Bowler reflectively; "seems rather a waste of jolly islands that."

"Yes; but the thing is they're hundreds of miles away from inhabited islands, so no one ever sees them."

"Except your uncle. I wonder he wasn't tempted to get out and take possession of one."

"That's just exactly what he said he was tempted to do," replied Gayford, stopping short excitedly. "He said very little would have tempted him to do it, Bowler."

"Oh!" was Bowler's only reply.

"And I tell you another thing," continued Gayford, "he gave me an old chart with the identical island he saw marked on it, and I've got it in my box, my boy."

"Have you, though?" said Bowler. "I'd like to have a look at it."

That evening the two boys held a solemn consultation in their study over Captain Gayford's chart, and Gayford triumphantly pointed out the little island to his friend.

"There he is," said he; "he doesn't look a big one there, but he's eight or ten miles across, my uncle says."

"That seems a fair size—but, I say," said Bowler, "how about getting there? How could any one find it out?"

Gayford laughed.

"You're coming round, then," said he; "why, you old noodle, you couldn't possibly miss it. Do you see that town called Sinnamary (what a name, eh?) on the coast of South Africa? Well, don't you see the island's dead north from there as straight as ever you can go? All you want is a compass and a southerly breeze—and there you are, my boy."

"But what about currents and all that?" queried Bowler, who knew a little physical geography. "Doesn't the Gulf Stream hang about somewhere there?"

"Very likely," said Gayford; "all the better for us too; for I fancy the island is on it, so if we once *get* into it we're bound to turn up right."

"Anyhow," said Bowler, who was not quite convinced, "I suppose one could easily get all that sort of thing up."

"Oh, of course. But, I say, old man, what do you say?"

"Well," said Bowler, digging his hands into his pockets and taking another survey of the chart, "I'm rather game, do you know!"

"Hurrah!" said Gayford. "I know we shall be all right if we get you."

"Who do you mean by we?" asked Bowler.

"Ah, that's another point. I haven't mentioned it to any one yet; but we should want about half a dozen fellows, you know."

"Don't have Burton," said Bowler.

"Rather not; nor Wragg—but what do you say to Wallas?"

"He's muffed quarter-back rather this term, but I daresay he might do for one."

"Well then, what about Braintree?"

"Too big a swell," said Bowler.

"But he's got a rifle at home."

"Oh, ah! all serene. Stick him down."

"What do you say to having them in, and talking it over before we ask any one else?"

This prudent proposition was agreed to, an extra spoonful of tea was put in the pot, and Gayford went out and conducted his guests in personally.

"The fact is," said Gayford, after having delicately disclosed the scheme on hand, and roused his hearers to a pitch of uncomfortable curiosity, "the fact is, Bowler and I thought you two fellows might like to join us."

"You'll have to wait till the spring," said Wallas, a somewhat dismal-looking specimen of humanity. "I've got my Oxford local in January."

"Oh, of course, we shouldn't start till after that," said Gayford, ready to smooth away all obstacles.

"Warthah hot, won't it be?" said Braintree, looking at the map.

"No, I believe not," said Gayford; "there's something about the Gulf Stream, you know, keeps it fresh."

"Wum idea calling an island fwesh," said Braintree, giggling. "It'll be a fresh start for it when we take possession of it, anyhow," said Bowler. "Of course you'll bring your rifle, Braintree?"

"Warthah," replied Braintree, "in case of niggers or wobbers."

"Hope we shan't quarrel when we get out," said Wallas. "That's the way these things generally end."

"Bosh!" said Bowler; "there's no chance of that—just like you, throwing cold water on everything. Wallas."

"If you call what I say bosh," said Wallas warmly, "it's a pity you asked me to join you."

It took some time to get over this little breeze and restore the party to good humour. This was, however, accomplished in time, and the consultation continued.

"We ought to have three more fellows, at least," said Bowler. "I tell you what, each of you pick one. Who do you say, Gav?"

"Well, I fancy young Wester might do," said Gayford.

"Warthah a pwig, isn't he?" suggested Braintree.

"He is a little," replied Gayford; "but he's very obliging, and fags rather well."

"All serene. Now then, Wallas, who's your man?" asked Bowler.

"Tubbs," said Wallas. Tubbs was one of the most hopeless louts at Swishford.

Gayford gave a low whistle; but he was too anxious to preserve the harmony of the party to offer any objection.

"Now you, Braintree?"

"I say, Cwashford. Jolly fellow, and knows French, too."

"Ah, but he is such a cad," said Bowler imploringly.

"Couldn't you think of somebody else, Braintree?" asked Gayford.

"Oh, have Cwashford. He's a wewy decent fellah. I like Cwashford, you know."

"Well, there's this to be said," remarked Bowler, finding there was no getting out of it, "it may be rather a good thing to have some one to keep in order; it will give us something to do."

"Yes, I expect you'll want it," said Wallas. "My opinion is it will be jolly slow out there."

"Not a bit of it. We shall have to go out every day and shoot our game—"

"With my wifle," put in Braintree.

"And then there'll be a log hut to build and the whole place to explore, and lots of bathing and boating."

"And no lessons to do at night."

"And we can get up concerts and penny readings, you know, for the winter evenings."

"And needn't get up till half-past nine in the morning."

And so they went on, till gradually the prospect became so delightful that even Wallas warmed up to it and expressed a wish that they could start at once.

It was, however, decided that they could not manage it this term, as they would have to spend Christmas at home and provide themselves with necessaries for their journey. As to the means of getting out as far as Sinnamary, at any rate, they had no anxiety on that score, for Captain Gayford, when he once heard the object of their expedition, would be sure to take them on one of his ships, and possibly afford them much valuable information as to their further route into the bargain.

Before the council broke up one solemn and momentous step was taken.

"What shall we call our island?" asked Bowler dramatically, placing his finger on the map and looking round on his fellow-adventurers.

There was a pause, and for a moment the founders of the new empire were wrapped in silent thought. At last Gayford said—

"I know—just the thing."

"What? What? What?" inquired three voices.

"New Swishford."

It is hardly needful to add that the name was there and then duly appended to the island on the chart in red ink, which done, the company separated to sleep, and heard all night long in their dreams the crack of

Braintree's "wifle" echoing among the waving woods and fertile valleys of New Swishford.

Chapter Two. Preparation

The week following the important consultation described in the last chapter was one of serious excitement to at least seven boys at Swishford.

Other fellows could not make out what was the matter, and as long as Bowler did not shirk the football match, and Gayford stuck up as usual for his house, they did not particularly care. It was certainly a novelty to see Braintree diligently reading a book in his odd moments, but when it transpired that the book was *Wobinson Cwusoe*, that wonder ceased. And even the surprise of seeing Crashford the lion lying down, so to speak, with Tubbs the lamb, wore away in time, and the conspirators were, on the whole, left undisturbed by Swishford to develop their plans for the eventful emigration of the coming spring.

The three last elected members of the band had fallen in promptly with the scheme, and were not a little elated at the honour conferred upon them. Crashford became quite mellow towards his old enemy Gayford, and actually paid back Bowler a half-crown which he had borrowed three terms ago. Tubbs, though less demonstrative, was equally delighted, and upset the inkpot over the chart, in his eagerness to exhibit to Wester their new home. (It was hardly worth noticing that Tubbs put his finger not on New Swishford at all, but into the centre of Peru, which he said he believed was one of the healthiest countries in all Asia.) Wester, who always made a point of agreeing with the majority, found no difficulty in rejoicing, wherever the place might be, and only wished they had not to wait so long as next spring.

"Why should we wait till then?" asked Crashford.

"Oh, it's better weather," said Gayford; "besides, Wallas is in for his Oxford local."

"Oh, that doesn't matter tremendously," said Wallas, who was beginning to think the world might after all go on if he did not pass.

"We can give him an exam, on the ship going out," said Bowler, "a Swishford local exam., you know, and offer a slice of the island if he passes."

"It strikes me," said Braintree, "a square mile of tewwitowy is warthah a wum pwize for a chap."

"But, I say," said Wester, "isn't our winter the same as their summer? so if we start now, we shall just get out in the warm weather."

"Never thought about that," said Bowler; "what do you say, Gay?"

"I know my uncle generally likes those parts not in the warm weather," said Gayford. "But then, he's been at sea all his life."

"By the way, when does his ship start?" inquired Wallas; "something depends on that, doesn't it?"

"So it does," said Gayford. "I forgot that. He got home a fortnight ago, and he gets six weeks at home. That'll bring it to the end of November."

"Just the very ticket; we must start then, I say."

"But how about my wifle if we don't go home at Cwistmas?" asked Braintree.

"Oh, bother! Couldn't you get it sent up somehow, or couldn't you fetch it next Monday?—that's the term holiday, you know."

"Hold hard," said Bowler, "I've got another plan for Monday. You know we ought to get our hands in a bit before we start, and try and find out what we really want and all that sort of thing. Now, my idea is for us to get the coastguard's boat for the day at Sound Bay (you know there's never any one there to look after it), and sail across to Long Stork Island, and knock about there for the day, just to see how we get on. Of course, we shall have to come back before six; but we must make believe we've landed there for good, and see how we manage. And, of course, if we get on there, we're bound to get on at New Swishford, for it's a far jollier place than the Long Stork."

Bowler's proposition was hailed with acclamation. His hearers were just in the humour to put their enthusiasm to the test, and the notion of a picnic on the Long Stork as a sort of full-dress rehearsal of the capture of New Swishford suited them exactly.

They proceeded immediately to discuss ways and means, and found that by putting their pocket-moneys together they could raise the very respectable sum of forty-one shillings. Reserving the odd shilling for the possible contingency of having to "square" a coastguard for the use of the boat, they had two pounds to devote to the purchase of stores, weapons, and other necessaries; and, as Gayford pointed out, of course anything they got that wasn't eatable would come in for New Swishford.

A sub-committee, consisting of Bowler, Braintree and Wester, was appointed to expend the funds of the adventurers to the best advantage, and meanwhile each member was asked to report what else he could contribute in the way of stores to the general need. Before the end of the week the list was handed in, and as the documents might some day be of immense value to the future historian of New Swishford, I quote them here.

Bowler.—A waterproof, a hat-box, a pair of cricket bails, and a fold-up chair.

Gayford.—The chart, a compass, jam-pots for baling out boats, an eight-blade knife, a hammer and tacks, and a chessboard.

Braintree.—The wifle (pwaps), *Wobinson Cwusoe*, gloves, and umbwellah.

Tubbs.—A crib to Sallust (sorry that's all I've got).

Crashford.—Clay pipe, pack of cards, a corkscrew, a strap, and *Hal Hiccup the Boy Demon*.

Wester.—Three tumblers, bottle of ginger-beer, and a bat.

Wallas.—A saucepan and two eggs, a rope, and Young's *Night Thoughts*.

At the same time the sub-committee reported the purchase of the following stores:—

> Fourteen tins of potted shrimps, 14 shillings;
> Ditto ditto peaches, 14 shillings;
> Ditto bottles of lemonade, 3 shillings 6 pence;
> (1 penny each allowed on returned bottles.)
> Four of Stodge's spice-cakes, 4 shillings;
> A fishing-rod, 2 shillings 6 pence;
> Flies for ditto, 1 shilling;
> One kettle, 6 pence;
> One crumb-brush, 6 pence;
> Total, 2 pounds.

This admirable selection of stores met with universal approval. Indeed, as regards the first four items, every one so highly approved that they wanted to take every man his share for safe custody to his own study. It was, however, thought undesirable to put them to this trouble, and the sub-committee were directed to continue in charge of these and the other voluntary contributions until the eventful day.

That was not long in coming round, though to the anxious voyagers it seemed long enough. The interval was spent in deep deliberation and solemn preparation. Braintree had his boots most carefully blacked, and Crashford practised boxing all Saturday afternoon with Rubble of the Fifth; Bowler and Gayford strolled casually round to Sound Bay, to see that the boat was safe in its usual place, and prospected the distant dim outline of the Long Stork from the cliffs. Tubbs, feeling he must do something to contribute to the success of the undertaking, wrote a long letter home, which he forgot to post, asking the forgiveness of his second sister, and adding, "Address for Monday, Long Stork Island." Wallas amused himself by reading over the directions for restoring life to the apparently drowned, and Wester tidied up Bowler's study and helped him make up the stores into seven equal brown-paper packages, writing the name of the owner of each on the outside.

This done, the preparations were pronounced as complete as they could be till Monday dawned.

The town holiday was an absolutely free day for the Swishford boys. There was no call-over in the morning, and, indeed, until the evening at eight o'clock they were their own masters.

Most of the boys availed themselves of their liberty by lying in bed an hour later than usual on the November morning, a practice which greatly favoured our heroes in their design of escaping a little before dawn.

Bowler was the first up, and went round to wake the rest.

"Howwid gwind," said Braintree, sitting up for a moment in bed and rubbing his eyes, and then subsiding again under the clothes. "Needn't get up yet, Bowler, it's long before cockcrow."

"It's just on six o'clock, I tell you, and it'll spoil it all if we don't get away by a quarter past. Do get up, there's a good fellow."

"Howwid waw morning," groaned Braintree. "I'd warthah—oh, vewy well, I'll get up."

And with a great effort he struggled out of bed and began to array himself. Bowler had a similar task with each of the other adventurers, and any leader less sanguine or eager might have felt his ardour damped by the evident want of alacrity on the part of his confederates to respond to the call to action.

However, once up, the spirits of the party rose, and they assembled in good-humour in Bowler's study, where by the dim light of a candle the seven brown-paper parcels were solemnly doled out, and a final review of the preparations made.

A few more articles, such as a whistle, a bottle of hair-oil (contributed by Braintree), a shut-up inkpot and pen from Wester, and a guide to the environs of Tunbridge Wells from Tubbs, were thrown into the common lot at the last moment, and stuffed into the pockets of the ulsters in which the boys had armed themselves against a rainy day.

All this being done, Bowler gave the order to march, which the party obeyed by taking off their boots and crawling downstairs on tiptoe to the front door. As silently as possible the great lock was turned and the bolts drawn, and next moment the adventurers, with their boots in one hand and their brown-paper parcels in the other, stood under the stars.

"Now stick your boots on sharp and step out," said Bowler. The order was promptly obeyed, and the dim gables of Swishford soon vanished behind them as they sped along the cliffs towards Sound Bay.

It was a good three miles, and in their ulsters, and weighted with their brown-paper parcels, the boys made slow progress. It was already dawn when, rather fagged and not quite sure how they were enjoying it, they reached the top of the path which led down to Sound Bay. The near approach to their journey's end revived them, and they stumbled down the stony path cheerily but cautiously, until at last they had the satisfaction of seeing the boat bobbing up and down in the little natural harbour close among the rocks.

The wily Bowler and Gayford had marked where the oars and sail were kept, and fetched them in triumph from their hiding-place. The seven brown-paper parcels were solemnly embarked and stowed away under the seats, and then one by one the heroes of New Swishford stepped on board, the painter was thrown loose, silent adieux were waved to the land of their birth, and their gallant boat, nimbly propelled by Gayford and the boat-hook, threaded its way through the rocks and made for the boundless ocean.

Chapter Three. Consternation

The "Eliza"—that was the name of the coastguard's boat on which our heroes had embarked—was a middling-sized sea-going rowing boat, which, if it was just big enough by a little judicious packing to hold the seven voyagers, could certainly not have accommodated more.

While Gayford, with the dexterity of an experienced bargee, shoved the boat along out of the creek, Bowler took upon himself the care of trimming the "ship," and stowing away all the baggage.

"As soon as we get out," said he, "we'd better lie down on the floor, in case the coastguards see us."

"Not much chance of that," replied Gayford. "They never get up till eight, and by that time we shall be halfway across."

"Suppose they spot us and give chase?" said Wallas. "What a row we shall get into!"

"They've not got a boat, I tell you, and I don't believe there's one they can get either," said Bowler.

"But they're sure to be on the look-out for us when we get back to-night."

"Let them. It'll be dark at six, and we can land in Rocket Bay, you know, and dodge them that way."

Bowler was evidently so well up in the arrangements, and had made such a careful study of all the pros and cons of the venture, that every one felt satisfied, and even the somewhat doubtful Wallas desisted from throwing more cold water on the expedition.

It was a raw morning with a little bit of a fog, and a cool breeze right off the land. This last point, however, gave great satisfaction to the leaders of the party. Once out in the open they would be able to hoist sail, and without the exertion of rowing make a straight track for the Long Stork—much indeed as would be the case when, with a southerly wind at their backs, they would before long plough the ocean from Sinnamary to New Swishford.

The fog also was decidedly in their favour, for it would help to screen them from the observation of any wakeful and inquisitive coastguard. In fact, the unusual combination of wind and fog seemed like a special sign of good omen to their adventure.

"Hope it's not wough outside," said Braintree, as the boat, now nearly out of the creek, began to dance a little at the prospect of meeting the open sea.

"Can't be rough with the wind off the land, you duffer," said Crashford.

"Can't it, though?" said Wester, as a wave lifted the prow of the boat and nearly sent it back on the rocks.

"I call that vewy wough," said Braintree, looking and feeling a little uncomfortable.

"Oh, it's only the ground swell," said Gayford; "we shall soon get out of that. Here, Bowler, old man, take an oar with Tubbs, and keep way on while I stick up the sail. Look alive!"

With some difficulty the oars were got out, and Tubbs made to comprehend what was expected of him. But comprehending was one thing with Tubbs, and doing was another thing. Just as he settled down to his oar, another wave lifted the boat and Tubbs with it, who clung wildly to the seat with both hands, leaving his oar to its fate. Luckily, Crashford was near enough to make a grab at it before it went, or the beginning of the expedition might have been marked by a serious catastrophe.

The unhappy Tubbs having been shunted, Crashford took his place, and with Bowler kept the boat's head steady till Gayford hauled up the sail, and the "Eliza" began of her own accord to fly through the water.

At the sight of the majestic sail swelling with the wind, and still more on perceiving a decided improvement in the pitching of the boat, the spirits of the party rose again, and Braintree actually began to hum "Wule Bwitannia."

The cliffs of Raveling loomed dimly out behind them, and ahead they could just discern the faintest outline of the land of their adoption.

"Upon my word," said Bowler, "this is jolly. It's just like the real New Swishford, isn't it, you fellows?"

"Warthah," said Braintree, "except my wifle to let fly at the seagulls with."

"But," said Wallas, "if the wind's off the land this side, it will be off the sea when we get over there, so I suppose it'll get rougher and rougher the farther out we get?"

This ominous suggestion had the effect of immediately damping the spirits of half the party, and Bowler and Gayford found it difficult to restore confidence in the much-abused ocean. The ocean, however, went some way to restore confidence in itself. For though it still continued restless enough to keep Braintree and Tubbs in a state of suspended enjoyment in the bows, it showed no signs of getting worse as it went on.

Bowler was jubilant. With his hand on the rudder and his eye on the compass, he kept the boat's course like a line, and fancied himself heading due north from Sinnamary. Gayford, with the sheet in his hand, and a careful watch on the sail, could easily delude himself into fancying the coast-line of the Long Stork was the veritable shore of New Swishford.

"Isn't it prime, old man," said he, "and won't it be primer still when the real time comes? I never guessed it would be so easy. Not a thing's gone wrong."

"No; and think of the lark of landing and collaring the island, too. I say, who does the Long Stork belong to?"

"Don't know—the Long Storks, I guess. They're the only inhabitants I ever heard of."

"Well, I'm sorry for them. But, I say, Gayford, it's just as well we have got some grub on board, for there's not much sign of forests and game, and all that sort of thing here."

Not much indeed! Long Stork Island was a barren rock about a mile long and half a mile wide, with a few scraggy patches of grass on its uninviting slope. No living creatures but the wild sea-birds patronised it in the winter, when the waves lashed over the island and sent their salt spray from one end to the other. Even they seemed to avoid it. But beggars cannot be choosers, and as the Long Stork was the only island of our heroes' acquaintance within reach, they had to take it as it was and make the best of it.

A decided sea was running on the landward side of the island as they approached it, and even such inexperienced navigators as Bowler and Gayford could see that there would be some difficulty about effecting a quiet landing.

"Better go round the other side," said Gayford; "it'll be quiet enough there out of the wind."

So the boat's nose was put out to make a circuit of the Long Stork.

"Look out, I say!" said, or rather groaned Braintree from the bows. "Don't make the boat woll. Why can't you wun her stwait in the way you—?"

His further observations were cut short, and during the rest of the time that the "Eliza" was rounding the stormy cape he and Tubbs and Crashford were in a decidedly pensive mood. At last the circumnavigation was accomplished, and in tranquil water the boat cruised along under the sheltered shore of the island. The sail was lowered, oars were put out, the invalids sat up, and Bowler, standing up in the bows, scanned the coast for a likely landing-place.

He had not to search long. A little natural pier of rock ran out invitingly, alongside which the boat was slowly and triumphantly brought.

"Now, you fellows," said Crashford, "here goes for first on shore. Out of the way, Tubby. Hurrah for New Swishford!" And he leapt on shore, half capsizing the boat as he did so.

Bowler found his authority unequal to the task of controlling the enthusiasm of his fellow-emigrants, and he had to let them land as they pleased, while he and Gayford grimly held the boat alongside.

When all but Tubbs were ashore, their patience could hold out no longer. They followed the general rush, Bowler crying out to Tubbs as he sprang ashore—

"See and make her fast, Tubbs, and land the grub, will you? We'll be back directly." And off he scampered with the rest, to join in the ceremony of capturing the island.

Now Tubbs was not the best man who could have been chosen to execute so important a trust as that laid upon him; and Bowler, had he been rather less excited at the moment, would have thought twice before he left him to perform it. In the first place, Tubbs could find no place to tie the boat up to, and as long as he sat in the boat and held on to the rock it was evident he could not land the grub. So he was in a dilemma. He did his best; he relaxed his hold for a moment and made a frantic grab at one of the brown-paper parcels. But it almost cost him his moorings, for the boat, taking advantage of its liberty, began to slide away out to sea, and it was all Tubbs could do to catch hold of the rock again in time to stop it. This would not do, it was clear. He pulled the boat along to its old position, and throwing the parcel ashore, meditated. He must wait till one of the others came to help him. Poor Tubbs! It was hard lines to see the rest of the party scrambling triumphantly up the hill, and find himself left here like a sort of animated anchor. Happy thought! How came he never to have thought of the anchor before? There it was in the bottom of the boat. It would be the simplest thing to jump ashore with it and fix it somewhere in the rocks where it would hold. No sooner was the brilliant project conceived than it was executed. Seizing the anchor in his hands, Tubbs stepped gaily ashore and triumphantly wedged one tooth of it into a crevice of the rock, where it would hold firm enough to keep a man-of-war in its place. He watched with a pleasant smile the "Eliza" as she drifted slowly out on the rope, enjoying the prospect of seeing her presently tug at the anchor, and then give up the attempt to get free and resign herself to her fate.

It was a longer coil of rope than he had imagined. The boat was twenty yards away at least, and still paying out. By the way, where was the rope? With a cry of horror Tubbs sprang to the anchor and began hauling in. The rope came in gaily, but not the "Eliza." She danced merrily cut to sea in a straight line for the North Pole, with the six brown-paper parcels on board, leaving her poor custodian to console himself as best he could with a loose end of rope, which had never been fastened to its ring.

What was he to do? After taking a few minutes to collect his ideas, by which time the boat was a hundred yards on its solitary voyage, it occurred to him he had better inform the others of what had happened. So he started in rather a low state of mind in pursuit of them. It was a long time before he came upon them, perched in a group on the highest point of the island, and singing "Rule Britannia" in a lusty chorus which sent the scared seagulls flying to right and left.

"Hullo, Tubby, old man, here we are! Got the grub safe ashore? Not been bagging any of the peaches, eh? You've been long enough."

Tubbs replied by pointing mysteriously to a little speck out at sea.

"What's the row? What is it?" asked Gayford.

"You wouldn't guess what that little thing is," said Tubbs.

"What is it? Can't you speak?"

"Well, if you must know, it's our boat. The anchor wasn't tied, you know!"

"The boat! You great booby!" cried one and all, springing to their feet and rushing in the direction of the pier, upsetting and trampling over the unhappy Tubbs as they did so.

"What on earth shall we do?" gasped Gayford, as he ran by Bowler's side

"We must swim for it," said Bowler. "It's our only chance."

"Can't do it. She's half a mile out."

"It's all up with us if we can't get her!" groaned Bowler.

They reached the landing-stage, and there, sure enough, danced the "Eliza" half a mile out at sea.

"I'll try it," said Bowler, flinging off his coat.

"What, to swim? You'll do nothing of the sort," said Gayford, seizing his friend by main force.

"I tell you it's our only chance," cried Bowler. "Let go, do you hear?"

"No, I won't, old man. We must make the best of it. It'll be more like New Swishford than ever now."

This last argument had more effect with Bowler than any other, and he slowly put on his coat.

"I vote we souse that idiot, Tubbs, till he's black in the face," said Crashford viciously.

"What's the use of that?" asked Bowler. "The fact is, you fellows," said he, "we're regularly in for it now, and the sooner we make up our minds what we shall do the better."

"Let's make a waft," said Braintree, mindful of his *Wobinson Cwusoe*.

"Where's your wood?" asked Wallas.

"Let's hoist a signal, anyhow," said Wester.

"No one to see it if you do," said Wallas.

"Let's have some grub," said Crashford.

This last suggestion met with general approval. They had had no breakfast to speak of, and after their voyage and excitement hunger was beginning to assert itself. The one brown-paper parcel rescued from the "Eliza" was forthwith handed in and pronounced common property. It happened to be the parcel bearing Tubbs's name, and contained, besides a seventh part of the provisions, Tubbs's voluntary contributions to the general store—namely, the crib to Sallust, and the guide to the environs of Tunbridge Wells. These, it was proposed and seconded, should be handed over to the owner as his share of the good things contained in the parcel, but Bowler and Gayford interfered on his behalf; and after having been reprimanded with a severity that took away his appetite, he was allowed to partake of a portion of potted shrimp and a potted peach, together with a small slice of cake. Bowler groaned to see what a hole even this frugal repast made in the provisions, and consulted Gayford in an undertone on the possibility of slaying a seagull and the merits of raw poultry generally.

Rather dolefully the provisions were packed up and deposited in a ledge in the rocks, while the party proceeded to wander about the island in search of board and lodging. The charms of Long Stork Island had fallen off greatly in the short interval, and the sea-fog, which was beginning to wrap it round and hide the mainland from view, seemed like a wet blanket both on the spirits and persons of the adventurers.

After much dreary search a hollow was found on the hill-side, which by fastening together three or four ulsters might be roofed over sufficiently well to keep out the rain or cold if required. As to food, the island provided absolutely nothing except the chance of raw poultry already mentioned and a few shell-fish on the rocks.

The day wore on, and the fog turned to drizzle and the drizzle to rain. They held out against it as long as they could, but had to take shelter at last, and herd together in their extemporised cabin.

Here a painful discussion ensued, "I hope you're satisfied now!" growled Wallas. "This is mess enough to please even you, Bowler."

"What do you mean?" retorted Gayford; "a lot you've done for the public good. There are plenty of seagulls about without you to croak, too."

"I wish my umbwellah hadn't gone out to sea," observed Braintree, shivering.

"By the way," said Crashford, "didn't I see it lying on the rocks. I'll just run and see," and off he started.

"When shall we ever get away?" asked Wester. "We may get starved here."

"They're sure to see us or find us out in a day or two," said Bowler.

"A day or two!" exclaimed Wallas; "do you really mean we've got to stay here without food or shelter a day or two? I wish your New Swishford was in the middle of the sea."

"So it is," dryly observed Bowler.

"Fine fools you've made of us with your humbug and child's play," growled the other.

"*You* don't want much making," retorted Bowler; "and if you want to talk any more, you can talk to some one else."

Wallas accepted the invitation, and growled all round till everybody was sick of him.

After a long absence Crashford returned without the umbrella.

"I couldn't find it," said he, sitting down. "It's gone."

"But you found the peaches, you blackguard!" said Bowler, springing up and pointing to some juicy remains still clinging to the delinquent's coat. And in his righteous indignation he dealt the traitor a blow which sent him out of the tent.

A fight ensued there and then between Bowler and Crashford, unhappily, to the disadvantage of the former, who was no match for the practised hand opposed to him. The company interposed after a few rounds, and none too soon for the damaged though still lion-hearted Bowler.

Crashford profited nothing by his victory, for it was decided unanimously to exclude him from the tent till he chose to apologise for his treachery; and meanwhile the remains of the slender provisions were taken into safe custody out of his reach.

The day wore on, and the rain fell heavier and heavier upon the ulster-roof over their heads. The wind whistled drearily above them, and the mainland was entirely lost to sight. As far as they were concerned they might be in the real New Swishford, a thousand miles from the nearest land.

They huddled together silently, no one caring much to speak. Only Braintree broke the monotony by shivering audibly, and the footsteps of Crashford, as he paced up and down outside to keep warm, added a dreary variety to the silence.

The afternoon drew on, and at last Bowler said—

"Better let the beggar in."

"Hadn't we better all turn out and see what's to be done?" said Gayford. "We shall only come to grief here. The grub won't hold out for another meal, and then it'll be something more than a joke."

"Come on, then, you fellows," said Bowler. And the roof was hauled down, and the party turned dismally out once more to seek their fortune.

Chapter Four. Consolation

Our heroes, who in all their anticipations had never calculated on anything but fine weather and unlimited rations and congenial occupation, began to entertain serious doubts as to the joys of founding an empire, as they trailed dreadily along in the rain after Bowler and Gayford. The weaker of the party had no spirit to suggest anything themselves, or to question what their leaders suggested; so they followed doggedly where they were led, neither knowing nor caring whither.

With Bowler and Gayford it was otherwise. They felt rather ashamed of themselves for having lost their heads earlier in the day and resolved now to atone for it in the only way they could. They put a brave face on the situation, and tried to impart their courage to their followers.

"I tell you what," said Bowler cheerily, as the seven stood again on the rocks at the water's edge; "it wants a good hour of dark, and the least thing we can do is to spend the daylight in looking for some proper place of shelter and something to eat, if we can find it. Suppose I and Tubbs and Braintree start to walk round this way, and you, Gayford, take the rest round the other way. If any of us find anything, we'll stop till the other party come up. I've got my whistle, so we'll be sure to hear one another."

It could do no harm, and it might do good, so the party tacitly fell in with the suggestion, and divided itself accordingly. Even Crashford was wise enough to feel he could gain nothing by sulking, and returned to his allegiance without demur.

"Can't we have something to eat before we start?" said Wallas.

"My dear fellow," replied Gayford, "I wish we could, but then we shall have nothing left for to-morrow."

Strange to say, Wallas disputed the matter no further, and turned with his companions to start on their tour of discovery.

Bowler kept whistling cheerily, and Gayford shouted in reply till the two parties were out of earshot. Then each walked on in silence, eagerly scanning sea and shore in search of hope. For Bowler's party there seemed very little prospect of anything turning up, for their way lay across bare ledges of rock, with perhaps a pool to wade, or a little cape to scramble across, but never a sign of food or shelter. Braintree did indeed announce that in one place he saw a "cwab" disappear into a hole, but the chances of satisfaction from that source were too remote to be pursued.

How they longed to be back under the roof of old Swishford, and to hear the cheery bell summoning the boys to tea, and how gratefully now would they have welcomed the wholesome plenty of that often abused meal! Alas! there were no cups of tea, or eggs, or bread-and-butter going on the Long Stork.

"Of course," said Bowler, "we could never be *quite* stuck up for grub as long as there's seaweed about, and if the rain goes on like this there'll be plenty of water too."

"You're wight there," said Braintree; "but seaweed and wain-water is warthah a spare diet."

"Anyhow," said Bowler, "we have got enough of the shrimps and peaches left for a good breakfast to-morrow; that's one comfort."

And they trudged on in that glorious prospect.

For an hour they toiled along the rocky shore until the daylight almost suddenly vanished, and the gloom of a damp November night fell upon them. What was the use of exploring further? Even Bowler lost heart as he stumbled about in the dusk, and heard Braintree shivering and chattering with cold beside him, and Tubbs's scarcely suppressed whimper of misery.

"Better get back to the rest as soon as we can," said he, taking out his whistle and blowing it again.

They listened, but no answer came, only the shriek of the gulls and the steady splash of the rain on the rocks.

"Never mind, we can't be long before we get round to them," said Bowler; "perhaps they've found a place, you know."

For another half-hour they toiled on, Bowler blowing his whistle every few minutes, but always without response.

"Where can they be? We're almost round at the place we started from, surely," said Bowler, "and—hullo, look out there!"

They had reached a sudden break in the coast about twenty yards across, with rocks on each side which dropped almost precipitously into the water, forming a serious bar to further progress.

They must either scramble down and wade or swim across, or else turn inland and make a long détour round the head of the chasm.

Bowler made a careful inspection of the rocks, and then said—

"I think we could do it; what do you say? If we went round we might miss the others."

"All wight," said Braintree, blowing his hands; "I'm game, so's Tubbs."

Tubbs said nothing, but stood by miserably, ready to follow Bowler's lead.

"I'll go down first," said the latter. "Mind how you come, the rocks are slippery."

He lowered himself cautiously down the steep rock, finding just enough to cling on to with his hands, while he felt his way down with his feet. He got to the bottom safely, and found firm footing in a ledge of rock close to the water's edge.

"Now, then," shouted he, "down you come, Braintree."

Braintree obeyed, and managed with difficulty to reach the ledge. Then Tubbs attempted. But he, poor fellow, clumsy at all times, and now utterly unnerved by the miseries of the day, was not man enough for the venture, and, after one feeble effort, begged to be allowed to stay where he was.

"Nonsense!" cried Bowler; "come on, old man, we'll help you down all right."

So Tubbs tried again. Had not the situation been so perilous, the appearance he presented as he clung wildly on to the rock with his hands, and kicked still more wildly with his feet, would have been ludicrous. But it was no time for joking. The two at the bottom piloted his feet as well as they could, and encouraged him in his downward career. But before they could reach him he slipped, and with a howl fell backward into the sea.

In a moment Bowler, dressed as he was, was in beside him, holding him up and striking out to where Braintree, with outstretched hand, waited to help them in. But it was long before they could haul his half-senseless form from the water; and by the time this was accomplished, Bowler himself was so exhausted that he in turn needed all Braintree's aid to land himself. At last, however, all three were on the ledge.

But what were they to do next? Tubbs lay still half-stupefied, utterly unable to help himself. The rock they had descended frowned above them, defying any attempt to return the way they had *come*, and between the ledge they stood on and the rock the other side twenty yards of uneasy water intervened.

"Could we swim across with him?" said Bowler, after a little.

"I'll do my best," said Braintree.

"The thing is," said Bowler, "the tide was dead out an hour ago, so it must be coming in now. Oh, what a cad I was to lead you into this, Braintree!"

"Shut up, old man, I say," said Braintree; and he began to take off his coat and boots.

Bowler did the same.

"We shall have to leave them behind," said he. "It can't be helped. Are you ready?"

"Yes. But I say, old man, if I get done up and have to let go, don't wait for me. I'm not much of a swimmer."

Bowler hesitated.

"If I could only be sure of getting *him* over," said he, pointing to Tubbs, "I might come back and—"

"Hullo! I say, Bowler, look there!" exclaimed Braintree suddenly, pointing out to sea. "Wasn't that a light? Blow your whistle, I say."

Bowler obeyed, eagerly gazing in the direction indicated by Braintree. There was neither answer nor light.

"I'm certain I saw something!" exclaimed Braintree. "Blow again, old man."

And once more the whistle sent forth a shrill cry seaward, accompanied by a loud shout from Braintree.

They waited in terrible suspense, but still no answer.

"You must be wrong," said Bowler.

"No, I'm not; blow once more."

And again Bowler obeyed.

This time, sure enough, he fancied he saw a glimmer on the water; but it might be only the lights on the mainland appearing through the lifting fog.

For ten minutes they kept up an incessant whistling and shouting, their hopes growing less and less as the time passed. At length, worn out and desperate, they had given it up, and were turning once more to prepare for their swim across. But as they did so the light suddenly reappeared, the time close to the shore.

Once more, with frantic energy, they raised their signal of distress, and after a moment's terrible silence had the joy of hearing a faint shout across the water.

"It's a boat!" cried Braintree. "Whistle again to show them where we are."

Again and again they whistled, and again and again the responsive shout, growing ever nearer, came back. Presently they could even distinguish the sound of oars, and at length the dim outline of a boat loomed across the entrance of the gulf.

"Where are you?" shouted a voice in the familiar tones of the Raveling coastguard.

"Here. We can see you. We're on the ledge here, Thomson!"

In a few seconds the boat was alongside, and the three boys were safely lifted into it.

"Where's the rest of you?" asked Thomson, as coolly as if this sort of thing was an everyday occurrence with him. "We want seven of you."

"I don't know where they are," said Bowler. "They were coming round this way to meet us. You'd better row round somewhere where we can land and look for them."

"Give your orders," said Thomson. "You've had your day's fun, and seemingly you're determined I should have my night's. Row away, mate." And he and his man turned the boat's head and pulled out of the gulf.

"I say, Thomson, have you got any gwub or anything?" said Braintree faintly.

"Grub," said the jocular coastguard. "What, harn't you found grub enough on this here island? Anyhow, if you do want something you'd better open that there bag and see what you can find."

Bowler was too anxious to discover the missing ones to feel much appetite for food, and kept blowing his whistle as the boat slowly coasted the island.

At length, to his unbounded joy, an answering shout was heard, and the shadowy forms of the four outcasts were seen standing on the pier from which they had started two hours before.

Jubilant were the welcomes exchanged as the heroes of New Swishford once more counted their full number, and ensconced themselves snugly in the stern of Thomson's boat round his wonderful bag of food.

It did not take long to chronicle the doings of Gayford's party. After about half an hour's journey they had been pulled up by the same chasm which had nearly proved too much for poor Tubbs. Finding it impossible to cross it, they had turned inland, and for a cheerful hour lost their way completely in the fog. At length, by means of walking in a straight line, they had come again to the coast, and after much searching had found the pier. And having found it, they resolved to keep it untll the other party completed the circuit and found them where it left them.

"And however did you find us out, Thomson?" inquired Gayford, after the repast had been done ample justice to. "Did your boat come ashore?"

"No, she didn't, young gentleman; and I can tell you you'll get to know how to spell her name tolerable well before you've heard the last of her."

"Oh, of course we shall get into a frightful row," said Bowler; "but how did you come to find us?"

"Why, one of you artful young scholards left a letter to his ma on his table, open for everybody to see, talking some gammon about a West Indian island, and saying you was going to lay hold of the Long Stork, to get your hands in. I can tell you you *have* got your hands in, my beauties. There's a cart-load of birches been ordered for you at the school already."

These awful warnings failed to counteract the satisfaction of our heroes at finding themselves nearly back again in the region of blankets and hot porridge. Bowler in the name of the party magnificently presented Thomson with the odd shilling reserved for his benefit, and expressed his sorrow it was not more. But, he added, if the "Eliza" ever turned up, he might keep everything he found on board, including twelve tins of shrimps and peaches, a bottle of hair-oil, a set of cricket bails, and a copy of Young's *Night Thoughts*; whereat Thomson was moved with gratitude, and said they were as nice a lot of articles as ever he came across, and he did not mind saying so.

An hour later our heroes were all in bed, comfortable within and without. They were let down easy for their day's escapade, and except for colds more or less bad, and a decidedly augmented bill at the end of the term to pay for a new "Eliza," as well as a regulation forbidding all sea voyages of whatever kind, they suffered no further punishment than the lessons of the day itself. To those lessons they added one more of their own accord, by resolving unanimously, that from that day forward they renounced all further claim to that eligible island commonly known as New Swishford.